Lord Danvers Investigates

A Lethal Spectre

DONNA FLETCHER CROW

Verity Press

real-life individuals. Detailed descriptions, seamlessly woven into the story, made the book believable as well as visual." ~ Becky

"A quick, entertaining read with believable characters." ~ Old movie fan

"Authentically Victorian." ~ Trinky

"Beautifully evocative and well-researched." ~ Sheila

"An entertaining read for all audiences. Highly recommended." ~ Janet

"The author's descriptive prose is excellent, and her grasp of history and her ability to put the reader into history is remarkable." ~ Amazon customer

"When you pick up a period mystery you do so because you want to experience all that period has to offer. Donna Fletcher Crow delivers on that expected promise, weaving details about clothing, decorative style, and odors—so many odors! Add taste and touch, and you have an idea of how thorough this author is when it comes to her ability to weave the threads of the mystery together. She writes with such attention to detail that you're constantly analyzing new evidence and never certain that you're on the right track. The surprise ending is truly that. I gave it five stars because of the intricacy of the storytelling, and the fact that this is a mystery that makes you think even after you've read the last word." ~ J L

To Felicity Margaret Kenyon
who is a writer

CHARACTERS

In England:
Lord Charles Leighton, 9th Viscount Danvers
Lady Antonia Danvers, his wife
The Honourable Charles Frederick (Charlie), their son
Sara Bevans, his nurse
Hardy, Danvers's manservant
Isabella, Lady Danvers's maid
Aelfrida, the Dowager Duchess of Aethelbert
Osbert, Duke of Aethelbert, her son
Miss Sophia Antonia Landry, her ward
Peyden, Sophia's maid
Soyer, the dowager duchess's butler
The Honourable Reverend Frederick William Leighton, Lord Danvers's brother
Miss Victoria Hever, charity worker, engaged to Frederick
Miss Cecilia Hever, her sister
Bracken, Danvers's butler
Jarvis, Danvers's coachman
Michael, Danvers's footman
Betsy, Danvers's upstairs maid

Mrs. Robinson, Danvers's cook
Lady Agatha Estella Burroway, Danvers's sister
The Honourable Arthur Emory Rannoch, Agatha's son
The Honourable Alice Rannoch, Agatha's daughter
The Honourable Beatrice (Bea) Rannoch, Agatha's daughter
The Honourable Margaret Leighton, Danvers's sister
The Honourable Eleanor Leighton, Danvers's sister
Captain George Bellingham
Lieutenant Thomas Anson
Colonel William Whitham
Padjma (Pamela) Whitham, his wife
Chandrika Johal, her sister
Faquir Johal, her husband
Lady Charmian Essworthy, London hostess
The Honourable Cyril Essworthy, her son
Lady Lucie Duff Gordon, London hostess
Sir Alexander Duff Gordon, Baronet
Bottle, Duff Gordon's butler
Lord Granville Levenson-Gower, leader of the House of Lords
Lord Ellenborough, former Governor-General of India
Gervaise, The Duke of Penthurst
Raoul, his valet
Sir Richard Mayne, Commissioner, Metropolitan Police
Inspector Futter, Metropolitan Police
Constable Lemming, London Bobby
William Thacker, host Devil's Dyke Hotel
Mary Thacker, his wife
George White, Chief Constable, Brighton Police
Monsieur Gaspard, floor manager, Brighton Pavilion
Miss Suzanne Howsham, Alice's friend
In India:
Emilia Landry, Antonia's cousin and Sophia's mother
Louisa Chalwin, Emilia's friend

Lydia Hillersdon

The Reverend William Heycock, Society for the Propagation of the Gospel

The Reverend Mister Moncrieff

Fanny Lindsay

Caroline Lindsay

Alice Lindsay

Rose Anne Greenway

William Joseph Shepherd

Azimoolah Khan

Nana Sahib

General Sir Hugh Wheeler

Captain John Moore

Lieutenant Mowbray Thompson

* Historical characters

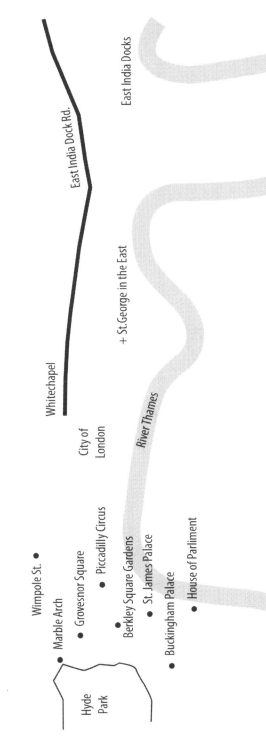

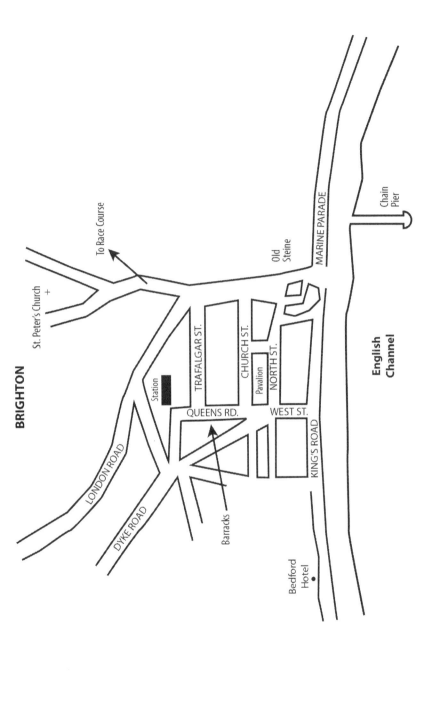

AFGHANISTAN

CHINA

Delhi ●

● Meerut

● Lucknow

● Cawnpore

BENGAL

R. Ganges

INDIA

❧ I ❧

I
t was only midmorning and already the heat was stifling. Hot wind seared and scorching sun radiated from the walls of the barracks behind them. The acrid smell of the buildings of the cantonment beyond, now reduced to black smoldering rubble—all their homes and possessions—stung every nose. Emilia Landry stood among the women and children who had been called from their homes in the civilian cantonment and gathered into the military entrenchment on the orders of General Wheeler.

They had been here a week now, hoping for the best; but fearing the worst. No attack had come on the entrenchment, but mutinous sepoys and vandals had ransacked the city, burned the officers' bungalows in the new cantonment, and, disastrously, seized the magazine where the army treasury, ammunitions and heavy guns were stored.

Emilia closed her eyes against the sight of the black smoke, and saw in her mind the pleasant bungalow she had occupied with her friend Louisa Chalwin and Louisa's veterinarian husband Edwin. Louisa had planted a lovely garden, complete with English roses that bloomed undaunted in the Indian summer. A magnificent old banyan tree shaded a summer house where Emilia loved to sit and read in the mornings and take tea in the afternoons. All a blackened rubble now.

They had been hearing dire reports for weeks. Revolt of the native troops at Meerut. Then at Delhi. And riots at Lucknow, only some sixty miles to the northeast. But no apprehension had been felt of treachery on the part of their own troops at Cawnpore.

This morning, however, Sunday morning, the seventh of June, Sir Hugh Wheeler, commanding general at Cawnpore, had received a letter from the Nana Sahib, declaring his intention of attacking.

Now everyone on the verandah of the barracks held their breath, as all in the entrenchment seemed to do. The tension of the soldiers, posted with leveled rifles around the circumference of the barricading mud wall, communicated itself to every person.

The mewling of a baby born only a few hours before vibrated on the air. The cry was cut off by the boom of a cannon. Women shrieked; children wailed as the ball struck the barrack behind them.

A bugle call split the air, sounding above the mayhem. The crack of shot was deafening as hundreds of rifles responded. The mutiny had come to Cawnpore.

A moan tore from deep in her throat and Lady Antonia Danvers sat up sharply. She was drenched in sweat, even though the early June night was cold in London. Tonia reached for the carafe of water by her bed and filled a glass to relieve her parched throat. What had she dreamed? How could such vivid horror have come from her own imagination?

She crossed the room and, pushing the heavy drapery aside, raised the sash on her window, letting a fresh breeze bathe her face. She breathed deeply of the blessed, moist air. Still unsettled from the terrors of her dream, Antonia returned to bed. The sky had lightened to silver, however, and the first notes of the dawn chorus rang in the garden before Tonia returned to an uneasy sleep.

She wakened far too late to share her morning tea with

her husband as was their custom. When she inquired of her maid she was informed that her lord would be out for the day, involved with his man of business and taking dinner at his club. She would have no opportunity to discuss the nightmare with Charles, although the phantom spectre continued to follow her.

As soon as the diminutive Isabella had finished her lady's toilette Antonia hurried upstairs to the nursery where she knew she would find the antidote to all her dismals.

The Honourable Charles Frederick Leighton clapped his chubby hands at the spinning top Nurse Bevans had set going for him. Tonia smiled at the sight and scooped her son into her arms, kissing him soundly on each chubby cheek.

"Has he had his airing yet, Sara?"

The nurse started to nod, but Tonia interrupted her. "Never mind, an extra won't hurt him. It is too lovely in the garden to stay indoors." The truth was, Tonia felt driven to be out in the reviving English air with her son. She was still feeling parched by the desert scene of what she could only think was an hallucination, for it seemed more that than a mere dream.

She would spend the day indulging Charlie's every whim. It would be a perfect day. Indeed, she was determined this would be the perfect summer, especially for Charlie. She placed her hand on her abdomen. This would be his last summer to be alone in the nursery. Being a big brother would undoubtedly be an excellent experience for the heir to Norwood, but for these few months, she wanted his time as lord of his realm to be perfect. Soon enough the weight and worries of life would encroach. Such a precious thing, childhood. It must be protected.

By force of will, Tonia managed to push her nighttime angst

to the back of her mind, and the entire day couldn't have been calmer or more surrounded by beauty. Her spirits were quite restored by the time Isabella had her attired for the evening's social engagement. Tonia made one last detour to the nursery to give a final kiss to the soft cheek of her sleeping son and run her fingers gently over his silky, blond hair. How fortunate they were—such a joy after she had believed for so long that she would be unable to bear a child, and then almost losing him in that dreadful fire last year. She gave a final, smoothing tug to his coverlet and, with a nod to Nurse Bevans, crossed the room and closed the door softly behind her.

The flounced skirts of her blue silk evening gown rustled as Lady Danvers swept down the curving main staircase. She found her feet moving faster with each tread, knowing every step brought her closer to Charles. She felt her mouth curve into a smile.

Lord Charles Danvers, awaiting her in the hall, returned her smile, then took the ruffle-trimmed mantelet Isabella was holding for her lady and put it around Antonia's white shoulders, fully bared as current fashion dictated. Antonia knew that if her maid had not been standing by, her lord would have kissed the back of her neck in the process, and she gave a slight shiver of delight at the mere thought.

Danvers escorted her out the Doric-pillared porch to the waiting barouche with his viscount's coronet on the side. As soon as they were comfortably settled against the maroon squabs of the carriage, and the pair of chestnuts were stepping smartly down Grosvenor Street under the steady hand of Jarvis, Danvers's coachman, Tonia gave a sigh of pleasure. "I can't tell you how I am anticipating this evening, Charles. I have never met the guest of honour, and yet her mother and I were the closest of friends in our girlhood. It's very odd, really." She lapsed into a brief memory of days long ago, laughing with her friend—Emilia's dark curls bouncing as they romped in the garden. How could they have allowed the years to make such a distance?

"Yes," Charles said. "I had an impression of mystery about this evening. Why ever is Aunt Aelfrida doing something so uncharacteristic as bestirring herself to give a Drawing-room for half of London?"

Antonia laughed. "And you accuse me of exaggerating, my love. Surely less than a quarter of London will be there. And only the top quarter at that. One could hardly expect anything less of the Dowager Duchess of Aethelbert."

"Still, I can't recall her having done such a thing in living memory. And who is this Miss Sophia Landry we are summoned to meet? I'm certain I can't have heard of her before."

Tonia saw again in her mind the flowing script of the engraved invitation fighting for space on the library mantel-piece amidst a veritable throng of stiff white cards summoning the Lord and Lady Danvers to the most brilliant events of the season: *The Dowager Duchess of Aethelbert requests the pleasure of your company at a Drawing-room on Monday, eighth June, at eight o'clock of the evening to meet Miss Sophia Landry.* "Aunt Aelfrida doesn't send invitations, she issues summons."

Danvers smiled. "Exactly. I wonder how many others have spotted that disparity? I expect most of the recipients will be so flattered to receive an invitation they won't stop to wonder if there is a skeleton in the closet."

"No skeletons, certainly. Aunt Aelfrida would not counte-nance that. Although it had occurred to me to wonder why she had undertaken such a charge."

"What do you know of Aelfrida's connection to the girl?" Danvers asked.

Tonia paused to think as the carriage turned toward Berkeley Square Gardens. "A rather sad tale, I only heard it once myself and that years ago—it's not the sort of thing children pay much attention to. Sophia is granddaughter of Aelfrida's oldest friend. Dore, my father called her when he recounted the tale to me. Staveley was the family name. Apparently this lady disgraced herself in her first season by marrying beneath her—a runaway match, no less."

"Aelfrida's friend ran off with a ne'er-do-well? That would have raised the eyebrows."

"I believe he was quite wealthy, but in trade. Something with the East India Company, maybe. At any rate, Dore was disinherited—with the Staveley fortune to go to a descendant who married according to their station."

Danvers shook his head. "I can only imagine what Aelfrida must have thought of the whole affair. And yet she has apparently kept touch with the family?"

Tonia's voice filled with nostalgia as she recalled days long past. "Dore died giving birth to a daughter. On the same day that my mother gave birth to me." She was quiet for a moment. "And my mother died shortly after that, too." Tonia paused. "That was how Emilia and I came to grow up together. You know, my love, I had never considered this before. Children simply take things so for granted, and Emilia came into my life when we were very young. We were enchanted by the fact that we shared a birthday..." She paused again, long-forgotten memories flooding her mind.

"So why have I never met this bosom friend of yours? Or even heard of her?"

Tonia shook her head. "Emilia and I made our come-outs together. Both under Aunt Aelfrida's sponsorship. We could have been twins, except for her black hair and my red. And then our lives took such a divergence. Emilia married in her first season."

"And so gained the inheritance?"

Tonia shook her head. "We all thought it would be so. She

was pursued by a marquess. But Emilia amazed us all by elop-
ing. A love match, apparently. But there was little money. He
was in the East India Company like her father. They went out
to India." She shook her head again. "We simply lost touch. I
did hear she had a daughter, in the first year after her
marriage. And then her husband died sometime later. I think
Emilia returned to England with her daughter and lived with
her people in Yorkshire or somewhere, but I was far too busy
with my social whirl to give it all much thought."

Danvers laughed. "*Le ne plus ultra*, you were—how well I
remember. Truly, there was never anyone like you, my love."

Tonia smiled, but her mind was still on her long-lost
friend. "You know, it's the oddest thing, but I received a letter
from Emilia only last week. It seemed so out of the blue, and
now I'm to meet her daughter tonight. It's so hard to believe
that Emilia's daughter is of age to enter society—when our
own child is still in the nursery. The years go with such frightening speed."

"And so Aunt Aelfrida has undertaken to launch the
granddaughter of her oldest friend." Danvers still sounded
puzzled as to the motivation, but Tonia could give no more
explanation. "Is the girl presentable, I wonder?"

"Her mother was a beauty. And since Emilia, like her
mother, married beneath herself, the Staveley fortunes are
waiting for Sophia."

"Oh dear, a noted beauty and an heiress—assuming she
marries well. Aelfrida will have her hands full. This should
prove a most interesting evening."

The carriage drew up before the Dowager Duchess of Aethelbert's Palladian house at the end of Berkeley Square Gardens.
Torches flared beside the pillared doorway and lights gleamed
from every window. The dowager duchess's liveried footman

handed Antonia out of the barouche before Danvers's own footman could spring down from the back of the carriage to perform the office.

A pair of bewigged footmen, in the knee breeches and silk hose such as servants would have worn when the dowager duchess herself was making her come-out, held the double front doors open, a maid took Antonia's wrap, and they ascended the wide staircase to the first floor reception room where the butler Soyer announced, without even glancing at the card Danvers handed him, "The Viscount and Viscountess Danvers," in a carrying voice that made all the heads in the already full room turn toward the newcomers.

They were barely into the room before Soyer announced the next arrivals, "The Baroness Burroway and The Honourable Alfred Emory Rannoch, The Honourable Miss Rannoch, and The Honourable Beatrice Rannoch."

Since they were staying with the dowager duchess, Danvers was surprised his elder sister and family hadn't already entered. His groan was audible only to Antonia as Agatha Estella cut a beeline straight to him, barely acknowledging greetings from any of the other guests.

"Charles, you must put a stop to this nonsense."

Danvers raised his eyebrows and surveyed the magnificent room fairly seething with the cream of London society. "Do you refer to Aunt Aelfrida's Drawing-room? What do you propose I do—yell, 'Fire'?"

Agatha's deepening frown did nothing to improve her already severe appearance; nor, indeed, did the unfortunate choice of the pea-green gown she wore. "Charles! I do wish you would be sensible. I refer, of course to Aunt Aelfida's proposal to introduce this—this nobody to London society. We shall all be quite sunk if she persists in this madness."

"My dear Agatha, I had no idea your standing in society was so precarious. Nor did I entertain any notion that my standing with Aunt Aelfrida was so certain that I could dictate her undertakings to her. I will admit to a certain curiosity, however. Perhaps you can enlighten me as to why Aunt Aelfrida should be going to so much trouble for the granddaughter of an old friend? It sounds highly unlike her."

Before Agatha could respond the great lady herself bore down upon them, demanding their attention with two raps of her ebony walking stick. Danvers bowed deeply. "Aunt Aelfrida, how fine you look. You are in health?"

"I am always in health."

Antonia made a slight curtsy. "Your diamonds are stunning, your grace." If anyone had doubted the dowager duchess's determination that the evening would make a splash in society, the fact that she had chosen to wear the Aethelsham diamonds would make matters quite clear. It should have been enough to quell even Agatha.

The dowager duchess was not interested in discussing her adornment, however. She turned to her eldest niece. "Agatha, keep your puppy away from Sophia. I have much better things in mind for her."

Agatha's strong features mirrored her dilemma between defending the heir to the Baron of Burroway's position as being unsurpassed and her horror at the prospect of her son dangling after a positionless miss. "I... I... How dare..." But the dowager duchess had turned her back and moved on to greet the Earl of Ellenborough whom Soyer had just announced.

Antonia pondered. It was clear that the idea of Agatha's son dangling after Aunt Aelfrida's protégé had never entered her sister-in-law's mind. So why did she object so strongly to Aunt Aelfrida bringing her out? Agatha would normally encourage any opportunity that offered a chance for her to present her daughters to the cream of society, especially since the painfully plain Alice, who had the misfortune to take after her mother, was now in her mid-twenties and would soon be on the matrimonial shelf. On the other hand, Beatrice, like her brother, had inherited their father's round blue eyes and curling black locks. The fact that a somewhat florid complexion was also part of the package was more attractive on Bea than on Alfred Emory.

The room, lavish with flowers and candles, and echoing with conversation, was rapidly becoming somewhat stifling. The dowager duchess, who had returned after greeting the earl, was well into ringing a peal over her viscount nephew's head on her favorite subject of family loyalty, so with a mere nod to her hostess, Antonia turned with relief to accept a glass of lemonade from a passing footman bearing a silver tray of drinks, and took the opportunity to continue across the room toward the guest of honour.

As she walked toward the small cluster of young people, of which Sophia was the center, Tonia couldn't help smiling when she saw that the scene before her displayed the validity of Aunt Aelfrida's concern. The Honourable Alfred Emory stood as if frozen in the circle of swains vying for Sophia's attention. His mouth slightly ajar, his eyes unblinking, he appeared to be mesmerized by the sight of Sophia's shining golden locks arranged with a fluff of ringlets over each ear and topped by a circlet of pale pink rosebuds.

Tonia stopped just short of the group to observe their interactions. She noted as well how accurate Agatha's calculations regarding her daughter had been. Indeed, Alice was sadly put in the shade by Sophia's radiance. Antonia considered whether the situation would be made better or worse in Agatha's estimation by the fact that Beatrice, who was permitted most social activities although her come-out wouldn't be official for another year yet, was such a perfect foil for Sophia's golden beauty. Bea, with her gleaming black side ringlets almost brushing her ivory shoulders, didn't appear to lack for attention in the circle of gallants clamoring to pay their regards.

Two young men, striking in their scarlet regimental uniforms amply adorned with gold braid, stood out among their rivals who were all dressed in the strictly correct evening habit of black tail coat and tight trousers with white silk waistcoat, and white linen shirt and cravat. Antonia did not know the older, quieter one, a captain if she read the stripes on his sleeve correctly, who stood at the back of the circle looking on. She was fairly certain, though, that she recognized the taller one as Lieutenant Thomas Anson, an acquaintance of Alfred Emory. This evening, however, the two young men appeared to be more rivals than friends as they vied for Sophia's attention. The young lady, though, looked to be more intent on visiting with Beatrice as the two young women sat with their heads together.

"I say, you ladies must come to the regimental parade in Hyde Park——" the lieutenant began.

He was cut off, however, by Alfred Emory who had obviously been badgering his brain for something to say. "What a topping idea, Anson. I shall escort the ladies." He had the grace to include both of his sisters in the invitation. "The dowager duchess ain't going to find it exceptional if my sisters come along." The footnote, directed to Sophia, received a scowl from Anson.

The dowager duchess might not have, but it was clear that the Baroness of Burroway, who arrived at her son's left shoulder in time to hear the invitation, found the idea entirely unacceptable. "Alfred Emory, I will thank you to secure me a glass of lemonade."

The young man had no choice but to obey.

The space left by his departure was filled by the dowager duchess who had led Danvers across the crowded floor to present her ward to Lord and Lady Danvers. "And you shall give a ball," she pronounced as Danvers was midway through acknowledging the introduction.

Before either Charles or Antonia could form a reply, Agatha mastered the conflicting emotions of disgust and aspiration that fought for ascendency on her face and turned to her brother. "Yes, Charles, that's the least you can do for Beatrice in her first season."

Antonia smiled at her husband's wisdom as he merely tendered a simple bow that managed to include all the ladies in the circle and walked away. Deciding to follow his example, she offered her brightest smile to Sophia, whose countenance mirrored the confusion she must be feeling, and retreated in Danvers's wake.

They had no more left the circle than a tall, middle-aged man with striking features in a slightly swarthy face strode into the room and, after making a bow to several of the ladies, cut a determined path to Sophia's side.

Antonia grabbed Danvers's arm. "Charles! Did you see who just came in?"

He gazed around the room. "Upward of a hundred people, I should judge, if the other rooms are as full as this one."

"No, Charles. There, bowing over Sophia's hand. How dare he show his face here?"

"Penthurst? I haven't seen him for more than a year— heard he was involved in some scandal. I wonder what brought him to town."

Tonia scowled. "It appears obvious to me. He seems to have his sights set on Sophia. Or at least on her fortune. Never mind he's twice her age."

Danvers considered. "If I recall correctly, his father died a year or two ago. Perhaps he's thinking it's time to do his duty by the family and survey the marriage mart. I would have had him down as a confirmed bachelor. I don't think he comes to London often."

"How dare he come at all? If he comes near me I shall cut him, and I'd thank you to do the same. He used my cousin abominably." But there was time for no more as Danvers moved on across the room.

At the far end of the reception room double doors opened onto a drawing room, likewise filled with small groups of splendidly arrayed, gossiping guests. Lord and Lady Danvers maneuvered their way across the room, stopping only briefly to acknowledge friends and acquaintances. The drawing room gave onto a dark-paneled, red-carpeted hallway. Beyond the hallway was the room Danvers was making for—the library.

The high-ceilinged room was ringed with two levels of leather-bound, gold-embossed books, the upper level reached by a circular stairway in the corner leading to an iron-railed gallery. A low fire burned on the grate of the fireplace at the far end of the room. Over the mantel a fine oil portrait held pride of place. Osbert, His Grace, the Duke of Aethelbert, the dowager duchess's son who had succeeded his deceased father to the title, displayed in all the finery of his ducal robes.

Beneath the portrait, lounging in a plum-colored plush chair, was the original of the portrait. His grace came to his feet at Lord and Lady Danvers's entrance. "Hullo, Charles, Cousin Antonia. I trust you are acquainted with the Earl of Ellenborough."

"Lord Ellenborough," Tonia smiled and nodded her head. "How agreeable that you could manage an evening away from the Lords." Aunt Aelfrida had done well, Tonia mused. Lord Ellenborough, who had been Governor-General of India more than a decade before, was well known for his insistent and sometimes fiery speeches in the House of Lords. He would not have left Parliament on a whim before the evening session adjourned.

"And you know Lucie and Alexander, I'm sure," Lord

Osbert continued and gave a sweeping gesture that indicated the newcomers should take a seat on the deep green velvet settee on the other side of the fireplace.

Tonia turned to the elegant, if strong-featured, dark-haired lady dressed in deep garnet satin. "Lucie, how charming to see you." The ladies brushed cheeks and took their seats.

Lucie, Lady Duff Gordon, only a few years older than herself, had been known to Tonia since girlhood. Lucie was a noted literary figure, having published several biographies and translations of books from the German. She was friends with such luminaries as John Stuart Mill, Tennyson, Dickens and Thackeray, who met frequently at the Duff Gordon home in Queen Square.

Tonia was wondering what could have interested this serious-minded lady in an event as frivolous as the come-out of a young girl of no position, when Lucie turned to Lord Ellenborough and asked, "Now, Edward, you must tell me—I only subjected myself to this squeeze in the hope that you would be here—what is all this brouhaha I hear about trouble in India? Surely it can't be true. Just the papers stirring up sensation I told Alexander this morning."

At the mention of his name her husband, who was a Commissioner of the Inland Revenue and member of Her Majesty's Privy Chamber, entered and presented his wife with the glass of Madeira he had apparently been commissioned to fetch for her. "Thank you, Alexander. I have just asked Edward to set us straight on all this nonsense about India."

The wavering flames from the fireplace added a grimness to the serious look already on the Earl of Ellenborough's handsome features. "Alas, Lucie, I only wish I could assure you that it is nonsense. On the contrary, I fear the situation is much more serious than we know."

"But surely any disaffection amongst the native troops is

limited to those in Bengal—which is hard enough to believe because they have always been so docile. The sepoy regiments in the Indian service have served faithfully and submissively for nearly a century. What could have changed that so suddenly?"

Before Ellenborough could answer, Lucie's husband continued her theme. "The fellows have always been happy enough to take our pay. And by all accounts they show a real aptitude for military discipline. Impossible to think they would mutiny."

"Mutiny?" Lord Osbert frowned and swirled the rich red port in his glass. "What twaddle! I read in the Evening Mail only last Saturday that 'somnolent tranquility, characteristic of the hot season, was brooding over India.' I believe I have the correspondent's words pretty much verbatim—quite poetic, I thought them." He took a sip of port before continuing. "I recall his assuring his readers that the greatest dangers are the risk of cholera and dysentery until the rains have come and gone. Unpleasant that, but hardly the stuff of mutiny."

The former Governor-General of India shook his head. "Certainly, your grace, I read the same article. Published sixth June, indeed, as you say. But did you note when it was written?"

The duke looked blank.

"I believe you will find that it was written on the eleventh of May. And if you had continued reading to the end you would have discovered a report of a telegraphic message containing intelligence which rather marred that profound picture of tranquility. I refer to the fact that the Bengal Cavalry are in open mutiny. The scoundrels have burnt down officers' bungalows and several officers and men have been killed and wounded."

Antonia hid her shiver in a sip of lemonade. *Officers' bunga-*

lows. Surely wives and children resided there also? She knew little enough about the vast continent of India from which the British Empire derived so much of its wealth, but she had recently begun to pay more attention to all things Indian since receiving Emilia's surprising letter. Surely Osbert had the right of it. Emilia had recounted in glowing terms how kind the Indian soldiers serving under British orders were. She recalled a particularly charming story of a sepoy teaching two young sons of a British officer to ride a pony.

But now the talk of trouble in Emilia's amiable world of military balls and officers' receptions brought fear to Tonia's heart. Lord Ellenborough was exaggerating, surely.

"I wish I could be of comfort to you, Lucie." Ellenborough turned to the lady who had opened this disturbing discussion. "But I fear that you, like most of our English, are too complacent. I much apprehend that the spirit of disaffection in India is widespread. I am privy to a telegraphic dispatch from Marseilles confirming the worst: Seven incendiary fires, sepoy cavalry in open mutiny, English officers shot and killed."

Alexander Duff Gordon set his glass of wine on the low table by his chair and leaned forward. "Balderdash! What do you mean alarming the ladies like that, man? Keep your warmongering for your speeches in Parliament."

"That is precisely what I did before coming here. You may read the account of my speech in the press tomorrow. I only hope our journalistic gentlemen report it accurately."

Lucie, whose features had flared at the suggestion that ladies should not be informed, turned to her husband. "Pray, do not be ridiculous Alexander. I am intensely interested; not alarmed. You know how dear I hold my friends in India. At least I'm persuaded that my charming Azimoolah Khan could never be disloyal. Nor his benevolent master Nana Sahib; 'The Gentleman of Bithur' they call him." She turned to

Antonia. "I am so sorry, my dear Tonia, that you were out of London when Azimoolah was my houseguest. Very grand-looking, he was. And you would have been as enchanted with his amiable manners as I was."

Tonia forbore to reply. She rather considered that she had had a lucky escape. If half the gossip she had heard of the suave Musselman's conquests in the bedrooms of Belgravia and Mayfair had any basis in fact, she was quite certain she would not have wanted to be placed in a position that would have required her to receive him. Although, she had to admit her curiosity was piqued.

Lucie Duff Gordon turned back to Ellenborough. "No, I am absolutely secure that there can be no uprising in Cawn-pore, whatever may be happening in some other far-off corner of the continent." She smiled complacently at Tonia. "Cawn-pore has the second-largest European society in India. My friends there assure me it is a most agreeable residence. In consequence of there being so many settled residents, the gardens rank amongst the finest in India. They give the city a very luxuriant appearance.

"And the faith is thoroughly established as well. The Society for the Propagation of the Gospel runs a fine orphan asylum in an old palace, and St. John's chapel, the soldiers' church, is as fine a stone structure as you would find in England. I am assured as well that shops offer every article of European manufacture necessary for comfort or even luxury."

Since that pretty well tallied with the impression she had received from Emilia's letter, Antonia allowed herself to be reassured.

With a snap of her black lace fan Lucie turned back to Ellenborough. "What are you suggesting? There can hardly be trouble in such a place as that."

"As to Cawnpore I have no immediate information." The earl inclined his head, the firelight revealing the ample grey in his formerly raven locks. "The immediate intelligence has come from Meerut."

Lucie considered for a moment. "Ah, that's all very well then. Meerut must be some three hundred miles from Cawnpore."

Antonia relaxed as the conversation continued around her. Emilia was safe, then. What luck that her friend was in Cawnpore. She had even mentioned in her letter how kind and obliging the Peshwa Nana Sahib was. Emilia had been among the European women, mostly officers' wives, to be entertained in his palace. She described "Saturday House," as it was apparently called: filled with carpets, tapestries, European chandeliers and chiming clocks. The description had made Tonia smile, sounding as it did so much like the Royal Pavilion at Brighton.

Still, the alarming reports Ellenborough had recounted to the others continued to disturb Tonia as Danvers's barouche carried them back to Grosvenor Square shortly after midnight. "Charles, what do you make of the matter of India?"

Danvers didn't reply.

"Pray, do not be like Sir Alexander and hold your opinion for fear of alarming me. I have always firmly believed that it is far better to be in possession of the facts of a situation than to be put in the position of imagining something far worse."

"Quite, my love. I have no intention of dissimulating with you. I simply do not know what to think. I do know, however, that there may be no man in London—in all of England— better informed on India than Lord Ellenborough."

"And why do you say that?"

"He has served in Parliament since before Waterloo. You'll realize, of course, he is very near my father's age. Ellenborough became Lord Privy Seal under Wellington. More to the present question, however, he was four times President of the Board of Control—overseeing the East India Company. That made him the chief official in London responsible for Indian affairs. He was an obvious choice then for the position of Governor-General of India.

"He is well known for his active interest in India." Danvers paused. "I seem to recall a few years back he agitated for the government of India to come under the Crown rather than the East India Company. Nothing came of that, of course—far too radical."

Antonia considered. "Does he have a family?"

"No. A melancholy story, I fear. His first wife died after a few years of marriage. My father knew her; said she was a frail beauty."

"And he never remarried?"

"Well, yes, he married." The sound of the carriage wheels on pavement and the smart clip-clop of horses' hooves filled the carriage in his silence.

"Charles, tell."

"There was a scandal. A son was born, but Ellenborough was not the father. Apparently other affairs followed. When her affair with some Germanic prince became public knowledge Ellenborough had no choice but to divorce her by Act of Parliament."

"Oh, the poor man!"

"Indeed. Forgive me for sullying your ears with such detail."

"Not at all, my lord. I thank you for an honest answer." She took his hand under the rug protecting their legs from the night air and held it in silence for the remainder of the journey.

Hours later, sometime in the small hours of the morning, Antonia jerked awake with a muffled cry on her lips. She held her breath, listening to the silence. What had so disturbed her sleep? She could just hear a faint snoring from her husband's chamber beyond her dressing room. Her beloved Tinker snuffled in his basket at the foot of her bed. She strained her ears. All was quiet in the nursery above them. If either Charlie or Nurse Bevans had stirred she would hear the footfall on the floor over her head.

Forced at last to breathe, she relaxed, and the images came flooding back: rioting dark-skinned men in turbans running through the night with flaring torches, setting fire to tidy bungalows; gunfire ripping the dark; the screams of women and children. A baby's sharp cry.

She was on her feet heading for the door when she realized the child's cry had come not from her own sleeping toddler upstairs, but from the fearful spectre she had conjured from the reports of the uprising in India.

2

*E*milia tossed on her straw pallet. Numb with fear and exhaustion, she had dropped into an uneasy doze. Incessant shot from rebel snipers pounding the walls of the barracks, however, soon made sleep impossible. Children sobbed and were comforted by their mothers or ayahs. It was encouraging that many of the native nurses had remained because they were Christians or out of devotion to their charges. Lydia Hillersdon's newborn infant's whimpers were stilled with gentle shushings.

Near-to four hundred women and children were huddled beneath the tiled roof of the barracks. Uncomfortable as they were—even in the night the heat was stifling—they had been assured there was plenty of food and medical supplies to last for a month, and General Wheeler intended to evacuate them to Allalhabad when General Havelock's relief column arrived. Dear God, let it come soon, Emilia prayed.

Rumors of the events of the previous day had reached the women in somewhat garbled form, the men wanting to shield them from alarm, but it was understood that the lieutenant Wheeler had sent to blow up the abandoned magazine had lost his life in the gallant attempt. That meant that the rebels had all of the English heavy guns and reserve ammunition at their disposal.

Daylight brought with it only a rise in the temperature. General Wheeler had ordered a cook-pit to be dug behind the barracks and the women set about stewing dahl from lentils, split peas and chick peas. Emilia took a hand shaping the flat, oval chupatties from flour, water and a little salt. Flour was plentiful, but the water had to be carefully rationed as a journey to the well exposed their valiant waterboy to enemy fire.

More trying than even the heat or the incessant noise of shot—the report of grape shot from the rifles or the boom of the nine-pounder guns—was the inability to bathe. In the oppressive, sticky heat, Emilia and all the memsahibs were accustomed to bathing and changing their raiment several times a day as a means of making life supportable. Now a mere mouthful of water was a precious thing.

By midmorning Emilia got up her courage to peer out the verandah where she could see beyond the mud wall surrounding the entrenchment. The scene made her catch her breath. The entire surrounding countryside seemed covered with men at arms, some on horseback, some on foot. She blinked, but the exercise did nothing to improve the vision. Indeed, it seemed to worsen as clouds of dust in the distance spoke of more gathering rebels. It made their own defenses appear Lilliputian.

Looking toward the cantonment, she saw a fresh billow of smoke, followed by a blaze of hungry, orange flame. At the sight, a groan, as of pain, went up from the men near her. St. John's, the soldiers' beloved church, had been set alight. Jonah Shepherd, standing near her, shook his head. "How heavy the hand of God is to bring such judgment upon us."

Emilia went inside, but there was no escaping the horror. As the day wore on the enemy fire increased. Every shot that struck the barracks was followed by heart-rending shrieks of women and children. Some were killed outright by bullets piercing the walls, or crushed by falling beams or masonry.

After one such salvo delicate little Mable Halliday, her friend's daughter, who had always been high-strung and frail, began tugging at her hair and screaming. When her mother reached her side, the girl was dead. Apparently from shock.

That afternoon Major Charles Hillersdon came into the women's quarters to visit his wife who was making a remarkable recuperation from her accouchement. After admiring their sleeping infant, Charles took his wife out to the southern verandah for a private word. "Will it be safe, outside?" Lydia asked.

"Yes, well out of reach of the rebels' batteries," he replied.

Emilia heard the musket ball fired into the entrenchment from the newly positioned battery. And she heard Lydia's scream of horror as it struck Charles Hillersdon full in the stomach.

But worse was to follow.

"Tonia, you look te—" Charles stopped himself with a cough before he said *terrible*. "Terribly peaked. Are you ill? Shall I ring for Isabella?" He leaned across the eiderdown and put a hand on her arm. She didn't feel feverish through the delicate white lawn sleeve of her nightdress, but her face, ringed with the tousled red-gold hair that never failed to allure him, looked as white as the embroidered percale pillowcase on which it lay. Except for the dark rings that circled her eyes like bruises.

Tonia always seemed so strong, so vibrant. It was hard to imagine her the childhood victim of consumption. His heart constricted. Could the dread disease have returned? Now, when they were in such anticipation of an addition to the nursery?

Betsy, the upstairs maid, had entered Lady Danvers's room at the usual hour that morning to open her curtains and light a low fire on the grate. She would return in a few minutes with the morning tray Lord and Lady Danvers liked to share in her ladyship's room. This morning, as yesterday, the activity had failed to rouse Antonia. Even Tinker seemed less frisky than usual, simply sitting up in his basket and cocking his head.

Tonia struggled to sit up and Charles arranged the pillows at her back.

Fear made him hesitant to voice his concern. "Our daughter?"

This brought a smile to Tonia's face. "You are so certain it's a girl, my love. No, I'm not ill. But I did have the most dreadful dream. Then I thought I would never get back to sleep again. I dreamed of Emilia again. I am so worried..."

"My love, I know you are concerned, but you mustn't fret. I realize you and Emilia were close, but—"

"We were close—like sisters. Closer than most sisters, I imagine. More like twins. It was the oddest thing—as girls we could always finish one another's sentences—almost before the other started hers. It was as if we could read one another's minds—knew what the other was thinking—feeling. Sometimes we would have the same dreams.

"Then we drew apart as adults—our lives took such very different turns. But of late—since she went out to India last winter, I've felt closer to her than in years. And then receiving her letter and meeting her daughter—

"Twice I have dreamt of her and wakened not knowing whether it was a dream or—some sort of message." Tonia shuddered at the thought. And Charles drew the eiderdown closer around her.

"Charles, how much foundation do you believe there is to Lord Ellenborough's concerns for India? Could Emilia be in danger?"

Danvers perched on the edge of the bed. "If it were anyone but Ellenborough I would write off the reports as hysteria over a smattering of restlessness on the part of the natives, or an inflated attempt to sell papers on the part of the press..."

"But?" Tonia encouraged him to continue.

Charles shook his head. "I don't know about the wider picture, but India is a vast country. I should think you could rely on Lucie's assurances of the reliability of her acquaintances as to the safety of your friend in Cawnpore."

"I do hope you're right. I wish she were safe in London right now, rather than racketing around India."

A brief knock at the door announced the arrival of their morning tray—tea for my lady and coffee for her lord—but the bearer accompanied his entrance with a surprising Irish lilt. "Ah, and the brightest of good mornings to ye, m'lord; m'lady." He nodded to each as he set the tray on the small round table in front of the window.

"Good morning, Hardy. And to what do we owe this surprise?" Danvers stared at his ebullient man, unsure that Tonia would be pleased to meet his valet's energetic manner this early in the morning.

"Betsy was a mite behind-hand this morning what with the Honourable Reverend Frederick arriving so much earlier than anticipated—"

"Freddie?" Danvers's stare darkened to a glare. "My brother wasn't expected until this afternoon."

"I believe he changed his plans and caught a train yesterday, m'lord. Something to do with Miss Hever and her sister. I understand it involved a milliner's appointment."

Now all shadow of her worries left Antonia's face. "Victoria and Cecilia are come too? How charming! Are they below?"

Hardy stiffened slightly. "I apprehend they are staying with some relations in, er—Upper Wimpole Street, m'lady." Hardy pronounced the address as if it had been located in the stews.

Tonia laughed. "Hardy! Marylebone is a perfectly respectable area. A trifle middle class, perhaps, but for the future wife of a clergyman it should do very well. I shan't blush to call on them there." Antonia made as if she would get out of bed. Hardy, taking the hint, backed out of the room.

"Tell my whippersnapper of a brother I'll join him at breakfast as soon as I've enjoyed my morning coffee with my wife, Hardy," Danvers called to his man's departing back.

A short time later, having assured himself of Antonia's recovery from the demons of the night, Danvers found Frederick making a hearty breakfast from the offerings on the sideboard. "Explain yourself, gudgeon. What do you mean, turning up at this time of the morning?" His words were softened by the twinkle in his eye. "Not that I'm not entirely glad to see you, you understand."

Freddie gave his brother the smile that had done so much to win supporters for the numerous charitable causes his church supported in the poorest part of York. "Don't start or I'll recount the entire journey in painful detail. Do you have any idea how many stops the Great Northern makes between York and London?" He held up his hand before Danvers could reply. "No, neither do I. I lost count somewhere south of Retford, but I assure you, I was fully awake through every one of the delays—scheduled and unscheduled. Didn't you receive my telegram updating my letter?"

Danvers shook his head.

"We came on a day early. Vicky did want to get her shopping in hand before I take up my placement, and with the Festival tomorrow—you've read about it in the papers, no doubt. Expected to arrive at an entirely respectable hour last night, instead of the middle of the night. Stout man, your Bracken. Sorry about waking him."

Following his brother's example, Danvers heaped his plate with scrambled eggs, boiled haddock and stewed tomatoes, then took his seat at the head of the table. The brothers ate in silence for a few moments, then Danvers asked, "And how did the Misses Hever hold up to such an ordeal? I hope you weren't required to minister to hysterical females the length of the journey?"

Freddie gave his brother a reproachful look. "None of it, I assure you! Vicky and Cece were much too busy calming their Aunt Dimity, who is attending them as chaperone, to take any thought for themselves. Besides, Charles, you know full well—"

"What undaunted ladies your intended and her twin are? Yes, little brother, I do. And I congratulate you." Danvers had not forgotten his admiration for the sisters' level-headedness through the anxieties of discovering the killer of inmates of Frederick's asylum for fallen women a year ago.

After the footman, standing by the silver urn at the end of the sideboard, had refilled both of the gentlemen's coffee cups and Freddie had taken another pass at the dishes offered there, Charles continued. "And how long are we to have the pleasure of your company, little brother? I believe your missive mentioned something about attending a meeting in London? And some faradiddle about working at the London Docks, but I'm quite certain you were joking. You've taken some strange notions into that head of yours, but becoming a navvie was never one of them so far as I am aware."

Freddie laughed. "I say, Charles, you should listen to yourself. You sound like Aunt Aelfrida. I most certainly shall be working at the Docks this summer. Well, very near them, that is, at St. George-in-the-East." In his enthusiasm he scooted to the very edge of his chair. "I've done a swap with another SSC priest—*Societas Sanctae Crucis*—the Society of the Holy Cross, you know."

Danvers rolled his eyes. He did not know; and he very much doubted that he wanted to. His little brother's extreme, ritualistic views had caused more than enough trouble in the past. Basic, safe, Church of England should be good enough for anybody. Why these Tractarians had to take it into their heads to stir up trouble, and why his brother should be one of them, was beyond him.

"George Walston—splendid chap, we were friends at Oxford—he'll take the services at St. Alphege's and oversee the work of the Magdalen House in York, and I'll get to work directly under Charles Lowder. It'll be the most magnificent experience!" Danvers considered that of all the adjectives in the English language 'magnificent' was probably the last he would have chosen for the experience Freddie described, but his brother gave him no opportunity to express his skepticism. "London's slums offer so much more scope for mission than York's. And Elizabeth Neale, sister of the hymn-writer John Mason Neale you know, has started a community of sisters, the Order of St. Margaret, to assist in the work, and—"

Unwilling to dampen Frederick's enthusiasm for work that was certain to become quickly enough a burdensome drudge, Danvers only said, "I do wish you would quit telling me I know things I don't know." He forbore to add, *and have no desire to know.* "Don't tell me Miss Hever, either one of them, is planning to join this order?"

Freddie had the grace to be shocked at the suggestion. "No! Certainly not! That would never do—they take vows of celibacy, you kn—Er, that is, not at all. Vicky and Cece will be more than adequately occupied shopping for wedding clothes. I do hope Antonia won't mind giving a hand in that?"

"She would be offended if they didn't ask." Antonia,

looking fresh in a morning dress of muted blue and brown plaid muslin, entered the room in time to answer for herself. "Hardy mentioned a milliner's appointment. I shall send a note offering my assistance."

Both men had come to their feet at Lady Danvers's entrance. She gave Freddie a brief welcoming embrace, and Danvers pulled out a chair for her. "Have you breakfasted, love?"

"Isabella offered a boiled egg and toast, but I'm not hungry yet." She took the chair Charles held for her. "I would much prefer to hear about Freddie's plans."

Danvers doubted that she would. He was confident that Antonia would be as dismayed as he was at the idea of Frederick taking up mission work at the London Docks so, leaning back in his chair, he steered the conversation another direction. "This meeting you're to attend, some festival I believe you said?"

"Yes, the SPG—it will be splendid." He paused at the blank looks on their faces. "Society for the Propagation of the Gospel in Foreign Parts, you know. Their festival, that is. You must come with us. I'll send a note to Aunt Aelfrida, too. You know... Er—that is, you see, Her Majesty has withdrawn her direct monetary support—a loss of ten thousand pounds a year to the society. That means we must be sufficient to raise our own support. It becomes incumbent upon the traders and bankers of the city..."

He continued describing the plans for the festival and his mission work until his hostess signaled to the footman to help her with her chair. His apology for running on was lost in the activity of all standing.

Antonia smiled. "I'm certain you are correct, Freddie. Your passionate enthusiasm will doubtless bring success to your efforts, but you must excuse me now. I need to dispatch a note to Victoria before I join Charlie and Nurse

Bevans in the garden." She moved toward the door, then turned back.

"We shall, of course, be delighted to attend your festival, Freddie. And you and the Misses Hever must be among our party at Lady Essworthy's musical soiree." Without waiting for an answer she swept on. "It promises to be a charming squeeze. Just don't tell Aunt Aelfrida the location of your new parish."

The gentlemen were no sooner reseated and Freddie relaunched into his theme quoting statistics of the splendid missionary efforts of the SPG, especially in India, than Hardy entered to inform their guest that his room was ready. "I took the liberty of unpacking for you, sir."

"Oh, that wasn't the least necessary, but I do thank you." He turned to Danvers, "If you'll pardon me, brother, I'll just go settle in. If you'd care to show me the way, Hardy."

"You may refill my cup, Michael," Danvers directed the footman when the others were gone. "And fetch me the papers."

A few moments later Michael presented his lordship with two newspapers on a silver salver. "Thank you. That will be all." The footman bowed and departed.

Danvers picked up "The Gazette" first. Freshly ironed by the attentive Bracken to dry the ink, it was still warm to the touch. Danvers smiled as peace descended upon the room of which he was now the sole occupant. He sipped his sweetened, milky coffee and unfolded the paper.

The information he looked for held pride of place on the first page. "The news which has just reached this country from India is of more than ordinary import," he read. "The telegraphic dispatch from Marseilles in anticipation of the arrival of the mail announced the spread of a very serious spirit of disaffection in the native army of Bengal, which has already manifested itself in mutinous outbreaks in no less than three separate regiments."

He scanned on down the column: "General revolt of the entire native army... open mutiny..." Thinking of Tonia's concern for her friend in Cawnpore, Danvers read with interest the list of scenes of mutiny: Meerut, which Ellenborough had mentioned, Dinapore, Barrackpore, Agra, Lucknow... His knowledge of the geography of India was less than precise, but wasn't Lucknow somewhat close to Cawnpore?

He turned to the "Morning Chronicle," hoping to find a report on the speech Ellenborough had given before joining them at the Drawing-room last night. Ah, here, given prominence at the top of the page: "Imperial Parliament, House of Lords. The Lord Chancellor took his seat on the Woolsack at five o'clock." And the first item had been "Our Indian Administration" with a two-column report on Ellenborough's speech and the subsequent debate.

The earl presented the situation in India essentially as he had reported to them last night, but with the alarming details that "a regiment of cavalry, not more than four hundred in number, had been allowed to remain for a week in open mutiny in the face of an overpowering European force in their vicinity."

Ellenborough then went on to search for a reason for the cause of such unexpected behavior on the part of the formerly loyal native troops. The article reported that the speaker "could come, however, to no other conclusion than that the cause of all these disturbances was the apprehension on the part of the native population that it was the intention of the Government to interfere with their religion." Danvers shook his head. Was such a change of policy possible? Her Majesty's Government had always been scrupulous in assuring that there would be no interference with the natives' religion or customs. If Ellenborough's conclusion were correct, surely the natives had disastrously misconstrued some situation.

In reply, Earl Granville, the former Secretary of State for Foreign Affairs, had deprecated a discussion grounded on a telegraphic message—which might, and most probably did, exaggerate the truth. "The electric telegraph, one of the most wonderful applications of modern science, was yet attended with some inconveniences, and one was that statements were received the accuracy of which could not be relied upon," the paper summarized his speech.

Danvers set the paper aside with a sigh, He could only hope that Granville was correct and the reports were exaggerated. He hated to consider what it might mean if Ellenborough's informants were correct. A bloodbath in India was unthinkable.

3

"**W**e are so fortunate to be in London for the festival!" The following day, Victoria, sitting beside her sister in Danvers's barouche, almost bounced on the seat in her excitement. "I have never been to St. Paul's before, and Freddie says they are to perform Handel —just as they did at the Crystal Palace last night. The chorus will be smaller of course, but I'm confident it will be just as fine."

Antonia started to make a noncommittal answer, but the dowager duchess preempted her. "That remains to be seen. It is, however, most proper in you as Frederick's intended that you should hold such enthusiasm. As a vicar's wife, you will doubtless be required to attend a great many such events."

The dampening speech did little to quell the girl's pleasure. "Oh, I do hope so. And Freddie is to be in the procession. Right behind the bishops. I'm certain it will be splendid."

"Much more appropriate for the son of an earl—even a younger son—than his usual activities. Do I understand correctly that Frederick's plan is to work at the Docks this summer?"

Tonia smiled. So much for keeping the information from Aunt Aelfrida. If the dowager duchess's observation was intended to subdue the girl's effusion, however, the effort was lost on the bride-to-be.

"Oh, yes. It is such a splendid opportunity for him." She sighed. "I can't help wondering if it's quite the thing for me to spend such an effort on finery when the need for charity workers is so great. But Freddie says we owe it to our families."

"I should think so. I will not be disgraced—"

The dowager duchess got no further with her ecomium to family honour because at that moment they arrived amid the bustle of carriages at St. Paul's Cathedral.

Lord Danvers handed the ladies out of the carriage and, with Antonia on one arm and Aunt Aelfrida on the other, led the way up the great front steps toward the portico with its two levels of paired columns. Once inside, he heard Victoria and Cecilia gasp at the sight of the magnificent white and gold nave. They craned their necks at the sweeping arches of the side aisles and the interior of the great dome soaring before them.

There was no time, however, to dawdle as an usher led them across the black and white marble floor to their seats. They were barely seated when the procession began. Their program informed them that the imposing choir which processed by them singing Handel's "The Lord Gave the Word" consisted of the united choirs of St. Paul's, Westminster Abbey, St. George's, Windsor, and the Chapels Royal.

The clergy were led in by the priest in ordinary to Her

Majesty, followed by the canons and minor canons, the officers of the Society for the Propagation of the Gospel and the Church Missionary Society. The dean of the cathedral, in splendid gold cope, led clergy and an impressive list of bishops from all over the United Kingdom. Danvers was certain he would have missed his own brother's presence in the august assembly had not he received such a compelling nudge and only slightly subdued squeal from Miss Hever beside him. The procession was concluded by the chaplain to the Lord Mayor.

At the close of the opening prayers the congregation sat for the readings from the Book of Job and the Psalms. Since his brother's involvement was Danvers's only motivation for attending the festival, he found his mind wandering to current events. How might the reported turmoil in India affect matters in England? In his own family, even?

The sermon was preached by the Lord Bishop of Salisbury on a text from Joshua, but Danvers didn't bring his mind back to the present until the Secretary of the SPG was called on to give a report on the work of the Society for the Propagation of the Gospel in Foreign Parts. "The society has now been pursuing its course for one hundred, fifty-six years, endeavoring to plant the Church of Christ among our countrymen abroad and among the heathen. When the society was first founded there were probably not twenty clergymen of the Church of England in foreign lands. Today there are almost three thousand in fields as widespread as India, China and Canada."

In keeping with events in the news of the day, the speaker presented a report from India. The society's work at Cawnpore was in the hands of the widowed Reverend William Haycock, a former printer who had become a missionary at some sacrifice of income. Haycock, the speaker assured the congregation, was a man of patient, laborious, unostentatious habits, well-versed in scripture and the native languages. He had done good work in ministering to the Indian population and had established a Christian congregation among the natives at Cawnpore. He was assisted in the work by Reverend Cockney and by Mister Willis, who would soon be going to Calcutta to receive ordination.

Special prayer was solicited for Reverend Haycock who, in his last message to the board had reported that on his return to the station from depositing his two motherless sons in school, he was warned by a Musselman cleric that the English would "soon feel the sharpness of the Mussulman's sword." Haycock's servant begged him to leave India before it was too late. The missionary, however, was standing by his flock, but he had entrusted the mission's communion plate and altar cloth to a neighboring landlord. His elderly mother had also chosen to stay, as had Reverend Cockney's wife and child.

In addition, prayers were requested for the Reverend Moncrieff, the pastor of the soldiers' church, who also ran the Free School for local children.

As the concerns for India mounted, Danvers felt Tonia tense beside him. He took her hand and was surprised at the fervor with which she clung to him. She must be more concerned for her friend in Cawnpore than he realized. He did not like having her disturbed by unhappy thoughts in her delicate condition. He wondered if he should take her home now, but such fears were put away as the service moved on to a stirring culmination with the "Hallelujah Chorus" sung by the combined choirs.

At the conclusion of the recessional, Victoria sat, still enraptured. "Oh, wasn't that wonderful! Such exhilarating music. And the thought of those dedicated missionaries toiling in foreign fields. Did you not find it thrilling?" Her question was general.

Aunt Aelfrida answered with a brief nod. "The music was very fine. All this enthusiasm for the Gospel in foreign parts, though—I am unaware of there being any want of heathen in our own land."

❊ 4 ❊

How much longer could this go on? Emilia had lost count of the days. Had it been only a week since the rebels opened fire? It felt like a month—or a lifetime. The pleasant days of strolls by the Ganges in the cool of the evening, watching the birds and flirting with young officers, were certainly a lifetime ago. Literally for many of those officers. How many of the attractive, lighthearted young men she had teased and shared stories of home with and danced with at balls now lay dead beneath the scorching sun?

She looked around her. Officers' wives and daughters, who always dressed in the height of fashion and kept a fastidious toilette, now sat on the floor or on broken furniture of the barracks in tattered clothing, begrimed with dirt, emaciated in countenance. She observed the wife and daughters of General Wheeler. Such a short time ago they had been beautiful. Their features were now chiseled with deep furrows; haggard despair replaced the sparkling smiles of a month ago. Even the valiant Mrs. Moore, wife of Captain John Moore, the Acting Deputy Commander of the Entrenchment Defense, was weakening. She was indefatigable in her efforts to comfort others and attempts to amuse the children, but she could no longer hide the exhaustion that slowed her every movement.

Some of the women were sinking into the settled vacancy which bespoke insanity. Some babbled with confused imbecility, others raved, some gave in to wild mania. Emilia was determined not to be among that number. She must cling to her sanity. She determined to take refuge in her memories and her faith. She reached back, before her marriage, to those long-gone days in green and pleasant England. Gentle days where the only gunshot ever heard was the discharge of a fowling piece during pheasant hunting season while she was herself engaged in a game of croquet on a green lawn.

She recalled one especially pleasant, long-ago afternoon, strolling on the beach of the rugged, Cornish coast, laughing with fascinated chills to their host's accounts of smugglers who made use of the numerous caves around the cove in their wiles to avoid the revenue men. One particularly large wave had struck the rocks with such force that it had sent a refreshing spray of cool water over their party.

She held her face up, as if such rejuvenating moisture could reach her now. A volley of shot struck the wall above her head, sending a rain of dust down upon her.

What strange turns her life had taken. What if all those years ago her suitor's impetuosity hadn't launched her into the arms of Robert Landry? She had shocked the polite world by running off with Robert in her first season—a mere Writer for the East India Company, fresh from his training at Haileybury—when she could have captured a marquess. Still, they had been happy years, even if following her husband had required leaving her life in England behind. Happy years, but all too few of them. She forced her thoughts away from such dangerous territory to the simpler days of her childhood.

Tonia. All memories of her childhood were filled with happy days spent with her cousin. They had shared everything. Every dream; every thought. Often without even needing to speak the words. If only she had paper and pen she would write to her dearest friend now. Communicating with Tonia could provide a much-needed escape from the barbarity around her. She would not write to her daughter—

thank heaven that lovely child was safe in England. She would not have her know such horrors existed as Emilia herself was experiencing.

Try as she would to hold on to visions of such pleasant days, though, they faded with the intrusion of cries of the distressed and wounded around her. She turned to her other source of strength, and picked up her prayer book, turning to the Psalms. Why do the heathen so furiously rage together... Thou shalt bruise them with a rod of iron: and break them in pieces like a potter's vessel... Blessed are all they that put their trust in him.

Even as another shot tore into the barracks, Emilia determined to survive.

That evening, the Danvers party arrived late enough at the elegant residence of Lord and Lady Essworthy in Cavendish Square that the main crush of carriages delivering fashionable guests had moved on and Antonia was able to alight from their barouche without danger to the wide skirts of her floral-print silk gown. A lady harpist was regaling the company with a lilting air when their hostess came forward to greet the new arrivals. "Tonia, my dear, the height of fashion, as always." She admired Tonia's gown, then looked at Freddie and the two young ladies following Lord and Lady Danvers. "And how good of you to bring your guests with you."

Tonia couldn't help noting their hostess's admiring glance at the young ladies' coiffures adorned with the confections that testified to the success of their morning's expedition to the milliner. Victoria looked particularly fetching with a frill of pearls, roses and lily of the valley. And Antonia was equally pleased with her own selection of velvet ribbon and flowers over her looped braids.

Danvers was presenting his brother to their hostess when

the dowager duchess's party arrived. Lord Osbert, doing his duty to escort his mama and Sophia, greeted Lady Essworthy and bowed to Antonia then took himself off to the smoking room, as far away as possible from the reception room where most of the guests were gathered to hear the musical presentations prepared for the evening.

Sophia, however, was effusive in her appreciation to their hostess and obviously delighted to meet young women near her own age when Victoria and Cecilia were presented to her. They were no more than introduced before the young women were deep in a chatter of feminine exchanges. Until the dowager duchess intervened. "We will take seats at the back of the room. I hope your musicians are up to snuff, Charmian," she addressed Lady Essworthy. "I will not be caterwauled at." She paused to allow the gentle strains of the harp to fill the anteroom, then nodded. "That is quite acceptable. Won't interfere with conversation in the least." She swept into the reception room.

Her protégé looked torn between following her sponsor and continuing her chatter with Victoria and Cecilia. "Don't worry, Sophia, we'll all go with you," Antonia assured her, then secured the girl's comfort by sitting on the love seat next to Aelfrida and allowing Sophia and her new friends to take chairs a bit apart.

Giving equal attention to the music and to the dowager duchess's pronouncements on the company she was busy surveying through her lorgnette, Antonia enjoyed watching out of the corner of her eye as a cluster of eligible males gathered around Sophia and her companions. *Bees to clover*, she thought, a smile curling her lips.

The strains of the Bach harp sonata came to an end and repartee around the room lulled in the sudden quiet, to be followed by polite applause. A break in the entertainment allowed the guests to move more freely around the room or to make their way to the dining room for refreshments.

"Oh, here comes that encroaching Anson." The dowager duchess frowned at the young man in a scarlet tunic approaching the circle around Sophia. "Charles, do something to head him off. I'll not have him dangling after Sophia."

"Don't you dare, Charles!" Agatha approached at quick-march pace, her daughters Alice and Beatrice a few steps behind her. "I shall be only too happy to have Anson cut Alfred Emory out of that girl's sights. Aunt Aelfrida, you must be all about in your head to have brought her into polite society. Setting a cat among the pigeons, that's all you've accomplished." Danvers's eldest sister scowled at her son, sitting on a delicate empire chair between Sophia and Cecilia Hever.

Antonia was about to intervene when Anson sketched a sort of half salute to a newcomer, likewise in regimental uniform, this one wearing a red sash across his chest, proclaiming him to be an officer of his Light Infantry regiment. Tonia recognized him as the quiet officer who had accompanied Anson at Aunt Aelfrida's Drawing-room. She was about to request that he be presented to her when she became aware of the direction of his gaze.

And more startling still was the return that the Honourable Alice Rannoch made to his silent homage. The shy smile and sparkling eyes only half hidden by Alice's ivory lace fan achieved the miracle of turning the plain girl into something approaching a beauty. *Well, well, how interesting.* Now Tonia must make the man's acquaintance.

Lady Danvers rose and turned to her husband standing with his brother. "Charles, you must make introductions. Lieutenant Anson I have met, but not the other."

Danvers stepped forward and made a general introduction

of Lieutenant Thomas Anson and Captain George Bellingham to their party. Again, Tonia's sharp eye noted that Captain Bellingham's bow was just the slightest shade deeper to Alice than to any of the other ladies. How would Agatha react when she realized what was afoot? From all appearances, Tonia thought her sister-in-law should be delighted, but with Agatha it was never possible to predict.

Tonia considered what she could do to take a hand in matters, then turned to the half circle of chairs occupied by the young ladies of their party. "Would you ladies care to accompany me to the refreshment room?" Before any could answer she added, "You may escort us Captain Bellingham." She placed her hand lightly on the captain's arm and turned without waiting to see who chose to join them.

Among the press in the corridor she encountered Lucie Duff Gordon, being escorted from the dining room by a grey-haired, mustachioed man whose military bearing would have proclaimed him to be an officer even if his regimental uniform had not. The R below his rank insignia indicated his retired status. Captain Bellingham saluted the gentleman, but did not stop. Tonia could no more than nod to Lucie in the crush.

Once across the crowded reception room and equally thronged hall, they entered the long dining room lit with scores of candles in crystal chandeliers and adorned with tall floral displays on Grecian pillars between each of the floor-to-ceiling windows. Now Tonia could turn and assess the success of her ploy. She was not surprised to discover that Alice had, indeed, chosen to follow her lead, as well as Sophia and Cecilia, followed by Lieutenant Anson. The fact that Arthur Emory had apparently been waylaid by his mother told Tonia that Agatha was sufficiently distracted by fears for her son's attachment to Sophia that Alice and Captain Bellingham would not come under Agatha's scrutiny for the moment.

The length of the center table held a staggering selection of jellies, ices and macaroni molds as well as miniature savory tarts and pies of every description. Sugared almonds, sculpted marzipans and meringues completed the assortment. On a separate table, near the French doors leading to the terrace, a three-tiered fountain poured forth a refreshing wine punch. Sophia, apparently new to such a gastronomical display, seemed grateful for Anson's presence at her shoulder as he advised her on her choice of delicacies. Careful in doing his duty, however, the lieutenant also carried Cecilia's plate for her. This arrangement conveniently left Alice to Captain Bellingham's attention.

The footman assisted their party by filling crystal goblets from the fountain's gentle flow, then offered to show them to tables on the terrace. Tonia was especially happy to escape the noise and heat of the room. Anson, Sophia and Cecilia took chairs at one small round table, leaving Antonia to chaperone Alice and Bellingham at another, an arrangement she found most satisfactory since she hardly felt she was well enough acquainted with the captain to abandon Alice to his attentions unaccompanied. Although she did fear serving as duenna for this taciturn pair might require rather an effort on her part.

She was delighted, however, to discover that in this secluded company the elder Miss Rannoch lost the frightened field mouse aspect she had formerly presented. She deftly managed to engage the reserved officer in conversation about his army duties. "Light bobs—that is, Light Infantry," he answered in reply to her query about his regiment. "Currently billeted at Wellington Barracks."

Alice awarded a pleased smile to this information, undoubtedly thinking, as Tonia was, that such a fortunate situation was likely to make a favorable impression on the lady's mama. "Oh, near the palace! Have you seen the queen?"

"Often enough as she comes and goes in her carriage. Prince Albert has visited the barracks more than once—splendid fellow; interested in everything. Wellington's the regimental headquarters, you see."

Alice made an approving remark.

"Certainly, it's a desirable enough posting. Won't last, though. The rumor is we'll be moved to Brighton soon." He smiled at his companion in a way that made Tonia think they had both forgotten her presence. "Don't bandy this about, but I wouldn't be surprised if we're posted to India before too long—if half the reports one hears from that direction are true."

A look of concern filled Alice's face. Tonia suddenly wondered how she could have thought anyone with such an animated countenance was plain. Yes, a rather high forehead for which the current fashion of hair parted in the center was unflattering, too prominent a nose and too strong a jaw—all inherited from her mama—but the soft blue eyes that became luminous in Thomas Bellingham's presence easily outshone any defect.

"Oh, don't worry, we're sure to miss all the fun. The chaps already there will have put down any bother long before we could reach the subcontinent." Bellingham spoke soothingly and Tonia fervently hoped he was correct. She had surreptitiously read the morning papers abandoned by her husband. The reports did not reassure her.

Antonia's desire to know more about the situation for her friend in India overcame her instinct to remain as invisible as possible for the sake of the two in front of her. "Captain, I have read such conflicting reports. Do you have any information as to what could make the formerly loyal sepoys revolt?"

It was unclear whether his startled look was for this reminder that he and Alice were not alone, or his surprise that a high-born lady, a viscountess, even, should be enquiring about such matters. He blinked, his forehead furrowing, then answered in measured terms, "Information? No, my lady. I fear there is little that could go by such a precise name."

After a slight pause Antonia followed up her query. "I sense that there is more you could say on the matter, however. Pray, do not hold back in deference to my sensibilities or to Miss Rannoch's. I am certain Alice would agree with me that imagination is always capable of conjuring up far worse than any reality. I am most concerned for my very particular friend in Cawnpore. We quite grew up together, made our come-out the same season..." Her voice trailed off as images of that distant summer rose before her eyes: The aching neck from holding one's head stiffly erect to balance the long tulle veil falling from one's floral headdress, the effort of hiding one's nervous tremors produced by fear of tripping over the long train on one's court dress—or worse yet, collapsing in one's curtsy before the queen.

And then it came back to her with bittersweet sharpness that forced a smile to her lips even now: Emilia calming everyone's fears with the mocking jokes she made on herself, pretending to commit some terrible gaffe before Her Majesty. That was Emilia, always ready and able to put others at their ease, even at her own expense.

Tonia came back to the present, realizing that Captain Bellingham had yielded to her urging and was explaining more of the situation in India. "You do understand the unique position of the British Army in India?" His question was directed to Alice.

She sighed. "Alas, I fear I understand very little. Mama allows my sister and myself only the society papers and Arthur Emory is quite useless when it comes to imparting information. Papa, of course, cares only for his estates in Scotland." The look she gave the captain would have melted a

47

heart far harder than Tonia suspected his was. "But I would so like to understand."

With a brief nod, he explained how the East India Company had grown in less than two centuries from a trading concern to become the agency for the British Government in India. "In order to keep the peace, the EIC recruits its own Indian troops. They're one of the largest standing armies in the world. But all sepoy units—that's to say, all native soldiers —serve under regular British officers and are supplemented by British Army units—Queen's troops, we call them."

"So you believe the sepoys are mutinying because they serve under British officers?" Antonia asked.

"Only indirectly. All that was really just background. The thing is—I understand something about this because Light Infantry use rifles—not the old muzzle-loaders which were woefully inaccurate, but Lee-Enfields which reduce loading time and are much more accurate." In spite of his reticence the captain couldn't keep a ring of pride out of his voice.

Antonia stole a look at Alice. If the conversation was boring her, as it certainly would most females, Tonia would change the subject forthwith, no matter how interested she was or how happy Captain Bellingham was to inform her. The shine, however, had returned to Alice's eyes. Tonia was convinced that very little Captain Bellingham could do would bore Alice. "And the problem is?" Tonia felt safe to urge him to continue.

"The cartridges have to be torn open with the teeth for rapid reloading. But they are greased with tallow or lard—an abomination to both Hindoos and Musselmen. I heard a report last April that of the elite native cavalry in a drill in Meerut only five members of the regiment would take the cartridges—even after they had been permitted to tear them with their fingers so as not to defile their caste. The recalcitrant sowars were imprisoned and held for court-martial."

"Meerut," Tonia broke in. "Lord Ellenborough said that was where the fires and slaughter were."

"That's right. Soldiers and military wives assaulted, killed with knives and stones; a pregnant infantry wife..." Captain Bellingham's cheeks flushed as scarlet as his tunic and he stuttered to a halt, realizing the solecism he had committed in opening such a topic. "That is... I beg pardon—"

Antonia felt a surge of compassion for the young man who, no doubt unexpectedly to himself, had been doing so well socially. "Think nothing of it, Captain. I beg you." She indicated her desire to rise and the captain sprang to assist with her chair. "Alice, we have been far too long from our party. We must return to the music. I am quite amazed your mama has not sent your brother in search of us."

The words were no more out of her mouth than, indeed, Arthur Emory appeared in the doorway of the dining room, looking heated and harried as if he had conducted a lengthy search. Tonia approached him with her brightest smile. "Arthur, how kind of you to come to escort us back to the music. I am afraid your sister and I quite forgot ourselves visiting with our friends." She took his arm and turned toward the drawing room. "Such a pleasant evening, is it not?"

They were still in the hall when the sound of a most unusual musical instrument accompanying a charming soprano singing voice drew Antonia to quicken her step. "Oh, how entrancing! What is it, I wonder?"

At the front of the room a beautiful, kohl-eyed, dark-skinned woman swathed in bright pink and gold silk sat on a gold velvet cushion with a long musical instrument balanced between her left foot and right knee. Her hands moved freely as she plucked the strings with a metallic pick, accompanying herself in a plaintive song evoking such hope and yearning that Antonia instinctively felt it must be a love song.

Moving quietly so as not to disrupt the performance,

Tonia resumed her seat by the dowager duchess and smiled to note that the distinctive performer had caught even that lady's attention. With Aunt Aelfrida, however, it was impossible to tell whether attention equaled approval. As a matter of fact, though, very few people were now talking. The entire room seemed wrapped in the enchanted web woven by melody and indecipherable words.

The applause that followed seemed more than the usual polite acknowledgement as the performer rose gracefully from her cushion, bowed to Lady Essworthy's guests with her hands folded palms together in front of her, then picked up her long-necked instrument and left the room.

"Who is she?" Antonia inquired of their party generally.

Agatha replied in flat tones. "I believe she is the sister of the woman Colonel Whitham claims is his wife." Her tightly closed lips left no doubt as to her opinion of that arrangement.

Lieutenant Anson, who had returned Sophia and Cecilia to their party earlier, nodded. "Your information is quite correct, Lady Burroway. Colonel Whitham is newly retired from service in Delhi. He has brought his native wife, her sister, and her sister's husband with him. As well as some native servants, I believe."

Agatha's eyebrows rose. "What a very curious ménage that that must be."

The dowager duchess sniffed. "I am shocked that even such a care-for-nothing as Charmian Essworthy would have the effrontery to bring such a woman before polite society."

Antonia frowned. "But the music was captivating. She's quite lovely."

"Lovely?" Aelfrida raised her lorgnette to inflict a quelling glance on Antonia. "I can only assume it escaped your notice that she is *dark*." The final word hung in the air.

A small shiver seemed to pass between Aelfrida and Agatha.

Surprisingly Captain Bellingham spoke up. He gave a slight bow, then stood stiffly erect as if giving testimony before a judge. "It is my understanding that the ladies in question—" Aelfrida gave a startled cough at the lieutenant's use of the word ladies, but he soldiered on. "I believe they are from a very fine family. I have been given to understand that Padmaja Whitham and her sister—Chandrika Johal her name is—are daughters of a rajah."

"What nonsense! She was doubtless his *bibi*." Fortunately, a string quartet, the next item on Lady Essworthy's musical agenda, had launched into a vigorous number because Lady Agatha Estella had not bothered lowering her voice at the scandalous word.

"Agatha! One does not know of such things." But the glimmer in the dowager duchess's eye clearly said she knew. And wanted to know more.

"What's a *bibi*?" Beatrice blushed the delicate pink of her gown at the reprimanding look she received from the dowager duchess. But she did not withdraw her question.

Antonia turned to the girl. "I believe it is a Swahili word meaning lady."

Agatha straightened her already impossibly straight back. "Lady? I hardly think that is the common usage."

Beatrice looked as if she were about to sink in confusion. Antonia came to her rescue. "It is said that in India the *bibis*, ah—entertain European men." Tonia turned back to face her seething sister-in-law. "Charles informs me that the word can also mean wife, and Captain Bellingham assures us that is the case in Mrs. Whitham's instance. Since Colonel and Mrs. Whitham are married I can see no reason why one should not call on her."

"Antonia, you can't mean it." Agatha's voice rose an octave

with shock. "What if she is wrapped in one of those silk curtain things?"

"It is called a *sari*." Tonia hoped that would be the end of the exchange. She was uncomfortably aware that she had already said far too much on the subject for this polite gathering.

Agatha, however, did not take the hint. "And her face— what if she wears paint? And a diamond in her forehead? Where will you look when you are introduced?"

"I will look her in the eyes, I expect." Antonia knew argument was futile, but she couldn't resist. She threw caution to the wind and continued. "I have heard that Queen Victoria never goes anywhere without her two Indian attendants. And it is well known how fond Her Majesty is of her great India diamond. Does not that make Padmaja Whitham a diamond of the first water?"

"An apt allusion, surely, since their children must have eyes as black as coal."

Antonia couldn't help being grateful for Agatha's remark. Nothing else could have so surely drawn Aunt Aelfrida's outrage from herself. Tonia rose and shook out the lace-edged tiers of the skirt of her silk gown. "I must seek out our hostess to thank her for a most instructive evening." With a small nod to ensure that Danvers and the others of their party followed her Antonia swept from the room, the swinging of her birdcage hoop below her still-slim waist ensuring the grace of her exit.

A few minutes later, at the bidding of the footman dispatched by Lady Essworthy's butler, Jarvis pulled the Danvers's carriage to the door and the party arranged themselves against the cushions of the well-sprung conveyance, Danvers and Antonia, in the back seat *vis-à-vis* Victoria and Cecilia. Freddie leapt up to the driver's box where the coachman joined him after unfolding the calash top to protect the passengers from the night air.

Tonia was anxious to report the extraordinary conversation she had held with Aunt Aelfrida and Agatha, but judged it would be best to wait until the Hever sisters were safely delivered the short distance to their lodgings in Upper Wimpole Street, so she filled the journey with general observations about the company and the music. Both of the young women were enthusiastic with their praises, so Antonia judged the evening to have been a success for their guests.

They were clipping briskly back down Wimpole Street with Freddie now on the more comfortable seating facing his brother and sister-in-law when Antonia began. "Charles, I had the most singular discussion tonight. I declare it would be funny if it were not so alarming. As if the reports one reads in the newspaper aren't disquieting enough—"

Her words were lost in the commotion of a shrill whinny from the horses, a sharp cry from Jarvis, and a heaving lurch of the carriage that threw Tonia across Danvers's lap. For one heart-stopping moment as Danvers's high-spirited pair reared again, Antonia was certain the carriage would topple and spill them onto the granite cobbles. "Whoa. Easy there," Jarvis's gentling tones did as much to soothe her alarms as it did the horses'. The fact that the coachman had sustained his perch on the box was testimony in itself to his superior skill as a driver.

Even before the carriage was stilled, Danvers and Freddie sprang over the side without even bothering to open the door. Tonia clung to the side of the vehicle as the horses backed and side stepped, too skittish to settle as Jarvis continued his efforts to quieten them.

"Hold them, Jarvis. Don't get down," Danvers ordered.

"No, my lord." The coachman was obviously making a great effort to keep his shaking voice steady for the sake of his cattle, but Tonia could hear the note of alarm. "I don't know how it happened, my lord." His voice rose in intensity. "Truly, I don't. He just lurched outta the dark. Come right at us afore I could do owt."

Antonia, listening in increased alarm, heard Jarvis draw a deep breath. "Is 'e breathing, my lord?"

※ 5 ※

anvers regarded the bloodied figure in the dim
circle of gaslight that managed to illumine the
cobbles of Wimpole Street despite the gathering
patches of fog. Even in the obscure light it was impossible to
avoid the sight of a deep cut from an iron horseshoe on the
man's dark-skinned forehead above his neatly trimmed black
beard.

Danvers dropped his head in his hands and covered his
eyes, but still the horror did not go away. The whole thing
had been only an instant. A mere flash of time. And a life had
been taken. How was it possible that his own horses could
kill a man? They had not been going at any pace at all. The
visibility was no worse than on any other night on a quiet
London street. Better than on most, as the fog had only
begun to gather.

He tried to think. Had he seen anything? Heard anything?
He had been listening to Antonia's account of the evening.
She was going to recite a troubling conversation she
had had...

He looked up as his coachman repeated his question more insistently. "My lord?"

"Breathing? No, Jarvis. I fear he is not."

Danvers gave himself a shake and rose stiffly, the cold of the paving stones sinking into him. "Freddie," he turned to his brother. "I fear it is too late for a doctor. We need the police. There should be a bobby around the hackney shelter on Oxford Street. It's not far. Can you—" He gestured in the direction.

"Yes, certainly. Anything. But, as a vicar, shouldn't I..."

"Last rites, you mean? I don't think it would be appropriate." Danvers stooped again and retrieved a fallen object from beneath the driver's box.

He held out a Sikh's turban. Formerly white, of the finest cotton, its unraveling twist was now muddied and blood-stained.

In less time than Danvers would have thought possible Freddie returned at a jog with a fresh-faced bobby in a stovepipe hat and blue swallowtail coat following close on his heels. "A man dead, my lord?" He addressed Danvers, then added, "Constable Lemming, at your service, sir."

"A dreadful accident. I can't understand how it could have happened." Danvers gestured toward the crumpled body lying face-up in the street. Jarvis had managed to soothe his team and had pulled the conveyance to the far side, out of the way.

The young constable paused and took a visible gulp of air before dropping to his knees to examine the bloodied form. It seemed obvious to Danvers that the fellow had little enough idea how to go about matters, but he was making a brave show of it.

Somewhat gingerly, Lemming felt the victim's arms and legs, straightening them from their twisted positions. Then he rolled the body over. After a few moments of further examination he stood.

"It were an accident. I swear. There weren't nothing I could do." Jarvis's voice barely carried across the street. "D-did I kill 'im?"

"Not unless you stuck that in him." Lemming pointed.

Danvers took a step forward and leaned closer to the body. In the dim light he could make out the handle of a dagger protruding from the fine wool of the man's well-tailored coat.

"I propose you summon aid, Lemming." Danvers took control. The victim was well beyond the reach of any help, but it was clear that the constable was in need of support.

"Yes, sir. Ah, thank you, sir. That is, I—" He stumbled to a stop and pulled an alarm rattle from his belt. Gripping the wooden handle he whirled the metal rectangle around above his head, gaining vigor with each swing. Jarvis tightened his grip on the reins as the horses side-stepped at the ensuing clacking sound.

The clamor, however, was successful in summoning help. A street urchin was the first on the scene. Lemming sent him skittering toward the Oxford street shelter. "Tell whoever's there to hie it to Scotland Yard. Tell 'em to send an inspector." The lad was just in earshot when he added, "And a mortuary cart."

In spite of Charles's best efforts to convince Antonia to allow Frederick to secure a hansom and escort her home, she staunchly refused on the grounds that Charlie would be long abed and there was nothing she could do at home but try to imagine what was happening here. So Charles joined her in the carriage where she took the opportunity of filling the time by finishing her story about what she had learned of the

Hindoo woman at Lady Essworthy's soiree, and Agatha and Aunt Aelfrida's regrettable reaction to her.

"And now this poor man—dead under our carriage wheels." She stopped with a shudder. "All this on top of the horrifying reports in the news. It's like some terrible web of doom."

"Tonia—" Charles put his arm around her.

"No, I'm sorry. How melodramatic that sounded." She shook her head. "But you must see what I mean. Everywhere one looks one finds some new anxiety from India. It makes one wonder. Where will it end?"

Far quicker than Danvers could have expected, a growler arrived bearing a police inspector and his sergeant, with the self-important urchin perched up beside the driver.

Giving a squeeze to his wife's hand, Danvers left his carriage to greet the Inspector. As the gaslight struck the features of the officer, Danvers strode forward with a cry of relief. "Inspector Futter. How glad I am to know this grisly matter is in such competent hands." He shook hands with the police officer who had been involved in so many of their past cases.

"Ah, my lord, what a piece of bad luck for you to be tangled in this fracas. Not that I'm not pleased to see you, though." He turned as Antonia likewise descended from the carriage. "And Lady Danvers." He raised his top hat, revealing his still-boyish, white-blond mop of hair.

"And how is your family Inspector?" Tonia asked.

"Ah, the nipper's so grown you wouldn't recognize him. Well, I guess you wouldn't anyway, since you never actually saw him." Tonia was certain that if the lighting had been more revealing it would have evidenced Futter's proclivity to blush.

"And Mrs. Futter?"

"Thank you, my lady. My Marianne is, er—blooming again." This time the blush was visible.

Tonia expressed her approval of the increasing Futter family, but before more could be said the rattle of iron wheels on the cobbles announced the arrival of the mortuary cart, a small wooden conveyance with a hooded leather covering held up by a wire frame, pulled by a single horse.

At this reminder of the matter at hand, Futter offered a final word to Lady Danvers and turned to his work. He squatted down on the cobbles and examined the body. After some consideration he drew the dagger from the victim's back. The blood-smeared, wickedly sharp blade was strangely curved, unlike anything Danvers had seen in England. The inspector held it up in the light. "*Quatar*, I believe this is called. Very helpful. I'm thinking this should limit our suspects to one of the Hindoo persuasion." He handed the evil-looking dagger to his sergeant.

"Or to someone who wants to make it look as though the crime was committed by someone from India," Danvers suggested.

Futter looked surprised at the viscount's words, but he did not disagree. He nodded to his sergeant that the body could be placed on the cart.

While the constable and sergeant were about their grim task, Danvers and Jarvis gave as clear an account of the happenings as they were able to do. "And the fellow seemed to come from over there?" Futter stepped toward the clump of bushes bordering a front garden.

Jarvis agreed. "I don't think he were exactly walking— more-like lurching. I didn't rightly see 'im, but as I think back on it, I sort of 'ad an impression of someone who was two sheets to the wind, if you takes my meaning."

Futter, as was always his practice, made meticulous notes of all that was told him, then turned to pace the distance from the bloodied spot on the cobbles to the bushes. After noting the span he began poking around in the bushes. Jarvis summoned the street boy to hold the horses, then unhooked one of the carriage lamps from the side of the barouche and brought it over to aid in the search. "Watter ye lookin' for?"

Futter poked at the bushes with the truncheon he pulled from his belt, then bent over. "I can't rightly claim to have been looking for this, but it will do very well." He held up a leather wallet that appeared as if it could have been made from crocodile skin. "Hold that lamp over here," he directed Jarvis. Raising the wallet in the light, he lifted the flap. "Empty. Must'a been robbery." Under the flap was a name stamped in gold. "Faquir Johal." Futter nodded. "I was thinking he must be a Musselman."

"I believe you'll find he was a Sikh," Danvers said.

"Begging your pardon, my lord, but is there a difference?"

Before Danvers could explain about the characteristic turban, Tonia stepped forward. "Johal, did you say?"

"That's what it says here. Does the name mean anything to you, my lady?"

"I think I know who his wife, or sister, might be. There can't be many of that name in London." She explained about the woman who had sung so beguilingly at Lady Essworthy's musical evening such a short time ago.

Futter made more notes. "Thank you, my lady. That could be very helpful." He closed his notebook. "I don't think we need to detain you any longer."

"Yes, take me home, Charles. I'm cold."

Charles put his arm around Antonia to lead her back to the carriage. "Tonia, you're shaking. Have you taken a chill?" He signaled Jarvis. "Bring all the rugs for Lady Danvers."

Even when she was wrapped securely in the woolen travel rugs the coachman brought from the box on the back of the carriage, Tonia continued to shake violently. "You've had a shock, my love. A brandy cordial and a well warmed bed are what you need." Danvers spoke as bracingly as he could, but he was concerned. Tonia had never been of a nervous disposition. She had faced far more distressing—even dangerous—situations than this in the many encounters they had had with violent death. He must take more care of her. After all, she was in a delicate condition.

"Yes, that would be best." Charles could hear the tightness in her voice that told him she was struggling to suppress her anxiety.

Was she worrying, too? "Tonia." The dark of the night allowed him to place his hand on her abdomen. "Are—are you quite well? Is there pain?"

She drew a wavery breath. "No, Charles. Your daughter—or son—is quite safe. It's as I said earlier—calamity everywhere. And I feel we are becoming enmeshed in it."

Charles did his best to make a bracing reply, yet he couldn't keep unsettling thoughts at bay. Was there truth to Tonia's fears? Were entangling shadows reaching out to them?

❧ 6 ❧

The weary weeks dragged on. Near-to three that they had been in the Entrenchment; two of them under this incessant firing. But Emilia would far sooner believe it was a matter of months. And still the horrors mounted. The ground, baked hard in this furnace of beating sun, was far too hard for digging graves. At first, bodies of the slain had been dumped into a trench, but that had filled long ago. Now the number two well, from which no water was drawn because of its exposure to the enemy, became their burial chamber. Every night the bodies were collected after dark and dumped into the well. Emilia had heard a whispered report—certainly not meant for feminine ears—that some two hundred and fifty bodies had come to rest there.

Nor was it only soldiers who found their final resting place in so unceremonious a manner. One of the cannon balls that constantly arced and bounced into the Entrenchment struck the inner verandah off Lydia Hillersdon's chamber and buried her in an avalanche of bricks. She was pulled out, but her skull was crushed. And so she joined the remains of her eviscerated husband.

It seemed that little worse could happen, and yet it did. The thatched roof of the second barrack, used largely for a hospital, had been a cause for concern from the first, and precautions had been made to shield the thatch with tiles and bricks. That night, however, as Emilia was doing her best to entertain the Hillersdon's orphaned daughters while cuddling the sleepless infant so recently deprived of its mother, she heard a whoosh of flame and a cry from the direction of the hospital barrack.

Clutching the infant, she ran to the verandah and saw the whole barrack in a blaze. Soldiers ran from every corner of the Entrenchment to help carry the wounded from the inferno. Women and children who had been sheltered there ran into the yard clutching their few belongings. Now the already-crowded, tile-roofed barrack must serve as hospital.

They learned the next morning that forty-two sick and wounded men had perished in the charred ruins of the hospital. Their precious reserves of water and a week's rations were lost. But far more disastrous was the loss of all the medical stores. Not one surgical instrument was saved. There would now be no means of extracting bullets from the wounded or dressing mutilations, save wrapping the lacerations in a fellow officer's torn shirt.

Further, the remaining barrack would not accommodate the whole party. There was nothing for it but that numbers of women and children should go out into the trenches. Emilia's small corner was required for hospital space, and so she exchanged her pallet for the bare ground of a trench.

Her throat choked at the tenderness with which a young infantryman, using two sticks and his discarded tunic, erected a makeshift sunshade over her head when the sun beat its hottest the next day. She smiled her appreciation, too exhausted to find words. He moved on down the trench to take up his position in the defenses.

The shade provided a blessed respite from the searing heat. Emilia closed her eyes and felt herself begin to drift. She had managed no sleep last night and very little since the siege began. Her mind drifted to Antonia. One of their favorite pastimes as girls had been *daydreaming and dozing in hammocks at the foot of Baron Barstow's garden...*

An enemy bullet tore through Emilia's overhead covering. Her startled cry shattered her reverie and jerked her back to reality. Helpful as it had been, the sunshade served as an attraction for enemy fire. Besides, this was no time for daydreaming. Emilia observed her sisters up and down the length of the trench. None were giving themselves up to despair. Instead, they busied themselves in teams, handing ammunition to the men, often with an encouraging word, distracting the children with simple games, and giving what comfort they could to the wounded.

When evening came there seemed to be a lull in the firing. Annie White, who had taken refuge near Emilia in the trench with her infant twins, seized the opportunity to walk with her husband under the cover of the wall, carrying a twin in each arm. Emilia smiled at the comfortable picture they made in that moment of peaceful family time.

A single shot pierced the quiet. The bullet passed through Private White, killing him and shattering both of Mrs. White's arms. The mother fell beside the lifeless body of her husband, her babes still in her arms, one of them severely wounded as well.

Emilia sprang to her side as others rushed to help. She picked up the uninjured infant and ran with it to the makeshift hospital, thinking that she would feel the bite of a bullet at any moment. She reached shelter, breathless and heart pounding, but with great relief. The mother and wounded babe were carried in a moment later. Without medical supplies there was little to be done for them except to make them as comfortable as possible on a pallet. Emilia pulled off her petticoat and tore it into strips. She thrust a handful of the impromptu bandages to the ayah who had remained faithful to a friend's infant. Together they did what they could to staunch the blood and bind their patients' wounds.

The shattered mother's arms would no longer hold her babies, but, by a careful bunching of the straw, Emilia and her helper were able to lay one babe on each side of the prostrate mother so that they could suckle her breasts. Through her haze of pain and distress, Annie White managed a weak smile.

What horrors were left to happen? It seemed it could get no worse. And yet it did. The very next day, the ayah who had helped Emilia tend Annie White emerged briefly from the barrack hoping for a breath of fresh air for the baby in her arms. She had taken no more than three steps when a round shot tore through both her legs, shattering them.

Too stricken even to cry out, Emilia watched as a nearby soldier picked the infant off the ground, suffused in its nurse's blood.

The children were a constant concern. Their suffering from thirst was the most intense of all. Infant cries for drink were perpetual—until they became too weak to cry. Children sucking on pieces of old water bags became a common sight. Emilia saw children with scraps of canvas and leather in their mouths, desperately trying to get a single drop of moisture upon their parched lips.

And confining the children, no matter how necessary, was impossible. The youngest, too young to understand the danger and desperate for freedom, would run away from their mothers and play about under the barrack walls. Not even the smallest children were spared the enemy muskets.

As if the deaths from bullets and cannon balls weren't enough, sunstroke and fever took a severe toll on all. Headache and drowsiness would be followed by vomiting and gradual insensibility, ending in death.

Dear God... *Emilia began, when she learned that all three of Charles and Lydia Hillersdon's orphans had died in this way. Her mind, however, numbed by accumulated monstrosities, could form no more words. Was God there? Did he care? She groped for her prayer book in her pocket.*

When her eyes were too blurred with fatigue to read the words, she simply held to it as a tangible source of comfort. Without faith she would have nothing. She had to hold on. And yet...

The Reverend Mister Haycock had been accustomed to bring out his aged mother every evening onto the veranda for a short relief from the fetid atmosphere within. One evening the old lady was severely wounded. Her acute sufferings overcame the son's reason. He died raving, in his mother's arms. If faith was not enough for a missionary, what hope did Emilia have?

Still, the station chaplain, the Reverend Mister Moncrieff, remained indefatigable in the performance of his ministry of mercy with the wounded and dying. Emilia was heartened as she saw him going from post to post, reading prayers to the men standing to arms.

The services were short and interrupted by enemy fire, but there was a terrible reality about them. Emilia well knew that for one or more of each little group she observed gathered around this faithful pastor, it would be the last time. How many went into eternity with "Though I walk through the shadow of death thou art with me" *sounding in his ears more loudly than the enemy fire?*

Antonia's foot struck a hard object in her bed, jarring her awake even before Betsy could enter to open her curtains to the morning sunshine. Her toes explored the glazed pottery surface, then she smiled as memory flooded back. A stone water bottle, cold now, but piping hot when she had gone to bed with her feet against it last night. Ever since they discovered that poor dead man five days ago, Isabella had been assiduous in fulfilling her lord's demand that her lady's bed be well warmed and supplied with hot water bottles. It was a wonder Tonia hadn't been required to sleep on a bed of stones like some ancient saint.

She reached above her bed and gave a single sharp tug to the tapestry bellpull. Isabella's response was so quick Tonia suspected she must have been lurking in the hallway outside her door, listening for any movement. She could scarcely have ascended the three long flights of stairs from downstairs in that time.

"Did you sleep well, my lady?" Having arrived before the upstairs maid, Isabella, perfectly attired for the day with a frill of starched white linen on her dark hair and stiff white collar and cuffs on her neat black dress, tugged open the long velvet window coverings, allowing sunshine to flood the room.

"Exceedingly well, thank you," Antonia lied. If she refused to dwell on her disturbing dreams, surely the spectre would fade faster. "Please bring my peach dressing gown and my cream lace cap. I wish to look my best for my lord." The silk gown she had worn on their honeymoon in Scotland was outdated, but it was Charles's favorite.

And she could tell by the twinkle in his eye when he entered her room a few minutes later that the effort had not been wasted on him. She poured his coffee with exactly the amount of cream he preferred and added a generous scoop of demerara sugar before pouring her own tea. She placed a slice of dry toast on the floor as invitation for Tinker to nestle at her feet.

Danvers took a drink, then replaced his cup and opened his mouth, but Tonia held up her hand before he could speak. "Before you ask, I am quite fine. I can't think how I could have caused such concern when we found that poor man. One would think me the shrinking-maiden heroine of a penny dreadful. No more presentiments of calamity, I promise."

She took a sip before continuing, "I do believe, however, that there is a pattern to these recent alarms. I should like to understand more of what is going on."

Before she could continue, however, Isabella re-entered with a letter on a silver salver. "Begging pardon, my lady, but I thought perhaps you would like to see this."

Tonia took the missive and gave a cry of delight. "Charles, here is another string to the pattern. It is a letter from Emilia."

"Ah, excellent. Hopefully it will put any lingering misgivings to rest. Do open it now."

She looked doubtful, but he reassured her. "You can read any interesting portions out to me."

She smiled and broke the seal. After only a few moments of silent reading she exclaimed, "Oh, it sounds perfectly delightful. She says that Cawnpore can become a dust bowl in the dry season, but that at the moment it is still pleasant and green. 'Especially the broad boulevard known as the Course lined with shade trees where officers and ladies ride out in the evenings.' I declare, she makes it sound like Hyde Park.

"And they must be very near the Ganges. 'The water is very low now and the Indians grow melons, cucumbers and other vegetables on the islands in the river. Cranes migrate to the sandbars, looking like old gentlemen in white waistcoats. Just last evening a party of us drove to the river to watch the pelicans. They hunt in flocks, beating fish into the shallows with their great grey wings, then scooping them up in their pouches. I am persuaded there is nothing like it in England.'"

"She sounds very content," Danvers observed.

"Yes, she does, indeed. I can't wait to share the information with Sophia—although doubtless she will have received a missive of her own." Tonia turned the sheet of thin paper. "Apparently April is a particularly agreeable time there. She says the calendar is crowded with officers' balls. 'Louisa is all things most charming and an energetic sponsor. She sees that I get introduced to the most handsome officers and am invited to the gayest events.'"

Tonia lowered the page she was reading from. "You remember my mentioning Louisa—the friend who persuaded Emilia to go out to India with her last winter." Danvers looked blank, so Tonia explained further. "Louisa Chalwin, wife of the veterinary surgeon to the regiment, was returning to India from home leave. She had persuaded Emilia that it was far the best place to..."

Danvers chuckled. "To get a husband. Heaven help the officers."

Tinker's ears perked up at the sound of laughter, then he returned to his toast. "Well, she has been a widow for something like fifteen years," Tonia said in reply to her husband's derision, then returned to her friend's letter.

"Oh, this is interesting. Lucie Duff Gordon mentioned Nana Sahib the other evening at Aunt Aelfrida's. I believe he is the local rajah. Emilia describes attending a breakfast at his palace twelve miles along the Ganges. 'We were escorted into a dining room lined with life-size portraits of the maharajah himself, interspersed with pictures of children, English beauties, and "our noble Queen," as the rajah referred to her. The menu was extraordinary—game pie, anchovy toast, mutton chops, sardines and—most remarkably—Fortnum and Mason marmalade.'"

"Stop, you're making me hungry," Danvers interrupted her recitation.

"Am I boring you, my love? You did say I might read out parts."

"Certainly I did, pray continue. It is most refreshing after the more recent reports one hears."

Tonia scanned the page to the end and summarized for him, "It appears that Lucie Duff Gordon must be quite correct in describing Nana Sahib as a gentleman. Emilia mentioned in his hearing that the thing she misses most about home, apart from her daughter, is the piano she was required to leave behind. The rajah has lent her one of his own. 'Louisa and I spend many happy hours singing duets at the piano which now graces her parlor.'"

Tonia returned the letter to its envelope. She would not bother her husband with the interesting detail that Emilia was fretting over a perplexing hair loss, which she was attempting to remedy by rubbing onions on her scalp. Tonia determined to write to Emilia by return post to recommend Isabella's pomatum receipt which she had cut from "The Englishwoman's Domestic Magazine": olive-oil, spermaceti, oil of almonds and essence of lemon. Tonia had found that it made her own auburn tresses shimmer in the sun. And it certainly smelt a great deal better than onions.

"So, does this put your perturbations to rest?" Charles interrupted her ruminations.

"A perfect antidote." Tonia lifted her teacup to her lips, telling herself again how very silly she was to place meaning on mere dreams. They were undoubtedly the result of her delicate condition.

"What are your plans for the day?" The question brought her back to the present.

"I shall spend the morning with our son. He has expressed to Nurse Bevans a particular desire to sail his new boat on the Round Pond, but it seems that Nurse has a somewhat morbid fear of waterfowl."

"Ah, then you'd best take Michael with you to beat any encroaching creatures off, and his long arms are certain to come in useful if the boat sails beyond reach."

"An excellent plan. I shall do so. Then this afternoon I intend to call on Lucie Duff Gordon. I am intrigued to learn more of her Indian acquaintances."

A short time later, Antonia smiled at the sight of her son, dressed in a short blue frock with a sailor collar as if he were at the seaside, prancing and clapping his hands in delight as Michael, proper in his footman's attire of tailed coat, waistcoat and stiff, high collar, set the prized toy yacht with its fine rigging and green and white hull afloat on the pond. Tinker, scampering in circles on the sandy bank and yapping at the ducks and swans, was enjoying it as much as the young master.

"Mama, see her go!" The breeze caught the tall white mainsail of the model craft and sped it toward the rounded corner of the bank to their left. Charlie began racing along the sandy shore of the ornamental Lake, Tinker at his heels.

"Darling, be careful!" Tonia called after him, adoring the still-toddling gait of his leaping run. In spite of his infant chubbiness it was already clear that her son would grow to match his father's tall lankiness. "Don't get too near the water!" Tonia lifted her skirt and hurried after footman and nurse already in pursuit of their charge.

At the far end of the pond the yacht joined a veritable regatta of white sails set afloat by young sailors attended by their nannies. It was fortunate that Charlie's boat sported a small red pennant from the top of the mainsail or they would not have been able to know which one was theirs. For a moment Tonia feared their boat would end in a tangle with three of the nearest craft. Then a shift in the breeze sent them all skittering toward the far shore.

Charlie and Michael darted ahead. His mother started to follow the clutch of amateur seamen when a cry from Nurse Bevans, accompanied by a series of growls and woofs from Tinker, made Tonia turn back. "Go away! Nasty birds!" Sara Bevans was shaking her skirts vigorously at an aggressive white goose that seemed to have taken a fancy to her.

Rather than discouraging the bird, her futile efforts served to call more of the flock to aid the feathered attacker. Nurse Bevans shrieked and turned as a gaggle of honking fowl approached.

In her haste she tripped over the hem of her skirt and

would have plunged to her knees if Antonia had not caught her. Fortunately, at that moment two children armed with bags of bread crusts appeared further along the beach, drawing the assailants off.

"Oh, my lady, forgive me. I'm sorry. I'm sure I don't know what came over me, but those horrid, squawking creatures—"

"Don't give it another thought Bevans. Are you certain you're quite unhurt?"

The nurse nodded and straightened her flat, black hat that had tipped to a rather rakish angle over one eye.

Tonia directed her to wait in the carriage with Jarvis and hurried on around the pond to join her son. "See, Mama, mine's fastest!" Charlie pointed and began his bouncing jog to keep up with his speeding craft.

At that moment a fresh breeze whipped the bright blue, beribboned tam from the boy's head and flung it into the pond after the sailing boats. "Oh!" Charlie cried out and started after his hat.

Before she could even order her son to stop, the child was in water over the depth of his high-top, buttoned boots. "Charlie!" Tonia yelled and looked for Michael. The footman, however, was now on around the pond, keeping pace with the boat.

There was nothing to be done but plunge in after the boy herself. Balancing on one foot Lady Danvers reached down to remove her kid boots.

At that moment Charlie tripped and began shrieking, splashing wildly at the water. "Charlie!" Tinker leapt into the pond with a single bound. Tonia, with one boot partly unbuttoned, darted forward. Before she could reach the water, though, a firm hand on her arm stopped her. "Allow me, my lady," a masculine voice said in her ear.

A moment later, a very dripping Honourable Charles and his wayward tam were returned to the trembling viscountess by a young man wearing likewise sodden blue trousers beneath his scarlet regimental tunic. Tinker followed, planting himself at Tonia's feet before proceeding to shake his long, golden hair free of moisture.

Tonia took the bedraggled Charlie into her arms and wrapped him in her cashmere shawl. He snuggled against her shoulder. "Lieutenant Anson, I am much indebted to you."

The lieutenant touched his hand to his tall black shako with its gleaming gold crest on the front. "My pleasure, my lady. It was fortunate that I happened to be nearby. We just finished morning drill for the parade." He gestured toward Hyde Park on the other side of Kensington Gardens. "May I be so bold as to repeat my invitation for you to view the salute in honour of Her Majesty's ascension to the throne? I believe I can promise you a good show."

"Oh, yes, I recall your mentioning it at Aunt Aelfrida's Drawing-room. I am certain it will be a fine spectacle." Tonia didn't commit herself. She recalled the earlier invitation being directed to Aelfrida's ward, but she wondered if Anson's roving eye had now focused more on Victoria's twin sister.

"And would be made all the finer by your attendance, Lady Danvers." He sketched a bow.

Tonia laughed. "I shall do my best, Lieutenant. And thank you again."

"May I be of further service, my lady?"

"If you would be so good as to inform our footman Michael that I have taken Master Charles to the carriage and wish him to meet us there with that troublesome boat, I would be most obliged." She tipped her head toward the group of enthusiastic sailors on the other side of the pond where the single liveried footman was easy enough to spot among the various children and nannies.

"It would be my pleasure." Anson sketched a bow. Before he turned to his task, however, he raised an arm, as if in signal to two men standing on the grass beyond the beach, seemingly telling them to wait for him. Or was he signaling to the tall, dark, impeccably dressed man she just glimpsed before he pulled back behind a tree?

Carrying the now-settled Charlie, Tonia turned toward the Carriage Drive. Her way took her directly past the two men Anson had appeared to signal. A low growl from Tinker as they drew near made Tonia look up. Her gaze lighted directly on the nearer man. Like his companion, he wore a rough tweed jacket and knotted neckerchief below a flat cap, as most common laborers, but Antonia was surprised to note that both men had the coffee-with-cream complexions and black eyes of Asians.

Unlikely that the lieutenant would have dealings with them, so she put the strangers out of her mind. The outing party returned to Grosvenor Square with Charlie fully recovered from his dunking and anxious to recount his adventure to anyone who would listen to him. Once home, Tonia breathed a sigh of relief and turned her son over to the care of his nurse for dry clothes, lunch and, hopefully, an afternoon nap. Tinker, likewise, was given into the care of the footman for a thorough grooming.

Lady Danvers went on to her own apartment. Isabella was dismayed to find her lady wet to the skin where she had clutched the soaking Charlie to her. "Don't fuss, Isabella. Everyone is quite unharmed, thanks to the lucky arrival of Lieutenant Anson on the scene." Antonia explained their morning adventures while her maid unhooked her from her dress and rubbed her with a soft Turkey towel. "I shall wear my magenta taffeta with the black braid, Isabella. Has his lordship returned?"

"No, my lady. He went out right after you left. With Mister Frederick. I heard him tell Bracken they would lunch at his club. My lord took Hardy with him, too. Something about going to the docks. Could that be right, my lady?"

"Yes, quite correct Isabella. Thank you for such a thorough report. I shall take luncheon on a tray in my room. And I shall ask you to accompany me on my afternoon call." She gave her maid a significant smile. "I know you will enjoy a good gossip with Lady Duff Gordon's servants. I am particularly interested to learn more about Azimoolah Khan who was her house guest a year or two ago."

Isabella's eyes gleamed. "Oh, yes, my lady. I shall most enjoy that."

When they arrived at Number 8 Queen Square, Westminster, a short time later, Tonia was startled to find a black wreath on the door and draperies drawn over the windows. "I was not aware there had been a death in the Duff Gordon family. How puzzling. When I saw Lucie at the soiree recently she was not in black." Tonia alighted from the carriage. "Wait for us at the end of the street, Jarvis. This may be a shorter visit than I had intended."

Tonia ascended the shallow steps under the ornamented portico of the red brick terraced house, then hesitated. Still, she had come this far, surely a short call would not be inadmissible. She extended a kid-gloved finger and pushed the small button beside the doorknob. The contrivance proclaimed that the Duff Gordon household was equipped with the most modern of inventions, a wired doorbell which one could merely push to sound a buzzer inside the house, making the handsome lion's head brass doorknocker obsolete.

The Duff Gordon butler opened the door with a solemn face, but admitted the callers into the marble-floored foyer. Antonia handed him her calling card. "Has there been a death in the family? I was with Lady Duff Gordon only recently. She mentioned nothing."

The butler glanced at the card in his hand and deemed the newcomer worthy of an explanation. "A friend of the family, my lady. Lady Duff Gordon is in the parlor, if you would care to come this way."

"Thank you, er—"

"Bottle, my lady."

"Thank you, Bottle. And then if you would be so good as to escort my maid downstairs."

Bottle bowed his agreement to the plan and led the way across the hall to the parlor, pausing at the door. "Lady Danvers, my lady."

Lucie put her book aside and rose to meet her guest. "My dear Antonia, how good of you to call. It has been so dreadful. You cannot imagine. The police have been here, asking the most impertinent questions. They even had the temerity to ring at the *front* door. Of course Bottle sent them around to the servants' entrance." She turned to the butler in the doorway. "Bring us some tea, Bottle."

The butler departed with Isabella. Tonia sat on the maroon velvet settee her hostess indicated. Lucie resumed her place in the dark blue Queen Anne chair and smoothed the folds of her severely cut black gown, its tailored lines giving her a rather mannish look. Tonia recalled the rumor that Lucie smoked cheroots and wondered if the bold image was perhaps part of her friend's bluestocking image.

A soft light glowed from the globes of gaslights in the darkened room, highlighting the bindings of several heavy tomes scattered on various tables. Tonia suspected they were Lucie's heavy-going translations of Greek and German works, then brought her thoughts back to the present. "I am sorry for your bereavement—a friend of the family, I understand?"

"Simply unbelievable, isn't it? To think that it happened

while we were all at Lady Essworthy's. I cannot forgive myself for not insisting that Faquir attend the soiree with us. What business could possibly have been more important than his wife's singing?"

Antonia shook her head, looking solemn, but harboring a certain satisfaction. As she thought, Faquir Johal had been the husband of the enchanting singer. But had he been a house guest of the Duff Gordons? How had that come about? She phrased her question as discreetly as she could manage, but she needn't have equivocated; her hostess was very direct.

"Colonel Whitham—you saw me with him at Lady Essworthy's—is an old friend of Alexander's. Making his home in London since his retirement from India." She gave a throaty laugh which seemed to be quite at odds with the accoutrements of mourning around them. "He's set the cat among the pigeons, I can tell you. I find his Indian wife most amiable. Very high caste. But, of course, that means little among the high instep crowd of London society.

"Mrs. Whitham's sister and her husband made the journey out from India with them. Her husband has, er—had some position with the East India Company. We asked Johal and Chandrika to be our guests since the Whitham's house is quite inadequate."

"I thought Chandrika's singing was charming." Tonia offered the trite comment to keep Lucie talking. If the young woman was in the house, where was she? Perhaps secluded in mourning?

Lucie smiled. "Yes, indeed, it was. But the poor creature is beyond distraught at the moment."

Ah, that must confirm Tonia's supposition. She shook her head. "And to think—that poor man died under our carriage wheels."

Lucie appeared surprised until Tonia explained the

circumstances of their finding the body. "Oh, my dear. How dreadful for you. You must have been quite distraught."

Bottle entered with a heavy tea tray which he placed on a low table near Lady Duff Gordon. Tonia asked for one lump of sugar in hers, then continued. "Yes, I will admit it quite overset me. It seemed to bring the spectre of the terrible reports one hears in the news so close to home." She took a sip of tea. "But this morning's post brought a most reassuring letter from my friend in Cawnpore."

"I think you can be quite at ease about your friend there. My dear Azimoolah assures me his great friend Nana Sahib is the finest gentleman. And very European in his ways."

"Yes, I regret more than ever that I did not meet the Khan when he was your guest. Do tell me more about him."

Lucie's face softened at the memory. "I don't know when I have met a man with finer manners. And so well educated. Fluent in both English and French."

"Surely that is most unusual for a Musselman. How did it come about?"

"Azimoolah and his mother were rescued from certain death in the famine that struck India some twenty years ago, when they stumbled into a mission station in Cawnpore. When he finished his education he served as secretary for several British officers, then for Nana Sahib."

"Ah, the maharajah."

"Yes, that's right, although peshwa is the more exact title, I believe. It's a rather tangled tale. Let me warm your tea, my dear." Tonia gladly extended her cup. "The hereditary peshwa had received a most liberal treaty from the British after the mutiny last century—a luxurious palace and a pension of something like eighty thousand pounds to be paid by the East India Company. Peshwa Baji Rao II had no sons, so he adopted Nana Sahib, a trusted official.

"The East India Company doesn't recognize adopted sons

—a policy which has greatly enriched their coffers—so Nana Sahib did not receive the pension he felt owed to him. A grave injustice, to my mind." She took a sip of tea before continuing. "So Nana Sahib sent his secretary Azimoolah as head of a delegation to London to present his case to the East India Company. He desired to petition parliament and to meet the queen." Her sigh indicated that such exalted plans had come to nothing.

Tonia shook her head to clear it. Thank goodness Lucie's tea was good and strong—she needed it to help her follow such a tangled skein of yarn. "But how did he come to lodge with you?"

"My dear friend John Stuart Mill introduced us. John is Examiner of Indian Correspondence at the East India Company." Her face fell momentarily and she sighed again. "Such a waste. The most brilliant mind of our day, set to work for commerce. But the truth of it is that true intellectual work is very little appreciated in our age." Her gaze rested momentarily on her own scholarly works.

"You were saying about Azimoolah Kahn?" Tonia prodded her.

"Oh, yes." Lucie gave a small chuckle at the memory. "He showed up at our house in Esher with his secretary one snowy day two winters ago. Our Maurice was amusing himself throwing snowballs in the garden. The sight of two black men, dressed in frock coats and top hats coming in our gate gave him quite a fright, I can assure you. But they proved to be most delightful.

"Of course, I insisted that Azimoolah be our guest. He had the most inquiring mind I have ever met, and so quick. Incessant questioning on political economy and all the social sciences. I quite felt I had become a university lecturer. I can't begin to tell you how many volumes I procured for him to devour." She took another sip of tea and returned her cup to the saucer with a clink of china.

"He arrived in this country with a prejudiced dislike of the English which he made little effort to hide from me, but I pride myself that I can confidently say he returned home an enthusiastic Englishman with very reforming notions for his own people."

Now that Lady Duff Gordon was well launched on her subject Tonia felt little need of prompting her, but she was curious to hear more about the social life of this very singular visitor.

The lady obliged without cue from Antonia. "He was so very grand-looking and amiable, it's little wonder he was such a social success." She gave an almost coy smile that was much at odds with her strong features. "He called me his 'European Mother.' I took him to a great many Drawing-rooms, to dinner parties, the opera..." For a moment she seemed lost in her memories.

Antonia was intrigued, but felt she was to learn little more from the lady on that subject. "The inheritance for his master? Did he gain anything of his object there?"

Lucie shook her head. "Sadly, no. Lord Dalhousie, who enunciated the Doctrine of Lapse when he was Governor-General of India, stood firm on the policy that adopted sons could not inherit. Dalhousie is a very shrewd man where the company's interests are at stake. He must have taken over five or six princely states for the East India Company under that policy. Goodness knows, Nana Sahib was rich enough as it was anyway, but it must have been a severe blow to his vanity."

"So Azimoolah Kahn returned home empty-handed?" Tonia drained her cup and set it aside.

"Alas, yes. There was no one left to whom he could appeal. He was a brilliant social success, but I fear a political failure."

Antonia stood. "My dear Lucie, how gracious of you to give me so much of your time on this sad day. I must be on my way, but, um—" She looked around the room, showing her discomfort. "Before I go... Your powder room?"

"But of course, my dear, just at the top of the stairs and to your left."

Tonia lifted her wide skirt and hurried up the stairs. She was truly in need of the use of a water-closet, but more importantly, she had been intrigued by the creaking floor-board over her head. Certainly it could be merely a servant, but somehow a feeling of stealth communicated itself to her.

At the top of the stairs the matter became more intriguing yet as the unmistakable sound of muffled female sobs struck her. Hardly surprising in a house of mourning for a violent death, but then, why the effort to keep it hidden?

She rapped softly on the door of the room from which the sounds emanated. The whimpers stopped instantly, but there was no reply. "Please, may I help?" Tonia said softly.

At first she thought there would be no answer, then she heard a slight rustle and the sound of a key turning in the lock. The door opened the merest crack. Tonia could just make out a pair of dark eyes peering at her.

"Chandrika?" She was certain it must be woman who had entertained them so beautifully at the soiree. "I am so sorry to intrude on your grief. Is there anything I can do for you?"

The door opened wider to reveal a small woman clad in a dark green sari. She was little more than a girl, red-eyed with streaks of kohl running down her soft bronze cheeks. Tonia had not realized that night how young the singer was. But the thing that startled Tonia was the look of fear in the wide eyes. And, in spite of the girl's attempt to control herself, she was trembling. She gave the appearance not of a woman mourning her dead husband, but of a girl afraid for her life.

Tonia stepped into the room and closed the door behind

her. She took the girl's hand, startled at how small it felt in her own. Hardly larger than Charlie's. "Don't be afraid, my dear. You are among friends—your sister, Mrs. Duff Gordon, Lady Essworthy... Whatever it is, they will help you."

"No!" Sheer terror gripped the girl's features. "I must hide. I will be made to burn. My husband die. I must burn with him."

Tonia fought to control her own shock. She had heard of the abominable practice of suttee where a wife was committed to death on her husband's funeral pyre. She considered shaking the girl to calm her rising hysteria, but instead reached for the glass of water beside the carafe on the bedside table. "Here. Drink this."

The girl made an attempt, shaking so she spilled half of it in the attempt.

"That's better. Now, listen to me. You are in England. We do not burn people. Living or dead."

Chandrika shook her head in dispute, but Tonia continued. "Do you hear me? It is not done. We are a Christian nation. Suttee is a heathen practice. It is not done here. You are safe."

Doubt filled the girl's eyes, but she was calmer.

"Furthermore," Tonia continued, "I am certain the hideous practice is no longer legal in India. I quite clearly recall reading that it was outlawed there many years ago."

"Yes, illegal, but done anyway. Among devout of high caste. My husband, he very faithful. His name has meaning 'of saintly ways' in our tongue. The *Ik Onkar*, All One, knows. To be a widow is a terrible thing. There is no place for such a one."

Tonia could only repeat. "You are safe. We do not burn people in England."

After the briefest stop in the powder room Tonia took her leave of Lady Duff Gordon. There seemed to be no reason to hide her strange interview from her hostess. "I encountered your guest. She seems to be under the impression she will be required to commit suttee. I fear my attempts to reassure her met with little success."

Lucie sighed. "The poor girl is in shock. I asked if she would like to be returned to her sister, but that only set her off worse. I fear we'll get little sense out of her until the police conclude this dreadful business. Of course, they are holding the body at the moment, so there can be no funeral arrangements of any kind. I think she thought they were coming for her when that inspector came to the door this morning. I will try again to talk sense to her."

Antonia felt the entire situation was highly unsatisfactory, but could see nothing she could do about it. She had come seeking answers, but found herself leaving with far more questions. She could only hope her maid had had a more gratifying time of it. Once settled in the carriage she turned to Isabella. "Now, tell me all."

"Flora—the upstairs maid—that one is the greatest..." She paused and fluttered her fingers to pantomime incessant talking.

"Gossipmonger?" Antonia suggested.

"Yes. That exactly. I had only to mention the exotic Musselman, then sit back and listen. She was proud of the Maharatta as if she had made him popular. A very silly piece. You would not have her in your house. Of that I am certain. She would still be chattering if the housekeeper hadn't sent her sharply about her duties. But it is no matter. I grasp the seed of it."

"I believe you mean kernel, Isabella."

"Yes, thank you, my lady. The Musselman—the kitchen maid whispered that he was a true Indian prince, but the cook boxed her ears—he was very handsome. Very popular with the ladies." She paused. "Ladies from above the stairs..." Isabella seemed confused as to how to continue.

"Isabella, you are not suggesting that Lady Duff Gordon —" Tonia's eyebrows rose. "She must be at least a decade older than he."

"No, no. Lady Duff Gordon very intellectual. Younger ladies, ladies more..." Isabella seemed at loss for the word.

"Ah susceptible. I take your meaning. Receptive, high-born ladies. But was there anyone in particular?"

"Flora, she talk of a lady in Brighton."

"Brighton?" The Indian did get around.

"Horses, she say."

"Oh, racing. I understand. Kahn went to Brighton for the races and met a young lady there. But, pray tell, how did such a story make its way to the Duff Gordon below-stairs?"

"A cousin of Flora..."

Antonia laughed. "Why did I ask? Of course there would be a connection." There always was with servants. "Did Flora know the lady's name?"

Isabella shook her head.

"Well, never mind. Do proceed."

"The Maharatta, take rooms at The Devil's Dyke. The lady..."

Tonia smiled and nodded. "Rendezvous seems to be the word you seek."

"She told her maid she would marry and go to India with him, but her brother discovered her plan."

"What a lucky thing, indeed, for the young lady. I wonder how she would like to have become an item in a Musselman harem."

The carriage concluded skirting St. James's Park and crossed The Mall. Antonia remained silent the rest of the journey back to Grosvenor Square. What a perturbing stew of things she had learned today. If she had hoped to find information to make her more comfortable about her friend Emilia's situation, she could hardly feel that learning of the failure of Azimoolah Khan's mission would give reassurance as to the safety of the English in Nana Sahib's sphere.

And what of the tangled tale Isabella told of a conspiracy and romantic folly in Brighton? Surely that could bear on nothing at hand. Unless whoever stuck the *quatar* into Faquir Johal's back did so in revenge for Khan's inamorata or some other Englishwoman's honour.

Perhaps strangest of all was the distraught Chandrika's fear of being forced into suttee. Of course, there was no possibility of such a thing happening in England. But could the girl be in some other kind of danger? Simply her insistence that the abhorrent ritual was still being practiced in India could be enough to inflame English sentiment.

Where would it all end? Every way Antonia looked she could see darkness gathering.

7

Charles, who had been awaiting Tonia's return, smiled when he heard the carriage pull up. "Never mind, Bracken, I shall greet her ladyship." He had not seen her since early morning and concern for her still lingered at the back of his mind. That concern deepened when he glimpsed her furrowed brow. As soon as her gaze alighted on him standing at the foot of the stairs, however, her face lighted, raising his own spirits.

"How delightful to see you, my love." She gave him her hand. "And how satisfactory that we have no engagements this evening. I shall help Nurse put Charlie to bed, then join you in the drawing room as soon as I've changed for dinner."

"Shall I send my jackanapes of a brother packing?"

"Charles, how can you say such a thing about a man of the cloth? Certainly not. I shall be most happy for his company. His counsel may be just what I need."

Ah, so his first instinct had been correct. Antonia must, indeed, be in a quandary if she was seeking advice.

A short time later Tonia, looking refreshed in a yellow striped silk evening dress and a fluff of lace and ribbon indoor cap, joined the gentlemen in the drawing room. Without asking, Danvers poured her a small glass of her favorite sweet sherry. The low fire warming the cool June evening made the cut crystal sparkle. Tonia took a sip of the amber liquid, sank back against the cushions of her chair, and launched into an account of the strange meeting with Chandrika Johal.

"Afraid of being forced into committing suttee? What utter bosh!" Freddie spoke first. "What can have put such rubbish in her head? Even if she weren't safe as houses in England—"

"I told her that, and that it was outlawed in India decades ago, but she insists it is still practiced."

"If so, it must be on a very limited scale," Freddie insisted. "I believe it is one of the real successes that can be laid to the credit of our missionaries a generation ago. I have read the works of some of them. William Carey—what a splendid fellow."

Danvers swirled the liquid in his glass as a reflection of his whirling thoughts. "I am aware that the abhorrent practice was held up as a symbol of Indian degeneracy in order to gain support for greater British control. Be that as it may, I have no doubt it may still exist in more remote regions. What I would like to know, however, is: What has planted the notion in this young woman's mind?"

Tonia blinked. "You mean you believe someone might be using the threat in order to control her?"

Danvers nodded. "If so, it would be most instructive to know who and why. It could very likely bear on her husband's killing." After a moment's further consideration, "I believe I should mention the possibility to our friend Futter."

"Yes, but advise him not to attempt interviewing her on his own. The poor thing is far too frightened."

Before more could be said on the matter, Bracken

appeared in the doorway. "Dinner is served, my lord, my lady."

Over cook's excellent breast of grass lamb and green peas the conversation shifted to Freddie's mission work. "I couldn't be more impressed with the work in the St. George's parish. Besides all the regular services, they provide a school for the ragamuffin children that infest the wharves like rats, run a refuge for pros—er, uh, that is, for fallen women, and a hostel for homeless girls. And there's no end of plans—night classes, an insurance scheme for dockers, parish clubs..."

"What is your work, Freddie?" Tonia asked.

"I lead morning and evening prayers daily at the church and work in the mission, mostly with opium addicts. I hope to be having a hand in more soon. I can't begin to tell you the extent of the need."

She held up a hand. "No, don't try. You must show me. I would especially like to see the church."

"Could you manage tomorrow? Victoria and Cecilia are most anxious to go as well, but their aunt has been unwell, so hasn't been able to escort them."

Tonia was enthusiastic in her acceptance. Charles considered whether he should discourage the plan. He was certain Tonia had no idea of the squalor she would encounter. He disliked the idea of adding more dark scenes to those already plaguing her mind. Surely a woman in a delicate condition such as she should avoid such things. But Tonia seemed set on the idea, and quite brightened by it. He would have to hope that interest in Freddie's activities might serve as a diversion for her anxieties.

As Jarvis was engaged about a matter of his lord's equipage the next morning, Danvers instructed Hardy to drive them. "And a fine thing it is, m'lord. To my mind there's not enough doing in London. Far more scope when one isn't so hemmed in." Danvers smiled. He had suspected that his man had been chafing at being required to focus almost entirely on his valeting duties without the freedom he usually enjoyed in the country. "There's too much taking of hansom cabs, to my way of thinking."

His man's final comment assured Danvers of the correct-ness of his analysis. "Well, hop to it then, Hardy. We wouldn't want you losing your excellent skill with the ribbons."

In spite of the heavy traffic clogging Oxford Street, Danvers's pair of chestnuts clipped smartly along in response to Hardy's expert driving a few minutes later. Victoria and Cecilia appeared to be in danger of severe neck injuries as they looked from side to side at the hackney cabs, omnibuses, pushcarts, and vehicles of every description. The street was lined with a mix of residences and entertainment establish-ments. Theatres and public houses stood side-by-side, attracting all manner of humanity. Men carrying placards announcing a new revue at the Princess's Theatre circulated through the pedestrians, followed by the inevitable gaggle of street urchins. At every cross-street a ragged child stood with a broom, hoping to earn a few pennies by sweeping the way free of rubbish and horse-droppings for ladies in fine boots and long skirts.

As they continued eastward the nature of the buildings changed. Banks, counting-houses and other establishments of commerce proclaimed them to be in the financial heart of the British Empire. In Leadenhall Street they encountered a magnificent neoclassical building. A triumphant figure of Britannia ruled from the apex of its central tympanum, supported by an impressive line of Doric columns. A portly gentleman was being helped from a carriage by an attendant as two richly dressed men were coming down the steps of the portico. A number of other men, their attire proclaiming them to be clerks and merchants, were coming and going singly or in groups, giving an air of bustle and importance to the area.

"The new East India House," Danvers supplied when he noticed the Misses Hever's attention to the structure. "Home to the most powerful corporation the world has ever seen."

"What do they do here?" Victoria asked.

"Conduct all the official business relating to the Company —which now rules a population of eighty-five million Indians." Danvers paused, impressed himself at the magnitude. "Inside the building you would find a court, an auction room, offices, a library, museum—in short, everything needed to run the world's commerce. I think it fair to say that the directors control areas of the world a good ten times the size of England. Their ships ply all the oceans of the globe laden with rich cargoes, primarily from China and India. It's all run from here."

Both sisters' eyes grew wide at Danvers's description of the wealth and power emanating from the edifice they passed. He smiled. "But I hasten to add that beyond the grand public rooms, you would find, behind that fine façade, warrens of cubicles where a veritable army of writer clerks beaver away from sun-up to sun-down by the light of wavering candles copying dispatches with their quill pens. The same document over and over."

"All to a good cause, though." Freddie turned back from his seat on the driver's box to pick up the narrative. "It's England's destiny to be an agent of civilization—to take peace and prosperity, education and morals to the world. Commerce paves the way for civilization." His voice took on the ring of an adherent. "Where commerce leads, Christianity follows and the people are civilized."

Danvers hoped it was so. At least, he would say nothing to dim his brother's ardor.

As they neared the river, the gleaming white fortifications of the Tower of London loomed beside them, but Freddie appeared to be impervious to the surroundings as he continued. "I was privileged to hear a splendid talk on this very subject at the most recent SPG meeting I attended. Through the East India Company the way has been paved for missionaries around the world, making it possible to diffuse among the native peoples, long sunk in ignorance and misery, the light and benign influence of the truth."

Danvers smiled at the passion in his younger brother's voice. It was doubtless a good thing for the young to be optimistic. Indeed, it must be required of those who, like Freddie, felt impelled to work among the destitute. But he did hope such enthusiasm would not be blighted too soon.

Once they crossed Dock Street and left the fine buildings of British commerce behind them, the streets became rougher, the buildings grimier and the population crowding the narrow, dirty lanes, shabbier. The squalor of Whitechapel assaulted them from every side as warrens of small, dark streets branched in all directions. Danvers felt Tonia drawing instinctively closer to him as a clutch of half-clad youngsters, so smeared with dirt it was impossible to tell which were girls and which boys, ran alongside the carriage, holding out their hands.

Danvers reached into his pocket for a few coppers which he flung into the midst of the pack. They instantly fell to their knees, scrabbling in the muddy street. Tonia raised a lace-edged lawn handkerchief to her nose as the stench from the gutters wafted to them. Even Danvers was appalled. This was far worse than anything they had encountered in the Bedern area of York the year before.

Beggars and sellers of trumpery called out to them, creating an indecipherable cacophony. A man, drunk or dead, lay in the gutter. It seemed that every corner was inhabited by a dollymop or night flower lounging against a grubby wall exhibiting her wares with a low-cut blouse and skirt hiked above her boots. Cecilia averted her eyes, but Danvers was amazed to see the compassion with which Victoria regarded these poor unfortunates.

Then Jarvis turned a corner and, as if by magic, a tall, white square tower, topped by a round lantern, rose before them. Behind the imposing main tower, two smaller ones, topped by distinctive pepper-pot tops, stood against the sky. Victoria was the first to respond to Freddie's pointing arm. "Oh, it's, it's so—clean! Can it be real?"

"Quite real. Substantial in every sense of the word."

Danvers observed that his brother had certainly chosen the correct description for the impressive architecture before them. After the darkness, decay and destitution they had just passed through, this seemed nothing less than a vision of heaven, albeit in very solid stone.

"And vigorous." Freddie continued his panegyric for his new ecclesiastical assignment. "The rector is assiduous in his spiritual and temporal duties. He offers fifty-four services a week, and as a poor law parish they sponsor a sailors' rest asylum and an orphan girls' school and asylum. The Association for Promoting Cleanliness among the Poor offers baths and laundry..."

It was clear that the list would have continued, but Hardy brought the carriage to a stop before a broad, paved passageway leading to the church.

Danvers instructed Hardy to stay with the carriage as the surrounding area was less than salubrious.

The others followed the walk to an impressive flight of steps ascending to the main entrance under the tower. Inside, the visitors all craned their necks upward as every eye turned to the high, coved ceiling divided into bays by arches enriched with roses. Substantial columns and massive piers supported the roof and galleries railed by carved, dark wood. At the front, a richly decorated, coved ceiling capped the semi-circular chancel lighted by painted glass windows representing faith, hope and charity.

Danvers noted the gothic golden cross flanked by heavy, gold candlesticks—evidence of the high church rituals his brother was so fond of. He had heard rumors of strong, even violent objections to such practices in the parish. Yet, he couldn't help but admire the good order that met his eye everywhere.

To their right, a distance down the sanctuary, a stairway led up to an impressively carved, high pulpit. Victoria stood regarding it, head tipped back to give her full view around the brim of her bonnet. "Freddie, will you preach from up there?" Her eyes shone at the prospect.

Her face fell, however, when he laughed. "Sorry to disappoint, my love, but I am chaplain at the mission chapel across the way in Calvert Street." He paused before concluding, "And I shall live there. In a house nearby."

Danvers held his breath. He did hope Victoria wouldn't become distraught at the revelation. After all she and Frederick had met when she did charity work in his mission in York. She must have had some idea what was in store when she agreed to be his wife.

"How splendid." Freddie's future bride put her arm through his. "Tell me more about your work. Perhaps Cecilia and I can be of assistance."

Freddie smiled at his intended, but looked doubtful. "Vicky, you are marvelous, but this is London. You saw what we drove through. There are far worse places—"

"At least you must tell me more about the work you will be doing." She cut him off before he could protest further.

"Ah, well—" It was clear that Freddie would need little persuading. "The girls' school and asylum houses twenty orphan daughters of British seamen. They are clothed, educated and set forward in life. An equal number attend daily from the neighborhood. More than six hundred children have been rescued from the worst miseries of the orphan's lot..."

The commendation continued, but Danvers moved beyond reach of his brother's voice to join Antonia who was admiring the organ in its high, dark wood gallery at the back. "I must say, I believe my little brother has had the good fortune to choose a wife astonishingly well-suited to him." He shook his head. "I wouldn't have thought it possible."

Tonia turned to observe the couple at the far end of the aisle, standing in intent conversation as if alone in the church. She laughed. "Aunt Aelfrida's nephew a slum priest. Who would credit it?"

"Every year helpless orphans are rescued. Only last year when fire destroyed an East Indiaman on the way to Bengal..." Freddie's voice floated up the aisle to them.

"Charles, it seems that everywhere I turn of late I hear a reference to the East India Company. I am most interested to learn more of this seeming bulwark of our society."

"Bulwark of our economy it certainly is. The East India Company is by far the largest employer of workers in England, and doubtless in India and elsewhere, too." He considered before suggesting to Tonia and Cecilia, "Would you care to view their docks?"

"I should be most interested. Are they nearby?"

"Not a great distance. Some quarter of an hour eastward, I believe."

Cecilia said she would be happy to see more of this new world she was discovering. Fredrick and his intended, however, were still deep in conversation, so Danvers merely informed them of their plans.

"Yes, fine. Don't bother returning for us. I'll secure a

hackney when we are finished." Freddie barely gave his brother a look.

They found Hardy instructing a cluster of ragged children in the minutiae of carriage building. Two lads crouched under the carriage. "C springs those are called. You won't get a smoother ride in any vehicle than that. And the leather straps —Ah, m'lord."

The ragamuffins snapped to attention at the announcement of the arrival of the fine lord who owned such magnificence, one small lad hitting his head on the undercarriage. "I was just instructing—"

"Fine, Hardy, carry on. We wouldn't want their education slighted."

"Thank you, m'lord." Hardy placed his hand on the soft leather hood covering the back seat. "As it's such a fine afternoon I was about to put the top down." He depressed the spring catches on each side and folded it back. "A calash, it's called," he explained to his rapt audience.

"Oooh, like bellows," one urchin observed.

"Fine, end of lesson." Danvers distributed coppers into the grubby hands. "Now, off with you."

Once seated in the carriage, both ladies raised their parasols as protection against the sun and Hardy snapped the reins. They were crossing Wapping at a clipping pace along Ratcliffe Highway when the fierce roar of a wild beast tore through the air. This set up a cacophony of animal noises that caused Cece to drop her parasol and clutch the carriage wall with both hands. "What is it?"

Danvers smiled. "Don't be armed. I should have thought to warn you. Jamrach's animal Emporium." He pointed to the shop facing onto the highway. "I'm certain you are quite safe. Jamrach buys exotic animals from seamen and supplies menageries and circuses."

Cecilia visibly relaxed, although the roaring, growling and

bellowing continued. Hardy soothed his team then looked over his shoulder. "That Jamrach is an intrepid fellow. Were you hearing about the Bengal tiger that escaped?"

"Hardy—" Danvers gave his man a severe look. "This is no time to be frightening the ladies with your faradiddles."

"No, m'lord, as true as the day is long, it is. A small boy who was passing tried to pet it. The big cat picked the child up in its teeth."

"No!" The horror in Tonia's voice showed she was thinking of her own small boy.

"No, no—no fear, m'lady. Jamrach rushed out and, quick as Saint Patrick, thrust his bare hands into the tiger's throat. The beast let his captive go."

The look of horror remained on Tonia's face. "Did the child live?"

Hardy laughed. "Quite unhurt, he was. But his papa sued Jamrach. Had to pay several hundred pounds, he did. But, canny fellow that he is, he made it back on the sale of the tiger."

The hair-raising tale took them into Limehouse where the poverty of the area closed in on them again. Charles became more uneasy, especially after Hardy's alarming tale. He regretted his suggestion that they undertake this jaunt. Perhaps they should turn back now. As the road curved nearer to the river, however, a new sight met their eyes. A veritable forest of masts rocked in the wash of dark water beyond muddy flats left by the receding tide.

What at first glance appeared to be large lumps of damp earth soon showed themselves to be small humans rootling in the ooze.

"Whatever are they doing?" Cece cried. A small creature Danvers assumed to be a boy straightened up from his bent-over search waving what appeared to be a bottle. He placed the object in a tattered basket his companion was carrying and returned to his grubbing. Next to him a girl, if one could judge by the length of the mud-caked hair, sat crying, holding her foot aloft—perhaps cut by broken glass. Another forager ran from the water's edge with both hands full of black lumps that were most likely coal.

"Mudlarks," Danvers explained. "All manner of objects wash up at low tide, some thrown overboard on purpose, others by mishap. Coal falls off the barges."

Cecilia shook her head in wonder. "And they collect it? To what purpose?"

"To live. Everything they find they sell. It's meagre, but it is a living."

Cecilia looked incredulous. "But they're just children."

"Yes, but the occupation is preferable to many others that might be available to them such as chimney sweeping or factory work. At least they're in the fresh air."

Tonia, sitting on the left side of the carriage, had been observing the human traffic closest to her view. "What strange dress—Oriental, it appears."

"Yes, Chinese," Danvers informed her. "They come in off the ships. Many set up, er—business establishments in the area." He considered: Should he tell her about the opium dens that infested this area of London? An old man wearing a garment that looked like loose black pajamas shuffled down the street, smoking a long-handled clay pipe. A woman wearing a loose-fitting embroidered robe with black bands around cuffs and hem stood in a dilapidated doorway. She moved aside to allow the man to enter. The grimy windows obscured any view of what took place inside, but Danvers had read of such places. And the ruin of lives that resulted.

No, if Cecilia had not been with them he might have ventured to inform Antonia, but not an unmarried girl. She should not know of such things. He only hoped that Freddie would have the same sensibility as to what he chose to share with Victoria.

They drove through Poplar, above the sharp curve in the Thames that formed the Isle of Dogs, amid increasing traffic of heavy carts pulled by dray horses loaded with merchandise coming and going to and from the docks. The clomp of horses' hooves and the rumble of iron wheels on cobbles, as well as the occasional cry of costermongers that managed to rise above the clatter, made conversation in the carriage impossible.

They were almost to the docks when a space between tumbledown structures opened momentarily at a bend in the road. "Goodness," Antonia cried. "What magnificent buildings. In the midst of such squalor."

"Yes," Danvers replied. "East India Company's warehouses. Elegant, aren't they? Very important symbols of wealth and power."

The view disappeared as they drove on down a filthy street lined with dilapidated buildings and choked with ragged children, mangy dogs and the occasional pig. Chickens fled before the carriage, squawking and flapping their wings. Women with nearly naked infants in their arms scolded children and shouted at the animals, all with equal futility. The stench of a midden beside a dilapidated hut made Antonia cover her mouth and nose with both hands. A nearby standpipe was surrounded by gossiping women who had apparently come to draw water for their households. Children played in the mud around it, as caked to their knees as the mudlarks the carriage passengers had seen earlier.

Then another turn in the road brought an unbroken vista across open marshland, revealing the East India Docks. "I had no idea it would be so vast," Tonia said. The distance between them and the river held an immense basin filled with tall-masted ships, some awaiting a place at the dock, others lining the wharves. The road led to a gate in the high brick wall enclosing the enormous installation.

"Designed by John Rennie, the man who engineered the new London Bridge—" Danvers began, but his attention was taken by an enclosed Brougham approaching with some speed from a side road. "Best pull over, Hardy. This fellow seems to want to pass us. We're in no hurry."

His man complied and they proceeded to the gate at their comfortable pace. The uniformed and armed gatekeeper bowed and pulled back the heavily scrolled wrought iron gate when he saw the viscount's crest on the side of the barouche. Hardy pulled on into the yard and drew up near the other newly arrived carriage.

Danvers handed Tonia out and she walked to the back of the barouche where she stopped at the sight of the occupant emerging from the brougham that had nearly run them off the road. "Colonel Whitham. What a surprise to see you here." She advanced and held out a hand to him. "Colonel, I am so sorry for your loss. Mrs. Whitham must be most distressed."

He gave a sharp, military bow. "As are we all. Thank you, Lady Danvers. I fear, however, I have not the luxury of grieving. Business must be dealt with." His black arm band and the crepe around his stovepipe hat proclaimed the recent death in his family, but he bustled with determination.

Danvers joined his wife. "I didn't realize you had interests in the Company beyond the military, Colonel."

"I hope to become more active now that I'm retired. Might as well give them the benefit of my years of service in that blast furnace of a subcontinent. Can't spend all my time kicking my heels at m'club, you know." He bowed and strode off toward the largest of the warehouses.

A moment later, however, he turned sharply and came back. "Beg pardon. Don't know what I was thinking." He nodded to Tonia and Cecilia. "I take it you ladies are here for a tour. I know the premises quite well myself. May I have the honour?"

Danvers blinked. This was the same man who had been in such a hurry he nearly ran them off the road? "Well, if you have time, Colonel. I haven't been here before myself," he accepted tentatively.

"Right. Splendid layout, this." Whitham talked at a rapid rate as he walked quickly toward an elevated ramp that gave a clear view of the docks and river beyond.

Perhaps the Colonel approached everything at speed, Danvers thought, as he lengthened his own stride.

"That Rennie fellow knew his business. Of course, these were the third docks to be built, so the designers could learn from experience. One dock is for unloading imports—" Whitham pointed toward a basin containing several ships. From their slightly elevated position they could also see the wharf lined with holding sheds and heavy dray carts waiting to be loaded. A row of brick warehouses filled an area behind that.

"The other side is for loading exports." Again, a seemingly endless line of heavily-laden carts waited beside the dock to be unloaded by an army of stevedores. "Handle two hundred, fifty ships at a time, these docks can. Third basin, over there nearer the river, is a holding area for those waiting to come in —prevents clogging up the waterway."

Although talking about the docks, their host's gaze swept the traffic-choked Thames, where Tonia's attention turned as well. She knew little about nautical matters, but it did surprise her to see a fishing trawler rocking in the wake of a larger vessel that had just passed. Fishing in this muddy, congested river? She gave a small shiver at the thought of fish from such waters landing on her table. "I shouldn't care to eat the catch from that trawler," she said to no one in particular.

Their host jerked his head to the direction of her gaze. "No, no, my lady. No need to fear. No commercial fishing in the Thames. Merely delivering their catch to Billingsgate."

Whitham's attention seemed to be taken by an elegant yacht sailing past the docks, steam billowing from its distinctive blue and yellow funnel. After watching the craft's progress for a moment he pulled out his pocket watch and noted the time, then turned without comment to the closer scene. "Take a look at the imports, shall we?" His former air of haste now dissolved and he became an expansive host. "Plenty to interest the ladies—silks, spices, tea—"

"Oh, it smells like Christmas!" Cecilia cried as they neared the long shed where crates emitting exotic aromas were being unloaded.

"It does," Tonia agreed. "Cinnamon, cloves, nutmeg... What fun Cook would have here."

Their guide led them under the wide wooden roof of the unloading shed where they could observe a heap of crates in a heavy net being lowered by a derrick from the side of the ship. Stacks of similar crates were piled in a veritable mountain to one side. Dockworkers moved everywhere like ants, directing the derrick operators, stacking crates, moving them with hand trucks. Several clerks held boards where they wrote on sheaves of papers.

"Meticulous accounts, of course," Whitham said. "Everything that comes off a ship is weighed and counted, then put into a warehouse or loaded directly onto carts for onward travel. Even with that, though—"

He paused abruptly and pointed with pride to a vessel being unloaded, its gilded stern sparkling in the sun, the red and white striped Company flag riffling in the breeze. "East Indiamen are the finest ships to sail the seven seas. Equal or even superior to our Royal Navy, if you'll forgive me for saying so. As heavily armed, too, I'll add."

His chest seemed to expand ever so slightly as he continued his monologue whilst walking down the length of the bustling warehouse. "Empire's founded on trade, of course. India sends a quarter of her exports home. You'll see it all on these docks: rice, cotton, silk, jute, oil." He pointed to various stacks of cargo as he enumerated their contents.

Three triple-masted East Indiamen were being unloaded at that moment, with three others lined up to take their place. "Seeds, tea, coffee, teak, indigo, carpets... Tea trade alone's worth thirty million pounds a year." Whitham waved a hand at a mountain of large, square baskets with distinctive geometric patterns woven into their sides.

"Assam, India's finest. Company controls the whole region, of course." Whitham spoke with almost fatherly pride. A man in top hat and frock coat sat on a tall stool at a high desk accounting for every chest arriving at the dock. Another well-dressed man was directing a dockworker pushing a hand truck piled high with tea chests, apparently taking delivery of his order.

At the next unloading bay Tonia raised her head and looked around. "What is that delightful floral scent?" The air was heavy with an intense, sweet perfume. "Incense? Oil?"

Before Whitham could reply a crate toppled off a hand truck a nearby worker was pushing. The carton split open and several pottery bowls fell out, tipping pale balls the size of melons onto the wharf. The overseer shouted orders. Several men ran to retrieve the spilled cargo and clean up the broken pottery. The heady scent became almost overpowering.

"Opium, Lady Danvers," Whitham explained. "From Bengal. Very profitable monopoly—although supplies are down."

"It looks like quite a mountain to me," Cecilia observed.

Whitham shook his head. "This confounded uprising in India plays havoc with commerce. Strictly for medicinal purposes here, of course. The East India Company ships most directly from India to China."

Danvers frowned. Medicinal, indeed. Laudanum was taken as freely as tea for every complaint from headache to cough to amputation. Mothers were encouraged to drop "Mother's Friend" into the mouths of sleepless children. Fortunately, Antonia had the good sense to forbid Nurse Bevans using it on Charlie.

"Charles, did you hear me?" Tonia gave a small shake to his arm where her hand rested.

"What? Sorry, afraid I was rather wool-gathering."

"Those men." Danvers looked in the direction Tonia indicated by the tilt of her head. He saw two Asian men in deep conversation with the clerk at the counting table. "I saw them at the park yesterday. They seemed to be with Lieutenant Anson. What a coincidence to encounter them here."

Danvers observed the way they were dressed and shrugged. "Perhaps applying for a job."

There was no time for further observances, however, as, weaving around workers, cargo, and laden hand trucks, Whitham led the way back through the shed. The journey took several minutes and Danvers became concerned for Tonia and Cece as the crush of workers seemed to increase.

When they finally achieved the open air beyond the shed, Whitham stopped and pointed to a row of buildings along the outer edge of the complex. "I would be remiss if I failed to point out that we take every care of our workers. That building is a workers-only pub." He pointed. "Likewise, strictest control is enforced among both dockers and seamen. The next building is a private prison."

Antonia appeared to share Danvers's relief that their guide did not suggest they should inspect those amenities. "Thank you for your most enlightening tour, Colonel." She extended a gloved hand to their escort. "I fear we have kept you from your business far too long."

He took her fingertips and bowed. "Not at all, Lady Danvers. It was my privilege. I am only too happy for an opportunity to share an insight into the magnificence of our empire." He bowed to Cecilia. "Miss Hever, delighted to make your acquaintance."

With the air of having achieved a duty well done, Whitham turned and strode quickly off toward the outside of the unloading shed. Danvers was surprised to note that he seemed to be heading toward the men Tonia had pointed out to him a few minutes earlier. Was the colonel's business here with them?

"Did you notice how he spoke of the Company as if he were a director himself?" Tonia asked as they strolled back toward their carriage.

"Yes," Danvers nodded. "He seemed very proud of it. Although, I suppose serving as an officer with the Indian army does make him part of the Company in a way."

Just as they reached the barouche, Whitham's driver snapped the reins over the team standing next to Danvers's and the brougham pulled sharply forward to the back of the shed they had just been inspecting.

Hardy observed the carriage making its way to the far end of the long building, then harumphed. "Strange thing to my thinking—in such a hurry he was to get here he almost ran us off the road, then takes all that time as if showing you through an art exhibit."

"I expect he found it much more engrossing than an art exhibit, Hardy." Danvers handed the ladies into the carriage.

Hardy gave his full attention to driving until they reached Upper Wimpole Street and Miss Hever was duly returned to Aunt Dimity with promises from Antonia that she would call to take both of the Hever sisters on a shopping expedition one day soon. Once the horses were turned toward the familiar route to Grosvenor Square, however, Hardy returned to his usual communicative self, talking over his shoulder. "I am thinking you will be interested to know, m'lord, that I took the opportunity to engage Whitham's groom, who is most fortuitously named Driver, in a comfortable natter."

Danvers smiled. "Ah, you mean you interrogated the fellow? Do tell, Hardy. I suspect an interesting tale."

"More like perplexing, to my way of thinking. It seems the colonel makes regular visits to the docks every day or two, most precise as to the hour. Driver isn't knowing why—or at least won't say. Didn't mean to be giving any information, of course, that was just by way of apologizing for nearly running us off the road. Most particular, his colonel. Could just be his military habits, of course. Out in India with him, Driver was —colonel's batman, he said, and very proud of it, too."

Danvers laughed. "Leave it to you to get the fellow's pedigree, Hardy."

Danvers passed the matter off, but later, reading the latest alarming news from India in the day's papers, he did wonder briefly what interest the retired officer had that took him journeying to the docks on a regular basis. The question was soon forgotten, however, as he read of the continuance and extension of disaffection among the native troops.

The debate continued in the House of Lords over the propriety of Governor-General Canning's support of missionary activity in India, but the more serious issue seemed to be reports of the aversion of the sepoys to the greased rifle cartridges they were required to load. Apparently Captain Bellingham had been correct in his explanation.

As Danvers read more about the burning of barracks, hospital, officers' quarters, and sepoys' houses, and the resultant deaths of several British officers, he began to fear that the former intimations of trouble had been understated.

One editorial was most instructive, if disquieting: "At length the black cloud ominous to the continuance of British power in India has collected and burst over that half ruined country... in all the great military stations, the native troops are in a state of mutiny... disaffection spreading with rapidity... by far the greatest shock that the British Empire in the East has ever experienced..."

Danvers folded the paper and tucked it carefully away. He did not want Antonia, already concerned for the safety of her friend, to be upset by this.

8

Antonia was still enjoying her morning visit to Charlie in the nursery the next day when Sophia burst in with the ribbons of her bonnet flying. "Oh, Lady Danvers, do forgive my intrusion—Bracken did try to escort me, but I'm afraid I outran him on the stairs." She brandished a heavy, vellum envelope with the gold wax seal broken.

"From the Lord Chamberlain?" Tonia asked, abandoning the line of toy soldiers she and her son had been marching up and down the carpet in an enactment of the regimental parade they would attend later in the day.

"Yes!" Sophia pulled the stiff, engraved sheet of stationery from the envelope and handed it to Antonia, her fingers trembling with excitement. "I did not think it would come. My name can mean nothing to the Lord Chamberlain. I did not think it possible."

"You forget, Sophia, who it was that sent your name to the Lord Chamberlain."

The girl gave a little trill of a giggle. "Yes, Aunt Aelfrida reminded me of that when she saw my surprise at the letter."

Tonia could only smile. The Lord Chamberlain having the

temerity to refuse the Dowager Duchess of Aethelbert was unthinkable. "Even so, my dear, were it not evident that you clearly 'wear the white flower of a blameless life,' even Aunt Aelfrida's imprimatur would not have been enough." Antonia breathed a quick thanksgiving that Sophia's mother's and grandmother's improvident marriages had not been an impediment.

Antonia perused the missive. "Yes, indeed. Very proper. You are to be presented at the Queen's Drawing-Room on the ninth of July." She thought for a moment. "Goodness, that gives only two weeks to get ready. I am complacent, however, that Aunt Aelfrida will have all well in hand."

"I believe her grace's dressmaker was informed almost as soon as I arrived in London. We have not yet chosen the fabric, though."

"Never fear. You may rely on it that Madame Elise will do you proud."

"The dowager duchess said you will attend me."

"Aunt Aelfrida said what?" Antonia sputtered, but suppressed her initial reaction. She did not want to dim Sophia's excitement, even though she had little fondness for the discomfort and fatigue of a royal Drawing-room. The possibility of pleading her parlous condition occurred to her. Truth to tell, though, she was feeling fine with none of the early morning discomfort that had attended her time carrying Charlie. "Then it appears I must have a new gown as well. It would have been thoughtful of her grace to have informed me earlier. No doubt the matter slipped her attention." More likely, however, it was what Aunt Aelfrida had planned from the first.

"We're going to see the soldiers march today," Charlie, who had apparently been ignored for quite long enough, announced.

"Yes, so am I. Won't it be splendid!" Sophia knelt on the carpet and picked up one of the toy soldiers.

"That's Lieutenant Anson," Charlie informed her.

"Oh, I didn't know they had names." Sophia replaced the lieutenant in his rank. "And is Captain Bellingham here as well?"

Charlie pointed out the captain and Sophia assisted in moving the troops forward. Charlie then brought out three toy cannons and lined them up beside the regiment. "The guns will be very loud. You won't be afraid, will you? You may put your fingers in your ears if you wish."

"Thank you for warning me." Sophia prepared to shield her ears.

"They are only booms. They won't shoot anyone," Charlie said reassuringly. "Tinker can't go, though. He would be afraid."

Charlie made a repetition of booms, even rocking the guns back in imitation of recoil. "It's for the queen. Mama says we will have forty-one booms, but I can only count to ten."

"You can count to ten? That is prodigious, indeed."

Nurse Bevans returned from below stairs where she had been taking her morning tea. "Master Charlie, we must put our soldiers away now and get ready for our outing."

A short time later Charlie sat proudly on his papa's knee in order to make room for Sophia to sit beside Nurse Bevans in the Danvers's carriage. In spite of the crush of onlookers coming to celebrate the queen's accession day, they had barely entered Hyde Park when Sophia spotted Beatrice and Alice, escorted by Arthur Emory in his stylish landau.

Luckily, Jarvis found a spot along North Carriage Drive

where they could view events from the comfort of their plush seats. Nothing would do for Charlie, however, but that they walk onto the grass to get closer to the proceedings. Antonia consented. "But you must stay with Nurse Bevans. No running off," she warned. "Take care, Sara," Tonia cautioned the nurse. "There is such a crowd." Tonia watched as her son skipped across the grass to the barrier marking the parade ground.

A moment later Arthur Emory strolled by with a fashionably bonneted sister on each arm. "Do come join us, Sophia," Bea invited. A slight breeze ruffled the lace of her parasol and fluttered the blue ribbons of her bonnet.

Arthur extended his hand to help Sophia from the barouche. She took his arm to stroll across the grass with Beatrice and Alice following. Antonia raised her parasol and sat back with a sigh. She smiled at her husband, quite happy for a peaceful moment.

Peaceful was hardly the word, however, when the band of the Honourable Artillery Company marched into the park with all seventy-some of their musicians playing "The Grenadier Guards," a splendid sight in their scarlet tunics and bearskin busbies as they marched across the park, then to the far side of the parade ground where they formed a single line and continued to play.

After a brief concert of celebratory music, the troops from the Wellington Barracks marched before the spectators in magnificent precision. The crowd of viewers all around the park clapped, cheered and waved small Union flags. With all the others, Antonia applauded their faultless discipline and felt a swell of pride. She raised a gloved hand to shade her eyes and sought to pick out their acquaintances in the unwavering rows of marching men, but to her eye they all looked alike.

This did not appear to be the case, however, with the younger ladies of their party. Tonia saw Beatrice raise her arm and wave with a white handkerchief fluttering from her hand. There was, of course, no flicker of recognition from any of the strictly drilled troops, but Alice soon joined her sister in saluting one of the marching men. The positions changed as the troops pivoted to march to the far side of the park to line the perimeter of the field. Antonia smiled as the young ladies continued to beckon to their officer friends, in spite of the fact that any recognition could have been impossible at that distance.

All else was forgotten in the next moment, however, as seventy-one horses of the Queen's Troop Royal Horse Artillery thundered into the park. The pounding of their hooves shook the earth and drowned the playing of the band. Six horses pulled caissons to which were attached thirteen-pounder field guns from the Crimean war. Artillery officers marched on and detached the guns. The horses galloped off and five artillerymen dropped to one knee behind each gun.

With the precision of a stately quadrille, the officers' white gloves moved in unison behind each gun. A powder cartridge was shoved into place, the trigger pulled. A mighty boom shook the earth and a cloud of white smoke issued from the barrel. While the empty shot was removed and the gun reloaded, the process passed to the next gun. Load. Pull. Explosion and smoke. Reload.

Up and down the line for twenty-one shots, the Royal Salute marked the day on which Her Majesty began her happy reign. New cartons of ammunition were carried onto the field for a succession of twenty more shots, signifying that Hyde Park was a Royal Park. The air was filled with smoke so thick as to obscure the band standing beyond the firing position. Antonia's eyes watered and her nose stung. Her ears rang from the reverberations of the barrage.

She closed her eyes and put her hands to her ears. Instead of blocking out the discomfort, however, the scene shifted in her mind and she was no longer in a green park surrounded by elegantly clad ladies and splendidly uniformed officers. The ground around her was brown and arid. Dust choked her throat. The shells exploding around her were not mere ceremonial powder but deadly cannon that ripped through buildings and tore at men's flesh. She gave a small moan and slumped against the seat of the carriage.

"Antonia! Are you all right?"

She felt Danvers's arm around her, holding her up. She blinked, and the scene cleared. The last of the shots rumbled forth. The smoke dissolved. At a signal the kneeling artillerymen bounded to their feet and gave a jumping turn to face the back of the park. The cavalry thundered onto the field again. The shining black horses made a sweeping turn so that each caisson arrived at precisely the spot for those on foot to reattach the guns. The horses galloped off. The infantry retired with their ammunition cases. The regiment marched smartly across the field, followed by the band, still playing a lively march.

The world returned to normal, but Antonia struggled to order her mind. Which vision had been the reality? The splendor of gleaming horseflesh, scarlet uniforms and waving flags in a green park spread solidly before her. Yet the horror, fear and pain of the parched desert would not let her go.

"Tonia, my love, are you ill?"

She shook her head, more to clear it than as a reply to Danvers. "It must be the sun. I felt rather faint. I should like to walk a bit, Charles." She was gripped by a strong desire to feel the gentle softness of the grass under her feet. To walk in the shade of the trees ringing the park.

"Let us find Charlie and Nurse Bevans," Tonia said.

They turned in the direction they had last seen them, before the billows of smoke obscured their vision, but had taken only three or four steps when Sara Bevans rushed toward them out of the lingering clouds. "My lord, my lady! Master Charlie—he's gone! The smoke—I closed my eyes only for a moment—"

"Which direction?" Charles demanded.

"I—I didn't see, but he loved the horses. He might have followed."

Charles spun in the direction the horses had gone. Tonia lifted her skirt and lengthened her stride in an attempt to keep up with him, but in that crowd it was impossible to stay together. "Charles, go on. I shall look further here," she called.

In a moment he was swallowed by the throng. Tonia stood, looking wildly around her, her heart cramping in her throat. It would be impossible to spot a small child in this sea of humanity. If only she could see a police officer or someone to help. Where were Arthur Emory and the rest of their party? All was a blur of moving bodies and chatting holiday-ers, appearing insubstantial in the haze of smoke still hanging over the park.

She had to make an effort. She stumbled forward a few steps, then caught sight of a familiar face. Colonel Whitham's sturdy build and grey mutton chop whiskers presented a comforting vision. He would help her. She followed as quickly as she could, but he was too far ahead for her to call out to him, and with his military stride, he covered the ground more quickly than she could.

She soon saw, though, that he appeared to be making for the Serpentine. Yes, Danvers had more than once taken their son out in a row boat on that long body of water on the far side of the park. Could Charlie have remembered that and headed for it once the horses he was following disappeared?

She clapped a hand over her mouth to stifle a cry. The thought of a small, intrepid boy and all that open water... She broke into a near-run. Even so, the colonel lengthened the distance between them. He disappeared behind a clump of bushes.

Tonia's throat burned and her breath came in gasps. She rounded the shrubbery, expecting to see Whitham's back well ahead of her.

Instead, she nearly bumped into him. "Colonel Whitham, I—" she halted as she realized they were not alone. She had apparently interrupted a meeting. "Your grace," she acknowledged the Duke of Penthurst. "Forgive me. My son has wandered off..." Even as she launched into her explanation, Tonia registered the fact that she had interrupted Whitham in the act of handing a folder of papers to Penthurst. Had the colonel not withdrawn the packet in such a furtive manner, it was unlikely she would have noted the motion.

The Duke of Penthurst made a slight bow to her. "Lady Danvers, may I offer my assistance? The young master? You believe he came to the water?"

"Yes. That is, I don't know, but I do need help looking for him." In her fear for her son Antonia's antipathy to the duke was forgotten.

"It would be my pleasure." Penthurst turned to his errand of mercy.

Before he could begin, however, Sophia and Arthur Emory hurried up. Sophia was breathing rapidly and Arthur glowing with perspiration from their haste. "We saw you making off in this direction. Lord Danvers, he has the boy," Sophia said between gasps for breath.

"Oh, thank you!" Antonia turned to retrace her steps, then stopped. "Your grace, thank you for your offer. Forgive my interruption." Even in her hurried words she perceived the low bow Penthurst was making to Sophia, her return of a deep curtsy, and Arthur's scowl. Antonia took time for no more, but hurried back to her son.

She found Charles holding a delighted Charlie. "It was as

Bevans thought; he followed the horses, but made little headway before they disappeared. He was howling for the horses, so a kind passerby took him to a mounted police officer."

"And you found him there?"

"It was more a matter of him finding me. The policeman took Charlie up before him in the saddle. From that vantage Charlie pointed me out."

"Oh, Charlie, you mustn't... You gave us such a fright." Words failed her. She turned toward the carriage.

They had returned Sophia to Berkeley Square Gardens and were almost to Grosvenor Square when Tonia finally relaxed her hold on her son and allowed her mind to play over the events of the day. "Charles, I encountered a most strange scene near the Serpentine. I don't know what it means, but Colonel Whitham was giving a folder to Penthurst, which he withdrew when I approached. It was most likely perfectly innocent, of course, but the whole thing had such a clandestine air about it. I expect I'm just being silly, but with the colonel's brother-in-law's awful death, and then his sister-in-law behaving so oddly..." She took a deep breath and shook her head. "Oh, I just don't know."

❧ 9 ❧

On the evening of the twenty-first day of the siege Emilia was holding a tin cup with a few drops of precious water to the lips of a wounded man in the trench when she noticed a strange quiet. Firing on both sides had ceased. She looked up, seeking the reason for this oddly alarming silence. At first she held her breath, then began slowly to breathe again. It was inexplicably eerie. After weeks of incessant cannonade, explosions and anguished cries of the newly wounded, how could silence be even more frightening? And yet it was.

After almost two hours of uneasy quiet, the lookout in the crow's nest shouted. "There's a woman coming across!"

"A spy," a man near Emilia muttered and raised his rifle.

"No!" Lieutenant Thompson, standing next to him, knocked his rifle away. "She is waving a white wand." Thompson lifted the woman over the barricade and she all but fainted in his arms.

"Rose Anne!" Emilia recognized the exhausted, tattered lady as Mrs. Greenway, the matriarch of a wealthy merchant family. The Greenways resided at Cawnpore, but had fled to a nearby town where they had a factory when the mutiny began. It was obvious that their escape had been to no avail. The woman was without shoes and *stockings, her threadbare dress her only garment. Her earlobes were red and swollen with infection where her earrings had obviously been pulled out. Emilia remembered what fine, expensive jewelry Rose Anne Greenway had always worn. And how proud she had been of it.*

When Mrs. Greenway had recovered somewhat she handed Lieutenant Mowbray Thompson a letter. "To the Subjects of Her Most Gracious Majesty Queen Victoria," Thompson read out the inscription. He handed the letter to the second in command of the post, Captain John Moore.

Moore opened it and read, "All those who are in no way connected with the acts of the Governor-General, and are willing to lay down their arms, shall receive a safe passage to Allahabad."

Moore looked up and held the brief missive out to Thompson. "It is unsigned."

The lieutenant looked at it, frowning. "Azimoolah Khan. I have seen his handwriting."

"Is it a trap? I find it hard to believe Nana Sahib could behave without treachery," Moore replied.

Thompson shook his head. "Wheeler must decide."

For two days the Entrenchment rang with rumors. General Wheeler, still hopeful of relief from Calcutta, opposed the idea of treating with Nana Sahib.

Yet there were only three days' rations left in store. The condition of the women and children was beyond deplorable.

The enemy held their fire for two more days. On the twenty-sixth of June, Mrs. Greenway returned to the Nana's camp, bearing the message that General Wheeler would treat.

Thompson passed the word to the native officer stationed nearest the Entrenchment, and almost immediately a splendidly arrayed Musselman rode proudly up to the English camp. A black, curly beard bristled beneath his fine white turban, and his gleaming white robes rippled with the movement of his red-gold Arab stallion.

Emilia had no idea who he was, but she heard the intake of breath and the murmurs of those around her who did. "Azimoolah Khan." The senior English officers went out to meet him and the officer of the Nana's cavalry that followed behind him.

Those nearest the wall heard the terms and relayed them to their fellows along the trench and further back. In exchange for the surrender of the garrison's money, guns and ammunition, Nana would provide the garrison with a flotilla of covered boats for their safe passage to Allahabad.

Moore replied that before General Wheeler could even consider such a proposition, Nana would have to agree to supply the boats with enough flour to sustain them. Azimoolah grandly offered to supply not only flour but sheep and goats also.

Moore further insisted on transport for the women, children and wounded for the mile to the Sati Chowra boat landing and that each man could proceed under arms and equipped with sixty rounds of ammunition.

Azimoolah replied that His Highness would probably accept Moore's conditions, then whirled his steed in the sand and rode off with his robes flying.

By mid-afternoon a sowar returned to report that Nana had agreed to all conditions. They would embark in the morning.

Emilia breathed an immense sigh of relief along with the rest of the camp. Water. Her first thought was water. Now they could go to the well without fear and drink their full. Along with every able-bodied person in the Entrenchment, she rushed to the formerly danger-ously exposed well. Repeated shelling of the well over the past weeks had knocked copious amounts of mortar and brick dust into the water, but even cloudy as it was, no nectar could have been sweeter.

And food—that night double rations of chupatties and dhal were served around. Everywhere she looked Emilia saw faces lightened, hope shining from formerly dull eyes.

Still, anxieties persisted. Could so vicious an enemy be trusted? Emilia heard the murmurs around her. "Do you think it will be all right tomorrow?" "Will they really let us go down to Allahabad in safety?" Even the words spoken as questions sounded too good to be true.

But the document was agreed and signed. Tomorrow they would go free.

"I will wear my ruched silk bonnet today, Isabella," Antonia said as her lady's maid put the finishing touches on Lady Danvers's hair. She had endured another disturbing dream last night, but she would not allow such a phantasm to spoil her day. A walk in the park with Charlie and Tinker would drive the phantoms away.

"And may I suggest your cashmere shawl?" Isabella held out the deeply fringed wrap. "It is a cool morning."

Tonia accepted, along with her netted purse and gloves, and was making for the door when the upstairs maid entered with a knock and a curtsy. "Beg pardon, mam; the Dowager Duchess, mam."

"Here?" Tonia looked around. It would not be beyond Aunt Aelfrida to invade her dressing room. "Downstairs, mam." Betsy curtsied again and fled.

Indeed, the Dowager Duchess of Aethelbert was awaiting Lady Danvers in the front drawing room with her ward in tow. She looked Antonia up and down. "Ah, bonnet and shawl, excellent. You are ready then?"

"Ready, your grace?"

"You shall accompany us today. If Sophia is to be presented at Her Majesty's next Drawing-Room there is no time to be lost."

Tonia smiled with relief. For once Aunt Aelfrida's dictates fitted her plans. "Excellent. I am to escort Freddie's intended in trousseau shopping this morning. We can accomplish both most readily." She turned to Bracken who was waiting to open the door for them. "You may tell Jarvis we will not need his services today."

The dowager duchess sniffed. It was obvious she did not care to have others' plans achieve a purpose before her own were announced. Once Victoria and Cecilia were collected from their Wimpole Street lodgings and all were settled in her ladyship's luxurious landau, however, there was little doubt that the expedition would be a lively one. The three young ladies, seated with their backs to the driver's box, chatted with animation about wedding plans and the upcoming Drawing-room.

"Presented to Her Majesty? I declare, my knees would shake so I couldn't stand," Cecilia said.

The dowager duchess rapped her walking stick. "Nonsense. I will not have you suggesting that the future Duchess of Penthurst resembles a quaking aspen."

Tonia noticed Sophia's dismayed look—whether for the prospect of her presentation or for the idea of marrying the Duke of Penthurst, she was uncertain. Tonia was tempted to ask whether the duke had, indeed, offered for Sophia, but since she was quite certain they had not met above twice, she feared even Aelfrida would take the remark for the cheek it would intend.

The dowager duchess's reprimand, however, served to turn the conversation. Victoria pulled a newspaper clipping out of the purse hanging from her wrist. "Aunt Dimity cut this from 'The Examiner' this morning. 'A newly arrived shipment of Brussels lace, flounces and trimmed handkerchiefs, nearly half-price and especially adapted for wedding trousseaux,'" she read, then held the clipping out to Antonia.

The dowager duchess, however, intercepted it. She fumbled for a moment in the folds of her wrap before producing her lorgnette and examining the offending piece of paper. "'Compton House, Frith Street, Soho.'" Her voice and her eyebrows rose with each word. The paper was duly crushed and consigned to the cobbles of Oxford Street. "Frith Street, indeed. I fear your aunt must be all about in her head."

Her ladyship's carriage pulled to the side at the confluence of Oxford Street and Regent Street. The two liveried footmen standing at the back hurried to open the door which bore the crest of the ancient house of Aethelbert. The dowager duchess processed to the shop where the entry was being held open by a tail-coated, top-hatted doorman.

A bowing attendant walked backward, escorting the party to comfortable chairs at a table in the rear of the showroom. The young ladies' eyes grew wide at the sight of shelves running up to the ceiling on each side of the shop, stacked with bolts of fabrics. Every color imaginable gleamed from the walls in a garden of stripes, checks and bars. In front of the shelves were cases displaying an endless assortment of ribbons, trimmings, parasols, gloves, and hosiery. As accustomed as Antonia was to such display, she still found it easy to understand the awe and confusion these girls were feeling.

"We require court dresses for the viscountess and this young lady," Aelfrida informed the attendant. "Silk *moiré*."

The attendant bowed. "An excellent choice, your grace. Her Majesty wore a train of black silk trimmed with ruches of crepe at her Drawing-room last week, as you no doubt read in 'The Times.'" He snapped his fingers for a clerk to bring bolts of fabric to present to her ladyship. "And if I might add, Her Majesty's train was trimmed with bunches of black flowers fashioned of feathers—"

"I shall have gold brocade, trimmed with gold silk flowers," Antonia intervened. She had no intention of appearing in black feathers.

"Of course, Lady Danvers." He bowed. "Excellent taste, your ladyship."

The dowager duchess quelled him with a look. "And white silk glacé for my ward." She indicated Sophia.

The attendant bobbed yet another bow. "Ah, yes. The Princess Royal wore a train of white silk glacé, trimmed with bugles. Perhaps your young lady—"

"Pearls."

With considerably less demand, Antonia simply raised a gloved hand to an attendant and explained Victoria's need for bridal attire.

"Quite, my lady. We have an excellent selection of new Honiton lace mantillas in the style Espagnol. They are much in demand just now for bridal attire. For the scarf, we have them in Brussels and Honiton." He produced a velvet-lined tray, displaying samples.

Victoria drew back as if afraid to touch them, but Tonia selected a length of Brussels lace and held it up.

"Excellent choice, my lady, and a veritable snip at only twenty guineas." He murmured near to her ladyship's ear.

Tonia dropped the length of lace when she saw Victoria blanch.

The attendant observed the bride-to-be's reaction as well. He turned briskly and returned with a somewhat less grand tray. "Imitation Brussels scarves from one to five guineas, mam." His bow was considerably stiffer.

Tonia glanced at the inferior tray. "Have you nothing in *Point Duchesse?*"

"But of course, my lady." This time the bow was deeper.

Victoria gasped at the beauty of the unbroken scrolling pattern of flowers and leaves displayed on black velvet. Tonia draped it gracefully around her future sister-in-law's shoulders. "You will have few enough trumperies as the wife of a slum priest, my dear. It shall be a gift." She could have sworn tears sprang to the girl's eyes.

At the other end of the table the dowager duchess was

examining court lappets obtained to supply the special needs of the shop's discriminating clientele attending Her Majesty's Drawing-Rooms. She held up two long strips of lace designed to hang from the top of the coiffeur and extend over the wearer's shoulders. Her sniff held a distinct note of disapproval.

The tray of lappets disappeared to be replaced by a selection of *mouchoirs en suite*. The tiny, lace-edge handkerchiefs fared no better than the lappets, however.

"The silk you may send to my dressmaker." The dowager duchess presented the attendant with a stiff, white card bearing the direction of London's most elite modiste and swept from the shop, leaving the others to follow in her wake and a footman to deal with such grubby details as the direction of her grace's bill.

"Hayward's, laceman to the royal family," she directed her groom when the carriage appeared at the curbside as if by magic.

They drove along bustling Oxford Street to a shop displaying the royal warrant in gold over the door. Here the lappets in *Point d'Alençon* exactly suited her grace, as did the delicacy of the *mouchoirs*—necessary in case one should be required to wipe one's brow in the presence of Her Majesty. "These will do very well for you, Antonia."

"I thank you, Aunt Aelfrida." Antonia hid her amusement with a deep nod of her head.

As they waited for the driver to pull their carriage forward, the Misses Hever and Sophia gazed at the grand building standing directly opposite Hayward's. Its golden stone gleamed in the midday sun as people entered and exited busily under its pillared and pedimented portico that extended out to the street. Antonia noticed the young ladies' interest. "You are admiring the Pantheon. It was once described as the most beautiful building in England."

"What is it?" Victoria asked.

"Originally it was for assemblies and the performance of operas. Sadly, now merely a bazaar, albeit a very busy one."

"It sounds like fun. Could we shop there?" Cece asked.

Antonia glanced at the dowager duchess. "I think not." Cecilia's lively features dimmed. "Perhaps we might view the architecture, however. Purely for educational purposes."

Her grace assented on the provision that both footmen would attend the young ladies in her place. "*I* will not be jostled." She directed her charges to be seated in the landau and her coachman to drive on to Marble Arch where he could turn the carriage and deposit them on the opposite side of the street.

The maneuver was accomplished in only little more than double the time it would have taken them to walk the distance. With an appropriate air of *noblesse oblige* the dowager duchess announced, "I shall await your return."

Duly chaperoned by footmen, the others were soon standing in the great barrel-vaulted hall, with their necks craned upward at the ornate ceiling and crystal chandeliers.

"Sadly, little of the resemblance to the Roman temple remains," Tonia explained to her charges. "The original ceiling was an enormous dome reminiscent of the ancient prototype. It was unfortunately destroyed by fire."

The young ladies' attention, however, quickly shifted to the five wide bays circling the room where every conceivable item of merchandise seemed to be offered for sale. Antonia glanced at their attendant footmen—potent reminders that Aunt Aelfrida was waiting for them. She began shepherding her charges toward the exit when Sophia, walking just in front of her, stopped so suddenly Tonia all but trod on the girl's heels. "Sophia—" she began, then followed the direction of the young woman's gaze.

There was no doubt about it. The tall gentleman in the

high silk hat and frock coat of exquisite cut was the Duke of Penthurst. Tonia's instinct was to shield the girl from his view, should he glance in their direction, but she quickly saw that there was little danger of that.

The gentleman's attention was entirely taken by the elegant creature he escorted on his arm. The deep rows of lace on the flounces of her crinolined skirt and the lace, flowers and fruit adorning her hair looked far more appropriate for an afternoon soiree than for a shopping expedition. Tonia refused to allow herself to name what the face paint she wore would be appropriate for.

Tonia stepped to the fore and walked briskly to the exit without looking to either side. Once they were resettled in the carriage and Tonia was confident that the noise of traffic and the young ladies' chatter would prevent her being overheard, she turned to Aelfrida and quietly informed her of the incident.

The dowager duchess made a dismissive sound that in a lesser mortal would be transcribed as, *Pooh*! Then said, "That does not signify. He is a man. The connection will be of convenience for Sophia."

"I do not understand, Aunt Aelfrida. Why are you so determined on this—alliance?" She settled on the word because she could not bring herself to consider such an arrangement as marriage.

"Simple practicality, my dear. Sophia has money. She needs a title to overcome her background. Penthurst is the most eligible duke in the marriage mart. Since there are no royal dukes available he will have to do."

"But Arthur Emory—"

"Bah! A barony, and a Scottish one at that. I intend a dukedom for her. It should have been her mother's."

Such bald pragmatism left Antonia speechless. The explanation gave no clue, however, to the deeper puzzle. Why was the dowager duchess going to such effort to help Sophia? Loyalty to the memory of the girlhood friendship Aelfrida had reportedly shared with Sophia's grandmother—so like her own with Sophia's mother—was all very well—and interesting how history seemed to repeat itself—but it hardly seemed a satisfactory explanation.

She determined to lay the puzzle before Charles when she got home. He had had enough experience with Aunt Aelfrida's machinations, he was certain to be able to provide an insight.

When she arrived back at Grosvenor Square, however, Bracken informed her that Lord Danvers was closeted in the library with Inspector Futter. "My lord asked that I request that you join them when you returned, my lady." Bracken was already moving toward the library to open the door for Tonia.

Both men stood when she entered the library. "Ah, Tonia, excellent timing. Inspector Futter has called especially to request your assistance."

"If you could be so kind, my lady. I wouldn't presume to ask, but you did suggest that Mrs. Johal not be interviewed on her own." Futter rubbed his hand backward through his white-blond hair. "The truth of the matter is that I've got nowhere. The woman skitters like a rabbit if I so much as enter a room. I thought her sister might be of help, but Mrs. Whitham is worse. She pretends not to understand a word I say, although I'm convinced she speaks excellent English. I did try talking to Lady Duff Gordon, but she seems to think anything I ask is an insult to her friend that Azimoolah fellow."

The inspector shifted his weight to his other foot and cleared his throat. "So, Lady Danvers, the thing is that we're pretty much at a standstill..."

"And you were wondering if I would speak to Chandrika for you," Tonia concluded.

Futter nodded. "As it was your advice, my lady. I thought—"

"Of course. Let me ring for refreshments for all of us, then I will be happy to undertake an afternoon call. Chandrika is still staying at the Duff Gordon home?"

A short time later Antonia ascended the steps to the crepe-draped door of the house in Queen Square, still uncertain how she might contrive to interview Chandrika alone or, indeed, what she could possibly learn from the girl that would be of use to Futter. But, as he said, it had been her own suggestion that got her into this, even if all she had in mind was that Futter be accompanied by a woman when he attempted to question Chandrika.

The butler opened the door at Tonia's ring and accepted her card. "I do apologize, Lady Danvers, but Lady Duff Gordon is not at home."

"That is quite all right, Bottle. Actually, it is your house guest I have come to call on."

Well trained, though he was, the butler seemed to have considerable difficulty concealing his surprise at this information. "If you would care to wait in the parlor, my lady. I will inquire whether Mrs. Johal is at home."

It was clear to Tonia that Lady Duff Gordon truly was away, but that the second reference was a mere politeness. "Please explain that I spoke to her shortly after her husband's death and I wish to know how she is faring." Antonia hoped that the description would be enough to identify her to Chandrika. And that the identification would be reassuring.

Apparently it worked because a short time later there was a light step on the stair and Chandrika entered wearing a plain white sari which Antonia assumed was the Indian color of mourning. She rose and took the girl's hand in both of hers. "Thank you so much for seeing me, my dear. You were so distressed when I was here before. I felt I must find out how you are getting on. Of course, I know it must be difficult..."

Chandrika sat at one end of the settee, allowing Antonia to take a chair across from her. The girl kept her head bowed, but raised her eyes to Tonia, a gesture that emphasized their startling size. "I am much calmer. As you see. I thank your ladyship."

"I am so glad. And you understand that you are quite safe?"

Tonia wished that the brief nod of the widow's head had given her more reassurance on the issue.

"The English do not practice suttee. Nor do they allow it. I understand."

The answer sounded rote. Had the girl memorized it as something to reassure herself with? Or had she been forced to give that answer? But mostly, Tonia wondered, if Chandrika was not afraid of being burnt on her husband's funeral pyre, what was she afraid of?

Bottle entered with a tea tray which he placed on the table near Chandrika. In her graceful way which seemed to emphasize the jerkiness of her former words, she poured a cup and added milk and sugar without asking, then looked at her guest. "This is finest Assam. Lady Duff Gordon drinks nothing else. I prefer it with a pinch of cardamom." She held out a tiny bowl of the aromatic spice.

"Yes, please. That sounds delightful." Tonia hoped that sharing a beverage would help the girl relax. She took a sip. "Oh, this is lovely. Is it customary in India to take your tea flavored with spices?"

"Many do, yes. My sister, she prefers cinnamon."

Tonia smiled. She had been looking for a way to bring Mrs. Whitham into the conversation. "Yes. It must be a comfort to you to have your sister here at this difficult time. Do you see her often?" Tonia still thought it strange that Chandrika chose to stay with a friend rather than with family.

"She is my half-sister. Her mother was Eurasian; mine full Asian. Padmaja takes more easily to western ways. She no longer wears the sari. Pamela, she wishes to be called." The wooden quality had returned to Chandrika's sentences.

Ah, a rift between the sisters. Tonia would like to know more. She leaned forward in an attitude of attention, murmuring encouragement to the speaker.

"She says it is more comfortable for her English friends. I think it is that her husband demands it." Chandrika took refuge in her tea cup as if to keep herself from saying more.

"Yes, Colonel Whitham can be most, er—decisive," Tonia agreed, then added, "We met him a few days ago at the East India docks."

Chandrika coughed as if choking on her tea, causing the contents of her cup to slosh over her white robe. She jumped to her feet. "Oh, so awkward of me. Please forgive." She fled from the room.

Before Antonia could make her own exit, sounds from the foyer announced the arrival of Lady Duff Gordon. A moment later she entered the library. "My dear Antonia. I do apologize. I had no idea you intended to call."

Tonia stood. "Actually, I called to see how your guest is doing. The poor creature appears to be a bundle of nerves. It must be a strain for you, having her here."

Lucie smiled. "As you say, but I believe the situation will continue until the police settle this dreadful matter. She bursts into tears if one so much as hints that she might return to her sister's home. I believe she is afraid of the colonel. And, of course, there is no possibility of sending her back to her own people in India until this matter of the disaffection among the troops is settled."

Tonia blinked at her friend's euphemism for what the newspapers were calling murder and mayhem. Danvers had of late turned protective male and begun keeping the papers from her. Perhaps he believed it to be his duty in response to her delicate condition, but she was quite certain it meant that the news was ominous. And it certainly spurred her to sneak glimpses of the news columns while pretending to read only the society notices.

After a few more comments Tonia took her leave of the Duff Gordon home, but continued to ponder all the way back to Grosvenor Square. Had she learned anything that could be of value to Inspector Futter? It seemed that her interview had only raised more questions; or deepened ones that already existed but lurked unformed in her own mind.

Chandrika was no longer afraid of suttee; and why she had ever been seemed a mystery. But the girl was inordinately afraid of something—or someone. It was apparent that there was trouble between the sisters. But how could that possibly bear on the murder?

"**M**y love, you look quite fagged." Danvers met her at the door. "What was that fellow Futter thinking, sending you to do police work?"

Tonia handed her shawl to Bracken and asked him to bring a tea tray to the parlor. She protested that she was not fatigued; yet she was most grateful for the small needlepoint stool Danvers put under her feet. "But I am perplexed, Charles." She recounted the occurrence at the Duff Gordon home. "I do believe Chandrika knows something, but I can't fathom what it is."

"Do you believe she is in danger?"

"I am certain she believes she is. Whether or not there is any truth in the matter..." She ended with a shake of her head and a small sigh. "I expect simply the warning of harm would be sufficient to terrify her. If someone has threatened her, it is unlikely they would be required to carry it out."

Danvers pondered as Bracken brought in the tea tray and served. Charles waited while Tonia availed herself of three of the cucumber sandwiches and a thick slice of Cook's special plum cake, heavy with currants. When the color began to return to Antonia's cheeks he felt comfortable to continue. "So, my lovely detective, who do you suspect could be menacing Chandrika? Is Padmaja a possibility?"

"It's certain there is conflict between the sisters—half-sisters, as she made clear—but I can't imagine the matter leading to violence. I suppose her sister's husband must come under consideration, but Colonel Whitham seems so dignified, it's hard to imagine him stooping to anything villainous." Antonia added another scoop of sugar to the cup Bracken had served her.

"Yes, and the idea of him killing his own brother-in-law is quite beyond the pale. Although we, of course, don't know for certain that Chandrika's fears are linked to her husband's murder." Danvers was silent for a moment. "But who else does the girl even know in London? I don't suppose the Duff Gordons could be terrorizing her?"

"And holding her captive in their home? First with the threat of suttee and then with some new spectre?" Tonia laughed. "My love, what a gothic imagination you have."

"Speaking of vivid imaginations, are you quite certain you feel up to attending the opera tonight? I can easily send a note to Aunt Aelfrida."

"Oh, yes, *Don Giovanni*. I had entirely forgotten. Are we not to occupy the Duke of Penthurst's box? I fancy that may present quite as contrived a plot as that of Mozart's villain." She told him of the scene in the Pantheon that morning, then shook her head. "I do hate to see Sophia thrown to the wolves for the sake of a title."

"Does the girl care for Penthurst? The fellow cuts a fine enough figure, I suppose she could be rather dazzled."

"If anything is dazzling her I would guess it's Lieutenant Anson's scarlet tunic, but I don't think she would hold out against Aunt Aelfrida."

Danvers smirked. "Few can."

"What's puzzling me more is why Aunt Aelfrida is going to so much effort over the match?"

Now the smirk was a full guffaw. "And since when has a sensible motive been a necessary accompaniment to any of Aunt Aelfrida's vagaries?"

That evening, dressed in her favorite fuchsia and gold gown, her auburn hair done with gilt tissue roses, and her shoulders swathed in an amber velvet and satin opera cape, Lady Danvers appeared as if she had never known the slightest fatigue.

Charles kissed her lightly on the cheek. "And to think that by this time next year you shall be the mother of two. You are amazing, my love."

Tonia smiled. "I shall soon have to instruct Isabella to let my gowns out, but we shall do very well for the moment."

As they crossed the lobby and ascended the stairs of Her Majesty's theatre Danvers noted with pride how every head turned to admire Lady Danvers, and when they were ensconced in the Duke's elegant box in the dress circle to stage right, he noticed many a pair of opera glasses in the stalls below trained in their direction. The warmth of their host's look at Danvers's wife, however, gave him less pleasure, although Tonia's acknowledgement was nothing but the strictest propriety. Charles pressed her arm warmly before turning his attention to his program.

He had little opportunity to study the delights in store for them that evening, however, before the rest of their party arrived. Osbert dutifully escorted the dowager duchess and Sophia to the front seats in the box, then withdrew to stand in the back, from where Danvers was certain he would soon make a discreet exit.

Arthur Emory, arriving soon after with his sisters, seemed

less pleased to occupy the other rear corner when all the seats around Sophia were taken. "Mama has the headache," Beatrice explained to her great aunt. "So Arthur Emory offered to escort us. Was that not obliging of him?"

The dowager duchess gave her grandson a look intended to skewer him to the back wall and sniffed. "Bea, you may not sit by Sophia. That is the duke's chair."

Danvers, occupying the chair closest to the stage, jumped to his feet. "No, stay there, Beatrice. Our host can have my seat. I prefer to stretch my legs."

"Wretch," Tonia said under her breath as her husband left the chair next to her open for the duke. Danvers winked and gave her a reassuring pat on the shoulder. He had no doubt that his wife understood he was protecting Sophia and giving Tonia an opportunity to learn what she could from Penthurst. With the added pleasure of interfering with Aunt Aelfrida's plan, of course.

With the questions of his earlier conversation with Tonia still running through his head, Danvers was more than happy to take an elevated seat at the rear where he could observe. He could hear little enough of the conversation around him, however, as the buzz of chatter, the rustle of silk gowns and the swish of fans emanating from the theatre's red plush seats reverberated from the white and gold walls behind the five tiers of circling galleries. Even when the maestro raised his baton and the orchestra in the pit struck the first ominous chords of the overture, the commotion barely abated.

The overture soared to a lively frenzy before the culminating notes, and the heavy velvet curtain rose to reveal the nighttime scene of Don Pedro's sumptuous garden. A smattering of polite applause greeted the opening before the audience returned to their preoccupied clatter. Danvers noted that Sophia, though, who had apparently never seen such a spectacle before, seemed riveted with the scene before her.

She only turned with some apparent reluctance to Beatrice's whispered gossip and, after making a brief reply behind the folds of her fan, returned to watch the performance.

Danvers, who had so often in the past taken great delight in bursting into a favorite aria, realized how long it had been since he had indulged in this pleasure. For the moment he was obliged to content himself with singing along under his breath, but he determined he would return to his diversion at a more propitious time. For now, he had purposed to observe the interaction between his companions.

Only the briefest of sideways glances told Danvers that Arthur Emory seemed to be unaware of the production occurring on the stage below them. And he appeared to be likewise oblivious to the audience and even to the occupants of their box—except for the charming profile Miss Sophia Landry presented. The one quick glance the lady made toward the back of the box left Danvers unsure whether she was returning the smitten swain's look, or simply gazing to see who else was in the box.

The mortal wounding of Don Pedro, the cries of his daughter and the escape of Don Juan brought the first scene to a conclusion. A general bustle ensued when the gaslights were turned up at the end of the scene. Danvers smiled to note that the dowager duchess, quite blissfully undisturbed by the commotion on stage or in the house, had fallen asleep. A circumstance that undoubtedly had prompted Osbert to take his leave, as Danvers expected him to. In short order, however, there was a knock at the door of the box and Osbert's place was filled by two men in regimental dress uniforms.

Alice, sitting slightly behind her sister and Sophia, rose sedately and walked to the back of the box, fanning herself as if in want of air. As she swept past the newcomers Captain Bellingham turned and followed her at a leisurely stroll.

Danvers smiled at how prettily the maneuver was accomplished. He couldn't help but wonder what powers of suggestion Alice had used to persuade the forceful Agatha Estella that she was in need of a quiet evening at home. He wished the couple well.

His thoughts were less positive, however, at the display Lieutenant Anson made as he walked to the front of the box and bowed over Sophia's hand, presenting her with an orange from the sellers circulating on the floor below with trays of the golden fruit strapped around their necks. Sophia appeared to be delighted with the present and with the lieutenant's presence. Danvers heard his nephew beside him emit a sound of disgust somewhere between a growl and a moan.

Since no invitation to remain in the box was forthcoming from the duke, Anson was obliged to leave when the scene two curtain came up on the public square in front of Don Juan's palace. Don Juan and his servant were singing in vibrant voices of the dandy's conquests, a duet that made Danvers return briefly to his *sotto voce* vocalizing, when a movement at the door to the box told him that Alice had returned. In the soft glow of the light falling on the box from the stage he could see that she looked flushed and not displeased with herself. She, too, carried an orange, undoubtedly the gift of Captain Bellingham.

All other considerations fled, however, when the soprano singing the part of Elvira, Don Juan's discarded sweetheart, made her entrance. She was a startling beauty, above average height, with masses of black curls piled high on her head, and wearing a low-cut scarlet gown that revealed her considerable, er—talents. It was not the diva's charms that arrested Danvers's attention so much, however, as the Duke of Penthurst's reaction.

Tonia had been chatting with her host throughout the performance with enough consistency that Danvers could hope she had gained whatever information she wished to learn about the likely success of Aunt Aelfrida's machinations, but the moment Adelina Maria Fabrica—Danvers consulted his playbill to ascertain her name—came on stage, Penthurst turned his attention so sharply Danvers was certain he had broken off the conversation in the middle of Antonia's sentence.

Aunt Aelfrida woke with a start in the midst of Don Juan's attempt to seduce a peasant girl on the eve of her wedding. Without ado she stood and demanded the attention of all in the box with three raps of her ebony walking stick. "That is sufficient. Sophia, we shall leave now."

"But, your grace, it is not over. And it is so beautiful. I've never seen anything like it," the girl protested, her face registering the dismay she felt at being jarred from the story she was following with such intent.

Arthur Emory saw his chance. He stepped forward with a bow. "Aunt Aelfrida, I shall be happy to escort So—er, Miss Landry home at the conclusion of the performance. My sisters would be most happy of her company."

The dowager duchess obviously did not consider this offer worthy of a reply. Instead, she raised her head with a piercing look at the back of the box. "Where is Osbert?" Fortunately, preparations on stage for the peasant wedding had reached sufficient pitch to shield her demand from most of the audience.

Danvers stepped forward. "He was called away, Aunt Aelfrida. I shall be happy to accompany you." He considered it fortunate that Osbert had already succeeded to the dukedom or he would be in danger of being stricken from the will.

The dowager duchess and Sophia were duly delivered to

Berkeley Square Gardens and Lord and Lady Danvers continued the journey to Grosvenor Square in companionable silence, each lost in their thoughts. Once they were snug back in the sitting room that connected their adjoining bedrooms, however, Danvers turned to his wife. "I hope you didn't mind being dragged away from the opera, my love, but I did feel I should do what I could to save Osbert."

Antonia smiled. "On the contrary, I have been quite aching to tell you what I have discovered. Although he paid little enough attention to her, I believe Penthurst is quite amenable to Miss Landry's charms—by which I mean her fortune."

"He obviously, however, has no intention of allowing that to stand in the way of his other pleasures." Danvers's voice held a ring of censure. "Marrying a chit of a girl in order to finance one's peccadillos is really the back of beyond."

"Oh, yes—the Fabrica. We saw him with his opera singer at the Pantheon, did I tell you?" Tonia paused. "About his finances, though, are you certain he is in want? When I quizzed him on mundane matters such as his garden and country seat, he informed me of numerous improvements he is undertaking. I know gentlemen have ways of keeping up appearances in London even when they are, er, in dun territory. But do they usually undertake exotic landscaping schemes? He informed me he has engaged Joseph Paxton to build him a glass house so he can grow Cavendish bananas."

"Exotic, indeed. It seems Penthurst's finances will bear looking into." Charles, however, had a subject considerably closer to home on his mind. "But that is for later, my love. Attending the opera tonight brought to mind that I have long failed to serenade you as I was used to do."

Without further ado he burst into Don Octavio's lines:
A thousand strange thoughts
are whirling in my head.

What a day, my stars, this is!

When he paused to draw breath Tonia leaned over and ended the performance with a brief kiss. "Very true, Charles, what a day, indeed. If you will forgive me, I shall retire now."

Danvers sprang to his feet to offer his hand to help her to rise. They were almost to the door when Hardy knocked lightly and entered. "And were you calling, m'lord?"

"No, Hardy, I was—oh, come in, man." He had not realized before that his servant had such a tin ear. Danvers opened the door to Tonia's room and gave her a brief good night kiss, then turned back to his attendant. "Tell me, Hardy, are you in any way acquainted with the Duke of Penthurst's man?"

Hardy assumed an air of umbrage that would have done Aunt Aelfrida credit. "Jumped up poser to my way of thinking, if I may be so bold, m'lord. Raoul, he calls himself." Hardy gave extended emphasis to each vowel. "And no manservant, he'll thank you to know. A valet," again pronounced with lengthened vowels.

Danvers smiled. "I'll take that to mean you are acquainted."

Hardy sniffed, then unbent. "Not as what you'd call acquainted, but the Duke of Penthurst prefers the same glover as you, m'lord. I have more than once encountered his man in Robertson's or other haberdashery establishments, but I wouldn't care to answer for my position if I was to purchase yellow kid gloves for you, m'lord."

"Indeed, neither would I, Hardy. I thank you for your discrimination in seeing to my wardrobe needs. However, I fancy I may be in need of new gloves for, um—" He paused to consider the items on their social calendar for the upcoming days. "For the theatre, an afternoon levee, an assembly... Oh, dash it, Hardy, just get yourself out and about tomorrow and when you encounter this Raoul," Danvers felt himself likewise tempted to extend his pronunciation, "invite him to take refreshment with you and try drawing him out on the matter of his master's finances."

Hardy accepted the shillings Danvers proffered to finance this expedition and tucked them in his waistcoat pocket. "But your lordship is not considering affecting yellow gloves?" Even a man with such flexible opinions as Hardy seemed to find this a disturbing thought.

Danvers smiled. "No Hardy. My usual pearl grey and white will do me quite well, I thank you."

Charles sighed as Hardy closed the door behind him. The season appeared set to continue through July when Parliament would break up and London would become its usual somnolent ghost town—at least in the eyes of those who came to town only for court events and society entertainments. Until then, one could be quite assured of the frivolities continuing unabated.

He would dearly like to get Tonia out of town for a respite. This summer was supposed to be one of gentle rides in the park, languid hours with Charlie and plenty of rest for her within easy reach of her Harley Street physician—should he be needed.

Instead it was crammed with social events, charity work, and even a murder. And Charles suspected that the worrying reports that continued to circulate about affairs in India caused Tonia far more anxiety than she would admit. He must think of something. If only his brother, sister and great aunt could be made to lessen their demands on his time. But never mind that, he must put Antonia's needs before others.

Emilia had expected a blissful night of sleep, but after so many nights filled with shattering salvos the stillness was almost painful. Then the animals moved in. Creatures, previously kept at bay by the incessant firing of guns, prowled around the Entrenchment to feast on the remains of the dead left in the desert. Whether by actual hearing or in restless sleep pierced by uneasy dreams, she heard the jackals making their unsettling sounds: high-pitched howls, screeching whinnies and quacking barks.

She woke in the morning uncertain whether she had slept or not. At dawn the jackals had departed and left the field to vultures and various carrion-feeding birds. She shuddered as a hawk swooped over the camp with an eyeball in its beak. It crossed her mind to wonder what sort of omen the scene presented.

But there was no time for such meandering thoughts. All around her was a bustle of preparation for departure. People so weakened by injury, fatigue and near starvation could carry little. Those who had precious jewelry or heirlooms secreted them about their persons. Some dug up treasures buried in the ruins of the barracks. Emilia had her prayer book. She needed nothing else.

Most energy was expended in an attempt to make their

remaining fragments of clothing hold together to achieve a remnant of decorum. And above all, every effort was made to encourage the wounded and offer what assistance was possible to enable their transport, especially seeing that all were given full rations of water, although no food was served before starting out. At all costs, no wounded would be left behind, no matter how grave their situation.

As she walked out of the Entrenchment that had been her prison for three long weeks, Emilia looked back at their barrack. In the dazzling morning sunshine she gasped. How was it possible that it was still standing? The walls were riddled with far more gaping holes than there was standing masonry, most of the jagged gaps larger than doorways.

Sixteen elephants and seventy-some palanquins arrived to transport women, children and wounded. Emilia assisted the emaciated Louisa into one of the covered liters, borne by four bearers, and saw Fanny and Caroline Lindsey shepherded by their mother Kate into an elephant howdah, but Emilia insisted that she could walk. It was only mile to the ghaut and there were so many wounded to transport. She noticed Captain Moore and Lieutenant Thompson making repeat trips between Entrenchment and ghaut in bullock carts, loading and unloading wounded for whom it must have been excruciating to be moved.

The sepoys did not offer to help, but stood around, talking to the officers they had been firing upon a few hours earlier. Emilia heard them expressing loud astonishment that the English had held out so long. One near her said he found it utterly unaccountable. While unloading a wounded comrade at the ghaut, Lieutenant Thompson asked a sepoy how many the rebels had lost. More than a thousand was the reply.

Most amazing of all was hearing the formerly loyal sepoys inquiring after their old officers. Oddly, they showed signs of real distress at hearing of the deaths of their former commanders. Emilia could only shake her head at such inconsistencies of thought.

"Are we to go to Allahabad without molestation?" Shepherd asked. The man gave emphatic assurances that this was true.

General Wheeler with his wife and daughter, followed by Major Vibart, walked out, the last officers to leave the Entrenchment. Some of the sepoys who had served under the major insisted on carrying his property for him. An entourage of cavalry escorted the major's wife and family down to the boats with the most profuse demonstrations of respect.

Emilia hesitated when she saw that there were no wooden planks for gangways. Everyone, men, women, children and bearers of the wounded, had to wade knee deep through the crocodile-infested water to get into the boats. Still, all plunged ahead. By nine o'clock of the morning the last of the forty boats was loaded.

Captain Moore announced that as soon as all were aboard they were to push off as quickly as possible and make for the other side of the river. Major Vibart stepped onto his boat and shouted the order. "Off!"

But none sailed.

The flat, overcrowded boats sank perhaps two feet and sat, stuck on sandbanks in a Ganges that was at its lowest.

The native boatmen all hurled their oars into the water, jumped over the side of their vessels, and waded to the shore.

Emilia screamed and pointed to the roof of their boat as green-grey smoke billowed from the thatch. When flames broke out, the treachery became apparent. Before jumping, the boatmen had secreted burning charcoal into the thatched roofs of most of the boats.

Now the troopers who had escorted Major Vibart and his family to the ghaut with such courtesy opened fire with their carbines. As best they could the English returned fire from their burning boats. All not disabled by wounds jumped out of the boats and endeavored to push them afloat, but most were entirely immovable. Now, from the ambush in which they had lain concealed all along the banks, it seemed that thousands of men fired upon them.

Emilia grabbed Louisa's hand and together they waded out into *deep water up to their chins to lessen the probability of being shot. The balls whizzed past them thick as hail. All around them women and children, their hair and clothing ablaze, tumbled over the sides of their boats and into the water. Many were cut down by the sepoys' fusillade. Others took refuge behind the hulls of the stricken boats. "God have mercy upon us," Louisa cried.*

Within a few minutes the water was red with blood and the air thick with smoke from the heavy firing of the cannon and the blaze of the burning boats. Emilia held her breath as long as she could, then choked on the breath she was forced to draw in with a sob.

Panicked elephants trumpeted, horses squealed, mothers and children screamed and shrieked as round shot crashed into the burning boats.

Women sobbed and prayed, many of them sinking into the putrid river from the weight of water and blood in their gowns as a stream of sowars came surging out from behind the Sati Chowra village, brandishing sabers and pistols and shouting, "Deen! Deen!"

The faithful Reverend Mister Moncrieff stood before the charging band with a prayer book in his hand. "We English do not put captives to death, but imprison them. Spare our lives, and put us into prison,' he challenged. A sowar struck him across the neck and he fell face forward into the water.

All along the bank sepoys and sowars clubbed the wounded with musket stocks or chopped at them with sabers as they wallowed, exhausted, in the bloodied mud. Villagers came out to plunder the weapons, treasure boxes and little parcels of jewels and money people had tied into their clothing. Some yanked rings and earrings off women lying dead or wounded in the water. Amid all the chaos, Emilia and Louisa somehow found strength to crawl out of the shallows. Together they collapsed on the bank.

It had all been the work of less than an hour. A bugler sounded the ceasefire. Some one hundred, twenty women and children remained on the riverside, sobbing and praying in their torn, scorched and gory gowns. Many of them were wounded with bullets and sword cuts, their dresses wet and full of mud and blood. Some still wore soggy bonnets and straw sun hats with crumpled, dripping brims.

Emilia, her dark hair hanging in sandy scraggles, clung to Louisa. Near them lay Kate Lindsay, reeling with a bullet in her back, attended by all three of her daughters: Caroline, Fanny and Alice. The captives were taken to Nana Sahib's headquarters where he ordered them incarcerated in the main hall of Savada House, the former SPG's orphan asylum, under heavy guard.

Too exhausted to talk and too crowded to find any real comfort, the captives attempted to bind up the worst of their sisters' wounds and find space for the most severely hurt to lie down. The tomb-like silence was relieved only by sobs and the moans and cries of children.

Late in the afternoon the rebels brought in about seventeen male fugitives from a boat that had drifted across the river. On Nana Sahib's order the men were bound together with rope and taken outside. For the women and children locked in the gloom of Savada House there was no escaping the ricocheting sound of the shots as the last of their menfolk were executed.

That night, as the grieving women lay down on the stone floor of their new prison, the heavens opened and the rain that had held off for so long poured down, raising a suffocating steam from the parched plain.

Tonia was still struggling to wash away images of a river running with mud and blood the next morning as she and Charles played with their son in the nursery.

"The seashore?" Antonia blinked at her husband's surprising suggestion. She pressed her hands to her temples, as if to force rolling blue waves to cleanse outrage.

"Just a few days—to escape the heat and noise—" Danvers began.

Tonia drew a deep breath and her mind cleared. "Yes, what a charming idea! It would be delightful above all things.

I can't think of anything Charlie would enjoy more. But what of the theatre tonight, and Lady Bramwell's rout, and I promised Freddie—"

"Look," Danvers interrupted her with a nod toward their toddling son who had gone to his toy shelf and extracted the tin sand bucket and spade, which he now held triumphantly aloft.

Tonia laughed. "That's decided then. Freddie and Lady Bramwell can wait."

Danvers swept the grinning child from the floor and held him aloft. "The seashore it is. I shall tell Hardy to acquire train tickets to Brighton. Will tomorrow be too soon for you to be ready?"

"Train tickets?" Antonia asked. "Won't you take the aerostat?"

Her husband's face clearly showed the appeal the proposal held for him. "Not in your delicate condition, my love. As much as our son might enjoy it, I don't believe our daughter is ready for such an adventure yet."

Tonia put her hand on her abdomen with a warning look at Danvers to be careful what he said in front of Charlie. His sharp ears picked up everything and were much too tender for the topic of childbirth. "Charlie is too young for your adventures as well, my love. But I'm confident Hardy is as anxious for an ascent as you are. Charlie and I shall do very well on the train with Isabella and Nurse Bevans."

Tonia smiled at the alacrity with which her lord agreed to her proposal. "Excellent plan. I shall inform the Bedford to have their best suites ready for us."

In the end the arrangements demanded considerably more than Danvers had at first envisioned. Antonia mentioned their plans that afternoon when they were gathered in the withdrawing room with their callers for afternoon tea. As soon as Sophia heard of the scheme, her face filled with wonder at the notion of an excursion to the seashore. "Do you mean to say you have never been to the beach?" Antonia looked at the girl in amazement as she passed her a freshly filled teacup.

Sophia opened her mouth to explain, but Aunt Aelfrida cut her off. "That's what comes of being brought up in Yorkshire. The gel needs broadening, Antonia. You shall take her with you. It will be no bother. I will send Peyden with her." It was quite clear that the dowager duchess herself had no intention of going any place that would involve getting sand in her own shoes. Her magnanimity in sending her under lady's maid was marked.

But that was only the beginning. Alice, having chosen to take her tea in the farthest corner of the parlor, spoke in a choked voice, "Brighton? You mean to say you're going to Brighton? Tomorrow? Oh, if only..." Tonia was certain she saw tears in the young woman's eyes. What was there about Brighton to make her weep?

"Yes, that is the plan. Would you and Bea care to accompany Sophia as well—if your mother will permit, of course?" Tonia felt it would be rude not to extend the invitation, even though she and Charles had envisioned a quiet getaway.

Agatha made no objection. Tonia turned to the other young ladies who had gathered with the family party at Grosvenor Square. Cecilia and Victoria, however, demurred. "Oh, I couldn't possibly leave Freddie. His work is going splendidly. The shelter for fallen women is almost as successful as the Magdalen Asylum—"

It was clear that Vicky would have gone into more detail had the dowager duchess not cut her off with a sharp clearing of her throat. Duly warned off, Cecilia merely nodded agreement with her sister. The work at St. George-in-the-East was

far too important to abandon for a jaunt to a bathing spot—
no matter how fashionable.

Tonia couldn't have been happier than she was to see Charles
standing on the platform waiting for her when she stepped
off the train at Brighton Station the next afternoon. Danvers
and Hardy had left shortly after dawn that morning in order
to catch the most propitious currents, so Lord and Lady
Danvers had missed their usual morning tête-à-tête. "Did you
have a good ascent?" She asked after exchanging greetings.
The question, though, was a mere formality, for Charles's
glowing countenance told her how much he had enjoyed it.

With his customary bustle, Hardy had a row of carriages
awaiting them, and soon the entire party and their luggage
was deposited before the grand, ionic porticoes of the
Bedford Hotel, said to be the finest late-Georgian building in
Brighton after the Royal Pavilion itself. Splendidly uniformed
footmen bowed their progress into the marble Grecian Hall
under its wide, glazed dome. The concierge welcomed them
and escorted them to their splendid ocean view suites occupying the entire second floor of the west tower. Their host
explained that the servants' rooms were located behind the
tower, but carefully assigned so that my lord and my lady had
only to tug the bellpull near their beds to summon their
attendants. The smaller pull beside the fireplace would
summon a member of the hotel staff—with alacrity, it was
understood.

Danvers assured him the arrangements were perfectly
satisfactory, then suggested that, as soon as the ladies had a
chance to wash off the soot of the journey, they refresh themselves in the tea room, leaving Isabella, Peyden and Hardy to
unpack.

Charlie was wild to get to the beach and Tonia promised

him that if he was a very good boy and took a nap for Nurse Bevans they would take him to the beach afterward. "And if you are very, very good, we might even find a Punch and Judy show."

Tonia and Danvers with their three young charges were seated at a round, white linen-draped table surrounded on three sides with palms, and Danvers was giving the waiter an order for tea and cakes, when a sharp intake of Alice's breath made Tonia look up. Tonia was seated with her back to the entrance, but it was clear from the sparkle in Alice's eyes and the blush on her cheek that someone significant had entered.

It was also clear that the transformation to the girl's countenance did not include a look of surprise. In the very little time that it took two officers of Her Majesty's Light Infantry to make their way across the room Captain Bellingham and Lieutenant Anson were bowing to the company at the Danvers table.

"Lady Danvers, how splendid to see you here," Bellingham said.

"Yes, and what a surprise." She looked at Alice. "Although I believe it may not be such a surprise for all of our party." She hadn't decided yet whether to be reproving or amused.

"May I hope it is not an unpleasant surprise, ma'am? I do believe I mentioned the matter of the regiment's impending transfer when we met at Lady Essworthy's."

Ah, yes, the matter had been mentioned, but it had made little impression on Tonia.

The officers stood as if at attention. Anson had only spoken the briefest of greetings to Sophia and Beatrice, but it was clear he would like to say more. There was nothing for it but to invite the gentlemen to join them, especially as there were empty places at their table.

The gentlemen accepted promptly. Anson reached into the breast pocket of his scarlet tunic and produced a stiff white engraved card which he presented to Antonia. "Lady Danvers, may I hope that you and your party will join us at the regimental ball at the Pavilion tomorrow night?"

Tonia took the card with a simple, "Thank you." One glance at her young charges, however, left little doubt that there would be no peace without an acceptance. "I shall be delighted to attend." She was rewarded with gratified smiles around the table. From all except her lord, but she had little doubt of her ability to bring him around.

The tea and cakes arrived and were consumed with dispatch. Neither of the officers knew how long they would be in Brighton, but they were anxious to be off to India. At the mention of the impending posting Alice's face fell. "Oh, are you certain it's to be India? We hear such dreadful rumors..."

"More than rumors, I fear. The news is—" Captain Bellingham looked at the ladies around the table, choked and reddened. "Er—that is, most anxious to get out there and lend a hand. Our fellows are encountering a spot of bother with the natives."

Antonia hid her concern with a swallow of tea. What had Bellingham been about to say? Was there more bad news?

"You have just arrived, Lady Danvers?" Anson broke into her reverie. "Might we have the honour of escorting you to see the Pavilion this afternoon? I'm confident you'll agree that the restoration has been magnificent. Terrible ruin it was, you know, until the town purchased it a few years ago. Back to its old glory now. They have concerts, exhibitions, bazaars—no end of events and meetings. And the pleasure ground—"

"You are well informed, Leiutenant," Antonia observed.

"Thank you, your ladyship. My home is near here, you see."

"I thank you for your invitation, Lieutenant. I fear Lord

Danvers and I are fully engaged for the afternoon." All three of the young ladies' faces lost their look of excited expectation. "But I am certain others of our party will be happy to accompany you."

Thus freed from her duties as duenna, the rest of the afternoon was given over to enjoying the beach with Charlie. Clad in sailor frock and sandals, with Nurse Bevans in attendance, Charlie busied himself filling his sand pail with the small stones that comprised the beach while Antonia relaxed in the canvas beach chair Danvers secured for her. Even though she had chosen one of her narrower crinolines for the excursion, her wide skirt filled the chair and flowed out over her brown leather half boots. The ribbons of her bonnet fluttered in the sea breeze.

Tinker scampered in happy circles around the group, barking at any seagulls that dared to venture too close. Danvers sat reading "The Brighton Gazette" in a chair a little apart from Antonia's. With a sigh of contentment, she adjusted her parasol to shade her eyes and delicate complexion and enjoyed the sight and sound of the waves rhythmically lapping the shore.

Seagulls cried overhead, children called and laughed, sunlight danced on the white fringes of the swelling sea. Tonia smiled at her son as he emptied his pail yet again, forming an ever larger mound of pebbles, and set to filling it again. After a few minutes she felt her eyelids growing heavy. She let her mind drift with the surf.

After a few moments, though, it was not the sun-sparkled English Channel that filled her vision, but rather a muddy, stagnant river washing a sun-parched bank with strange long grasses growing along the edge. And it was not the delight of children's calls that sounded in her ears, but cries of terror and something much harsher.

The brown water around her streaked red as if with blood. A turban-clad figure rose from the vegetation on shore. The sound of a shot jerked her awake.

Charlie. Her eyes widened at her first thought, but her son played happily a few feet away from her under Sara Bevans's careful supervision.

Tonia shook her head and looked around her, confused by the dark visions in her mind and the beauty before her. Had she only dreamed, or had she heard a shot? Then she blinked at the sun in her eyes and realized she had dropped her parasol on the stony beach. That must have been the sound that wakened her.

She stood and surveyed the shore. She could see nothing amiss. Clumps of holidayers relaxed and frolicked as far as she could see. At the edge of the shore to her left was a row of bathing machines doing a brisk business, conveying adventurous ladies modestly into the water to experience the healthful properties of seawater without the necessity of displaying their persons. Bathing machines for men operated further up the beach.

To her right the magnificent Chain Pier extended into the ocean, its series of four arches connected with looping suspension chains. A packet boat from France docked at the end of the pier and its debarking passengers were strolling the length of the pier, mingling with visitors who had paid the admission to enjoy the experience of walking over the ocean. As far as she could see there was nothing to have caused the alarms of her dream. Tonia determined to put it out of her mind.

The rustle of a newspaper being folded and a crunch of pebbles brought Danvers to her side. He stooped to retrieve

Tonia's dropped parasol and handed it to her. "I believe we promised our son a puppet show."

"Puppets!" Charlie had been studiously attending to his mountain building, but at his father's mention of a new attraction he flung his pail away and ran to Charles, who swept his son off his feet and whirled him in the air to a peal of delighted giggles.

Nurse Bevans was freed to return to the hotel with their beach accoutrements while the others, stepping carefully on sand and stones, strolled down the beach toward the pier. The wood and metal structure extended across the beach from the ocean to deliver promenaders directly onto the Marine Parade along the Steine. Underneath the pier, they paused to marvel at the heavy, intricate pylons supporting the underside, one structure for each of the four arches above, the final complex framework at the edge of the shore where the waves lapped the pebbly beach.

Tinker was kept busy performing his self-appointed task of guarding his humans from encroaching seagulls. "Tinker, come here. Don't go into the water." But Tonia was too late. The red-gold terrier had scampered off in pursuit of a particularly intrepid bird and was thoroughly dowsed by the surf swirling around the pylon structure.

"Heel," Tonia ordered her dripping pet when he scuttled back up the beach crestfallen, but with his tail still wagging. At least he stayed closer as they continued. To their right, where the beach met the concrete wall supporting Marine Parade at street level above, a row of booths offered a variety of delights such as little dishes of pickled oysters, whelks, and periwinkles; papers of salted herrings; bottles of ginger beer; or glasses of donkey's milk. And, beyond that, surrounded by a group of children and adults shouting instructions to the performers, was the attraction they sought—a mobile puppet booth covered in checked bed ticking.

Danvers dropped pennies into the bottler's container and swung his son up to his shoulders for a clearer view. Antonia smiled as Charlie squealed with delight at the characters she had known since her own childhood. The red-hatted Punch squawked at the skeleton, dispatching him with a single brandish of his bat. Judy, in her blue gown and mob cap appeared, holding her baby, which Punch promptly took from her, holding it upside down.

Judy screamed and ran out, bringing in the constable, who righted the baby before Punch ran the officer off. Charlie clapped his hands and squealed. The show proceeded along traditional lines as a series of glove puppet figures—clown, doctor, horse—made their appearance, only to be beaten off by Punch, until the final villain, the crocodile, came with open mouth, threatening to swallow Punch whole. Punch beat the crocodile off with his stick, to approving cheers from his audience. "That's the way to do it." Punch squawked and bowed to another round of energetic applause.

Tonia laughed and clapped with her son until, in her mind, a crocodile lumbered menacingly from the waters of her earlier dream. As the vision rose she stumbled backward and might have fallen had a strong pair of arms not steadied her. She turned and drew a sharp intake of breath at the sight of her rescuer. "Lord Penthurst. I had no notion you were in Brighton."

He tipped his top hat and sketched a bow. "How fortunate that I am, my lady. Do take care. This pebble beach can be deuced—that is, can make for precarious walking."

He started to take his leave, but Danvers had turned at Penthurst's voice. "Ah, Penthurst. What brings you here?"

"I have a horse running tomorrow. Duke's Delight—a charming filly. She's one of the fastest I've bred, if you're looking for a tip." With a touch to the brim of his hat he turned and strode through the crowd the bottler was gathering for the next show.

Charlie set up a plea to "walk on the ocean," pointing to the pier stretching invitingly out over the waves. Charles looked at Antonia. "Are you fatigued, my love? Would you prefer to return to the Bedford?"

"Not at all, Charles." She forced a smile. She did not want him to guess that she would prefer to blame fatigue rather than her worrying dream for the slight stumble a few moments ago. This strange apprehension—she would almost say presentiment—was much harder to bear.

They were walking back past the various stalls and booths toward the stairs leading up to Marine Parade when Charlie, still perched on his father's shoulders, pointed and cried out, "Ice cream."

Tonia was amazed; she had never seen the like. Mrs. Robinson had, on occasion, made the delectable treat from *Mrs. Mary Eales's Receipts,* hand-stirring the bowl of custard and cream set in a basin of ice and salt, but confessed to her mistress she was not entirely comfortable with the process since Mrs. Beaton did not include such a recipe in her *Household Management*.

But here, an ingenious vendor was producing the product with small, hand-cranked freezing machines. He sold the results in tiny paper cups with wooden spoons. Of course, they must partake. Charlie's day was quite complete when, licking the delectable treat off their spoons, they walked the length of the pier, hearing the swelling of the ocean below them and the call of seagulls over their heads. Antonia smiled at her son's delight, although she had to admit that she found the combined motion of swelling water below, scudding clouds above, and sailing birds and boats all around them to be rather dizzying.

At the end of the pier they encountered a windowless

wooden building with a tall tower on top. "Oh, yes," Danvers said. "The camera obscura. I have heard that it is most interesting." He paid their admission and they entered the small, dark room with a large, white table in the center. Images of people strolling along the beach moved across the table.

It took Tonia a moment to realize that this was no magic lantern show, but that they were seeing actual people as they walked along the beach. The guide explained how the top of the tower contained a mirror set at an angle. It reflected the light downward passing through three lenses, one of them magnifying, to project the images before them on the table. "Charlie, just look!" Tonia pointed to the projected images as children ran before them on the table flying a kite. She felt less comfortable with the scene, however, when a couple, thinking themselves unobserved, walked hand in hand, then paused and kissed.

A matron on the other side of the table drew in a shocked breath and Tonia was about to suggest to Charles that he set Charlie on the floor when the mirror rotated. The scene shifted to an unbroken panorama of the English Channel. The packet boat from France that had earlier unloaded its passengers now steamed back toward Dieppe. A few pleasure craft sailed jauntily along and fishing trawlers rocked gently further out. One sleek craft in particular caught Tonia' attention. A double-masted yacht with a blue and yellow funnel rocked at anchor a distance beyond the pier. It flew the Union flag and a smaller flag undoubtedly identifying its owner, but Tonia couldn't make out the device.

Another tilt of the mirror brought into view a more secluded part of the beach on the other side of the pier. Tonia thought it almost deserted until a flash of red caught her eye. Surely the scarlet tunic of an officer of a Light Infantry regiment. She tugged Danvers's arm and pointed to a group of figures standing in the angle of the wall, carefully out of the view of any strollers that might venture onto that side of the beach. Only the tilt of the camera obscura mirror revealed their presence. The image was from some distance, of course, and yet the likeness was unmistakable. She had understood that Lieutenant Anson was to spend the afternoon squiring the young ladies of their party around the Royal Pavilion. What was he doing in what appeared to be a clandestine meeting on a secluded part of the beach?

The mirror continued its rotation, revealing the two men against the wall Anson was talking to. Or was he perhaps yelling? His gestures indicated a considerably heated encounter. Antonia wondered if the men might be the lieutenant's dark-skinned acquaintances from the Round Pond. Or was it merely that they were standing in deeper shadow?

Another slight shift of the mirror revealed a tall, black-clad gentleman walking rapidly down the beach away from the group. Had he also been part of the meeting? His purposeful stride did not indicate a stroll merely to observe the scenery.

Charlie interrupted her thoughts with a cry of delight. "Mr. Punch!" He clapped his hands. Her focus returned to the projection on the table just in time to see that the figure she assumed to be Anson had struck one of the other men, knocking him onto the rocky beach. Thank goodness Charlie thought it a play-acted entertainment. She would not want her son's innocence sullied by such violence.

"It is time for Charlie to return to our rooms." Tonia turned toward the door without waiting for a reply. "And I shall have a rest with one of Isabella's cucumber skin refreshers. This salt air can be drying to the complexion." She put her hand to her cheek. The truth was, the disturbances of the afternoon had now left her more fatigued than she cared to admit.

In the lobby of the Bedford they encountered Hardy

awaiting their return, "It's the aerostat, m'lord. That bumbling farmer who agreed to store it in his barn—well, I'm not right certain how it came about, but—"

"Are you telling me there has been an accident to my aerostat, Hardy?" Danvers had already turned toward the door to see to the matter when he bethought himself. "Antonia—"

She laughed. "Go on. See to the repair of your toy. Charlie and I can very well ascend the elevator on our own." She laughed again at the look of relief on her lord's face.

Antonia left Charlie in Nurse Bevans's care with instructions for his dinner—no sweets since he had already consumed his own ice cream and half of hers. "Lord Danvers and I will look in on him before we go to the theatre tonight, but don't keep him up if he is sleepy."

She was almost to her own room when she heard sobs coming from the room occupied by Sophia and Danvers's nieces. Oh, dear, had one of their charges had her heart broken already? She knocked gently on the door. "It's Antonia. May I be of help?"

In a moment the door opened to reveal a red-eyed Sophia. Antonia took the distressed girl in her arms. "My dear, what is it? Did that cad Anson—"

Sophia drew in a ragged breath and sniffed. She dabbed at her eyes with one hand. Antonia closed the door behind herself and produced a soft linen handkerchief. She guided the girl to the rose brocade settee occupying one corner of the room. "Now, tell me, my dear. Have you been insulted? Charles will—"

Sophia blew her nose, then shook her head. "No, no. It's nothing like that. It's very silly in me, I know. But today was such fun. Mama told me she loved sea bathing so much—" She choked on a stifled sob. "I have been worried about Mama. I miss her so dreadfully. I hear rumors, but no one tells me anything, and it has been so long since there has been a letter."

Antonia was amazed. Sophia spoke of her mother so seldom... She looked at the girl with a new admiration. Had she been putting on a brave front all this time? And said nothing? She took the distressed girl into her arms, debating in her mind what to say. She opened her mouth to voice soothing platitudes: Homesickness for her mother was perfectly natural, but nothing to worry about; Sophia was fatigued by the journey to Brighton and the excitement of exploring a new place...

Yet Antonia herself had been missing her friend of late and held similar worries for her safety. Perhaps the best approach would be to face the matter squarely.

"My dear, take courage. There is trouble in India, yes. But we know very few details. What we do know is that the trouble is at places which are some distance from Cawnpore."

Sophia responded only with the slightest nod of her head.

Tonia had taken a surreptitious look at Charles's newspaper on the beach and the words still burned in her mind: "The Sepoys are fully possessed with a frantic belief in the intention of Government to convert them to Christianity. Accordingly eighty-five men of the regiment refusing to handle the cartridges were tried by court-martial, and sentenced to various terms of imprisonment with hard labour. On the 9th their sentences were read out on parade and the offenders marched off to gaol. Up to this time disaffection had shown itself only through incendiary fires in the lines, hardly a night passing without one or more conflagrations. But on the 10th it appeared at once in all its strength. Towards the evening of that day, while many of the Europeans were at church—for it was Sunday—"

She stubbornly argued with herself. That news was nearly two months old. But the letter she had received from Emilia, on which she had placed so much comfort, telling, as it did, of gay balls and entertainments and their charming Nana Sahib, had been written well before that.

The newspaper article had gone on: *Many officers murdered, Colonel Finis the first victim of the outbreak. Other officers fell with the colonel or in the terrible moments that ensued. The whole body now thoroughly committed to the wildest excesses—rushed through the cantonment, slaying, burning destroying. Every house fired. Every English man, woman or child that fell in the way pitilessly massacred...*

It's not Cawnpore, Tonia repeated over and over in her mind. Two months ago—the English officers would have put a stop to it all weeks ago. Of course they would. And the Cawnpore cantonment was under the protection of their gentleman maharajah Nana Sahib.

But Tonia could not find the confidence to give voice to these hollow assurances.

⚜ 12 ⚛

Emilia *shifted slightly to focus the thin slat of light onto her prayer book.*

My God, my God, look upon me; why hast thou forsaken me: and art so far from my health, and from the words of my complaint?

O my God, I cry in the daytime, but thou hearest not: and in the night-season also I take no rest...

O go not from me, for trouble is hard at hand: and there is none to help me...

My strength is dried up like a potsherd, and my tongue cleaveth to my gums: and thou shalt bring me into the dust of death.

For many dogs are come about me: and the council of the wicked layeth siege against me...

Deliver my soul from the sword...

Emilia closed her book with a sigh as the last rays of light seeping through the bolted shutters died. This evening, the third of July, if she reckoned properly, they had been herded down the steep steps of Savada House and carted two and a half miles through the ruins of their former station to a new prison.

Now nearly two hundred women and children were crammed into the former home of the mistress of a European official. The Bibighar, it was called, "The House of the Ladies." Narrow rooms and cupboards surrounded a small courtyard, open to the rain, where a single Mulsuri tree grew. The house had long ago been looted of its furnishings, so there was no furniture, not even straw for pallets; only coarse bamboo matting of the roughest fiber, moldering in the steamy climate, covered the tamped clay floors.

The indomitable Mrs. Moore had organized a rotation for space under the roofed verandahs, for there was not room enough for everyone to lie down at once. Emilia and Louisa would have the next turn to get what rest they could lying prone in the courtyard, soggy as it was from the monsoons that drenched it daily. For now, Emilia leaned against the wall with a small girl's head in her lap. She gently fondled the golden curls, dulled though they were from the mud of the Ganges. Poor, fatherless child. What was to become of her? Of all the children? Thank God Sophia was safe in England. *Emilia drew her knees up to make room for Louisa, leaning on her shoulder, to extend her legs. Using her prayer book as a fan Emilia swatted at the swarm of mosquitos that replaced the daytime flies at sundown.* Lord have mercy, *was the only prayer she was capable of breathing.*

The fetid air hardly moved since the shutters were fastened tight against escape, yet in the stillness, over the whimpers of distressed children and soft moans of those suffering from wounds, a wavering voice rose in a familiar evening hymn, "As now the sun's declining rays." A few more joined in, feeble, but distinct, "At eventide descend." Emilia drew what breath she could and added her weak voice, "So life's brief day is singing down to its appointed end."

Antonia awoke gasping for air. She gave such a sharp yank to her bellpull she was amazed it didn't come off in her hand. Far quicker than one could imagine Isabella traversing the hotel halls, her maid was at her side. "My lady, you have the headache? You are unwell?" Distress clouded the small, sharp-featured face.

"Open the window, Isabella. It is stifling in here." The diminutive maid stood on tiptoe to reach high up on the heavy velvet drapes that covered the tall, floor-to-ceiling double French doors. She pushed the drapes open to the morning sunlight, then threw the windows open. Refreshing sea breezes wafted in, ruffling the net curtains under the velvet drapes. Without being told, the maid poured a glass of fresh water and handed it to her lady.

"Thank you, Isabella, I dreamt—I don't quite recall—but I was suffocating." She breathed deeply of the fresh, salty sea air blowing in over the balcony. "The air was so close. Hot. Heavy. And it stank. There were shutters on the windows. Nailed shut..." She shuddered.

"My lady had a bad dream. Perhaps the eiderdown fell over her face..." Isabella spoke soothingly as Sara Bevans might to Charlie.

"Doubtless that is the truth of the matter, Isabella." Church bells pealed, borne into the room on the breeze, reminding Tonia that it was Sunday. "I shall wear my blue muslin with the white collar to church, Isabella. And the blue sateen bonnet."

When Lord and Lady Danvers collected their charges a short time later to escort them to church Tonia was happy to note that Sophia's eyes were bright and her smile ready. Thank goodness for the resiliency of youth. The barouches ordered from the livery stable awaited them beneath the *porte-cochère*. My lord and lady with the Honourable Charlie and the three young ladies in the first carriage were followed by the servants in the second. They made a stately progress along

King's Road and turned up Old Steine, where both levels of the newly erected Victoria fountain cascaded with silver droplets in the morning sun.

They passed the glistening white confection of onion domes and minarets of the Royal Pavilion on their left. Tonia glanced at Sophia, hoping this India-inspired vision wouldn't bring a return of the girl's fears, but the young ladies on the seat facing the Danvers had their heads together, no doubt giggling over their beaux. They continued on up the Grand Parade to the top of the long green triangle of Steine Gardens to where the perpendicular gothic tower of St. Peter's was pealing forth welcoming bells to Sunday worshippers.

Tonia alighted from the carriage and looked up at the tall tower of soft grey Portland stone surrounded by sharp pinnacles pointing heavenward. "What a lovely building."

"Yes, it was designed by Sir Charles Barry who is overseeing the reconstruction of Westminster Palace," Danvers replied.

Tonia nodded; she could certainly see the resemblance to the clock tower on the houses of parliament, still being rebuilt after the disastrous fire twenty years before. A peal from the organ drew Antonia forward, but she paused when she realized the others had stopped to greet a group of red-coated officers. The gentlemen very properly made their first bows to Lady Danvers, but then quickly turned their attention to the young ladies who were all smiles for the newcomers.

Tonia bristled. Couldn't they turn around without running into the regiment? Then, after Alice proceeded toward the open door on the arm of Captain Bellingham, Anson and another officer Tonia didn't recognize brought a smile to Sophia's face by competing for her arm. Tonia relented, deciding the presence of officers might be no bad thing if it cheered her charge.

Sophia accepted the offer of the unknown officer and the lieutenant bowed to Beatrice. The party filed in to the long pew near the front to which the usher escorted Lord and Lady Danvers, the officers taking seats across the aisle. The seemly service of Matins was efficiently accomplished with a sermon that lasted only slightly over an hour, freeing the worshippers to the warmth of a Sunday afternoon.

As their group stood outside the church chatting, Danvers inquired of Bellingham about their accommodation in the Church Street Barracks. "Pleasant to be so near the Pavilion," he suggested.

The captain made a face. "Afraid we drew the short straw, my lord. These barracks were thrown up in haste during the war with Boney. Never intended for extended use."

"But haven't they been improved? Surely Parliament—"

"Only enough to keep them standing, I'm afraid. The Cavalry Barracks at Preston," Bellingham gestured toward a village just north of Brighton, "they made that a show piece for the cavalry. Infantry and artillerymen have to muck in here. Only a few officers; most of the troopers are Irish." He shook his head again. "Fight all night. But then, that might not be so bad if they take it out on the pandies when we get to India. If they don't kill each other first."

Tonia realized she wasn't meant to hear this conversation, but even Captain Bellingham's soft voice didn't keep the gist of it from her ears.

"Have there been incidents?" Danvers asked.

"More than one. Fights, shootings even. And threats nightly. They get drunk, you know, and we're so crowded. Still, we won't be here long. Word is we'll be on our way to India next week. Of course, the fun's sure to be over by the time we get there."

One of the other officers reminded Captain Bellingham that they were due back at mess in less than a quarter of an hour. They bowed to the ladies and marched down Marlborough Place toward their ramshackle barracks. Tonia noticed Alice's soft blue eyes following Captain Bellingham's retreating back. "Did you visit the Pavilion yesterday, or only the gardens?" she asked her charges.

When it was established that the young ladies had not yet viewed the splendors of the newly refurbished royal pleasure palace of the previous century, Tonia suggested they take Charlie with them but allow the servants the afternoon off to enjoy the beach for themselves. On the understanding that Isabella would take Tinker with her as he had been shut in the hotel room all morning.

In a few minutes the party alighted from their carriage and walked between the twin gateways of the south entrance. Each arched gate on either side of the walkway bore an onion dome topped by a ball and a spire. Tonia stood before the amazing concoction, gazing upward toward the Pavilion beyond. From where she stood she could count no less than twenty such oriental-domed structures of various sizes, and she knew those were only a fraction of the whole.

Since the young ladies had visited the pleasure ground the day before, they merely paused to enjoy the strains of a military band playing in the garden, then went directly to the Octagon Hall, a small, domed room with grey walls, where Danvers paid their admission fee of sixpence apiece. Next was the cool sea-green entrance hall with entablature of Chinese designs decorating the walls. Sophia, Alice and Beatrice regarded the strangeness of the decoration with awe, if not recoil, at the dragons coiling above them.

Perhaps noticing their consternation, an attendant stepped forward. "If you will indulge me?" He looked at Danvers who nodded his assent and the guide explained, "In the latter years of the previous century, the Prince Regent had a great fondness for Brighton where he felt free to indulge his, ah—more extravagant tastes. He had a pavilion built on the grounds of a former royal property. After Wellington's victory at Waterloo in 1815, the prince engaged the architect John Nash to enlarge and redesign the pavilion. It is Nash's work you see today.

"Our good Queen Victoria, however, had no fondness for Brighton and no use for the Pavilion, it being inadequate to accommodate the numerous royal family. Our queen, quite understandably, prefers her quiet retreat on the Isle of Wight. So the entire edifice fell into decay and disrepair until the government sold it to the city of Brighton seven years ago. I think you'll agree they have done a fine job of restoration and the property is a great asset for civic events. May I direct your way to the north drawing room? I believe you'll find it houses an admirable collection of museum pieces."

Without waiting for their assent, the attendant walked across the hall to a long corridor hung in chinoiserie wallpaper and lit by overhead skylights. "Sadly, most of the original decorations have been dismantled, but there is considerable public agitation to make an effort to have them restored. You will find this interesting, though." He pointed to a small Chinese commode against the wall. "Not actually bamboo as it appears, but English made, simulating bamboo."

His listeners seemed suitably impressed so their guide moved on into the banqueting room. A gasp of astonishment from the visitors visibly pleased their host. "Breathtaking, is it not? We are most fortunate that our incomparable gasolier survived the ravages of disrepair that afflicted so much of the building."

Tonia blinked at the amazing sight of a high dome filled with gigantic painted and sculpted plantain leaves from which an enormous winged dragon hovered at the apex, supporting a lighting device which their guide pronounced to be, "a ton of unparalleled beauty." The fixture was a cascade of crystals and jewels, encircled by more silver dragons, each with an open lotus blossom in its mouth. Around the perimeter of the room hung smaller gasoliers of lotus blossom design. Such splendor made Tonia glad that, in spite of her reluctance, she had accepted the officers' invitation to the ball tomorrow night. She much hoped that refreshments would be served in this room so she could see the full effect at night.

The guide led them on into a long room with walls decorated in a busy and colorful chinoiserie pattern, and columns entwined with gilded serpents and topped with scalloped canopies, making them look something like an oriental potentate's parasol. "This room was used by the Prince Regent as a sitting room where he loved to regale his guests with anecdotes of well-known personalities. As you can see, it now serves as a museum of oriental curiosities. Our most interesting piece is on loan to us from East India House."

Tonia didn't need the guide's sweeping arm to call her attention to the attraction as Charlie cried out, "See the kitty!"

Tonia looked, then drew back with a gasp at the shocking sight of a Bengal tiger with a life-size European man in its mouth. "Tippu's Tiger," the guide announced. "A mechanical toy created for Sultan Tippu, ruler of the kingdom of Mysore in India in the previous century." He moved to fold down a flap on the far side of the tiger, revealing the keyboard of a small pipe organ. "Sadly, demonstrations are offered only on Wednesdays, but I am certain you would be highly entertained if you wish to return. Mechanisms inside the automaton make one hand of the man move as he emits a wailing sound accompanied by grunts from the tiger.

"The tiger was the personal emblem of Sultan Tippu and the unfortunate fate of the Englishman expresses his hatred of his enemy, the British of the East India Company. The mechanical tiger was discovered in his summer palace after

East India Company troops stormed Tippu's capital in 1799..."

"Charles, take Charlie away this instant," Tonia ordered, but their son had already flitted to the other side of the room to inspect an intricate ormolu clock with Chinese figures.

Their informant continued to talk as he moved across the floor to the next room, but Tonia could only think with horror of the poor fellow represented by the toy. It brought back to mind the story Hardy had recounted of the Bengal tiger escaped from Jamrach's Menagerie who took a small boy up in its mouth. Fortunately, the child had been saved by the menagerie owner, but it was clear that the message of Tippu's automaton was *Death to Englishmen*.

Their host led on to the music room, a chamber that exceeded even the banqueting room for magnificence. Although the crimson and gold murals of Chinese landscapes were dulled and pealing from neglect, they still gave a shimmer of elegance in the light of the lotus flower gasoliers that seemed to float overhead. But the scenes of oriental splendor brought only visions of burning cantonments to Tonia.

She couldn't help wondering if the Englishman being mauled by Tippu's tiger was a warning. And yet, it had not been an Englishman but an Indian who had died under the wheels of the Danvers's carriage. She wondered how the police were proceeding with their investigation. Had Inspector Futter solved it yet? She hoped so for Chandrika's sake. Tonia resolved to call on her when they returned to London.

❦ 13 ❦

By noon the next day Antonia realized Charlie was very nearly reaching the end of his two-year-old patience at being cooped in a hotel room. "Very well, Bevans, his sailor frock. And his straw hat with the ribbon." The child had wakened that morning with a stubborn determination to go paddling in the ocean, which no amount of distractions could override for long. Although the day was warm and sunny, Tonia judged the morning breeze to be too chill and was hoping to delay the adventure until the temperature might rise.

Antonia had returned to her room to don the broadest brimmed of her hats to serve as protection against the sun when Sophia, Alice and Beatrice knocked on her door. They were clad in fashionable crinolined dresses and bonnets, appropriate for sight-seeing or shopping, but each carried a bulging carpetbag. At Tonia's invitation the girls entered her room, but seemed reluctant, embarrassed, even, to introduce the business they had come about.

"I am going to the beach with Charlie," Tonia said. "What are your plans for the afternoon?"

Beatrice giggled. Sophia spoke. "Lady Danvers, we—well, that is, since we're at the seashore... We want to go sea bathing."

"It is said to be very healthful," Alice urged.

"Oh, I see. That is what you have in your bags—bathing dresses?"

"Yes." Sophia opened her bag and pulled out a light blue garment piped in maroon. She held it up to show that the full skirt fell to her knees and the sleeves were full-length. "And these—" The bloomers were voluminous, but fit tight around her ankles to prevent riding up in the water. Both garments were made of a heavy flannel.

She reached into her satchel once more and produced a white cotton cap to cover her hair with a large blue bow on the top. "Is it not charming?" Madame Elise made the whole from a plate in 'The Ladies Magazine.'"

"Madame Elise? You don't mean to say that Aunt Aelfrida ordered her dressmaker to make you a bathing costume?"

"Oh, yes, she said it was quite the thing. Although," Sophia paused and blushed, "she did say that in her day ladies did not bother with such encumbrances. They bathed quite, er—"

Tonia smiled. "Yes, so I've heard. An invigorating experience, no doubt."

"And she told Mama to have bathing costumes made for us as well." Alice held her bag aloft.

"Please, won't you come with us?" Sophia pleaded. "You do have a costume, don't you?"

Tonia sighed. Yes, she had one, but the very thought of sea bathing brought back to her those long-ago days in Ramsgate when the daily ten minute sea bath was *de rigeur* for those being treated for consumption. "Well, yes, I do, but I really don't think—"

Charlie burst into the room, "Paddling!"

Tonia hugged her demanding son. If those childhood treatments had not been successful they would not have Charlie now. And Brighton was much warmer than those frigid mornings in Ramsgate. "Just a minute, darling, Mama is almost ready." She turned to her wardrobe and folded her bathing ensemble into a bag.

They chose a row of bathing machines not far from the pier and selected the end vehicles so Tonia could have the pleasure of watching her son paddle to his heart's content under Nurse Bevans's watchful eye. She knew that further up the beach Charles would be enjoying a vigorous swim. He had left the Bedford more than an hour earlier in his top hat and frock coat, carrying nothing with him, as men did not require bathing costumes.

Tonia entered the rear door of the tiny canvas hut on wheels. By the light of its single window she placed her street clothing on a high shelf where it would be out of the reach of the surf and donned the dark green flannel bathing dress with cape and bell sleeves. It was cut in the style of a paletot coat and fell only a little below her knees, so she also wore striped Turkish pants, full at the knees and tight at the ankles. The paletot had weights cleverly sewn into the hem to keep the garment from floating up in the water. A pair of light canvas slippers and a flat-brimmed black straw hat tied under her chin completed the outfit.

She knocked on the door to signal the dipper that she was ready to enter the water. Tonia stood at the seaward door and watched as the machine was pulled into the sea by a sturdy brown pony. The wide iron wheels rolled easily over the sand and the water was soon level with the top step. The driver unhitched the pony from the machine and left Tonia with a clear, sun-sparkled view of the sea before her.

The dipper offered her strong arm to help Tonia descend into water above her waist. She squealed as a gentle wave washed the cold surf even higher, but she had to admit it was exhilarating. She spread her arms for balance and waded deeper, savoring the sights and sounds of birds, boats and bathers all around her. "Mama!" Charlie's high-pitched voice called from the edge of the surf behind her. "Look at me!"

She peered around her machine and saw her son paddling happily in water above his ankles while Nurse Bevans, her skirt tucked up, hovered behind him.

Squeals and shrieks of delight from the other side of her machine told Tonia that Sophia, Beatrice and Alice had likewise descended into the swelling water. She joined them and entered gently into their games, splashing one another and flinging handfuls of water toward the sun for the simple pleasure of watching the droplets fall in golden beads.

After half an hour Antonia turned back toward her bathing machine. The weight of her water-logged costume made her movements heavy and she was happy for the firm grip with which the dipper held her while she ascended the stairs. As soon as she was settled in her little cabin she pulled the cord that raised a small red flag, signaling the driver to return and pull her back to shore. The young ladies could remain in the water as long as they pleased, but she, for one, would be happy to get back into street clothes and spend the rest of the afternoon in a canvas beach chair watching Charlie paddle.

Dried and dressed, she emerged from the machine, tipped the dipper, and walked across the pebbles to the stall renting chairs. A flash of light, as if reflected from a mirror, caught her eye and drew her gaze to the Marine Parade above the seawall. A tall man in a dark coat leaned against the stone parapet and held a most unusual instrument to his eyes, sweeping the beach.

Tonia was fascinated. She had never seen the like. The two black tubes looked to be twin telescopes, although somewhat shorter, and connected over the nose. She frowned. Was the man engaged in some sort of peeping Tommery? Surely most of the females would be sufficiently protected from such prying by their bathing machines? She checked to be certain her charges were shielded.

Or was the man innocently using his novel instrument to view the seascape, just as they had done at the camera obscura? She gazed out to sea and saw several small sailboats tacking in the breeze like large white birds. Beyond them were the fishing trawlers she had seen before. A larger boat caught her eye with a billow of white steam as it navigated westward across the horizon. She recognized it as the yacht she had seen through the camera obscura.

When Tonia returned her gaze to the top of the seawall the man and his optical instrument had gone. She turned her attention to admiring the cairn of pebbles that Charlie was constructing until it was time to summon the entire party to return to the Bedford to prepare for the ball.

A few hours later there was nothing about the ladies of the Danvers party to suggest they had been engaged in anything as raucous as sea-bathing when they descended the staircase to the Grecian-style lobby of their hotel. Antonia smiled, surveying her charges, thinking how very much they looked like a flower garden with Sophia in pale yellow, Beatrice in the pink that set off her dark locks so well and Alice, careful not to choose a color that would overpower her soft brown hair and light blue eyes, in palest mint green. All of which, Tonia knew, allowed her own glowing amber taffeta, which she was aware bought out the golden lights in her copper hair, to stand alone in their company. The gleam in her lord's eye above a lifted eyebrow reinforced the accuracy of her perception.

A gold and coral sunset sky made the domes and minarets of the Pavilion radiant as the Danvers's carriage approached up East Street. Danvers helped the ladies alight, then offered his arm to Tonia to lead through the twin gates. The walkway was lined with flaming torches and the garden hung with Chinese lanterns, aglow like butterflies among the branches of the trees.

"It's enchanted," Sophia breathed softly, as if she were afraid of breaking the spell, her words reflecting Antonia's own thoughts.

Danvers presented their invitation in the entrance hall and all the party were given dance cards in the form of tiny fans listing the evening dance program with space to write the name of one's partner next to each dance using the tiny pencil attached. Danvers promptly inscribed his name on Tonia's card for the Grand March and first waltz before they proceeded into the Corridor. Tonia drew in her breath. The long gallery by daylight had been interesting, if slightly shabby and sparsely furnished. Now, however, lit by a multi-plicity of flickering candles, lanterns, oil lamps and gasoliers, and alive with officers in splendid red and gold dress uniforms and ladies in multi-ruffled, wide-crinolined ball gowns, it was even more of a fairyland than the garden had appeared.

Beatrice giggled nervously behind her fan, to be rebuked by Alice. "Pray, sister, show some deportment. You don't want the officers thinking you a schoolroom miss."

Antonia looked in the direction Beatrice indicated and saw Captain Bellingham with several officers she didn't know.

As she watched, Lieutenant Anson joined the group with an attractive young lady in a blue gown on his arm. She looked up at the lieutenant and Tonia was struck by how much the two resembled each other.

Captain Bellingham noted the arrival of the Danvers party and led the others across the hall to present his fellows to Lady Danvers. "Lieutenants Vickars and Incham, my lady."

Anson joined them. "Lady Danvers," he bowed, "may I have the honour of presenting my sister Annabelle."

Tonia acknowledged the introductions with a nod and presented her charges. She had to smile at how neatly the captain cut out his lieutenants in being the first to inscribe his name on Alice's card. It was little surprise that the officers all turned to Sophia, as she looked like flickering candlelight in her pale lemon dress with yellow roses tucked in her blond curls. Vickars and Incham were out of luck for the first two dances, however, as Anson had stolen a march on them, so they turned to Beatrice and teased each other for space on her card, Vickars managing to sign first while Incham greeted Annabelle Anson as an old friend.

Tonia realized that undertaking to chaperone three unattached young ladies was going to be a considerable challenge. She cast a careful eye over Sophia's card to be certain she had allowed Anson no more than three dances, although she was inclined to be more lenient with Alice.

Captain Bellingham suggested they move on and led the way to the drawing room where Mr. Walton, the Master of Ceremonies, appeared to have been looking out for them. He approached Danvers and bowed over the long walking stick which was his badge of office. "My lord, my lady, may I request that you honour us by following our host, General Howsham and his lady in the Grand March?"

Lord and Lady Danvers assented and were led to the top of the Music Room, next to the musicians, where the Master of Ceremonies introduced them to General and Mrs. Howsham. Antonia chatted with the general's wife as the line of couples formed behind them. "I am told that the regiment will soon be going to India. Will you accompany your husband?" Tonia asked.

The general's lady looked surprised that she should ask. "By all means. I always accompany my husband. We have two sons in the Hussars. The older is married, and his wife always accompanies him as well, although I've warned them that it will become more difficult when their children start school. I always managed, however. Military families always do."

Tonia murmured an appropriate reply. It was clear that Mrs. Howsham had as stiff a backbone as her husband. "And you are not concerned by the alarming reports in the news?"

"My dear, there are always alarming reports in the news. Were there not, people wouldn't buy the newspapers. There is nothing the British Army cannot handle—especially a pack of native troopers who get above themselves." Mrs. Howsham smiled at a young lady with brown ringlets who was being led into the line by an officer. "That is Suzanne, our youngest. She is much anticipating getting to Cawnpore. I don't mind telling you that she has an understanding with a captain in the Guards."

It was clear she would have gone on, but the line of dancers now extended the length of the wall and around to the second so the Master of Ceremonies nodded to the conductor and the musicians began Mendelssohn's "War March of the Priests" from *Athalie*. The ball was officially opened. At another nod from Mr. Walton the general and his lady began the procession. Lord Danvers presented his right arm to Antonia, she rested her finger tips in the crook of his arm and they moved forward in time to the martial music, stepping on the left foot with each accented beat.

They marched twice around the room before the Master

of Ceremonies gave a twirl to his walking stick, indicating to General Howsham that the pattern could be varied. Of an obvious military mind, the general's variations consisted merely in cutting back and forth side to side, across the golden dragons swirling on the blue carpet underfoot.

The room was already becoming stuffy and Tonia was most grateful when, at the end of the Grand March, several of the officers moved to open the tall French windows giving off onto the veranda. Tonia was glad they were not there in the days of the Prince Regent. It was said he had a horror of night drafts and always kept his rooms close and overheated.

The waltz was next. At the opening notes of the sweeping Strauss melody, Danvers placed his hand on Antonia's waist and swept her onto the floor. Her skirt swayed like a bell and she felt herself barely touching the floor as she whirled around and around. The dancing flames of candles, the lotus shaped gasoliers floating overhead, and the gigantic golden serpents and flying dragons ringing the ceiling below the central dome, spun with every turn of their steps until Antonia could feel herself quite transported to Kubla Khan's palace at Xanadu.

When the dance came to an end Tonia asked Danvers to lead her to one of the gilded chairs lining the wall and to secure her a glass of punch. "Are you fatigued, my love? It may be our daughter is not ready for so much dancing yet?" The sparkle in his eyes reflected his happiness with his wife's delicate condition.

"I am certain she likes it as much as her mother does, but now that you put me in mind of my condition, perhaps you had best bring two glasses of punch."

Danvers was no more than a few steps departed when Lieutenant Anson was at her elbow. "Lady Danvers, may I ask the pleasure of the next dance?" He glanced at his card. "It is to be a polka, I believe."

Tonia laughed. "You flatter me, sir, to ascribe me so much stamina. I believe I will forego that energetic dance, however."

"Ah, all the better. If I may be permitted to bear you company, that is?"

Tonia pushed her wide skirt aside to make room for him in the next chair. Before he could sit, though, his sister's partner for the preceding dance returned her to her brother, and the chair was taken by the young lady.

"Are you enjoying the ball, Miss Anson?" Antonia inquired.

"Oh, yes, your ladyship."

"I understand you live near, so you must have opportunity to attend many such events."

"No, I have never... That is, I have been... I—"

"My sister has been indisposed for some time, Lady Danvers." The lieutenant came to his sister's rescue. "She is just recently returned to society."

Tonia could see that the girl did look strained. "I am very happy to hear that you are recovered, Miss Anson. The Pavilion is quite splendid is it not? I believe one could quite fancy oneself transported to India." Tonia endeavored to shift the conversation to safer ground, but Annabelle's confusion seemed to increase with the new topic.

"Oh, India." She swallowed. "Oh, yes, I—" Antonia could have sworn that tears sprang to the girl's eyes. "Mon Cher..." She whispered the last words.

Fortunately, Lord Danvers reappeared at that moment. With great skill he had managed to circle the crowded room bearing three cups of punch.

"Well done, my love. I believe you did that without spilling a drop."

"I sincerely hope so. It would be a shame to blot this exquisite carpet." Danvers turned to offer a glass of punch to

Annabelle Anson, but before he could speak her brother whisked her away with only the slightest bow to Lady Danvers.

Antonia gratefully emptied her first cup of punch and set the glass cup on the silver tray of a passing footman. "What a very odd young lady. She seemed quite overset by the mention of India."

"Perhaps not so odd if the rumors are true that her brother is to be posted there in a few days."

"Yes, surely that is it. And Lieutenant Anson mentioned that she had been unwell." Still, Tonia continued to ponder as she began on her second glass of punch.

The Master of Ceremonies announced the Lancers. Across the space of the room couples began forming rectangles of four partners. "Would you care to dance, my love?" Danvers asked.

"Alas, it is one of my favorite dances, but I think I should prefer some fresh air." In spite of the doors standing open, the room, so full of active bodies and blazing lights, was overheated. Danvers offered his arm and they strolled onto the balustraded terrace running the length of the back of the Pavilion. The long promenade overlooked the lawn that was well protected by trees and bushes from Old Steine Street. As in the front garden, this was charmingly lit with swags of Chinese lanterns looped from tree to tree. A few couples strolled in the grounds, but Tonia was content to remain on the balcony.

The lively strains of the fifth and final figure of the Lancers floated through the open windows when a couple emerged from the doors at the far end. A few steps brought them closer and Tonia was surprised to see Sophia holding the arm of one of the few men besides Danvers who was not in uniform. The severe cut of his tailcoat made an elegant picture against Sophia's gossamer gold.

Tonia was less enchanted with the vision, however, when light from the window showed that her charge's partner was Lord Penthurst. When the couple reached them the gentlemen bowed to each other. "I believe the Lancers is coming to an end. Next will be the Allemande, let us return to the ballroom." Tonia's words were an invitation, but her voice indicated a command. Sophia returned with them obediently, but the duke followed as well.

It had not been Tonia's intention that the duke should be Sophia's partner for the dinner dance, but there was nothing she could do about it now.

Antonia and Danvers joined a line of couples. When the music started they extended their paired hands forward and paraded the length of the ballroom, walking three steps, then balancing on one foot. On the other side of the room another line, which Antonia saw all of her charges and their dance partners had joined, was performing a livelier version of the dance with three springing steps and a hop.

The lines moved back and forth the length of the room several times, then Mr. Walton announced that the supper room was open. Just as Antonia had hoped when they visited the Pavilion as tourists, this was to be in the Banqueting Room. She knew how privileged she was to take supper there, for Aunt Aelfrida had recounted to her how, in the days of the Prince Regent, no lady attended a banquet in this sumptuous room for the simple fact that the prince did not have a lady to act as hostess.

Tonight the long banqueting table in the center of the room was draped with white linen, and a great many branched candelabra ran its length illuminating the variety of dishes offered. Danvers escorted Tonia to a chair at one of the many small, round side tables set around the room and turned to the buffet to secure her refreshments. After some time he returned bearing a plate filled exactly to her liking with chicken, tongue, *fois gras* and sole mayonnaise. He set it in front of her and departed again, as gentlemen all around the room were doing for their dinner partners, and returned in a moment with a tall, amber glass of champagne for each of them. As politeness required, Danvers did not sit, but stood guard behind Antonia's chair, ready to procure any tidbit she might require.

When the more substantial refreshment was consumed, he returned to the buffet and secured a plate of trifle, tipsy cake, jelly and blancmange for his wife, and a second glass of champagne for himself. Tonia looked around the room for her charges. With something of a twinge of conscience she realized she had done very little chaperoning this evening.

She spotted Sophia at a table across the room with Lord Penthurst standing at her back—as was inevitable, since they had danced the dinner dance together. At the far end of the room she saw Bea and Alice at a table, awaiting the return of their escorts from the buffet. She did not know the officer serving Beatrice, but, inevitably, Captain Bellingham presented Alice with a selection of delicacies. Antonia did hope they had not committed the impropriety of spending the entire evening together. Although, if the captain was soon to depart for India, she could well imagine the temptation. Anson did not appear to be in the room. Perhaps he had taken his sister home.

Couples drifted in and out of the room. The strains of a quadrille floated to them from the Music Room, indicating that the dancing had resumed, but Tonia had no desire to move. She noticed some officers who had finished serving their partners and restored them to the dance, now returned to secure sustenance for themselves. And, if her younger days were anything to judge by, she knew that many of the young ladies who had eaten and gone off to join the quadrille, would find their way back later as well, since the buffet would remain open until the ball ended sometime before dawn.

Antonia felt, though, that for her the pleasures of the evening had been quite adequate. "My love, do secure yourself a plate of food before we depart."

Danvers's eyebrows rose and he started to object, but she stopped him with a nod of her head. Not three tables away, General Howsham was enjoying a plate piled quite high with ham and slices of fowl while his wife ate delicate bits of her jelly. "It seems our host has set the pattern. It would be impolite not to follow his lead." Danvers smiled and went to do his wife's bidding.

"Shall I order our carriage brought around, my love?" he asked when he had finished his repast. "You do look fatigued."

"How ungallant of you to say so. But, yes, I am ready to retire. Will you request the Master of Ceremonies to inform the others to meet us in the Entrance Hall when the quadrille is over? I don't see them here, so they must be dancing."

In a few minutes the young ladies were obedient to their summons, although all three faces clearly showed with what reluctance they had left the glittering affair. Alice was characteristically quiet on the journey home, but Beatrice babbled most of the way, barely pausing to draw breath. Only after Danvers's nieces were handed out of the carriage did Antonia have opportunity to ask Sophia about her evening.

"Oh, it was charming!" The girl answered with such enthusiasm that Tonia didn't know whether to be glad to learn that Anson's departure had not dampened her spirits, or to worry that she might have enjoyed her time with Penthurst too much. Tonia considered. Was she being unfair? Could the man be repentant of his past? Could his suit be honourable? Title, wealth, manners—few chaperones would ask for more in a partner for their charges, no matter that he was old enough to be her father.

Sophia clasped her hands, her eyes shining in the gas lanterns lighting the front of the Bedford Hotel. "If only Mama could have been here. She would have loved it so. That would have made it perfect."

Antonia couldn't have agreed more wholeheartedly.

🎋 14 🎋

A few days later, Emilia woke after a few hours' sleep to the news that, amazingly, the women and children crowded into the Bibighar had been assigned a Bengali doctor, and they were to be supplied with fresh clothes. A cook had been sent to them from the fish bazaar to prepare better meals. The children were even served a swallow or two of milk.

The next evening Emilia and Louisa were among the women Nana Sahib allowed to emerge from the Bibighar to sit in the evening air. This was a more welcome relief than even the mouthful of meat and sip of wine that had been served them at their daily meal. This was more like the behavior of the Nana Sahib who had allowed Emilia to play on his piano those few months ago that seemed like another lifetime.

"What a blessed respite." Emilia filled her lungs with the fresh air. "I wonder, why has Nana Sahib allowed this?"

"I suppose he realizes our worth as hostages," Louisa replied.

They were joined by Fanny, Caroline and Alice Linsday, nieces of Major Lindsay who, like so many young women of their age, had come to India seeking husbands. "How is your dear mama tonight?" Emilia inquired. She recalled all too vividly seeing the lady fall in the *shallow water as she was shot at Sati Chowra and her daughters' subsequent attempts to relieve their mother's suffering.*

Fanny shook her head. "The wound festers. At least the Bengali doctor has provided a clean dressing, but I fear the worst."

Alice, once the most handsome of the Lindsay daughters but now noticeably pale in the evening light, sighed. "It is all my fault. It was my urging for an upper life that brought us all to India. And now look what it has come to, Aunt Lilly dead, Uncle Willy dead, George dead..." She strangled a sob. "I don't know how I shall bear it."

Caroline took her hand. "Courage, Alice. We shall bear it. We are still alive. We shall bear witness. This will not last. I heard our sepoy guards talking of the rapid advance of Havelock's forces. The British army will revenge their dead. And we shall bear witness."

Emilia looked at these young women, only slightly older than her own daughter back in England. How many times had she thanked Providence that Sophia was in that gentle, green land, enjoying the delights of a London season. She couldn't imagine how it would increase her own anxiety to see Sophia enduring all that these young women had.

And for the first time, seeing the dreadful suffering of the little ones around her, she gave thanks that she had birthed no more children after Sophia. For so many years it had been a heartache that she and Robert had been blessed with only one.

Those few improvements to their condition were all they were to see, however. Their primary overseer was Nana's favorite concubine's serving girl, a woman with a temperament so fierce and imperious that she was known as the Begum. She had a virulent hatred for the fine English ladies who in past years had looked on her as a servant. She chased off any faithful servants who attempted to smuggle food to their ladies, and every day led some of the women prisoners off to grind gram flour from chickpeas.

These were mere pinpricks, however, compared to the infestations of lice. Women snipped off each other's hair with scissors from the embroidery kits a few had secreted in their belongings. When even the fresh clothes Nana had provided became fouled with sweat, mud, blood and worse, the women made a pathetic attempt at laundry in the small amount of water a servant brought in a single, dripping bag from the well. They hung their laundry in the thorns of the Mulsuri tree and crowded beneath the dripping fabric to shelter from the burning sun.

Then cholera struck. Borne by contaminated food and water. Victims of the disease suffered bouts of violent, watery diarrhea that led to rapid dehydration and death. In the steamy confines of their prison there was no privacy, no way to isolate the sick, no protection for those not yet infected. The bodies of the dead were dragged out by servants and thrown into the river.

Alice Lindsay was among the first to succumb. She died of cholera three days before her mama died from the infected wound in her back.

Then Louisa fell ill. After all they had been through, escaping the starvation, bullets, falling masonry, drowning and cutlass slashes that had carried off so many, this was a crushing blow to Emilia. The heat, hunger, grief, and claustrophobia closed in on her.

She dropped down beside her friend, too spent to offer any poor comfort. Instead, Louisa took Emilia's hand. "God will help us all," she murmured. Those were her last words.

Danvers entered his wife's room the next morning with a spring in his step. He took a deep breath in preparation to serenading her with a cheery "*Awake, my love and with the day*—" but the tune died on his lips.

After yesterday's exertions he was not surprised to find her still abed, but the drawn look and deep shadows under her eyes alarmed him. "Tonia, are you ill?" He crossed the room and perched on the side of her bed.

She pushed herself half upright against her padded head-board. "Do not be alarmed. I did not sleep well, that is all." She shook her head. "I had the most dreadful dream. Pray, ring for Isabella. I shall be much better after my morning tea." She smiled at the red-gold terrier who stood by her bed looking up at her. "And Tink will be far happier after his morning outing."

Danvers did as she asked, but a few minutes later when they were enjoying their morning beverages together he was still concerned. "I fear you have been over-doing severely. Sea bathing and a ball all in one day..." He took a sip of coffee. "Please, Antonia, promise me you'll have a quiet day today. Complete rest. Nurse Bevans can take care of Charlie."

"Oh, yes, Charlie will be quite happy spending the day on the beach. But Sophia, Beatrice, Alice..."

"They were chattering about visiting Hannington's today. Surely Peyden would be sufficient chaperone for visiting a department store."

Tonia smiled. "I fail to see the enticement, when they can go to Harrod's in London, but it should be an innocent enough amusement. What of you, my love? What are your plans?"

Danvers noted that she made no objection to his suggestion that she have a quiet day. He strove to hide that, though pleased, he found the fact alarming. "If you are quite certain you can do without me, I had thought of going to the races."

"Thinking of having a flutter on Penthurst's mare, are you?"

"I can assure you, I'll not be taking that fellow's advice on horses. As a matter of fact, Hardy tells me the rip in the aerostat has been repaired, and I was thinking of making an ascent to test its soundness. Viewing the races from the air should prove considerably diverting."

"Just don't frighten the horses, my love."

Charles drained his coffee cup and kissed his wife. "You're certain you'll be comfortable on your own?"

Tonia smiled. "I shall have Isabella and Tinker and Mr.

Dickens." She pointed to the latest issue of "Household Words" containing the final installment of *Little Dorrit* resting on her bedside table. "What more could I ask?"

Danvers brushed aside a red-gold curl peeping beneath Antonia's lace cap and kissed her on her forehead. He stopped in his dressing room only to pick up his hat, gloves and walking stick before going out into the midsummer morning.

Approaching the Church Street Barracks, where Hardy had assured him he had located a convenient gas main, Danvers had no difficulty spotting his man. The fully inflated red and yellow striped aerostat was tugging impatiently on its mooring ropes, surrounded by the inevitable gaggle of small boys that were always drawn to such a scene. "Can we go up fer a penny, Mister?" a red-haired lad called out.

His idea received an enthusiastic chorus of importuning seconds, but Danvers merely smiled and waved them on. "Not today, but you may watch us ascend. All ready, Hardy?" He turned to his man.

"All right and tight, m'lord. We've a good stiff breeze blowing in from the sea. Should just make the first race. Telescopes are in the gondola."

Danvers stepped over the wicker side of the basket to a repeated chorus of requests to be taken along. "I could help yer," one hopeful shouted.

Hardy jumped in and pulled free each of the three grappling hooks securing them to the ground. Their admirers waved and shouted with enthusiasm. Once over the nearest buildings the aeronauts saw the troops at the Church Street barracks drilling on the parade ground, ranks and files in scarlet tunics stepping smartly across the green field to the cadence of the drummer.

The racecourse lay a short distance to the north east. They had no trouble maneuvering the aerostat to the north in the increasing strength of the breeze from the channel, but finding a current to take them to the east was more of a problem. Hardy experimented with various flap settings, each time tossing a tissue over the side to determine the direction of the airflow. "Shall we try a mite higher, m'lord?"

Danvers agreed and Hardy emptied the sand from two of the ballast bags hanging on the outside of the gondola. He tossed out another scrap of light paper and cheered at the results as the paper floated due east. "Ah, that'll be doing first rate."

In a few minutes the long expanse of Whitehawk Hill was beneath them with the two mile racecourse stretching across the downs. It was a fine scene, a field of perhaps a dozen horses streaking across the green with the blue sea in the distance. Even from this height Danvers could hear the pounding of hooves on the sod and the cries of the crowd.

Appealing as the view was, though, it was impossible to tell which horse was which from that height. "Can we take her down to viewing level, Hardy?" The plan had been to throw out their grapnels beyond the viewing stand and watch the proceedings from their private ringside seat.

"I'll try, m'lord, but I'll not vouch for the currents. We can go down right enough, but there's no maneuvering in this draft."

Danvers gave a tug to secure his high black hat. "I do believe the winds are increasing, Hardy. Still, see what you can do. I am curious to see how Penthurst's horse performs." He held the first grappling hook ready to toss over the side when they reached the proper level. "Just a little lower, Hardy. This should catch in a few feet."

Hardy valved to allow a little more gas to escape. They sank to the level of the grandstand. Just as Danvers was ready to throw out the anchor, however, the airflow shifted and a strong wind bore them upward again. "She's a stubborn one today, m'lord. Are you wanting me to deflate the aerostat? I'm thinking it's the only way we'll get her to stay down if you're wanting to visit the race."

Danvers looked at the billows of white clouds racing over the downs in the pellucid blue sky. "Never mind, Hardy. I think I'd far rather enjoy our ascent."

"Right you are." Hardy was obviously pleased with the decision. He gave up attempts to navigate and let the aerostat float over the South Downs at the will of the wind.

A short time later, Danvers shifted his gaze from the sky to the ground beneath them. "Hardy, get out our maps. What is that distinctive v-shaped valley below us?" He pointed to a yawning, abrupt gash in the smooth slope of the Downs. The deep ravine with its steeply sloping sides appeared to have been cut with precision and covered with smooth turf. In all his aerostat journeys over England he had never seen anything quite like it.

Hardy opened his instrument box, unfolded the map, took a reading on his compass to determine their direction, and peered through a sextant to measure the altitude of the sun. He quickly calculated their latitude and pointed to their precise location on the map. "Devil's Dyke, that is, m'lord."

"Hardy, you are a sore loss to the Royal Navy,"

Hardy glowed at his lord's compliment. "True, but I'd not be fancying a life at sea."

"And do you happen to have any knowledge of just what the Devil's Dyke is?"

"Well, m'lord, I've heard tell that it was dug by the devil so as to allow the sea to rush in to submerge the churches of the Weald."

Danvers observed the remarkable formation below them. "If that was his plan, he wasn't much of the engineer. The dyke seems to be entirely closed at both ends."

"Well, the histories do depart at that point, m'lord. As to

whether a rooster crowed, or an old woman, disturbed by the digging, lit a candle, or whether the devil stubbed his toe on a rock, is a matter of debate."

"Hardy, you are priceless." The high point of the Downs above the dyke was crowned by a low white structure with smoke curling from the chimney. It appeared to be some sort of hostel or inn, as several carriages were parked around it. A paddock behind contained a number of horses. "Hardy, set us down there. It seems to be a hostelry where we can refresh ourselves and hire transport back to Brighton."

Hardy began valving to release the gas and the aerostat sank to earth. "Well done, Hardy. Hardly a bump." And Danvers saw that he had been right in believing the building to be a hostelry. *Devil's Dyke Hotel*, the sign over the door read, and under that, *host, Wm. Thacker*. "Secure the aerostat then come in for refreshment, Hardy." Danvers turned toward the door. "Oh, and speak to the ostler about hiring a cart or some conveyance. Failing that, obtain shelter for the aerostat in a shed and engage his best saddle horses."

The public room was occupied by three or four convivial groups, apparently out on a holiday. The host approached Danvers bowing deeply, a single glance having obviously informed him that a member of the upper orders was to be among his patrons. "Welcome to our establishment, my lord. I deeply regret that our humble hostel has only one private parlor, and it is occupied at the moment. May I hope to offer you a table in the corner? As you see, it is quite secluded."

"That will do very well." Danvers inclined his head.

The host led the way across the room to a pleasant table near a leaded window looking across the Downs and wiped the table vigorously with the towel he carried over his arm. "The chops are very good, my lord. And my wife's apple tart with fresh cream is said to be the best in Sussex."

Danvers agreed to the offered fare and ordered a glass of

the house ale as well. The landlord was quick to serve his aristocratic guest with the best in the house. "I hope that will please you, my lord." He set the tall glass of amber liquid before his guest. "If I do say so myself, Prince Albert found it most acceptable. 'Full-bodied and fruity,' he pronounced it."

Danvers's eyebrows shot up questioningly.

"Oh, aye, His Majesty were here. Not as we were supposed to know. But of course, I recognized him." The host tapped the side of his nose knowingly with his forefinger. "Incognito, he was. With only two companions. Very interested in wonders of all kinds as our good prince is, he naturally wanted to see our geographical marvel. Came by horseback. Very affable gentlemen.

"Of course, King William and Queen Adelaide had been here—before my time, that was—and our good Queen Victoria herself before she married. Well, not to our humble inn, you understand, but to the dyke."

Danvers was suitably impressed with the royal pedigree of the area, but was wishing his garrulous host would allow him to savor his chops and tart in peace, when Thacker added, "And two summers ago we had an Indian prince. Very grand he was."

Now Danvers was all attention. "Azimoolah Khan?"

The host slapped his thigh. "That's the one! Are you for knowing him?"

"Only by reputation."

"Oh, very grand I can assure you. Stayed here upward of a fortnight. And his manners and dress—better than most Englishmen—saving yourself, of course, my lord. Came here with a group of friends—out racing on the Downs every day, they were." Encouraged by Danvers's rapt attention Thacker expanded on his information. "If your lordship will pardon my saying so, the young ladies seemed much enraptured, but it's not for me to be commenting."

He would likely have said more, but a guest at another table snapped his fingers, demanding mine host's attention. Thacker departed with a bow, leaving Danvers deep in thought. When Hardy entered a few minutes later he reported success in securing the hire of a conveyance for themselves and the deflated aerostat. "It's not what you'd be calling a fine carriage, m'lord, but it's sound, with plenty of room for the aerostat."

"That's fine, Hardy, but I have another task for you first. The good lady of the house, one Mrs. Thacker, is something of a prodigy with her apple tart. Be certain to order some with your pie and beer, then contrive to sweet-talk her on the pretense of—well, you'll know best what pretense. The thing is, Thacker himself just told me that Azimoolah Khan spent some time as a guest of this establishment and entertained ladies here. It seems just possible there could be a connection to that poor Hindoo fellow who died under the wheels of our carriage."

Hardy turned to his task with a twinkle of delight in his eyes. Danvers noted him a short time later seated at the bar, chatting to a rosy, stout woman in a ruffled mob cap and copious apron. Danvers allowed Thacker to bring him another glass of his excellent ale, as he judged the matter could require some time.

Slow though Danvers was in sipping his libation, Hardy was still deep in conversation when Danvers had emptied more than half his glass. He hoped his man was gathering information worth his spending the better part of so beautiful an afternoon sitting in a remote country inn. He was thinking of going out for a walk when a door at the back of the room opened and two rather roughly-dressed men exited the private parlor with a third behind them.

Danvers turned so sharply he all but knocked his ale over. What the devil was Lord Penthurst doing at what appeared to be a clandestine meeting in this obscure place? Especially when he had a horse running in Brighton?

"Penthurst!" Danvers was on his feet and striding across the floor before he thought what he was about. "Penthurst. What are you doing here?"

The duke blanched, but recovered quickly. "Danvers. I could ask the same of you. Out of the way place, eh?"

Danvers scowled. "I trust you didn't come here for the excellence of Mrs. Thacker's apple tart. Especially when you have a highly favored horse running today."

"I hope you took my advice and backed her. Pretty little runner, she is."

"I find it extremely odd that you would be here rather than at the racecourse." Danvers's voice was hard. He would not be sidetracked.

"Should I be flattered that you take so much interest in my affairs?" Penthurst's voice stopped just short of the insolent.

Danvers realized there was little to be gained from this ill-thought-out confrontation. "I can assure you, flattery was not my intention." He bowed. "Allow me to wish you a good day, sir." He turned on his heel and strode to the bar. "If you have finished your repast, Hardy."

The condition of the farm cart and the bone-shaking jolting of its iron wheels over the rutted road did little to improve Danvers's humor as Hardy drove the plodding pair along the well-worn way across the Downs back toward Brighton. "Well, Hardy, I hope to goodness you learned something of value."

"Most interesting, I assure you, most interesting. Apparent it is that our host's wife found Azimoolah as romantic as a good number of English females seem to have. A lucky thing for us, because she paid a great deal of attention to his doings."

DONNA FLETCHER CROW

"Do tell, man." Danvers felt the ire Penthurst's oily demeanor had raised in him begin to wear off.

"I heard my fill of what a fine gentleman he was, how nice his manners, how finicking his demands for fresh laundry, clean linen, hot water—who would have thought a heathen would worry so much about bathing?"

Danvers forbore to remark that there were some who didn't expect fastidious hygiene from the Irish. "Yes, yes, I'm not interested in his personal habits—however nice they may have been. What about his activities?"

"Very fond of the ladies, our Musselman was. Entertained rather a bevy—not that Mrs. Thacker approved of such goings on in her establishment. 'Respectable, we are.' She must have said it half a dozen times. But I noticed she didn't put a stop to any goings-on.

"I'm by way of thinking she enjoyed it for the eavesdropping. Not shy about telling me all she knew. The young ladies would ride out from Brighton and canter over the Downs with the Khan. 'A pretty scene,' Mrs. Thacker was calling it."

"Anyone in particular?" Danvers inquired.

"One, it seems. Apparently their cantering continued indoors where Mrs. T could overhear. 'Mon cher Goody' the young lady called him. Rode out often, it seems. Only she left her groom outside, if you take my meaning. Mrs. T heard Azimoolah telling his 'catch crumb' how he would introduce her to his master in India, but she must keep quiet about it for the moment. The girl pledged she wouldn't even 'tell her father confessor.' What a load of rubbish, I say."

"Rubbish, indeed, Hardy. I don't suppose the garrulous Mrs. Thacker managed to discover the young lady's name?"

"Apparently Azimoolah addressed her as 'my charming Miss A.'"

The cart jolted over a particularly deep rut. When the

creaking conveyance had settled, Danvers asked, "Anything else?"

"Letters. Mrs. T said he wrote reams of letters."

"To young ladies? Planning rendezvous?"

Hardy shook his head. "To his boss in India. That Nana Sahib I've heard talked about. Fat letters, like he was reporting something important. Or making plans."

"What sort of plans?"

"She didn't read the letters. Written in a 'nasty foreign tongue,' she said."

Danvers smiled. "I take it she would have been happy to read them had they been accessible to her. Pity. That might have been most instructive. Azimoolah was supposed to be in London presenting his master's case for inheriting his kingdom from his adoptive father—speaking to Parliament and the East India Company, not swanning about the South Downs with a harem."

"And there was one thing more, but I'm not knowing what to make of it—"

"Well, out with it, man."

"When you confronted Penthurst Mrs. Thacker looked up and was by the way of mentioning that that gentleman was often among Azimoolah's party."

Danvers was silent the rest of the journey back to Brighton. Whatever Nana Sahib's emissary had been about in London and at the Devil's Dyke, it was clear Danvers needed to know more about his mission. Surely seducing susceptible Englishwomen wasn't part of the official plan. So what other sidelines might the enterprising young man have got up to? And what could the Duke of Penthurst have had to do with it?

15

When Danvers arrived back at the Bedford, however, thoughts of untangling such intrigues fled from his mind as Antonia came to him in distress. "Oh, Charles, thank goodness you are come."

"What is it my love? Do you feel worse?"

"No, no, not at all. I've had a most pleasant day. That is, I did until Beatrice came to me in hysterics. Alice is quieter, but I'm persuaded her grief is more deeply felt. It's Sophia I'm most worried about. She is in an anguish of concern for her mother's safety, and her friends' unhappiness is making it all the worse."

Danvers issued a brief prayer of thanksgiving that Charlie was a boy. Perhaps he was wrong to be so desirous that the next one be female. He took Antonia's hands and led her to the settee. "Tell me, what is the source of all this anguish?" "The regiment is to embark tomorrow morning—"

"Oh, is that all? I thought it was a well-known fact their departure was impending. Why the sudden dismay?"

"But the thing is, someone left a copy of the 'Brighton Gazette' where one of the girls picked it up and read out the article about India. I can't help but believe they are right to be anxious—however inappropriate it might be for them to know about it. Perhaps we have done wrong to conceal the facts from Sophia... but, then, the trouble is, we don't know the facts."

Danvers took a deep breath. "Where are they? I'll try to talk some sense to them."

"Thank you, Charles. That is exactly what is needed. They are in their room. Isabella is tending to them with vinaigrette and rose water compresses. I sent Peyden to bed before she swooned."

Charles could only issue another thanksgiving that they were to return to London tomorrow. The sooner he could deliver his nieces to his sister and Sophia to the dowager duchess the better. He knocked more loudly than he intended on the door of the young ladies' room, but when he saw Sophia's wide, red-rimmed eyes in her drawn face, the rebuke about nonsensical vapors he had intended to issue died unspoken.

"Lady Danvers tells me you young ladies have encountered an unfortunate piece of journalism. Reading newspapers is an office for your fathers and older brothers. I shall, however, forego delivering a homily on the inappropriateness of young women undertaking such an enterprise. If you will be so good as to show me the offending article I shall endeavor to enlighten you on the truth behind its contents. And I hope to goodness that in future you seek proper counsel when you are in need of such information."

Sophia pointed to the table by the window, littered with the crumpled, tearstained pages of the latest issue of the "Brighton Gazette." "I had read such before, and Lady Danvers assured me all would be well, but this sounds as if it is getting worse and worse."

His eyes skimmed over the article: *Terrible mutiny of the*

troops... banks and treasury plundered... European inhabitants brutally massacred. Little question there was plenty to send a tender female into a fit of hysterics.

"'Wildest excesses,' it says, 'every English man, woman and child piteously massacred.'" Sophia spoke almost under her breath. It was plain she not only read the article in detail, but had also committed portions to memory. And worse, she was now reliving the scenes the words conjured in the mind of the reader. Alice gave a hiccough, sniffed and dabbed at her eyes. Beatrice hid her face in a sodden hanky.

Nothing to do but to meet the matter head-on. "You are quite right, the report is most serious." His words were met with a wail from Beatrice, causing him to raise his voice to a sterner note. "However, it seems that your governess was most remiss in her schoolroom geography lessons. Let me assure you that Meerut and Delhi—to which this article refers—are a great distance from Cawnpore where your mother is, Sophia. India is a vast continent, several times the size of England. If Cawnpore were London, it would be as if the events were in Germany."

Sophia raised hopeful eyes to him as though seeking more such comfort.

"Let me draw your attention to the final paragraph of the article." He rustled the paper to draw attention to his words. "The insurrection may be said to be confined within the walls of Delhi. Within these walls it will be—very possibly has already been—beaten down and trodden out."

He skipped to the final sentence. "Before many days are past, we may expect to hear that retribution, as merited, has been dealt to the insurgent soldiery."

Danvers crumpled the paper and thrust in in the bin. "There now, I do hope that has put paid to your vapors. I would also remind you of the time it takes for news to travel over such great distances as exist between England and India.

The events referred to in this story occurred two months ago and have, no doubt, been dealt with by the English Army weeks ago."

Sophia managed a smile, but the reference to the great distance to India brought renewed sobs from the others. Alice was the first to recover. She held her head up as if she had reached a determination. "I am certain you are quite right, Lord Danvers. I thank you for your good sense and for the geography lesson. The regiment is to depart from the Brighton Station tomorrow at noon. May we see them off?"

Danvers sighed. So much for his plans to depart for London tomorrow morning. Still, he was greatly relieved at what seemed like a reasonable request. Certainly worth a delay to restore equanimity. He granted the entreaty with alacrity then departed before any more difficulty could be raised. He had had quite enough aggravation for one day.

Indeed, there were no more alarms until their party gathered at the appointed hour for dinner in the anteroom of the Bedford's Palm Court to await escort to their table. Sophia and Beatrice arrived properly gowned, with little trace of red about their eyes. Apparently Peyden had recovered sufficiently to bathe her charges' eyes with cucumber water or whatever it was that Isabella used for lady Danvers in times of distress.

When Alice failed to make her entrance, however, Danvers frowned. "Your sister was not well enough to come to dinner?" he asked Bea.

"Oh, she is quite recovered, Uncle. Your clear explanation of matters was a tonic for her. She left shortly after you departed to do some shopping."

"Shopping?" Tonia asked. "But surely the shops are closed by this hour. Why has she not returned? And who bore her company? Was Peyden not needed for your dinner toilette? Surely Alice didn't go unaccompanied?" The scandal that could attach to such a situation rang in Tonia's voice.

"No, not at all. She was accompanied by Captain Bellingham."

Tonia's voice rose a pitch. "Alone?"

Before any further explanation could be made Alice appeared between the twin palms marking the entrance to the room. Her eyes were glowing and her flower-bedecked hat was just the least bit askew. "Where is your escort?" Danvers demanded in a voice that clearly said he would have words with the captain.

"Oh, I insisted he only see me to the door. He was due back at the barracks."

"What do you mean, I should like to know, by such behavior?"

Tonia held up a hand to silence her husband. "That can wait. Our seating is ready. Alice, go make yourself presentable and join us as soon as possible. There is no need to add fuel to the gossip your behavior is likely to incur." Several matrons' eyes were turned disapprovingly on them.

Tonia met the stares with a smile and nudged her husband. "Bow to Lady Markham, Charles," she said behind her fan.

Considerably later, with dinner concluded and the alarms of the day behind them, Danvers and Tonia relaxed in their sitting room and he regaled her with his adventures in the aerostat.

When he recounted the scene in the Devil's Dyke Hotel and Hardy's report from Mrs. Thacker Antonia became thoughtful. "Wait, Charles. What was that again?"

"Azimoolah and his friends rode regularly on

the downs—"

"No about his lady friends. A Miss A—who called him 'Mon cher Goody'?" She jerked forward in her seat and clasped her husband's hand. "Charles! It's Miss Anson. She got all teary-eyed when I mentioned India and she said something about 'Mon Cher...'"

She paused for another thought. "And she was just reentering society after a lengthy illness... What if it was something worse than an illness—something...," she gulped, "disreputable?"

Charles frowned. "Are you suggesting that Lieutenant Anson's sister was Azimoolah Khan's lover?"

"I'm very much afraid that I am, Charles. And that the results were disastrous."

Danvers nodded his head slowly. "So disastrous that her brother felt honour-bound to avenge her?"

"But Khan was back in India, so he took his anger out on an Indian who happened to be in London?" Tonia put her hands over her face. "Oh, it sounds preposterous when I say it like that. And yet, Annabelle Anson could certainly be Miss A, and she was most distressed."

Danvers considered, then gave a brief nod. "It is certainly possible. More than possible." His voice rose with each sentence. "I believe we may have just solved a murder. I shall inform Futter the moment we return to London."

"But that will be too late. The regiment leaves tomorrow. Anson will be gone."

Composing a message containing the facts of their discovery in concise enough a manner to send in a telegram was no simple task, but at last Danvers managed it and dispatched Hardy to the telegraph office. Satisfied that all was now in the hands of Scotland Yard, Danvers could sleep with as clear a mind as he had known since Faquir Johal fell dead under the wheels of the Danvers carriage.

❧ 16 ❧

The next morning Danvers woke with the same light spirit with which he had gone to sleep. He had to curb his desire to burst into song, however, because the bustle of getting their assorted party to Trafalgar Street allowed no time for serenading. The regiment was to march from the barracks to the station where they would board the train to Portsmouth and from there set sail for India. Danvers could only hope that whatever action Futter chose to take, here or in Portsmouth, wouldn't cause a disruption—to the army or to their own plans.

For the moment, though, the spectacle around him claimed his attention. Charlie was equipped with a small Union flag on a stick which caused Tinker to bark and jump at it with every patriotic flutter. The young ladies clasped white hankies to wave, as did many of the other ladies crowding the way. Beatrice was all agitation, insistent that they must secure places to provide a clear view of the line of march, while Alice seemed unusually quiet. At last they secured an acceptable position.

Trafalgar Street was an area of dense housing, the buildings on either side of the street rising several stories. The population was well accustomed to such spectacles in their street and gathered quickly when the sound of drums and pipes alerted them to the approaching parade. A young mother brought her considerable brood from a nearby house along with a baby in her arms. A number of children emerged from a first floor window to sit on a makeshift balcony apparently erected for just such a purpose. Washing hanging from building to building across the street fluttered in the breeze like bunting.

"Oh, here they come!" Beatrice squealed. With a skirl of pipes the parade turned the corner from St. George's Place into Trafalgar Street. When Danvers boosted Charlie to his shoulder the child waved his flag with vigor at the sight of the pipers with fierce red moustaches, swinging kilts, and ribbons fluttering from pipes and bonnets.

Next came the regimental ensign flying bravely from its standard with General Howsham riding proudly on a large bay horse. The regiment marched behind, four abreast. The tramp of boots on cobbles kept time with the drummers. The entire scene created an exhilarating, dizzying effect.

The pipers were almost even with the Danvers party when an inebriated man from one of the beer houses along the street rolled up his pants to resemble a kilt and joined in behind them in an unsteady jig. A young boy darted into the street and ducked down to peer under the kilt of the lead piper. He was pulled back sharply by his sister. At the back of the crowd a tall, bearded man in a stovepipe hat swept the throng with eagle eyes. Danvers was pleased that the local police were on the watch for the pickpockets that were certain to infest such a mass of humanity.

Sophia, Alice and Beatrice bounced on their tiptoes and

craned their necks. Beatrice cried more than once, "Oh, there he is! Lieutenant Anson!" Only to lower her waving arm with a sigh. "No, it wasn't him. Oh, why is it so hard to spot anyone? I swear, they all look alike."

Sophia managed to locate two of the officers she had danced with at the ball, but Alice remained the quietest. When Captain Bellingham marched by, so perfectly upright with his rifle over his left shoulder, his eyes fixed straight ahead, she kissed her fingers before fluttering them at him and then placing her hand over her heart.

When the parade had passed she turned to Danvers. "Please, uncle, may we go to the station to see them depart?"

Impressed by her controlled composure, he agreed. Hardy would be only a few streets behind them, waiting with the carriage at St. Peter's Church. They could drive down Gloucester Road and get to the station before the regiment arrived.

If Danvers had thought to escape the jostling crowds at the station, however, he quickly discovered his mistake. Even before the skirl of the pipes and beat of the drums told him the parade approached, the platform thronged with people scrambling for a view of the brave soldiers going out to the ends of the Empire for Queen and Country. From the eager faces and cheers beginning to rise, it was evident that favorable relationships existed between the military and the local community. Especially the female members of the community.

The maidens of the Danvers party were not the only teary young women on the platform. Danvers noted as well many women, a number of them with young children, carrying carpetbags and valises. Apparently wives and families of officers who would be following the drum with their husbands and fathers. He couldn't help but admire their brave smiles and stalwart bearing. Surely this was the backbone of the great British Empire.

It seemed that everything happened at once: Several baggage wagons, loaded high with luggage and heavy-looking crates that must have contained rifles and ammunition, arrived at the station from Queen's Road to the south, just as the parade marched in on Trafalgar Street from the east, and the train, Union flags flying from her engine, steamed up to the platform.

All semblance of military precision was abandoned as the parade broke ranks, the officers to find their families and either escort them onto the train or to bid a fond, poignant farewell. Young women threw themselves tearfully into the arms of troopers, then saw them to the carriages where the leave-taking could continue through the windows. Farther down the track the wagons were being unloaded and their mountains of gear stowed in the baggage cars.

Sophia stood wide-eyed, undoubtedly recalling her own experience seeing her mother off just a few months earlier. Danvers did hope the scene wouldn't trigger a renewal of her earlier fears, but her gaze seemed to be more one of pride.

"Oh, there's Lieutenant Anson! Come, I must bid him farewell!" Bea grabbed her sister's hand and tugged her further down the platform.

Danvers frowned. Did Futter not react to his telegram? Or were they planning to meet the train at Portsmouth? Surely the police wouldn't let a murderer go out to India? He started to suggest to Tonia that they should follow his nieces, but at that moment the drum and pipe corps, who would not be embarking, began a lively rendition of "Rule Britannia" at the other end of the platform and Charlie broke free from his mother's hold and darted in their direction. He was quickly caught, but by then Beatrice and Alice had disappeared in the throng.

It was little short of miraculous how quickly the confusion of the platform sorted itself out. The luggage carts emptied, then turned back toward the barracks. At barked orders from their commanders any regimental stragglers received a parting farewell and jumped aboard the train. It was amazing that, even with all the regiment on the train, the platform seemed more crowded than before, if that were possible. Perhaps more of the townspeople had arrived in time to wave the train away. The engineer released a cloud of steam, enveloping those on the platform and drawing delighted squeals from Charlie and many of the other children. The mighty iron wheels ground on the rails and the train rolled forward. The band played "The British Grenadiers," the crowd on the platform cheered, and the engineer gave three earsplitting blasts of the train's whistle. The train disappeared down the track.

With that, a profound silence descended. Viewers who moments before had been cheering or sobbing now turned, as if in formation, and filed from the platform. The pipers and drummers retreated to the barracks, their instruments silent.

Danvers couldn't say he was sorry to see them go. Whatever action the police chose to take or not to take was out of his hands. And the fact that their lives would now include fewer upsets from young ladies enamored of gentlemen in red tunics could only be for the good. "Let us collect our charges and return to the carriage as speedily as we can. The traffic is certain to be intolerable." Danvers's mind was already racing ahead to tomorrow. He would see their party to the train, then enjoy a leisurely, quiet ascent in the aerostat. He could picture in his mind the pleasant green fields slipping away far below, leaving all frantic, emotional scenes behind him.

His vision of floating placidly above a peaceful landscape under a cloudless blue sky, however, was interrupted by Beatrice's return from the far end of the platform. Alone.

"Where is Alice?" Antonia was the first to ask.

"I—I don't know. She's—she's gone!"

"Gone? What do you mean, gone?" Tonia demanded.

"Gone? Where?" Sophia echoed.

"I thought I saw Lieutenant Anson, but then it wasn't him, and I insisted on looking in every window. And when I turned back..." Beatrice shook her head and choked on a sob.

Danvers turned without a word and strode to the end of the rapidly clearing platform. He had had more than his fill of Beatrice's histrionics. The girl had undoubtedly lost sight of her sister in the crowd and imagined her vanished. He would find Alice looking perplexed in the thinning company, wondering where her sister had vanished to.

Danvers scrutinized those remaining around the station, especially the few clumps of females lamenting together the departure of their young men. But nowhere did he see Alice's soft brown hair tucked under a bonnet with blue ribbons.

Tonia, with Charlie in tow, Sophia and Beatrice following close behind, met him halfway back up the platform. "No sight of her," he said.

"She must have become separated from you in in the melee and gone back to the carriage," Tonia said, thrusting a dry hanky into Beatrice's hand. "We'll doubtless find her waiting with Hardy, wondering what's keeping us."

"Yes, of course, that's it. How foolish you must think me." Bea sniffed and turned toward the church.

When they arrived, however, Hardy was alone, waiting on the driver's box of the carriage.

"I suppose the silly girl summoned a hansom to take her back to the Bedford," Danvers said, before Beatrice could enact another Cheltenham tragedy, and handed the reduced party into the carriage.

At the hotel Tonia delivered an overexcited Charlie and Tinker to Nurse Bevans's care, then joined Danvers who had checked their suite without success. They were walking down the hall toward the young ladies' suite when the door burst open and Beatrice came flying out waving a sheet of heavy writing paper embossed with the Bedford crest.

Danvers caught her just before she hit the floor in a swoon.

❧ 17 ❧

"**M**arried?" Tonia read the missive for the third time. Peyden held a vinaigrette under the prone figure Danvers had deposited on the aptly named fainting couch in the young ladies' room, while Sophia put drops of lavender essence on Beatrice's wrists.

"How is that possible?" Danvers asked.

Tonia shook her head in wonder, then held out the sheet of stationery that had fallen from Beatrice's fingers, but Danvers did not take it, so she explained. "Yesterday afternoon, by special license. Alice writes that Captain Bellingham had obtained it some time ago from the Bishop of London with whom he has family connections. They had hoped not to use it, but your brother-in-law being in Scotland made it impossible for the captain to speak to Beatrice's father in the normal way. When the departure of the regiment became certain, they felt there was no alternative—either Alice went out to India then, or they would be separated for months. More likely years."

"Surely Agatha—" Danvers began.

"Would have refused. You know very well your sister had

much higher things in mind for her daughters," Tonia reminded him.

"But why elope? The match was entirely eligible—no matter what Agatha may have thought. Surely Alice could have talked her around. The girl could certainly have persuaded her father."

"I think that's what they were hoping, but time ran out on them. And they didn't actually elope. They were married by the vicar of St. Nicholas's Church next to the barracks with Lieutenant Anson and General Howsham's daughter Suzanne in attendance." Tonia looked up from Alice's letter. "I met her at the ball. A most sensible young lady, I thought. She will make an excellent companion for Alice in India."

Danvers's forehead furrowed. "You don't mean to say you approve of this hole-and-corner affair?"

Tonia sighed. "It is decidedly not what I would have chosen for her. But I can't help feeling they will deal very well together."

"But why didn't she tell us? Her mother should have been notified—"

"That is precisely why, love. She says she knew you would try to stop her." Tonia held the paper out for her husband to read for himself.

At the end he could only shake his head once more. "Ramshackle. I can't begin to think what Aunt Aelfrida will say."

Tonia considered. "I somehow suspect she will be pleased for Alice. As, the more I think about it, I am as well."

"So you don't think I should hire a horse and ride hell for leather to Portsmouth, storm the ship and drag her off?"

Tonia laughed. "What a romantic picture you present. But the distance is near-to fifty miles, is it not? And the ship is certain to sail with the morning tide. It does seem somewhat impractical." Tonia smiled at the look of relief in her husband's eyes.

Still, he shook his head. "What I'll say to my sister I can't imagine."

Before they could explore that grim prospect further, however, a tap at the door announced the Honourable Charles Frederick looking thoroughly refreshed with Tinker bouncing at his heels. "Beach!" He held out his sand pail.

"My lady, I do apologize for the interruption," Bevans, entering behind him, said, "but Master Charles is most insistent, and I didn't like to take him without your approval."

"What an excellent idea!" Tonia sprang to her feet. "A good, stiff sea breeze is just what we all need to rejuvenate us." She turned to the languishing Beatrice. "Come. A good, deep breath of fresh air is what you need."

There were few strollers on the beach so late in the afternoon. Most visitors to Brighton were still dawdling over a late afternoon tea or in their rooms dressing for dinner. Although the sun had not yet set, the sky was showing streaks of pink to the west and gaslights were being lit along Marine Parade and on the pier. Tonia suggested they satisfy themselves with the easier walking of the Marine Parade and merely enjoy looking at the beach below.

The suggestion was endorsed by her husband, but their son prepared to make his wishes known by drawing breath for a full-lunged, two-year-old howl. Antonia felt that being required to tread on pebbles would be far preferable to enduring more theatrics. Besides, Tinker had spotted seagulls on the beach and was already bounding down the stone stairway to the seafront.

Tonia put her hand on her husband's arm and waved the more energetic members of their party onward. Nurse Bevans could very well keep up with Charlie and Tinker. She and Charles would enjoy a more leisurely pre-sunset stroll.

"Oh, can we not go out on the pier?" Sophia looked longingly at the strings of fluttering pennants and swinging loops of Chinese lanterns enticing visitors to the attraction some distance down the beach from them.

"Perhaps later," was the best Antonia could promise. "It will be Charlie's bedtime soon." For now, Tonia was savoring the peaceful rhythm of the gentle, white-fringed waves lapping the shore and the soft crunch of shingle under their desultory footsteps. An occasional seagull squawk or sharp yap from Tinker merely punctuated the calm of the scene. All the entertainers and hawkers had folded their booths and gone for the evening. Only a few other strollers wandered along the surf some way ahead of them, silhouetted against the silver sea and pink sky.

When they drew near the pier a few notes of a tin horn floated out to them, followed by a clash of cymbals and bang of a drum. Tinker gave a series of barks and bounded away from the commotion. "Tink!" Tonia called. "It's only a one man band warming up."

The enterprising musician, who would hope to attract visitors converging on the pier after dinner, continued his clatter over their heads, but Tinker raced on toward the beams forming the support structure of the pier. Surf swirled around the sturdy poles extending into the sea just at the shoreline, and a flock of seagulls were feeding at its base— undoubtedly what had attracted the terrier, rather than the entertainer above their heads.

Charlie broke free from his nurse's hand and darted after Tinker. "Don't let him get his feet wet, Sara," Tonia called. "He'll take a chill."

Bevans caught up with her charge just before the surf could dampen his sandals. "Come away, now, Master Charlie.

That's nothing but a nasty bag of rags. The seagulls are welcome to it."

"Come on, Tink!" Charlie was obedient to his nurse's tugging, but the terrier stood firm, his barks and growls becoming more insistent.

Danvers's attention turned to the scene at the substructure of the pier. Tonia felt him stiffen and his arm jerk. "Bevans, take Charlie back to the hotel. Now." His voice left room for no argument. "And Sophia and Beatrice."

Sophia started to turn, but the command came too late for Beatrice who was walking closer to the shore. Her scream shattered what little was left of the peace of the evening.

"Beatrice!" Tonia started toward the commotion at the base of the support trusses. She felt Danvers's hand restraining her, but the light of the long twilight had shown her that it was no mere bag of rags causing Tinker's insistent clamor.

Beatrice bent down and scooped a handful of pebbles which she began throwing at the persistent seagulls. "Get away, you nasty creatures! Leave him alone!" The birds fled and Tinker backed off.

A swirl of surf receded and Tonia saw. "Lieutenant Anson!"

She turned toward Beatrice, certain the scene would bring on more hysteria, if not worse. Strangely, though, the girl's reaction to the terrible sight was anger. She lobbed another stone at a departing gull, then turned to the figure in the water. "Oh, just see what those horrid birds did to his face! Get him out before he drowns!"

Sophia reached Beatrice first. Tonia took both young women firmly by the arm and turned them away from the scene while Danvers saw to the body caught in the timbers of the truss. "Hush, Beatrice. It's too late."

Now the girl's anger dissolved into tears. "No. No, no."

Tonia hugged Beatrice and made soothing sounds, but over the girl's shoulder she watched Danvers pull the body from the water to the edge of the shingle. He removed his coat to place over the sad form and hailed two young men walking along the beach from the direction of the town. When the lads turned and took off at a purposeful run, she knew the police would soon be there.

"Beatrice." She held the girl at arms' length and shook her shoulders gently. "Bea, pull yourself together. I know this is a terrible shock, but Lord Danvers has summoned help. You'll need to tell us what you know. How was the Lieutenant when you saw him at the station? Did you see him actually depart on the train?"

Beatrice gave a ragged sniff, followed by a shudder of her whole body that told Tonia the girl was making an effort. "That's it, Bea, a nice deep breath. You can do this," Tonia encouraged her.

Beatrice shook her head. "I didn't see him at the station. I kept thinking I did. But the uniforms were all alike. I did see Lieutenant Vickars that I danced with and asked him. He said he was sure to be around somewhere." She sniffed. "I searched and searched, but there were so many people, and then all the steam and the noise. And I so wanted to give him my hanky. I sat up half the night embroidering my initials on it—so he wouldn't forget me... But I couldn't find him." The silent tears that spilled from her eyes and trickled down her cheek were far more affecting than her earlier, noisier demonstrations.

"And you, Sophia? You didn't see him, either?"

Sophia shook her head.

Both girls were shivering now, either from shock or the cooling evening air. "Wait. One minute." Antonia crunched across the pebbles to Charles. "What a terrible thing. I know you'll need to stay here until the police arrive. I'll take the girls to the hotel."

"Yes, that's best." He placed his hand on her arm. "Tonia, are you all right? You must take care." His eyes moved from her face to her abdomen.

She smiled. The warmth of his hand felt so good. "I'm fine, my love. I expect the police will want to speak to us later. I'll endeavor to have everyone calm for them."

Her words to her husband were brave, but as Antonia guided her charges back up the beach she could only wonder that one day could contain so many alarms. The familiar phrase from morning prayers came to her, *Preserve us with your mighty power that we might not be overcome by adversity*. If she were honest, she would have to admit that she was very near to being overcome.

A short time later, though, the restorative effects of Isabella's ministrations began to work, as, Antonia was confident, did Peyden's on Sophia and Bea. Tonia was more than happy to submit to her maid's insistence on a warm bath infused with oil of chamomile. "I do wish, my lady, I had a tincture of poppy oil for you. I was just reading in 'The Lady's Magazine'—the effects are most beneficial. It is so simple, merely grind a pound of poppy seeds and steep them for one hour. Most beneficial and safe even for infants. My lady would sleep for hours."

Tonia thought of the poor souls she had glimpsed on the pavement outside the opium den at the London Docks. "No thank you, Isabella. I shall do very well with a chamomile tea to accompany your bath infusion. Cook can keep her poppy seeds for her excellent cake."

"Shall I order your dinner served in your room, my lady?"

"Yes, please, Isabella. And for the young ladies as well.

Lord Danvers will join us as soon as he can." She did not want to recount the scene on the beach and she knew Isabella would not pry—no matter how curious she might be about the state of the ladies returning from a simple stroll by the sea.

Isabella had just finished restoring her lady's coiffeur and adorning it with a simple black velvet frill for the evening when the sound of male voices in the parlor told Tonia that Danvers had returned with the expected caller. Isabella was quick to assume her protective role. "I shall tell them you are not receiving, my lady."

"Certainly not, Isabella. I shall join Lord Danvers and his guest. Please be so good as to ask Sophia and Beatrice to join us as soon as they are able." And she hoped to goodness her charges could give some sensible answers without dissolving in tears. Tonia smoothed the skirt of her royal blue gown, held her head up, and entered the parlor.

Danvers came across the room to meet her. "Antonia, may I present Mister George White, Chief Constable of the Brighton Police."

The stout man with neatly trimmed side-whiskers, holding his black top hat in the curve of his arm, acknowledged the introduction. "I am sorry to intrude, Lady Danvers. His lordship has been most helpful in this dreadful matter. I understand you have some acquaintance with the—er, victim?"

"Won't you sit down, Chief Constable?" Tonia chose the settee for herself and made room for Charles. The policeman perched on the edge of a straight chair. "We knew Lieutenant Anson socially in London. I have asked that the young ladies in our charge who knew him better—in the normal course of social events, you understand—to join us. I don't know how much help they can be, though." She told him about Beatrice's unsuccessful search for the lieutenant at the station.

When Sophia and Beatrice entered a few minutes later, they were unable to add much to Tonia's account.

"When did you see him last?" Chief Constable George White removed a small notebook from his pocket and licked the end of his pencil.

"Monday. At the regimental ball—at the Pavilion." The young ladies gave a somewhat disjointed account of the social activities of the past days in Brighton.

"And how did the lieutenant seem? Within himself, that is. Was he in spirits?"

"He was always in spirits," Beatrice began, then choked.

"Did he give any indication that he was unhappy in the regiment? That he didn't want to go to India? Anything like that?"

Beatrice shook her head vigorously. "No!" She swallowed, then continued, more steadily. "No, never. He was most anxious to have us attend the parade for the Accession of the Queen. He was so proud of the whole garrison—" Her response was scattered, but definite.

"Did he have any enemies? Did you see him arguing with anyone?"

"No, he was very popular. Captain Bellingham was his closest friend. Everyone liked him. At the ball..." Her last words were lost in a sniff.

"Chief Constable," Danvers interrupted. "Are you suggesting Lieutenant Anson deserted—and committed suicide—because he didn't want to go to India?"

"We have to follow all possibilities. Anything like that is a matter for the military, but since his immediate superiors have now departed for India... Well, as I say, we have to explore all avenues." He turned back to the young ladies sitting in twin chairs beside the fireplace. "So you're certain the lieutenant didn't show the least reluctance to go out to India?"

For the first time Sophia answered. "Quite the contrary. I mentioned to him my concerns for my mother—she is in India, you see—and matters are..."

"Very grave." White nodded.

"Yes." Sophia looked at her hands folded demurely in her lap. "I have been most concerned. And he said—" She paused. "I'm not certain I should repeat it. It sounds—er, indelicate."

"Don't be missish, Sophia," Tonia said. "If you know anything that might be of help, it is your duty."

"Yes. Well, he said that was why he joined the regiment— that he couldn't wait to get to India and start seeing to the, er, I think pandies was the expression. Would that be right?" Sophia bit her lip.

Danvers nodded. "I believe it is military slang for the revolting sepoys."

Tonia reached over and squeezed Sophia's hand. "You did quite right to report the matter, but, pray, do not say the word again."

"Did the lieutenant give any reason for his, um, fervor?"

"He said something about his sister. And that they were all alike."

The chief constable held his pencil suspended above his notepad. "They? Sisters?"

"No." Sophia shook her head. "The pan... er, Musselmen, I think he meant."

"But surely he had joined long before the current crisis." Tonia found the whole matter very perplexing.

"He had been with the regiment for two years, I believe." Then a new thought seemed to strike Beatrice. "Has anyone notified his family?"

"That will be a matter for the Army." Chief Constable White closed his notebook and rose. "They know their whereabouts. Could be anywhere."

"No, they're here," Bea insisted.

"Here? In Brighton?" the Chief Constable asked. "How do you know that?"

"I met his sister at the ball—we all did." Bea looked around for confirmation.

Tonia nodded her agreement. "Annabelle. A charming girl. As a matter of fact..." Antonia gave Charles a significant look and nodded toward the door. She did not want to disclose their earlier suspicions in front of the young ladies.

"Indeed." White returned his notebook to his pocket. "Thank you for your time. If you recall anything more of importance, I trust you will call around at the station in John Street."

"I'll see you out, Chief Constable," Danvers said.

Tonia walked with them to the door. Once out of hearing of Sophia and Beatrice Danvers said, "I suggest you contact Inspector Futter of Scotland Yard. There is considerable background to suggest Anson may, indeed, have taken his own life."

"Impossible. One does not *garrote* oneself, my lord."

❧ 18 ❧

"What do you mean *married?* You were Alice's chaperone. Her guardian. Of all the incompetence I have ever known you capable of, you have exceeded yourself, brother. Married! And gone to India! India!" Agatha looked as if she would attack Danvers with her fan, but he stood firm.

Tonia had hoped that once they were safely back in London they could leave the alarms of Brighton behind them, but it was obvious such calm as she envisioned would not be achieved for some time yet. She had just a week to finalize the preparations she had set in place weeks ago for the masked ball they were to hold in Sophia's honour. Bother Aunt Aelfrida for getting her into this. Still, in all fairness, even Aelfrida couldn't have foreseen such events as these.

"We shall all be sunk socially. I must take Beatrice out of London immediately. I think Aethelsham will be best, Aunt Aelfrida. If you will permit." She held up her hand. "No, better yet, we shall go to Scotland. Thanks to your bumbling, brother, I shall never be able to show my face in London society again. And what Beatrice is to do for a husband after the scandalmongers finish with this family, I cannot imagine."

"Sit down, Agatha!" The Dowager Duchess of Aethelbert gave one sharp, imperious rap of her walking stick. Agatha sat. "You will do no such nonsensical thing. You will have the notice of the marriage sent to 'The Times' today. Saint Nicholas's church, did you say, Charles? That will do very well. Do not omit to state that since the groom is an officer in Her Majesty's Light Infantry and the happy couple has departed for India, felicitations may be sent here to Berkeley Square Gardens."

All color drained from Agatha's flushed face. "Aunt Aelfrida—have you taken leave of your senses? You can't mean to say that you approve of this—this—fiasco?"

"Whether I approve or not has nothing to say to the matter. It is whether or not society believes we approve. The only way to stop scandal is for there to be no scandal. Which will be the case unless you are such a ninny as to give tongues cause to wag."

Her mouth set in a hard line, Agatha rose and walked stiffly to the escritoire on the far side of the room. She drew out a sheet of the dowager duchess's crested, hot-pressed writing paper.

Danvers extended an arm to his wife. "That seems to be settled satisfactorily, so we will take our leave. Tonia and I have calls to make."

The dowager duchess sniffed and inclined her head. "Soyer will see you out." Agatha ignored them.

"Why the insistence on calling on Lady Duff Gordon, my love? I hadn't thought you intimates," Danvers asked, once they were settled in the barouche.

"Not at all." Tonia frowned. She had been asking herself

the same question. "I don't really know. Ever since we saw that disturbing Tippu's Tiger in Brighton, I haven't been able to shake the feeling that these deaths and disturbances all have something to do with India, and Lucie Duff Gordon is the person I know with the closest ties there." She paused, trying to sort out her own intuition. "Chandrika is the one I'm most anxious to see. I do hope Futtter has made headway solving her poor husband's death." She sighed. "I suppose Anson's death may confuse that matter more."

When they arrived at Number 8 Queen Square, however, the first thing Tonia noted was the absence of black crepe. "They have taken down the mourning. That must mean Chandrika is no longer with them." Then she saw the elegant carriage at the curb with the groom sitting on his box. "Oh, it appears Lady Duff Gordon has a caller. Do you recognize the crest?"

Danvers peered at the door of the Landau. "A cock gules. That will be Ellenborough. Excellent. Just the man if you want news of India."

The Duff Gordon butler showed them into the drawing room where the hostess was pouring a fresh cup of tea for her guest.

"Antonia, Lord Danvers, how good of you to call. Lord Ellenborough has been informing me of the recent debate on India in Parliament. One can learn nothing from the papers." She gestured at several newspapers stacked helter-skelter on a side table. "Do have a seat. One lump or two?"

Danvers handed Antonia's teacup to her and accepted one for himself. "Do pardon our interruption, but we would be very happy to hear the latest news."

Ellenborough shook his head. "As would all of London. Every particle of information connected with India is sought with the greatest avidity and anxiety. I trust you will forgive my quoting myself—but, as I reminded Parliament just this week, this anxiety has gone on increasing upon the arrival of every mail. No official information whatever has been published to satisfy the people who are left to depend altogether on such accounts as private letters afford. The public is wholly ignorant of the measures adopted by Government to meet this formidable insurrection which threatens the safety of our rule in India. Although every newspaper report states that the danger is now over, it appears on the contrary that the crisis is far from being past." The earl refreshed himself from his teacup after his long speech.

"Oh, hear, hear!" Lucie applauded. "And what reply did you receive?"

"Lord North said he wanted to know what measures Government were prepared to adopt to reinforce the army and asked that within three days they publish officially the information they have received." Ellenborough made a sound of disgust. "Predictably, Granville assured the noble earl that the Government were fully alive to the state of affairs in India and would take every means in their power to deal with it. Then he had the effrontery to claim that my speech would have the effect of making things wear a more gloomy appearance than was justified."

"Oh, iniquitous!" Lucy came to her feet and began pacing the room with her masculine stride. "Is it possible for things to appear worse than they truly are? I have heard rumors that Nana Sahib has joined the rebels—although I can scarcely bring myself to credit it. Surely so refined and respected an advisor as my Azimoolah would keep the peshwa loyal to his English friends. I really don't know what to think."

"I fear our Lord Dalhousie may have sadly miscalculated in denying Nana Sahib's petition to be recognized as the rightful heir of his adoptive father. After all, Hindoo law fully recognizes adoptive sons for that purpose. And what would it have cost the Company to allow Nana to style himself maharajah?"

Antonia struggled to follow Ellenborough's arguments, but she found little in the conversation to be of comfort regarding Emilia's situation.

"So you believe as I do, that Nana Sahib should have been paid his pension?" Lucy asked. "I confess that I supported Azimoolah's desire to be presented to the queen—I thought the very idea that he so wanted to hear her voice to be the sign of a most loyal subject. But when he applied to my husband, Alexander replied that it would be improper to present someone to Her Majesty who had come to England solely in order to advance a claim against the Company.

"I don't mind confessing that I was indignant. I could hardly believe that our court could take upon itself to prejudice a question of the kind. It would have been in the queen's interest to encourage Azimoolah in his attempt to behave like a civilized man—as indeed, all enlightened persons from the subcontinent should be." She sat down abruptly. "Forgive me, I stray. But I do fear a grave miscalculation."

"As do I," agreed Ellenborough. "If there is any foundation to the rumors, I believe it could be said that no pension —whatever the amount—would have been too much to keep Nana Sahib loyal compared to the cost of this mutiny."

Antonia shivered. In the silence that followed Ellenborough's speech she turned to Lucie. "Has your house guest left?"

"Yes, her sister convinced her to return to them. Colonel Whitham came for her last week. Chandrika was reluctant, but I must admit it was rather a relief. I simply couldn't understand what to make of her. Dear creature that she is."

Antonia could only hope that Chandrika had returned to her family under her own free will. She couldn't forget the vision of the terrified young woman cowering in her room.

Tonia had assured her that she could be in no possible danger in England. But was that true? Still, surely the girl was safer with her sister than with a friend.

"Have the police really made no progress on discovering her husband's murderer?" Danvers asked.

"Not that I have heard of. I do not believe they have released the body yet for burial. I know that was a great grief to the family," Lucy replied.

"Have you had any communication from Azimoolah since he returned to India?" Danvers asked.

Lucie's soft smile revealed the fond memories she still held of his visit. "Alas, no. But of course, he has been much taken up with affairs there. And now with the state of things... I should be most happy to have his direction, if only to send on the letters that arrived here for him. Of course it has been many months now, but one does feel responsible. I fear that young lady in Brighton has quite broken her heart over him. Understandable. Such a charmer—"

Tonia turned to her hostess. "Brighton? You have letters for Azimoolah Khan from Anna—that is, from a young lady?"

"Yes, two or three. As I say, it has been some time now, but I hate to dispose of them. Somehow one feels the post is a matter of sacred trust."

"Do you know her name?"

Lucie looked aghast. "I didn't open them."

"No, no. I intended no such implication, but perhaps your guest let a name drop when he was in your company?" Antonia's mind raced. She had been so certain of their conclusion as to the identity of Miss A. Then the fact that the lieutenant's death was murder rather than suicide had put their surmises in doubt. Finally, here could be proof.

"He was very discreet. Miss A was his only reference."

Antonia stole a glance at Charles. She stood. "We must

intrude no more on your time." She placed her teacup back on the tray.

Lord and Lady Danvers took their leave of Lady Duff Gordon and Lord Ellenborough, but didn't exchange another word until they were in the privacy of their carriage. "Charles, perhaps we were right after all. Perhaps we have solved it."

Danvers shook his head. "Or complicated it. If Anson did kill Johal, it still tells us very little about Anson's death."

"But letters—"

"Certainly Futter should be informed. Let me take you home, Antonia, then I shall proceed to Scotland Yard."

"No, Charles, take me back to Berkeley Square Gardens. I must see how Beatrice and Sophia are faring."

Much as she had expected, Tonia found the young ladies in the library, but their depressed spirits prevented them from giving anything but the slightest attention to the volumes lying open on their laps. "You are quite on your own?" she inquired.

"The dowager duchess had a call to pay, but I didn't care to go with her," Sophia explained.

"And Mama has taken to her room," Beatrice added. "She says we must remove from this house, but I do hope she will repent of the notion when her pique has passed."

Tonia had no doubt of it. Since the Baron of Burroway steadfastly refused to purchase a residence further south than Edinburgh, and his wife was too prudent to set up an establishment from her own income, there was little to be done but that Agatha live as a guest of family or friends in London. She had, however, sent Arthur Emory with some alacrity to lodge at his club the first time he cast an approving eye at Miss Sophia Landry.

"How fortunate that I find you unoccupied." Tonia put

more vigor into her voice than the occasion perhaps merited, but such languor was not to be encouraged in young ladies. She suddenly realized, however, that she was quite at a loss to suggest anything to stir them to activity. She had come with a vague notion of promoting enthusiasm for the Queen's Drawing-Room where Sophia was to be presented in two days' time. But now that she saw Beatrice's sad countenance she realized that the Drawing-room would not do at all, since the younger daughter of the Baron of Burroway was not to be of the party.

"As I am in need of occupation myself, would you care to join me for a stroll in the park?"

Sophia looked toward the window where the July sun was kept at bay by thick net curtains. "Thank you, Lady Danvers, but it is so uncomfortably warm. Surely it's much nicer inside."

As Tonia's next suggestion was to be a shopping expedition, she was again at a loss. "Yes, I am sure you are quite right." Happily, her eye alighted on the mantle where the engraved invitation to the fancy dress ball to be given by Lord and Lady Danvers in honour of Miss Sophia Landry next week sat in the middle of the row of such enticements to pleasure. "Besides, we doubtless need to be making preparation for events here. What plans do you have for the ball next week? Have you your costumes planned?"

Antonia feared she had made an unhappy choice of subject when Sophia sighed. "I had thought to go as an Indian princess. Mama wrote of the beautiful fabrics and lavish jewels the native women wear when they are entertained by the local peshwa. But with all the disturbance one hears of just now..."

"No! With Alice run off to that horrid place. I couldn't stand to be reminded," Beatrice cried.

"Quite right. We must rethink the matter. Bea, what had you thought of?"

To Antonia's astonishment, Beatrice burst into tears. "Oh, I had quite forgot! Alice—" It was some time before she managed sufficient control to continue. "Alice and I were to go as Regency ladies. Great Aunt Aelfrida said she has trunks of fine dresses in the attic." Beatrice interrupted herself with a long sniff and resort to her handkerchief. "She said we could make free of them."

"Well, there you are, then. Dry your eyes, girl. Sophia can very well take your sister's place in such a duo." Tonia wasn't entirely sorry that she was unable to keep a touch of asperity out of her voice. Perhaps it would stir her niece to some self-possession. Tonia tugged at the tapestry bellpull beside the fireplace.

Soyer entered in his best imitation of a pouter pigeon. "The dowager duchess has given the young ladies permission to search the trunks in the attic, Soyer," Antonia began even before he could enquire as to her ladyship's pleasure. "We shall be in need of lamps, and doubtless, dust cloths. Is the attic unlocked?"

"I shall see to it, my lady."

In a few minutes Antonia and her charges were climbing the stairs to the top story, led by a footman bearing two lanterns, and followed by a maid with a duster and a footman carrying a chair for Antonia.

The lanterns, placed on a credenza along the back wall, were a good idea for lighting dark corners, but the attic was far from the murky place Tonia had feared, since it was lighted from overhead by two skylights. Tonia quickly saw the folly of attempting to put the dusters to use, though. The first attempt by a maid to clean off a trunk raised a cloud of dust that made Tonia's eyes water and produced an explosive sneeze from

Sophia. "Never mind, Iris. Just leave the dusters. We'll employ them if necessary." She sat on the chair the footman had placed in the center of the room for her. "Thank you, Lukas, now if you would be so good as see if you could open those skylights. Some fresh air would be helpful. Then that will be all."

Earlier dejection entirely forgotten, Sophia and Beatrice turned to their job with vigor. The lid to the first trunk fell back with a clatter and a shower of dust. Sophia sneezed again, then knelt on the bare floorboards, oblivious to the dust being swept aside by her wide, moss green skirt. She held up a navy blue jacket with a double row of brass buttons in a style popular many years ago. It would have fit a boy of perhaps five years old. "How charming! Do you think this was Osbert's?"

Beatrice held up a white shirt with a round collar and a wide black bow at the neck. "This must have gone with that. I do find it hard to think of the Duke of Aethelbert wearing such a thing." She held the garment to her nose. "Oooh, it reeks of camphor." She waved her hand to clear the air.

Sophia dug deeper and pulled out a tucked and embroidered, long-sleeved white frock. Although the yellowing of the fabric proclaimed it to be from an earlier generation it was not unlike garments still worn by toddlers like Charlie before they were breeched. Antonia swallowed a lump in her throat at the thought of how soon her son would outgrow such garments and be wearing smaller versions of his father's clothing. She put a hand on her abdomen, so happy with the thought that early in the next year there would be another infant in the Danvers's nursery.

The lid of the trunk snapping shut brought her back to the present. "Who would have thought Great Aunt Aelfrida would be so sentimental as to keep such things?" Beatrice shook her head and pulled another trunk from the shadows to a position under a skylight. "I hope this will hold something more to the purpose. We can hardly go to the ball as infants." The brass fittings on this trunk were so heavily tarnished that they required an effort from the young ladies to push the creaking hinges open. When they peered inside, though, they both fell to their knees and began bringing items out with delight. Sophia held up a tiny, tasseled, beaded bag. "Isn't this sweet!" Even in the dim attic light the golden glass beads sparkled.

"That is a reticule. Unless I very much miss my guess, Aunt Aelfrida would have carried that to a ball when she was near to your age. I have often heard her refer to dancing at Almack's with Lord Danvers's father," Antonia said.

Beatrice found a similar item made of embroidered striped silk, suspended from a satin ribbon. "Oh, there's something inside." Bea snapped open the clasp and pulled out a dance card. She moved to be more directly under the skylight and peered at the dim writing. "Ah, here Aethelbert has inscribed his name. How romantic to think of the young duke being one of Aunt Aelfrida's gallants." She examined the tiny pages further, then frowned. "How odd, she gave Aethelbert only one dance. Someone named Staveley had the first and last dances and the dinner dance."

"Staveley?" Sophia asked. "That was my grandfather's name. Do you suppose he pursued Aelfrida before my grandmother?"

"Or perhaps he had a brother?" Tonia suggested. "Whatever happened, it's certain it didn't harm the friendship between Aelfrida and your grandmother, or Aelfrida wouldn't have undertaken to present you." Tonia spoke heartily, but she couldn't help wondering about old rivalries.

The young ladies, however, seemed to give the matter no more thought as they returned to the trunk. It proved to be a veritable treasure trove. Shawls of every description, fringed, ruched, and lace-trimmed followed one another from the depths, all to be draped over the arms and whirled about. Evening headdresses with jewels, feathers and tissue flowers came next, to be admired. "Oh, why didn't we bring a mirror?" Sophia lamented, holding a velvet band with bangles to her forehead.

Fans, parasols, gloves of every length all tumbled to the floor as the young ladies dug deeper into their hoard. Satisfied that her distraction had worked to great success, Tonia stood and wandered to the far end of the attic. One chest she opened contained a set of dinner china in an old-fashioned pattern. Another held blankets and embroidered linens—all reeking of camphor. She turned the latch and opened the double doors on a tall armoire standing near the back wall. "Ah, Sophia, Beatrice, do come see. I believe this is just what you were looking for."

Indeed, the high-waisted gowns in silk and finest muslin, all white, pastel or sprigged, offered a mirror into a past age. Best of all, standing next to the wardrobe, under a dust cover, was an oval pier glass. Nothing could have exceeded the young ladies' delight as they pulled out gown after gown, held them up to the mirror and practiced a dance step or two, complete with curtsy.

Finally, Tonia, aware of the passing time, suggested each girl choose two dresses to take to her room to try on. "If your choice needs some adjustment, I am confident Peyden can see to it for you. When you have selected your gowns you can come up again and find the proper accessories. While you are choosing I will just tidy a bit." She turned to the quite thoroughly ravaged accessories trunk and began folding a stole of Nottingham lace that had been left draped over a nearby covered chair.

Tonia placed it in the bottom of the trunk and reached for another when she saw an item that had been overlooked. A small book bound in red leather. She lifted the cover and saw that it was the daybook for The Honourable Aelfrida Chalfant for the year 1807. Fifty years ago. Antonia made a swift calculation. Aelfrida must have been sixteen or seventeen then—in her first season. The same age Sophia now was. And enamored with Sophia's grandfather, if the dance card was from the same season. And yet she had married Aethelbert.

Sophia and Bea made their selections and left the attic, but Tonia sat on, musing. How odd to think of the young girl who had worn these gowns and fripperies and kept her daybook tucked away in a dusty trunk. She had heard Aelfrida refer to how she had danced the night through with Wellington's dashing officers, but never a hint as to an earlier *affaire de coeur*.

Tonia flipped through the pages of the book she held. Like all ladies' daybooks of that time, it contained a wealth of useful information such as a table of weights and measures, a map of the United Kingdom, the Christian calendar for that year marking all the principal feast days, fashion plates, the monarchs of England, and space for a brief diary entry for each day. The young Aelfrida's entries were written in her precise hand with a well-sharpened quill.

Antonia scanned a few entries at random, not intending to read closely, but merely to get a feeling for the young lady who had written them so long ago. It was the ink blot, so out of place in this carefully inscribed volume, that drew Antonia's attention. *Sent S away. Must be firm. A mere Writer's pay will not serve. I will have A, do not believe D's heart seriously engaged.*

Was that bit of blurred ink actually a tear stain? And who were the people to whom the writer so cryptically alluded?

A light tread on the step made Antonia close the book and slip it into her pocket. "Oh," Iris gave a started cry. "I beg pardon, my lady. I did not know you were here. Soyer sent me to collect the lamps."

"That is fine, Iris. I am quite finished here. Please return these items to the trunk as well." She indicated the ladies' accessories strewn about the open chest.

"Yes, my lady." Iris bobbed a curtsy as Tonia turned to the stairs.

Antonia found her charges in Sophia's room, having laid aside their choices of Regency costumes for a perusal of the newspaper account of the Queen's Drawing-Room from the week before. "The Princess Royal, 'A train tastefully trimmed with white crepe; petticoat of white glacé. Headdress, wreath of white roses; ornaments, pearls and diamonds. The Duchess of Sutherland—a dress of rich black glacé with cordons of black crystalised violets *en tablier*...'"

"Oh, just think." Beatrice sighed. "How fortunate you are to be. I can picture it all—superbly gowned rank and beauty moving through lofty halls. Such magnificent elegance and supreme comfort... Mama says my turn will come, but I don't see how I am to manage to wait so long."

Antonia smiled at her *naïveté*. "Do not be filling Sophia's head with dreams of decorum and comfort, Bea. I fear the reality has less of the grand etiquette about it and rather more of the duty to sovereign and society than you would imagine. Why do you think Aunt Aelfrida has commissioned me to deputize for her? *She* would not submit herself to such discomfort." Tonia turned to Sophia. "Make certain that you get a good night of sleep and eat a nourishing breakfast beforehand. I shall call for you promptly at noon."

"So early? But the Lord Chamberlain's card said three o'clock."

"Yes, my dear, but we must arrive at Saint James's Palace by two o'clock."

"But we are less than a mile from Saint James's."

"As I said, my dear—a good night of sleep and a fortifying breakfast. You will have need of it."

She left the young ladies looking bemused, but Tonia's thoughts returned to her discovery in the attic. A leisurely stroll to Grosvenor Square was what she wanted at the moment. She needed to think.

She recalled Charles asking her why Aelfrida had put herself to the trouble to bring an old friend's granddaughter into society—a friend who died years ago and whose daughter, although once so close to Tonia, had been gone from their lives for many years. Had Tonia found the clue in the small book tucked in her pocket? Had Aelfrida cared deeply for a common Mister Staveley, but thrown him over for a duke? As the daughter of a baron, Aelfrida had a title, but had she been determined on one higher than a mere Honourable —whatever her heart might have said?

And who was the Duke of Aethelbert dancing with when Aelfrida was with Staveley? Had he been courting her friend Dore? Antonia smiled. It could be of little consequence now. Still, she found it interesting to ponder.

❧ 19 ❧

"**A**nother cup of tea, Aunt Aelfrida?" Charles smiled at his wife's efforts to obtain information from the dowager duchess as she took tea with them the following afternoon, but it was apparent that Antonia had met her match.

"Every young man in London was at my feet. What could anything so long ago possibly say to anything?" The dowager duchess set her teacup aside as a rejection of further refreshment.

The door to the drawing room opened and Bracken announced, "Miss Hever and Miss Hever." Since the young ladies were twins they both bore the honorific due to an eldest daughter.

Tonia sprang up to embrace the newcomers. "My dears, how delightful to see you. You must forgive me. I have woefully neglected you. Do join us." She gestured to chairs and nodded to Bracken to bring more teacups.

"Now, you must tell me all the latest of your wedding plans."

"I rather fear there is little to report, Lady Danvers. We have been so engrossed in our work of late," Victoria said.

"Work?" the dowager duchess brought her lorgnette into play as an indication of the unacceptability of such a concept.

"Oh, yes, we had no idea of taking a hand when first we came to London," Cecilia answered.

"But when we saw the need..." Vicky continued. "I'm sure no one could bear to turn their back. It is quite overwhelming—the poor, lost souls."

"Do you find the work harder than at the Magdalen Asylum in York?" Tonia asked. "You must not overtax yourselves, my dears. I shall speak to Frederick."

"Oh, no, Freddie is most solicitous in his care for both of us, although he pushes himself endlessly. It is just that I had never seen opium addiction before. Respectable women who suffer from coughs, sleeplessness, er—women's problems..." Victoria blushed and stole a glance at Aunt Aelfrida.

Bracken returned with more cups and Tonia offered tea to the newcomers then refilled Danvers's teacup also. While Vicky sipped the restorative liquid Cecilia took up her narrative. "They take it for relief and then the filthy habit gets hold and won't let go. Even among children. It seems that the devil works overtime to find ways to enslave people and these poor women... Of course, the men Freddie ministers to are in even worse state—there are so many more of them. The sailors are the worst, but you would be amazed—respectable Englishmen from banks and offices—"

Vicky set her cup down. "Oh, yes, I wish you could see—" She looked again at the dowager duchess. "Not that I would suggest that your grace visit the slums, of course."

The Dowager Duchess of Aethelbert rose with a rap of her walking stick. "Slums? I do not know of such things. Undoubtedly the product of laziness, sin and vice among the lower orders."

She crossed the room and turned back at the door which Bracken opened for her. "You shall call for my ward at twelve o'clock tomorrow."

Antonia spoke into the silence created by her departure. "I should be most interested to view your work, Victoria. You are going to the mission now, are you not?"

"Tonia, you must not think of taking a hand—not in your present condition," Danvers protested.

"No, my love. I quite agree. But I would like to encourage their fine efforts with my interest."

Danvers smiled. He knew better than to argue with Antonia when she was moved with virtue for good works—as with anything else she set her mind to. He would be best advised to go along without complaint, but it was certain to cost him. "I shall ring for Hardy to drive us."

When they arrived at Whitechapel, Vicky and Cece both took part in directing Jarvis to a red brick building two streets over from the white tower of St. George-in-the-East. The reception office was just inside the door. They were greeted by a woman in a dark green muslin gown with a small, white lace collar framing a face of ecru complexion, her rich, black hair done in the latest fashion.

"Mrs. Whitham, is it not?" Tonia said, her voice expressing her surprise.

"Yes, indeed. Lady Danvers, Lord Danvers, welcome to our poor mission. We are honoured."

"Miss Hever did not tell me you volunteered here. Although she has spoken glowingly of the fine work of the mission. She is most anxious that Lord Danvers and I take an interest."

While the others spoke, Victoria and Cecilia took long, white aprons from a row of hooks just inside the door and tied them on, enveloping the fashionable dresses they had worn to call on Lord and Lady Danvers.

"I understand your work focuses on treating victims of opium addiction?" Danvers asked.

"Opium, gin—er, more physical vices, as well as simple starvation," Pamela Whitham supplied. "We attempt to help all who come to us, although, victims of the vile opium habit are among the most difficult to reach."

"Why is that?" Danvers inquired.

"It is because the primary result of the drug is to produce depression and lethargy in the user." She spoke with careful precision, as one to whom English was not her first language. "The resulting languor means few are likely to come to us for aid. They just lie on their filthy straw mats until they are beyond the reach of our poor efforts. That is why our workers make an attempt to go into those evil dens and bring out the worst cases." She shook her head. "But most often we are too late."

She turned back to her desk and picked up a long, narrow booklet and handed it to Danvers. "This is the report of our work for the past year. You might be interested, my lord."

Rescued Lives, he read on the cover and smiled at the cunning chequebook shape of the publication, undoubtedly designed to make the reader think of writing a cheque for the work. As Vicky and Cece led into the large hall, lined with patient beds on each side, Danvers skimmed the information he had been given: *Out of five hundred, forty-three deaths in London in a single year, one hundred, eighty-six, including seventy-two children, were due to opium addiction... Opium suppresses pain, worry and sleeplessness, but these tortures return in increased volume when the opium wears off, thereupon the addict wants a stronger dose which produces an unending cycle of fear, anxiety, depression, irritability, delusion, paranoia, exhaustion, vomiting... The downward spiral inevitably ending in seizures, coma and death.*

The thought of the wasted lives sickened Danvers. As did the immensity of the problem.

At the end of the row of beds Cecilia stopped by a woman Danvers at first judged to be in her sixties. On second look, however, the fact that she held an infant to her breast and that her soft brown hair showed no grey led him to guess her true age to be nearer twenty. "How are you today, Martha?" Cece asked.

The woman moaned and twitched, scratching at her neck and arms. Danvers saw red gashes her nails had made in her flesh from the constant itching she suffered. Cece took a cloth from the deep pocket in her apron and wiped the woman's sweating forehead. A bowl of soup and an uneaten bread roll were on a table by the bed. "Have you eaten today? You must try for the sake of your babe."

"I tried. Truly, I did. I simply can't. My stomach..."

Danvers was amazed at the well-modulated voice. He did not expect such proper speech from one in such circumstances.

"A sad case," Victoria said in a low voice. "Her husband is in the regiment—sent to India before the babe was born. Martha planned to join him when the child was old enough to travel. From what we can make out of her story, she suffered from worry and sleeplessness after her husband was gone so she took laudanum. We believe she acquired an adulterated dose from her chemist—so strong as to be addicting."

"Does that happen often?" Danvers asked.

"It's impossible to say. We believe several of the cases here were quite unintentional—enslavement from taking over-strong formulas. The potency varies so much—in strength and in purity. It has even been suggested that owners of the vile opium dens contrive to strengthen the formulas to enslave people."

The ladies crossed to the other side of the room, pausing

at several beds for Vicky or Cece to soothe a brow, offer a patient a drink of water, or smooth the thin sheet over them. Danvers took the pamphlet Mrs. Whitham had given him from his pocket again. Victoria's words reminded him of something he had read there. Ah, yes, here: "Adulteration, which takes place in almost every ingredient dispensed in the drug and chemical line, is fearful to contemplate. All preparations of opium are amongst the articles to which this remark applies with peculiar force." The writer went on to urge readers to support Lord Granville's bill for the restriction of the sale of poisons, which "would vexatiously interfere with the drug trade throughout the country." Particularly in the case of opium where "everything depends upon the exact nicety of the dose ministered."

Danvers continued to consider the issues the brochure raised. If it was all a matter of mistake and mischance the dilemma would be difficult to deal with, indeed. But if unscrupulous persons in the drug trade were dispensing over-potent draughts of opium in order to cause addiction—and the poor souls thereby ensnared became enslaved to the drug —raising the profit of the trafficker...

Insidious, indeed. At a minimum he would urge Ellenborough and others he knew in Parliament to support Granville's measure. But surely more should be done.

The suggestive shape of the booklet worked. Danvers drew out his pocketbook and left a substantial contribution with Mrs. Whitham for the work of the mission before he and Tonia took their leave.

Tonia was quiet as the brougham bore them back toward Grosvenor Square, allowing Danvers's mind to wander over the evils they had just viewed. Opium, raised in India, but a curse to so many here in London. And the possibility of even rightfully administered doses being purposefully adulterated to cause addiction...

To whose benefit? The answer was obvious—to those who profited from the opium dens. And if the owners of the dens could be obtaining the drug illegally, it would amount to pure profit. But was that possible when he had seen how carefully the shipments were accounted for at the East India Docks? Yet, it seemed that the unscrupulous would always find a way.

The carriage lurched at an uneven cobble, making his throat constrict. Would he never be rid of the feel of the sickening thud when his carriage wheels hit a human body? It had been weeks ago, and still his stomach contracted at the mere thought of it. A small dog had once run under his carriage wheels and he had been many months freeing himself of the sensation—the clenching of his stomach, the sick feeling in his breast.

Even though the presence of the dagger proved the man's death was not to be laid at his own door, Danvers could not help feeling involved.

❦ 20 ❦

hey had no more than left Berkeley Square Gardens the next morning than the crush of traffic moving northward slowed. By the time they crossed Piccadilly and turned into Saint James's Street it was almost impossible to perceive that the wheels of the carriage were turning. "Oh, you were right, Lady Danvers. We should have left earlier! Will we ever arrive?" Sophia sat forward on the carriage seat.

"Sit back, my dear and do not give in to nerves. You will need your energy later." Antonia put a hand on the girl's shoulder. "Have I told you that your mother and I made our come-out at the same time?"

"I did not know! Do tell me about it." Sophia relaxed as she gave her full attention to Antonia.

"It was the first of the season, just after Easter, the year we both turned sixteen. You are aware that we share a birthday?"

Sophia squeezed Tonia's hand. "Yes, I do know. And I miss her less, just having you here, Lady Danvers. But, oh, I do wish..."

"Yes, and I daresay she wishes it as well." Tonia paused. Her dreams had again been disturbed last night: a sense of stifling heat, suffocating airlessness, gnawing hunger... She shook her head, making the three ostrich plumes attached to her coiffeur ruffle with the motion. "Two hundred debutantes were presented that day, but Emilia was the beauty. Her floral garland perfectly set off her shining locks." Tonia smiled at her companion's golden radiance. "Just as yours does, my dear —although her hair was dark. But it was her gentle kindness that shone the brightest."

"And my father?" Sophia prompted as the carriage inched forward.

"A love match, in Emilia's very first season—whereas I took so long to settle, I am certain everyone had given me up to spinsterhood." Tonia paused. "But surely your mother has told you of all this?"

Sophia shook her head. "I feel I know so little of my parents. I was so young when Papa died and I didn't like to ask Mama because it always seemed to make her sad. Did she love him very much?"

Tonia smiled. "Absolutely a love match, I believe. Your mother could have married a marquess." She fervently hoped that was the truth of the matter. At least she was spared from answering further as their carriage at last pulled up to the entrance of Saint James's Palace.

Built by Henry VIII on the site of a former leper hospital dedicated to Saint James, the forbidding, red brick walls with their crenelated parapets looked far more like a fortress than the principal ceremonial palace in the kingdom. The clock between the octagonal entrance towers said almost two o'clock. It had taken them nearly two hours to journey less than a mile.

And the crush of carriages in Cleveland Row was greater than anything they had encountered earlier. The footmen sprang off the back of the carriage and handed the ladies out. Tonia instantly swooped her long, gold silk train over her left arm and assisted Sophia to do the same before they could drag on the pavement or be trodden on by the tumult of humanity around them.

Up and down the street elegant ladies, all similarly clad in long trains over the most voluminous possible crinolined gowns, heavy with frills, embroidery and brilliants, pressed toward the entrance. The scene shimmered as wide-scooped necklines bared white shoulders below glittering necklaces of every imaginable precious stone. Puffed sleeves gave width to the shoulders in order to emphasize the slenderness of waistlines. Hands sheathed in long, kid gloves held bouquets, lace pocket handkerchiefs and enormous fans of ostrich feathers.

All was precisely as decorum and fashion dictated. Debutantes, like Sophia, who had not been presented earlier during the special days set aside for young ladies making their comeout at the first of the season, were all clad in purest white, and wore floral coronas to which were attached long tulle veils. They were accompanied by married ladies of high rank wearing tall white ostrich plumes in their hair and gowns of every hue.

Others were there for diplomatic purposes. Subjects of Her Majesty who would be traveling abroad and needed qualifications to be presented in foreign courts, must first be presented to the English court as a means of supplying the Master of the Ceremonies in Paris or other capitals with testimonials as to their respectability. The gentlemen of these couples—for they largely appeared to be couples—wore the highest robes of their office, whether clerical, judicial or military, many sporting numerous medals and honours and colorful sashes across their chests. Those without a uniform wore tail coats heavy with gold lace and metallic ornamentation above tight, white knee breeches and white silk hose.

Their ladies' gowns were of the same pattern as the debutantes, but in deeper hues of emerald, ruby and topaz, rich
with gold embroidery.

"Move on! Move on!" the policemen struggling to keep
order on the pavement called out. And the throng attempted
to obey, squeezing toward the dark funnel of the arched
entrance.

Antonia felt herself shoved from every side. "Oh!" she
cried as a Hessian-booted man next to her trod on her kid
slipper. She grasped Sophia's arm tightly as they were carried
forward by the sheer press of the crowd. It was imperative
that they maintain their footing. The consequences of falling
were unthinkable.

Momentarily blinded by the dark of the foyer, Tonia
blinked, then made out the narrow stairway before them.
"Move on!" This time the order came from a palace guard.
Somehow they managed to ascend the stairs to a small room
opening onto another small room and so on down the side of
the palace. Tonia and Sophia progressed as far as they could
until they halted in the Queen Anne Room. Perhaps fifty
seats had been provided for near-to double that many guests.
Tonia looked longingly at a lady sitting, somewhat smugly, it
seemed, on a campstool she had possessed the foresight to
bring with her.

Unbelievably, more comers squeezed into the chamber,
increasing the pressure from every side. The air was suffocating and Antonia found herself praying she would not faint.
If she could just lean her back against a wall for a moment, it
would give such ease. But there was no possibility of reaching
such a prop. Tonia looked at the ladies accompanied by
gentlemen and longed for her husband's strong arm to
support her. Why had she not thought to insist that the
dowager duchess procure a ticket for him, too? Even though
the thought of adding even one more body to this mass made

her shudder, the comfort of a male escort seemed inestimable. Her own presentation had been uncomfortable and it had seemed crowded with the two hundred debutantes to be presented to the newly married queen with her handsome, youthful husband standing beside her, but it was spacious comfort compared to this.

Tonia wondered how much longer they would be held in this pen. And how many were ahead of them? Would the barrier across the door ever be removed? And even if it was, would they reach the Presence Chamber in time? It was well known that the doors were closed at four o'clock and those left in the holding pen were shut out like the improvident virgins in the parable of the marriage feast.

They had been in the room for something approaching an hour when the bar across the doorway to the next room was raised, and again, the order, "Move on!" rang out. Impelled onward by the vexed multitude in the rear, Sophia and Tonia entered the room where their first cards were received. Quite to Antonia's amazement, although this required another stoppage in their progress, the gentlemen on duty were so alert and adroit in receiving the tickets that they were able to proceed without much difficulty toward the entrance of the next chamber.

Before they could reach the doorway, however, another impediment presented itself. A narrow bench had been fixed, most improperly, as if to increase the obstruction of the narrow entrance. Tonia managed to step aside, pulling Sophia with her, to clear the hindrance.

They were in the act of progressing to the next room when a burly, red-faced man in a deputy-lieutenant's uniform with a short lady on his arm forced his way up the side of the room. Tonia had no more than registered her shock at the man's boorishness in breaking all rules of order or good breeding when he shoved her sharply in his attempt to wrestle himself and the lady into the room before them.

"Kindly grant us a moment's grace, sir," she said. "We shall all be through without difficulty and you will follow in the line."

The determined oaf paid not the slightest attention to her appeal, but instead, put greater energy into his thrust, knocking Antonia into Sophia. She caught the girl entirely off balance. Sophia was propelled headlong toward the barricading bench.

Tonia drew breath to cry out, but quicker than she could do so, a gentleman in a black velvet coat and gold brocade waistcoat reached across the bench and caught Sophia before she could fall.

"Oh," Sophia gasped. "Oh, thank you—" She looked up and gave a little cry. "Lord Penthurst! What—How—"

"Delighted to be of service, Miss Landry. Viscountess." He nodded to lady Danvers. He drew forward a lady in a deep maroon gown with masses of dark hair supporting her ostrich plumes. "May I present my sister Morwenna. Going to Vienna next month. Needs her bonafides, although I must say, there has to be a better method of obtaining credentials than this mauling."

The offensive boor and his lady having cleared the entrance, the way was now open for Sophia and Tonia to proceed, with Penthurst and his sister to follow once they had maneuvered around the bench. At long last, they were in the Presence Chamber. Gorgeously gowned women and splendidly robed or uniformed men filled the hall, but all eyes were on the tiny woman standing at the head of the room, flanked by her tall husband in a gold-frogged military uniform and the Princess Royal in white glacé silk.

One of the lords-in-waiting stepped toward Sophia with his wand extended. "Lower your train," Tonia said in her ear.

With a graceful, flowing motion, the attendant hooked his wand under Sophia's train and spread it evenly to its full length on the floor behind her. "Remove your right hand glove," Tonia prompted.

The line inched forward. "Deep breaths, Sophia. You're almost there, and you're doing splendidly." Sophia rewarded the encouraging words with a shaky smile.

When they were near the top of the line a footman received their second cards and passed them to the Master of Ceremonies standing behind the queen's right shoulder.

"Miss Sophia Antonia Landry." Sophia stepped forward. She curtsied so low she was almost kneeling. The royal hand extended to her. Sophia placed her own ungloved hand below the queen's. Her lips brushed her sovereign's fingers.

Antonia put a gloved finger to her cheek, recalling clearly where she, as the daughter of a baron, had received a kiss from the queen. Sophia, however, would not receive that honour as she bore no title.

Sophia turned to her right to curtsy to Prince Albert, then to her left for the Princess Royal, then retired backward. Tonia held her breath as Sophia executed the intricate rearward succession of curtsies. They had practiced this maneuver endlessly, but the slightest stumble over one's train could bring disaster. At last the girl reached the threshold of the doorway. The official once more extended his wand, expertly lifting her train and gathering it over her left arm. The presentation was complete.

"Well done, my dear. You were perfection. We may all breathe easy now." Tonia led the way down another succession of small rooms opening directly into one another at the back of the wing, to descend a narrow stairway to a lobby where a mass of tired-looking, slightly disheveled people like themselves, were awaiting their carriages. Tonia noticed one lady with a rip in her gown where someone in the throng must have trodden on her skirt. Another was bemoaning a broken feather in her fan—undoubtedly another victim of the crush.

They had waited some time before an attendant called, "Lady Danvers's carriage." Tonia grasped Sophia's arm to keep from getting separated in the mass of people and attempted to move forward. They made little headway.

"Lady Danvers's carriage," rang out again after a few more minutes. The ladies continued to struggle, but were unable to make significant progress.

By the time her carriage was called for the third time Antonia began to despair. If they did not achieve it soon, the driver would be sent away. Then goodness only knew when they would see their conveyance again.

"This way, my lady," a familiar voice called to her and, miraculously, the Red Sea parted. They walked unimpeded to the carriage just before the equerry could direct Jarvis to depart to make room for others.

"Lord Penthurst, we are indebted to you yet again. I do thank you." There was no time to say more as the footman closed the carriage door and sprang up behind the barouche, even as it was already moving.

Both ladies sank back against the cushioned seat with a sigh. The clock high on the palace wall told Antonia it was past six o'clock. She couldn't remember ever being in a greater state of exhaustion. "Sophia, you were splendid." She turned to the frazzled girl beside her. "I do hope the ordeal wasn't too great."

Sophia sighed. "Oh, no! Never. It was marvelous. The queen—who would have thought she was so tiny? My hand looked enormous underneath hers. And Prince Albert!" She sighed again. "He was magnificent in his uniform. The gleam on his boots... Have you ever seen a more handsome man?"

Antonia was amazed that the girl had taken in such detail. Tonia's own presentation had been much of a blur to her.

"Except Lord Penthurst, of course," Sophia added. "Imagine him rescuing us twice. Such gallantry. It is as though Providence sent him to us."

Tonia was less positive. "It is certain we were in need of a knight errant." She could not but be grateful for the duke's timely rescues. Without doubt she would not wish to be trapped longer in that multitude struggling to exit. Still, she couldn't be entirely easy in the duke's presence. There was a coldness in his eyes... But surely she was just being silly. His manners were perfect. And if he was attempting to make up for past misdemeanors, surely that was to be admired.

"You have sent him a card for my ball, have you not, Lady Danvers?"

Sophia's words jerked Tonia's thoughts back to the present. She was quite certain Penthurst's name was not on her list. And it was late to be issuing an invitation only a week before the event. Still, such marked service was due a reward. "I shall see to it, my dear."

Sophia hoped the satisfied smile on Sophia's face was for the completion of the day and not for thoughts of the dark duke.

𝕊 2 1 𝕊

Emilia had no idea she would feel so bereft from Louisa's death. She had seen so much of dying, how was it possible for this one to make a yet more profound impact when she thought she was numb? She kept telling herself her friend was in a better place. Louisa was free from suffering, hunger, thirst, mud, mosquitoes, heat... the list was endless.

Still, to have endured so much and then to die when it must be only a matter of days, even hours perhaps, until Havelock's forces freed them—as surely they would. Still, Emilia was amazed that she could feel alone in such crowded quarters.

They had been imprisoned in the Bibighar for almost two weeks now, each day hotter and steamier than the last. And the deaths from disease continued. Every day they mouthed their prayers and watched as more corpses were dragged out.

Straggling prisoners from Fatehgarh, including three men and a teenage boy, had added to their numbers, so in spite of being decimated by death, they still numbered more than two hundred.

Emilia eased her aching body onto the rough matting that served as the only protection from the muddy ooze of the courtyard and sank into a restless slumber. She dreamed of Louisa, lovely in a rose-colored, wide-crinolined dress, dancing with her dashing husband at an offi-cers' assembly. Then the dream shifted and it wasn't Louisa, but rather Antonia being whirled around the floor by the most handsome man in the room while Emilia herself watched the door, hoping for Robert to enter and sweep her off her feet.

But dear Robert would not have been invited to so grand an event. Instead that persistent marquess bowed over her hand. She refused the dance and he turned away. Antonia saw it—as if she had felt Emilia's loneliness. With the briefest word Antonia excused herself in the middle of the dance and came to her friend's side, grip-ping her hand and leading her out the French doors and onto the terrace.

In her sleep Emilia extended her hand and scraped the coarse coconut matting, jarring herself awake. She groaned, and in her semi-conscious state continued to reach for her friend. Louisa. Antonia. Her hand grasped only air.

Perhaps an hour or more later she finally drifted into an uneasy doze. Until she was jarred awake by the shaking of the earth under her. Was it an earthquake? She sat up and looked around at the early morning light in the sky over the courtyard. Then she heard the muffled pounding of artillery.

Everyone around her was waking now. Sleep-dazed children cried, only to be shushed by their mothers. Women pushed their ears to the ground and to the outer walls of the Bibighar, listening to the distant rumbling like an echo of the Entrenchment barrages. Was this the relief forces? If so, were they winning over the rebels? How far away were they? Would they soon be freed? It seemed too much to hope for, and yet it was impossible to suppress all optimism.

After perhaps an hour the firing ceased. Did that mean the rebels had won? Surely not. The suspense continued into mid-morning. Then the clamor started up again. Closer this time. Now not only the earth shook, but also the very walls of their prison. Surely their rescue was at hand.

The Begum, however, shouting at the servants and spitting at *prisoners, grew ever more hostile. She stormed through the courtyard, kicking anyone in her way and hitting children or the wounded not quick enough to elude her. Would the rebels let their prisoners live to tell their stories? If Nana Sahib retreated, would he force the prisoners to march with him?*

Women hugged the children near them to quieten them. Little groups whispered prayers together. Emilia looked over the shoulder of the lady next to her and saw that she was reading a devotional classic called Preparation for Death: The Christians' defense against the fears of death, how to prepare ourselves to die well. *Emilia clutched her prayer book, but did not open it.*

A cry came from one of the women crouched near a window, peeping through the slats of the shutter. The four male prisoners were being marched up the footpath toward the riverbank under armed guard. Only a few minutes more and a volley of shots rang out.

The waiting seemed interminable. Evening was falling when the Begum marched into the courtyard with a gleam of triumph. "The Nana has sent orders for your immediate destruction." She delivered her announcement in a ringing voice, then turned on her heels and stamped out.

The proclamation was met with gasps and a few outcries, but for the most part the sobs were merely of fatigue. Emilia could feel only a numbed disbelief. Was it possible? After all this time? After all their grief and suffering? All their prayers? Were they now to be butchered within earshot of their rescuers' guns? Would God really allow that?

Caroline Lindsay managed to find a scrap of paper and the stub of a pencil somewhere. On it she recorded the sad chronology of her family's deaths, carefully noting the date of each. She tucked it into her clothes, as others were pinning children's names to their clothing. Women tore strips off their skirts and did what they could to barricade the doors by tying the doorknobs together.

The doctor, cook and servant who had served the women were dragged out. Shots rang out from Nana's executioners. There was now no one left but women and children for their captors to vent their violence on.

Emilia drew her beloved prayer book out of her pocket and this time opened it to the Litany. "O God the Father of heaven: have mercy upon us..."

"Have mercy upon us." *Several standing near gave the response.*

"Spare us, good Lord, spare thy people, whom thou hast redeemed with thy precious blood..."

"Spare us, good Lord," *came the response just as it was given every Sunday, Wednesday and Friday after Morning Prayers in the most peaceful of English village churches.*

"From plague, pestilence, and famine; from battle and murder, and from sudden death." *The double doors at the end of the courtyard were flung open with a crash. A harsh, imperious voice ordered the ladies out.*

No one moved. Those standing near pillars clung more tightly to them.

"Good Lord, deliver us." *The response was louder now, almost enough to drown out the Begum's order to the sepoys to drag them out.*

"From all sedition, privy conspiracy and rebellion..."

"Good Lord, deliver us." *The sepoys backed out, unable to budge the women.*

"In all time of our tribulation... in the hour of death, and in the day of judgment." *Emilia's voice rang more firmly. It was a small victory, but they had stood firm.*

"Good Lord, deliver us." *Now even the children were entering in.*

"That it may please thee to bless and keep all thy people..." *Her words were drowned out in a crash of splintering wood as rifle barrels crashed through the shutters, aimed at them. With a gasp, the prisoners tried to draw away, but there was no room to move.*

"We beseech thee to hear us, good Lord." *Only a few stalwarts now replied, engulfed in terrified screams.*

"That it may please thee to strengthen such as do stand; and to comfort and help the weak-hearted; and to raise up them that fall..." *Pressed against the wall, Emilia managed to carry on.*

"We beseech thee to hear us, good Lord." *The few responses were lost in a volley of shot. The layer of women and children nearest the windows fell.*

"That it may please thee to forgive our enemies, persecutors, and slanderers, and to turn their hearts." *A second volley scattered the prisoners to take what shelter they could in side rooms and behind pillars.*

There were no more shots. Aiming from outside as the gunmen were, they could not find their targets. The angry shouts of the Begum echoed through the courtyard, above the moans of the wounded. She cursed the gunmen as cowards and traitors. But they refused to continue the slaughter.

Emilia returned her book to her pocket and knelt to do what she could to bind the wounds of Mrs. Walker, the oldest of the captives.

A little before sunset one of Nana Sahib's bodyguards strode to the Bibighar with four recruits. Two of them wearing butchers' aprons and all armed with long, curved sabers. A mighty crashing against the doors pounded in every ear. The doors burst open.

The butchers lay to, slashing right and left with their swords. Women shrieked. Blood spurted.

Emilia opened her prayer book. "O Lamb of God: that takest away the sins of the world;

"Have mercy upon us.

"Lord, have mercy upon us.

"Christ have mercy upon us."

Drops of red blood spattered the pages of the prayer book.

Tonia woke to a great void. A sense of loss overwhelmed her. The weight on her chest and the tangle of her bedclothes told her she had slept badly, but she could not recall her dream. Still, the spectre hovered over her. What could have caused this sense of desolation?

She fought through the morass clouding her brain to the day before. Ah the Presentation. A trial, indeed, but, in the end, something of a triumph for Sophia. So that could not be the cause of the hollowness inside her. She clasped her abdomen with both hands—the babe—the tiny roundness, hardly larger than a cricket ball, filled her cupped hands. She let her breath out with a rush. All was well there.

Then a worse terror struck her heart. Charlie. She sprang out of bed, barely pausing to pull on her dressing gown and thrust her feet into slippers. She fled along the hallway and up the stairs to the nursery.

The sight that met her eyes made her heart lurch with joy. Charles, sitting on the carpet in the middle of the room, stacking blocks with their golden-haired son. "We're building a castle, Mama," the toddler called when he saw her.

Tonia smiled. All was right in her world. Her waking anxiety had been a mere fancy; no presentiment. She joined her husband and son for a spell of castle-building.

She could not linger long, however, no matter how great her delight. Lord and Lady Danvers's fancy dress ball, to be held in a few days, was to be the last grand event of the season, for tomorrow the court was to remove to Osborne House on the Isle of Wight and surely Parliament would soon adjourn this much-protracted session, bringing the season to a close. Which meant that every detail must be perfect. As the culminating occasion, every occurrence would linger in the mind of every guest, and the responsibility that all went smoothly was up to the hostess.

The invitations, of course, had gone out weeks ago—to

far more people than could comfortably be accommodated in the Danvers House ballroom, since not everyone invited would attend, and it was mandatory that the floor be filled. Likewise, more men than women had been invited, to assure partners for all the ladies. None of the young ladies must be left in the unthinkable position of sitting on the sideline with her chaperone.

Tonia spent the rest of her day seated at the escritoire in her sitting room, conferring with staff to make certain of every detail. Soyer assured her that the finest orchestra had been booked—indeed, it was the same one that had been employed by the Duchess of Devonshire for her ball in May. Indeed, my lady, the housekeeper had assured him that an adequate supply of the very finest beeswax candles had been delivered last week. The details of florist's instructions and the placement of potted palms, table centerpieces and display baskets required more time, but at last Lady Danvers was satisfied that all the floral arrangements would be in the very best taste.

The conference with Mrs. Robinson over every detail of the menu took the remainder of the afternoon. Although discussing the menu had been one of Tonia's first tasks many weeks ago when the ball was first planned, it was necessary to revisit every item again. Cook had not been able to obtain a sufficient quantity of Jerusalem Artichokes for the soup. Would her ladyship think Asparagus Soup acceptable? Although Tonia was partial to the more traditional white soup, she bowed to the necessity of a pale green starter, even though it was to be followed by the green of a lettuce salad.

"We could add an accompaniment of cheese fingers, to add color, my lady."

Tonia accepted Mrs. Robinson's suggestion and they moved on to the baked salmon with sauce hollandaise to be followed by roast chicken with potato rissoles and green peas, and timbales of ham with cucumber sauce.

Mrs. Robinson next placed the dessert choices before her mistress: Mousse au chocolate; Lemon-water ice; selection of cakes—Pavini Cake, Almond Queen-cakes, and Savoy cake.

"And surely, your magnificent sponge cake as well, Mrs. Robinson?"

Cook's pleasure with the suggestion was apparent. Since the choice of wines to accompany the meal would be the domain of Lord Danvers and Soyer, the conference with Mrs. Robinson completed Tonia's responsibilities. She sat for a moment with a satisfied smile, but after a few breaths it turned to a frown.

At that instant her lord entered his wife's sitting room. "Antonia, why the frown?"

A small sigh escaped her. "The ball. Everything possible has been done, and yet it seems there are still so many things that can go amiss." She paused, searching how to put her vague feelings into words. Then it all came pouring out. "Her first season is so important for a young lady, and, as the last grand event of the season, this marks the culmination for Sophia. I so want it to be perfect. But what if something goes wrong? She was so valiant at the Presentation—in spite of the crush—which almost defeated me, I'll admit—and then getting knocked over just before entering the Presence Chamber—yet no one would ever have guessed. She's simply indomitable. I only hope life rewards her for her courage." The frown had deepened by the time she concluded.

Danvers bent and kissed the furrowed spot between her eyes. "My love, why such a mother hen?"

Tonia attempted to make light of her tumultuous feelings. "I know—it is nonsensical of me. I suppose I was thinking of her mother's come-out—and mine, too. And what different roads life has taken us. I—I don't know—I've been missing

Emilia today. She feels so—so *gone*. I feel as if the whole responsibility of Sophia is on me somehow."

"That's certainly not the case officially—you are merely deputizing for Aunt Aelfrida. A fact you may well have forgotten since, in her typical manner, she seems to have very neatly offered to sponsor the girl, then shoved all the actual work off onto you."

Antonia thought for a moment. "That's odd, isn't it?" She smiled. "Not that she put the work on someone else, but that she involved herself in the first place. I still don't understand why Aunt Aelfrida took on the responsibility even in name."

After another pause Antonia added, "Did I tell you we found Aelfrida's daybook in the attic? From when she and Sophia's grandmother were in their first season? I looked at it a bit. Quite fascinating, really—like reading history. Then I laid it aside." She gazed around the room and spotted the small, red leather volume on a table beside the sofa.

She noted that Charles still carried "The Times" under his arm, as when he entered the room. "Were you on your way to the library, love? Do stay here to read; it's much cozier."

Danvers assented and they sat side by side on the sofa, each absorbed in their own reading for some time. At first Tonia skimmed the diary entries, noting similarities and differences in the coming-out process between today and two generations earlier. Then her reading slowed as the young Aelfrida began writing less about the whirl of events and more about her feelings. Tonia's attention was entirely consumed when she realized that the Dorothea so often referred to was Emilia's grandmother. "Charles, this is fascinating. Aelfrida had a rival for the attentions of the Duke of Aethelbert—and it was Emilia's grandmother." She sighed. "It's like reading a novel. And it seems that Aelfrida actually had tender feelings for Robert Staveley."

Danvers spoke from behind his paper. "Odd, isn't it? To think of Aunt Aelfrida as a young girl."

"Yes—and quite a flirt, at that." She returned to her reading and carried on to the end of the season, then looked back and read the final weeks of June again. "Charles—" The newspaper rustled and a pair of eyes appeared over the top. "I have the answer—as to why Aunt Aelfrida took on responsibility for Sophia."

"Well?"

"Restitution. Aelfrida was determined to have the duke for herself, so she encouraged her friend to run off with Mr. Staveley."

"Of whom Aelfrida herself was fond? What a tangled tale." Danvers shook his head.

"Yes, it is. But rather straightforward on Aelfrida's part, actually. She was set on a title—so pushed her friend into the arms of her untitled lover."

"And if I recall correctly, you mentioned that alliance ended in something of a disaster."

"Socially, yes. A pattern which Dorothea's daughter repeated. So Aelfrida is determined that it not be repeated by the granddaughter."

"The Dowager Duchess of Aethelbert feeling guilty?" Danvers's tone of voice told what he thought of that idea.

"No, I think it's more like expiation—giving herself a second chance to make things come out right. Rather like fulfilling a duty owed to her friend. And that explains why Aunt Aelfrida is forever throwing Sophia in the way of the Duke of Penthurst. Although I'm complaisant even the dowager duchess couldn't have engineered that fiasco at the Presentation."

"Do you think Sophia's affections were engaged?"

"By Penthurst? It's hard to say. I had thought she had rather special smiles for Lieutenant Anson—poor boy." She shook her head. "I do hope she doesn't have a *tendesse* for the dark duke. I can't like him." Tonia sighed. "Oh dear, this makes it all the more important that the ball go well."

Before more could be said on the matter, however, Soyer ushered callers into the sitting room. "Victoria, Cecilia!" Tonia cried, cutting off the butler in the act of announcing them. She crossed the room and took each young lady by a hand. "How delightful to see you." She showed them to chairs and instructed Soyer to bring tea and cakes.

The Honourable Reverend Frederick followed more slowly, to be greeted by his brother. "Freddie. How is your work progressing? Have you cleared the Docklands of vice yet?"

Freddie exhaled as he sank into a chair. "If only." He shook his head. "Polite society simply has no idea of the viciousness of the problem. Problems, I should say—there are so many. Of course, as a clergyman I understand that sin is at the heart of it all, but simply in human terms—the human misery..." He paused and ran his fingers through his hair. "Forgive me. I didn't come to carry on like this, but it can become rather overwhelming.

"It seems the suffering caused by opium-eating is among the worst." He held up a hand. "Oh, I know, it is supplied by every tobacconist, barber and chemist—in every formula for cough syrup, sleeping potion, even calming drops for infants —but I'm convinced it's quite wrong. If more people saw the poor devils... I'm convinced our government should take a hand in it.

"Forgive me. I'm not usually so morose. It's just that a case we had been working with—a young mother with three children—she seemed to be doing so well in throwing off her addiction... Vicky found her dead this morning, and now the children must go to the workhouse—and they are but babes." Freddie visibly pulled himself together when Soyer returned with the tea tray. "Anyway, I thought it best to bring Vicky and Cecilia here. They are greatly looking forward to your ball—it will do them good I'm certain."

Sitting between the newcomers, as she was, Antonia was privy to snatches of the conversation on both sides of her. From what she heard of Freddie's words and observed of Vicky's demeanor, she agreed that the girl was in need of a distraction, so set herself to talk of the ball. "And have you decided on your fancy dress?"

"We shall be our favorites from *Mother Goose's Melody*," Cecilia answered. "Vicky will be Bo-Peep, and I shall be Mary Quite Contrary."

"Excellent choices. That will be charming." Tonia handed a cup of tea to Cecilia and poured one for Victoria. "And what about Freddie?"

"I wanted him to come as Little Boy blue. But he declares he shall come as a clergyman."

"And what of your wedding shopping? Is it all in hand?"

"Oh—yes. All is quite in order, I think." She spoke as if she had forgotten that was the purpose behind her visit to London. "I have been rather busy of late."

Vicky's lack of animation made Tonia question her tactics of distraction. Perhaps the girl needed to talk about the day's experience. "Victoria, I am so sorry you had such a distressing day."

"You would think after all I saw at the Magdalen Asylum I would be more inured to it all, wouldn't you?" Victoria took a deep drink from her cup, then set it down with a clatter. "The madness and horror of the opium dens, though—"

"Surely you don't..." Tonia began.

"Oh, no, Freddie won't let us go near them. He says they are wretched holes—the opium-eaters lying on filthy mattresses in low rooms filled with smoke... It is quite easy enough to imagine. We see the results in those we care for in the refuge. The poor souls who seek oblivion in this hateful drug, then must suffer torture when they seek to free themselves from it. And Maud was doing so well. I thought. Then I gave her a mixture for her cough. It should have been fine—vinegar, treacle and laudanum—only ten per cent—I measured carefully. A surgeon who helps at the refuge said the laudanum may have been too strong. It's known to happen. Mostly by accident, but sometimes of a purpose—to make people want more. It's iniquitous."

Tonia agreed. So much suffering in the world. Even in their little corner of the most advanced city in the most civilized country in the world. And yet a man had died under the wheels of their own carriage and his wife went about in fear for her life. A dashing army officer was found slain in one of the nation's most fashionable watering places. And those like Freddie, working to bring light into dark places, were overwhelmed.

While she put all her energies into giving a fancy dress ball. And yet, perhaps in a small way, that effort was a stance against the blight of evil—to create beauty, joy, hopefulness was a strike for good. It had to be.

As was proper for the guest of honour, Sophia and the dowager duchess were the first to arrive just before nine o'clock. "Oh, my dear, you look lovely." Antonia kissed Sophia. Indeed, she had never seen the girl look lovelier. "The Regency style suits you perfectly." The high-waisted, white muslin gown adorned with pink rosebuds couldn't have set off Sophia's slim figure and ivory blush complexion better. It was clear that the evening's honoree shared none of her hostess's nervous worries.

The dowager duchess sniffed. "The gel does the gown credit. I, of course, was the toast of the *ton* when I wore it in my first season."

Agatha, Beatrice and Arthur Emory arrived almost on their heels. Beatrice made a charming companion for Sophia in the pale green muslin from Aunt Aelfrida's attic. The yellow roses in her dark hair were the perfect accent. The dowager duchess examined her through her lorgnette, then let it drop with a sniff of approval.

Agatha, Lady Burroway, came as a regal Queen Elizabeth in a stiff brocade gown, a high ruff and a blazing red wig.

Arthur Emory had chosen an admiral's uniform, splendid with gold braid and epaulets to do escort duty for his mother and sister. The sight of her nephew in such regalia made Tonia blink. She had been accustomed to thinking of him as a callow youth, but tonight he seemed to have achieved a new stature.

After that the guests arrived in such quick succession that, struggle as she might to greet each one, Lady Danvers was quite unable to keep track. Lord Ellenborough arrived as part of Lord and Lady Duff Gordon's party; Lord and Lady Essworthy, whom she had not seen since the evening of their levee, came with their son and daughter; Freddie with Victoria and Cecilia; Lord Penthurst with two or three young blades; Colonel and Mrs. Whitham with her sister... Tonia began to worry. One routinely issued more invitations than one could accommodate with no expectation that all would be accepted. Now though, she realized with apprehension that she had received very few replies of regret over the past few weeks. Oh well, a squeeze was a sign of a sure social success.

Indeed, when the orchestra struck the opening strains of the first of the fancy quadrilles there was little doubt that "The Times" would pronounce Lady Danvers's ball to have been one of the best of the season. The first set was to be performed by the highest ladies in attendance, so Lady Danvers, dressed as Britannia, with her lord in severest evening black, led the other couples to the center of the floor, while the guests stood in a ring around the sides.

Lord and Lady Danvers faced Lord and Lady Duff Gordon, both in rich Indian dress of bright silks and heavy jewels. To the right, Lord Ellenborough, as Sir Walter Raleigh, accompanied the Baroness Burroway. Lord and Lady Essworthy, as Columbine and Harlequin, completed the square. As the music carried her through the intricate set of figures—*balancé*, forward two, grand right and left—Tonia felt herself buoyed with the assurance that the evening would be perfect. How nonsensical she had been to worry so. The ball was set to be a triumph. Candles flickered in crystal, the scent of floral displays wafted on the air, the guests smiled.

The first set quadrille came to its graceful conclusion and Monsieur Gaspard, the floor manager, beckoned to the young couples who were to perform the second fancy quadrille. Tonia frowned when she saw that the Duke of Penthurst, splendid in black velvet, was partnering Sophia. Antonia had carefully arranged that Cyril Essworthy, down from Oxford, should partner her charge when Monsieur Gaspard instructed the young ladies in the figures of their exhibition dance last week. She saw that now, however, the Honourable Cyril, in scholar's robes, partnered Cecilia's Mary Quite Contrary. Ah, perhaps Sophia had made the change as a favor to her friend. Cece's smiles for her partner indicated that this might be the case. Although The Dowager Duchess of Aethelbert's smug look did make Tonia wonder if Aunt Aelfrida had somehow engineered Sophia's pairing. The square was completed by Victoria and Freddy and Beatrice partnered by her brother, although it seemed to the closely observing Antonia that Arthur Emory's eyes were far more often on Sophia than on his sister.

The couples acquitted themselves admirably, to the applause of all in the room. "Let us form a set," the floor manager directed as an invitation for the dancing to become general, and around the room gentlemen bowed to ladies to take part in the cotillion. Lord Ellenborough bowed over his hostess's hand. The earl was an excellent dancer, despite his age and the gravity of his demeanor. Tonia wondered if he had affairs of state on his mind and longed to ask him if there was news of India, as she had heard nothing for many days.

The pattern of the dance, however, moved swiftly from an

allemande to a promenade and there was no time for even a brief enquiry, let alone a serious discussion. When she had an opportunity, Tonia swept the room with a swift gaze, looking for Sophia. Aunt Aelfrida might be her official sponsor, but Antonia felt responsible. Ah, the young lady was dancing with Arthur Emory. In spite of Agatha's frowns, Tonia thought they made a handsome couple.

At the end of the dance Antonia's partner enquired if he could bring her a glass of punch. "Lemonade, please, Lord Ellenborough. Two cups, if you please. I have neglected my guests and I see Chandrika Johal standing alone."

She made her way to the beautiful woman whose plain white sari decreed her to be in mourning. "My dear, I am so honoured that you chose to attend tonight." She would have liked to enquire more into the woman's affairs, but hesitated to probe. "You are well?"

"My sister Padjma, she insist. Although I do not know if it is proper. Still, I try to obey. I do not dance, though." Tonia noticed that no such hesitancy seemed to hinder Colonel Whitham's Eurasian wife, dressed as an English bluebell. The colonel and his wife spun gracefully across the floor in a waltz.

Lord Ellenborough returned with the ladies' lemonade and Tonia suggested she take Chandrika to the terrace for a breath of air. The young woman seemed to relax in the quieter atmosphere. "You have returned to your sister's home?" Tonia knew she had, but wondered how Chandrika felt about it.

"Padjma insist." The rule of the older sister seemed inviolate.

"And you are no longer afraid?" Was her demeanor due to shyness and loss, or did the girl still harbor her unreasonable fear of suttee?

"My husband. We bury him last week."

"Chandrika, that is good news. So have the police found out what happened?"

The whites of Chandrika's large eyes seemed to grow larger in the dim light. "The inspector..."

"Futter?" Tonia prompted.

"Yes. That one. He comes to the house many times. Talks much with the colonel. Then we are told we may have the body." She spread her hands to indicate that was the extent of her understanding.

Tonia frowned. Did that mean the case was closed? Surely they would have been told if there had been an arrest.

Monsieur Gaspard was instructing the guests to take their partners for the *galop* when Antonia led Chandrika back into the ballroom. "Freddie, just the person." She was delighted to find her brother-in-law standing inside the French doors. Freddie would know how to make the young widow comfortable. Having a clergyman in the family could be a great convenience at times.

Tonia was less pleased, however, to note that Sophia was being led to the dance floor by the Duke of Penthurst, although it was impossible to read an understanding of the girl's feelings from her expression. Confusion? Apprehension? Acquiescence? Tonia could not guess it.

She turned to a cluster of chaperones sitting on small gold chairs in the corner. The ladies were deep in an enthralled discussion of the commentary that had appeared in the newspapers following the mishap at the Queen's Drawing-Room. Tonia would have much preferred it be kept out of the press, but they never missed reporting anything with the least connection to royalty. "The temerity of that odious man who suggested it is all the ladies' fault for choosing to wear skirts so wide, trains so long and headdresses so high. Would he prefer that our ladies appear before Her Majesty in servant's dress?" Lady Walker sniffed.

"The account I read asked why no use could be made of Buckingham Palace. It is certainly true that the apartments at Saint James's are utterly inadequate." Countess Burlingame snapped her fan shut.

"It is a shame that the doors must be shut at four o'clock, regardless of whether or not all the company has been received. I believe that is much of the cause of such great shoving and thrusting," Tonia joined the conversation. "It seems to me that if Her Majesty would receive her guests seated there would be no loss of decorum and she could venture to extend the time of the Drawing-rooms without fatigue." Fortunately, there had been no hint of Sophia's name in accounts of the unfortunate event, so none suspected Lady Danvers's close association with the situation.

"A very sensible suggestion, Lady Danvers." Countess Burlingame nodded. "But did you read the abhorrent remarks of that Irishman in the 'Cork Examiner'? I presume he fancies himself a wit, but such degrading nonsense should not be allowed in print."

A birdlike lady whose identity Antonia struggled to recall piped up, "Indeed, I read it. 'These complaints of the arrangements of Her Majesty's Drawing-Room are extremely disloyal. Ladies should rejoice in the opportunity of showing what they are ready to go through to show their duty to their Queen. If their clothes are torn off their backs in the crowd so much the better. It proves their devotion to their Sovereign, and what a willing sacrifice they make to do homage to her.' Of course, I dismissed it completely. I don't give such drivel a second look."

Tonia nodded to the group and continued on around the room, pausing to greet guests, chat with friends and welcome those she had not seen for some time. The *galop* came to an end and gentlemen claimed their partners for the second waltz. Again Tonia frowned as she saw that Sophia had granted Lord Penthurst a second dance. Either the young lady was being imprudent, or the gentleman overly importunate. Tonia wished she knew which it was.

Antonia was almost to the bottom of the room when she noticed a newcomer. What an unusual idea to choose a police inspector's frock coat and tall hat for fancy dress. Then he removed his hat and she saw that this was not a matter of fancy dress. What could have brought Inspector Futter here?

Danvers, approaching from the other side of the room, had apparently noted the inspector's entrance as well because he reached the foyer with Antonia. "My lord, my lady, I apologize." Futter looked around at the elegant company. "I had no idea. Colonel Whitham's butler said he was here, but I didn't realize..." He stumbled to a halt.

"You have information for the colonel?" Danvers asked.

"No. Well, yes, in a way, I suppose—That is..." Futter ran his hand through his pale straw hair. "It's, um, rather awkward, my lord. You see, the thing is—I'm here to arrest him."

Tonia gasped and looked around to make certain no one had overheard.

"Impossible," Danvers said. "What can you mean?"

"I'm very sorry, my lord. But we have been most thorough in our investigations. The murder of Mr. Johal, my lord."

"How is that possible?" Shocked as she was, Tonia was still careful to keep her voice very low. "Are you certain?"

"The evidence speaks clearly for itself, my lady. The colonel is involved in opium smuggling and his brother-in-law found out, so he had to be silenced."

Danvers's reply was stiff. "I believe the colonel is in the card room. I will fetch him with as little fuss as possible. You may use my library. Pray, be discreet."

"This way, Inspector." Tonia led the way down the staircase to the ground floor library.

A few minutes later Danvers entered with a red-faced Whitham striding before him. The colonel spoke before anyone else could draw breath. "What is the meaning of this outrage? I hope you can explain yourself. Lord Danvers has had the goodness to inform me of some nonsensical story that you have come to arrest me!" He sputtered to a stop.

Futter ran a finger around the inside of his high, starched collar. "I do regret, Colonel, that is my painful duty to—that is to say, yes." He cleared his throat. "Colonel Whitham, I arrest you on the charge of the willful murder of Mr. Faquir Johal—"

"Halt!" Whitham held up his hand as if commanding a battalion on parade. "Try not to make more of an a—" he looked at Lady Danvers and cleared his throat, "more of an idiot of yourself than you can help, man."

Futter looked nonplussed and Whitham turned to Danvers. "May I request, my lord, that a message be carried to Commissioner Mayne of Scotland Yard who can clear this matter up?"

"Very easily, Colonel. The commissioner lives not far from here." Danvers stepped into the hallway and requested a footman to send Hardy to him, then turned back to Whitham and indicated his desk. "You will find paper in the top drawer, if you wish to write a missive, Colonel."

By the time Hardy joined them the letter was written and sealed with Danvers's wax. "A matter of some sensitivity, Hardy," Danvers informed his man. "Take this to Commissioner Mayne." He gave him the address. "You may return with his written reply or conduct him here, as the commissioner prefers."

"Yes, m'lord." Hardy hurried out, obviously pleased to be called into service on what was clearly a matter of importance.

"Colonel Whitham?" Danvers looked at him with a raised eyebrow, inviting an explanation.

"Inspector Mayne will vouch for me. I have been working closely with him, investigating this matter of opium smuggling on behalf of the East India Company. For some time their shipments have registered a significant shortage. We have very nearly closed in on the leader of the scheme. I only hope to heaven your bungling hasn't tipped the fellow off." He glared at Futter.

Tonia heard the strains of the third waltz begin in the ballroom above their heads. This was the dance before dinner. When it was ended their guests would expect their host and hostess to lead into the dining room. She at least must return to her hostess duties. "Inspector—" she began, but got no further before the tall, double doors of the library crashed open. "Arthur Emory, what—"

"Forgive my bursting in like this, but it's Sophia. She's gone off with Penthurst."

23

I t took Danvers a moment to react. "What do you mean, gone off?"

"The dinner dance—it was supposed to be mine. I signed her card the first thing. I couldn't find Sophia in the ballroom, so I went out on the terrace in search of her. They were there—Sophia and Penthurst." He ground the name out between clenched teeth. "He told her he knew she had been worried about her mother, so he set his people to make enquiries. Apparently he has links to India—to the army— something. Anyway he said his man just brought him a telegram—her mother is arriving at the docks. He took her to meet the ship."

"The London Docks? Rubbish! Does the girl think her mother is sailing on a cargo ship?" Danvers was scathing at the nonsensical story.

"I know it's a lie. But Sophia didn't know. I called after her —gave chase. It was useless. They were already to the end of the garden." Arthur Emory looked at his muddied boots. "Penthurst had his carriage waiting outside the gate. They're gone."

Colonel Whitham spoke into the shocked silence. "Penthurst? The Duke? He's the fellow. Almost certain he's behind the smuggling. Haven't been able to get the proof, though. Slippery, he is."

"But Sophia—we've got to save her!" Arthur Emory brought the more immediate crisis back to focus.

At that moment Hardy entered with a distinguished-looking man whose impressive grey side-whiskers filled in his hollow cheeks and accented his sharp nose and thin lips. "Sir Richard," Danvers greeted the newcomer. "Thank you for coming so quickly. Colonel Whitham tells us you can clear up some—er, difficulty regarding an opium smuggling ring and the murder of Faquir Johal."

The Commissioner, who was well-known for his strict enforcement of the law, put his hands behind his back and drew breath for what promised to be a lengthy explanation. "The matter is one—"

Alfred Emory, however, would not be restrained. "Please, sir, Sophia—Penthurst has abducted her. He'll escape!"

A flush of anger suffused Mayne's fine features. "Penthurst? And you let him slip through your fingers?" He rounded on Futter. "After him, man! What are you waiting for?"

Whitham was first out the door. "My carriage!" he demanded of the nearest footman, then turned back to Futter. "Stop dithering, man. Come on."

"M'lord," Hardy was at Danvers's elbow, "I was after taking the liberty to call for your phaeton, thinking you might have need of it."

"Good man." Danvers was out the front door when he realized Hardy and Arthur Emory accompanied him. He gave a curt nod. Hardy sprang to the driver's bench by Jarvis. "East India Docks, Jarvis. And spring 'em, man!" Danvers called even before Arthur Emory was seated beside him.

"How do we know which docks?" Arthur Emory asked.

"If Penthurst is smuggling opium, you can bet it comes off the East India ships. Somehow he has some transferred to his own vessel. He must have a boat moored in the river near the dock."

"And he means to take Sophia aboard a smuggler's boat." Arthur Emory's voice was filled with agony. "But why? What does he hope to gain?"

"A forced marriage, I should imagine. I have known for some time that Penthurst is deeply in debt. And he gambles. Sophia is an heiress." Danvers answered.

"They have a good start on us." Arthur's grim tone matched the set of his features.

Once through the zigzag of London streets, they made good time along the Embankment, but the way slowed again when they entered Whitechapel. The streets were narrow and dark, some places slick with refuse. And, even at that late hour, the area teemed with humanity: Streetwalkers accosting sailors; old women selling hot pies and baked potatoes; young children, snatching at what they could and darting off down a dark alleyway. A stench of horse droppings, rotting food, and smoke hung low on the moist night air. And the sounds— raucous laughter, harsh arguments, babies' wails, cat yowls and dog barks... Charcoal braziers burned intermittently, producing light and heat and shifting shadows that gave Danvers the feeling they were driving through hell.

"What was Penthurst driving? Did you get a look?" Danvers asked.

"Not very clear. A closed carriage."

That went without saying, Danvers thought. One would hardly abduct a lady in an open barouche. Around every turn in the road he gazed intently in all directions, peering down every dark alley, for fear that their quarry might sense he was being followed and turn aside. Danvers was also puzzled that there was no sign of Whitham and Futter. The Danvers Phaeton should have overtaken the heavier police vehicle some time ago. Danvers was convinced that his carriage was the lightest and his horses the fastest.

When they neared the river Danvers kept a careful watch for any activity around a boat that might indicate a carriage having newly arrived or an intent to cast off. A few boats had lanterns lit on deck, but he could detect no sign they had been recently boarded. A fisherman and his wife sitting with their feet propped up, both smoking pipes, was the extent of the action.

Would it be worth taking the time to question them? He hated to delay, yet they would likely lose more time groping in the dark if they continued this blind search.

"Question them, Hardy—find out if they've seen a closed carriage in the last few minutes."

Jarvis stopped beside the wharf and Hardy sprang down. He approached the trawler. "Ahoy, Captain, and have you good folk been about seeing a coach approach the docks in the last little while?"

The thickly bearded seaman lowered his feet and his pipe, came slowly upright and walked to the rail. Danvers seethed with impatience as the man leaned forward, elbows on the railing, as if settling in for a lengthy yarn.

"Only it's a mite of a hurry we're in, if ye've seen anything," Hardy prompted.

Another puff on the pipe and a lengthy exhale of smoke followed. "Well now, can't rightly say I've seen any such in this past hour. What would you be wantin' to know fer?"

Danvers was berating himself as a fool for wasting time when Arthur Emory clutched his arm. "There, did you hear that?"

Danvers heard plenty of sounds, water lapping the wharf, wooden timbers creaking, rats skittering...

"That way—" Arthur pointed back down river. "A steam engine starting."

"Hardy!" Danvers shouted. His man sprang to the carriage even as Jarvis was turning the horses.

"Must have missed them in the dark." Danvers prepared to spring to action, praying the gangplank wouldn't be pulled up before they could reach the vessel.

"There!" Arthur Emory pointed to a pale puff of white from a smokestack, five or six moorings along.

Danvers frowned. It was impossible to be certain in the murky light, but he had the impression the funnel on the yacht was the distinguishing blue and yellow they had seen before.

Then a high-pitched sound took his attention. Was that a cry for help? Danvers wasn't sure. The shriek could have been a cat or seabird. Or a young woman.

Jarvis stopped the phaeton in the shadows a distance from the yacht. "Best not to give advance warning, sir."

"Good man, Jarvis. Stay with the horses." As he and the others jumped to the cobbles Danvers realized they were all unarmed. "See if you can avail yourselves of a weapon," he directed the others, indicating the piles of rubbish in front of the darkened buildings on their right.

Repelled as he was by the stench and the sight of rats feeding on the heap of debris, Danvers approached near enough to spot a broken chair protruding from the far side. As he reached toward it, a cat sprang out with a howl, almost making him lose his balance. The chair, however, yielded three solid oak legs he was able to wrench off to provide sturdy coshes. Hardy had likewise provided himself with a small, but lethal-looking bottle, its bottom broken off to leave jagged shards. He tucked the bludgeon in his belt and the bottle in a pocket to keep his hands free.

Keeping to the shadows, they moved forward. Danvers let

out a relieved breath when he saw that the plank was still in place. Now he saw Penthurst's carriage, concealed behind a dark, dilapidated building. Perhaps where Penthurst warehoused his contraband?

The thought had no more crossed Danvers's mind than a stocky figure emerged from the building carrying a large crate that Danvers could well imagine held several of the opium balls such as they had seen being unloaded at the East India Docks. That explained why the gangway was still in place. Hopefully they could slip aboard after that man—if only there wasn't another stevedore behind him. Danvers raised his hand in a signal for the others to follow him.

They had barely set foot on deck when the slamming of the hatch followed by heavy footsteps sent them diving for cover. The burly man who carried the cargo reappeared and disappeared into the darkness along the gangplank. Two men emerged from below deck and set about winding the winch that pulled the gangplank up. It was impossible to be certain in the dim light, but the men appeared to be of Eurasian cast. Possibly the two Antonia had pointed out to him on the beach in Brighton? The ones arguing with Anson before his murder?

The creaking ropes and scraping wood made a bleak accompaniment to Danvers's realization that the boat was about to set sail. And they had not been joined by the policemen. The task of rescuing Sophia and apprehending a gang of murdering smugglers was down to himself, his valet and an untried youth.

There was nothing to do but take things as they came. Which meant starting with the two in front of them. At least Danvers and his two had the element of surprise on their side. For the time being. They crept forward as far as they dared.

Danvers signaled to his men to wait. As soon as the gangplank was fastened in place along the side of the hull the villains turned back to the doorway. Danvers sprang, trusting the others to follow him. He grabbed the closest around the neck and gave a mighty whack with his stick. The man went limp in his arms.

Out of the corner of his eye, Danvers saw that Hardy had tackled the other man, knocking him to the boards, and Arthur Emory was delivering repeated swings of his chair leg as efficiently as if it had been a cricket bat. When both men were subdued they dragged them beyond the lantern light on the far side of a lifeboat. Arthur Emory brought ropes from a coiled pile and they tied the men securely. "Hadn't we better gag them, too—in case they come around?" The man Danvers had restrained emitted a loud groan, evidencing the wisdom of Arthur Emory's suggestion. Danvers and his nephew removed their own cravats for the purpose.

The engines chugged and Danvers felt the sway of the boat as it caught the current and moved further out into the river. The pilot's cabin was forward, where they were fortunately out of view. It was unlikely Penthurst would be there. Danvers would expect to find him in his cabin. With Sophia.

If only Danvers could know how many crew members they were likely to encounter. It was not a large yacht, and Penthurst would doubtless want to keep his smuggling operation to as few henchmen as possible. Still, whatever the odds, they must act swiftly if they were to rescue Sophia. Once the ship reached open waters the likelihood of help reaching them would be greatly diminished.

The most feasible place for Penthurst to have taken Sophia would be to his cabin, presumably on the deck below them. They had to make the attempt. Signaling for the others to follow him, Danvers crept across the deck to the hatch.

Holding his breath, he grabbed the iron handle and pulled. The rusty metal hinges groaned, but no burly accomplice rushed to see what was causing the disturbance. Danvers forced himself to breathe again.

Treading softly and holding tightly to the railings, they descended below deck. Indeed, just as he thought, the fine wood paneling of the hall, leading to double, highly-polished, oak doors with ornate brass fittings, told Danvers they had located the great cabin extending the width of the prow.

As quietly as he could, Danvers turned the handle. The lock did not yield. A muffled cry from the other side of the door propelled Danvers to knock urgently on the unyielding oak.

"What is it?" Penthurst demanded.

Hardy pushed forward. "Sorry, cap'n, er—yer lordship. Only it's a bit o' bother with the cargo."

The metal key scratched as it turned in the lock. Danvers and Hardy jumped back from the doorway as it was yanked open. "Blast you! What—"

Penthurst got no further as Danvers leapt forward and knocked him off his feet. The duke rebounded before Danvers and the others could enter the room. Sophia gave a sharp, sobbing cry and Danvers had a blurring image of Arthur Emory leaping to her side, but Penthurst took all his attention as the duke lunged toward him.

Danvers side-stepped neatly and this time sent Penthurst sprawling forward. Danvers raised his cosh.

"Allow me, m'lord," Hardy intervened and brought down a mighty whack which subdued their opponent. "Not quite the thing for a gentleman like yourself to be doing, I'm thinking, m'lord." Hardy grinned.

"Well done, Hardy. Find something to tie him up."

Before the job could be done, however, the door to the cabin burst open. A burly, red-faced crew member filled the doorway. Danvers gathered his muscles to lunge at the man. Then saw the pistol levelled at his chest. His bludgeon clattered to the hardwood of the floor.

"Found these two tied up on deck, yer grace." The man nodded to the hallway behind where the two crewmen they had overcome earlier stood none too steadily. The duke, still on the floor, groaned and pushed himself up to a half-sitting position. The newcomer pointed his weapon at Hardy. "There's brandy in the decanter. Minister to his lordship. And don't try nothin'."

Out of the corner of his eye Danvers watched his man go to the cut glass decanter on the table, pour out a snifter and take it to Penthurst. In the far corner he saw Sophia and Arthur Emory clinging to one another as if their lives depended on it—which they probably did.

The duke rose unsteadily to his feet and made his way to a chair, holding his head. "Blast you, Danvers. You'll wish you hadn't interfered before the night's over." He turned to the man with the pistol. "Well done, Mr. Mapp. I think it only fair now that Kabir and Parth should have the pleasure of returning the favor done to them earlier. We can make more, ah—permanent arrangements when we reach open waters."

The men set to do his bidding with the ropes that had formerly bound them. Danvers's mind was in a whirl. In the face of the unwavering firearm he could see nothing to do for the moment, so he submitted. Let Penthurst think he had won and perhaps he would overplay his hand.

The duke turned to observe the couple in the corner. "Most affecting. Young Rannoch makes a charming knight errant for the lady in distress." He advanced on the couple who shrank from him. "No need for that, my charming beauty. I'll not hurt you. When we reach my estate in Cornwall I can assure you of my most loving attention."

Sophia looked as if she might spit at him, then remembered her dignity. "How could I have believed you?"

"I must apologize for my little subterfuge, of course. It would have been much simpler if you had accepted my most forthright proposal of marriage. After all, many young women would delight in becoming a duchess. And you shall make a lovely one."

Sophia did not utter a word, but her stiff-necked posture defied him more eloquently than speech could have. She gently pushed Arthur Emory away and stood facing Penthurst squarely.

"No!" Arthur reached out to her.

The duke gave him a blow which sent him reeling into the wall. Arthur crumpled to his knees. Penthurst yanked two tasseled cords from the heavy velvet draperies that hung at the square-paned windows and bound him tightly. "If you would be so good as to join us above-deck, my dear." Penthurst seized Sophia's arm. "There's nothing like fresh sea air to clear the head."

The duke picked up Danvers's dropped cudgel and handed it to one of his men. "Do forgive my manners, I failed to introduce you to my, ah—associates. Lord Danvers, may I present Kabir and Parth." Absurd as it seemed, the men acknowledged the introduction with a *namaste*. Danvers did not respond.

"Keep our guests company, Parth, but don't shoot unless you have to. I have my own plans that will be rather more fun, I think."

When the others were gone the guard tucked his pistol into his belt and swaggered about the cabin, swinging his club and pausing on every circuit to kick at one of his captives or give him a sharp nudge with his club. Danvers bided his time. Parth eventually tired of his strutting and sat in the leather chair Penthurst had abandoned, his pistol near to hand on the table.

Most fortunately, the wide, plush captain's bed, which Danvers and Hardy were leaning against from their positions sitting on the floor, blocked part of their captor's view. Danvers shifted his body imperceptibly until, with his bound hands, he could reach the tail of Hardy's coat. With slow, cautious movements, he pulled the garment around until he could feel the pocket of the heavy tweed where Hardy had stowed the broken bottle.

Inwardly cursing the need for caution and his own awkwardness in working with both hands behind his back, Danvers eventually managed to slip the jacket from his man's shoulder, fortunately on the side away from Parth's view. From there Danvers was able to grasp the neck of the bottle and pull it out.

Hardy gave the merest twitch of his head to indicate that he understood. With Danvers holding the jagged end of the bottle sideways, Hardy maneuvered until he could rub his fetters against the shards. It was slow work, made slower by the need to pause every few moments in case their guard should become aware of any movement.

At long last Hardy worked through the rope. Fortunately, the noise of the engine and the creaking of the boat more than covered the sound of the rope falling to the floor. Cautiously Hardy took the bottle from Danvers and they repeated the process. Danvers tried to control his impatience. One careless slice of his wrist with that razor-sharp glass would do Penthurst's work for him. If only he had some sense how long they had been under steam. How long would it take to sail to the open water of the North Sea? He had more than once driven to Tilbury, where the Thames widened out, in less than three hours. If he could just know which way the tide was flowing he might have a better sense of their speed.

At last he gave a small jerk of a nod when he felt the bonds loosen.

Hardy uttered a pitiful groan and slumped sideways. The act was so good it alarmed Danvers. Had his man slit his own wrist in the act of cutting the rope? Then Hardy winked and Charles understood. "Parth, my man has fainted. Give him some brandy." Danvers tried to match Penthurst's rhythm of speech in hopes it would produce a more automatic obedience.

The guard looked at Hardy and shrugged. "Fine hero now. What do I care?"

"Do you think your master will be best pleased if one of his captives expires? I understood him to have his own plans."

Parth looked unimpressed, but came slowly to his feet. A splash of amber liquid from the decanter landed on the oak table as well as in the glass. He crossed the room to his captives and dropped to one knee beside Hardy, bending forward enough that his thick, black hair fell in his eyes.

The glass was almost to Hardy's lips when he twisted his body, pushing hands and bound feet against the floor, and gave Parth a head-butt that sent him reeling.

Danvers propelled himself forward to his knees and threw himself across their stunned guard. Danvers felt Hardy sawing at the fetters binding his ankles. In a moment he was free. "The pistol, Hardy," he directed his man who had like-wise freed his own feet.

"M'lord?" Hardy sounded concerned, but he handed his master the weapon.

Danvers smiled. "Not so bloodthirsty as all that, Hardy." He raised the butt and gave Parth a mighty thump. "That should see to him for a while."

Hardy was occupied freeing Arthur Emory, so Danvers tucked the pistol in a pocket and set about binding their former captor. "Above deck now, I think," he said to his companions.

They stole out of the cabin and up the stairs. Danvers held his breath when they reached the hatch. There was no way to know what was on the other side of the heavy barrier. His only hope was to open it as quietly as possible and attempt peeking out.

The action produced no results, however, because he was able to see only a narrow strip of vacant deck and beyond the rail a dark void which he assumed to be the River Thames. He thought he heard voices to his right, but they were indistinguishable. He was aware of Hardy and Arthur Emory close behind him. They would follow his lead, he knew.

He pulled the pistol from his pocket with a firm grip, threw his weight against the hatch and propelled himself forward onto the deck to see Sophia struggling in Penthurst's arms. Danvers no more than registered the scene than Penthurst pulled back with a sharp cry of pain that had nothing to do with Danvers's presence.

Sophia gave a shout of triumph. Then, as Arthur Emory appeared on deck she flew to his side. "Ha! I bit him." She wiped away a smear of the blood she had drawn. "There was a boat," she gestured toward the darkness beyond the railing. "I shouted. He put his hand over my mouth."

"My brave love," Arthur hugged her.

"Hardy, you may bind my lord of Penthurst." Danvers raised the pistol to a more threatening level. "I suggest you refrain from attempting to call your crew to your aid, Duke."

"And why would his lordship be needing to do such a thing, I'm wondering?" Danvers recognized Mapp's gravelly voice at the same moment that he felt the flared muzzle of a blunderbuss in his ribs. The pistol Danvers held clattered to the boards of the deck.

Penthurst gave a shout of triumph. "The most interesting

game of chess I've ever had the pleasure of playing, Viscount. I thank you. I do believe this is checkmate." He strode to Sophia and pulled her from Arthur Emory. "Which means I take the white queen. For some reason, my dear, these gentlemen seem to be laboring under the impression that you are unhappy with the state of affairs. Perhaps for the health of your noble protector you would like to inform our guests that you are happy to become the Duchess of Penthurst."

Sophia made a strangled sound.

"Louder, if you please, my dear. Our guests weren't able to hear you and Lord Danvers is, I am certain, most anxious for your reply."

"I—"

She got no further, for at that moment the yacht's steam whistle blew three sharp blasts over their head, causing everyone to startle, including Mapp.

The moment Danvers felt the gun waver he leapt aside, then swung around with clenched fist extended. He caught his assailant in the jaw and he staggered backward. Danvers followed for another blow and another. He had not boxed since university days, but the technique and rhythm instilled then was still with him.

When at last the man was subdued, and Danvers safely in possession of the firearm, he was able to look around and take in the amazing scene of Penthurst and the others of his gang being handcuffed by Futter and three Second Inspectors from the Thames Division of the Metropolitan Police, while Hardy gave Colonel Whitham a spirited account of the night's adventure.

"Can't tell you how happy I am to see you, Inspector," Danvers greeted Futter as one of the Thames Division officers saw to manacling Mapp. "I was afraid you'd miss all the fun."

"Glad to be here, I can tell you. By the time we arrived at

the dock *Penthurst Pride* was in the middle of the river. We had to commandeer a steam launch from these fine folk," He swept his arm to the port side where Danvers saw the fisherman Hardy had interviewed earlier. "The rowing galleys supplied to the Marine Policing Unit are entirely inadequate for police duty."

Danvers shook his head at the swift turn of events. Nothing made sense, but he was exceedingly glad to be alive.

❦ 24 ❦

Still in her ball gown, Antonia paced the floor of her sitting room. In spite of the absence of the host and guest of honour, the ball had continued until dawn. Even now she could hear the dawn chorus outside her window. Where was Charles? What had happened? How could they possibly be gone so long?

"My lady, please, won't you change?" Isabella indicated the nightdress she carried over her arm. "You need to sleep."

"Don't be ridiculous," Tonia snapped, then sank into a chair. "Forgive me Isabella, I know you mean well. But I couldn't possibly rest not knowing—" She bit her tongue. She would not say 'Whether Charles is alive or dead.' "Not knowing what has happened," she finished.

Isabella returned the silken gown to her lady's bedchamber, then came back. "You will allow me to bring a tray? Tea and toast?" Antonia opened her mouth to refuse, then Isabella added, "For the little one."

Tonia sighed. "Very well, Isabella."

When her maid had gone Antonia dropped her head into her hands. In order to keep her fears at bay she forced her mind back over the night. Even in her distraught state, the memory of the scene after dinner when the absence of several of their party was discovered brought a shaky smile to her face.

Aunt Aelfrida had been the first to spot her ward's absence. She cornered Antonia in the ladies' powder room. "Eloped? With Penthurst?"

Tonia had shrunk from the scathing outburst that was certain to follow, and even now could feel the jolt of surprise when the dowager duchess gave an exclamation of triumph. "Aha! A runaway match. And with a duke. I was determined to set her grandmother's folly to rights, and I have done so."

Before Tonia could reply Agatha Estella entered in hysterics, followed by Beatrice making feeble attempts to calm her mother. "Eloped! Two of my children! What could I have done to be treated so? As if Alice weren't enough, now to have Arthur Emory run off... Oh, 'how sharper than a serpent's tooth it is to have a thankless child.'" She sank onto the nearest sofa in a semi-swoon.

"*Arthur?*" The dowager duchess gave a reproving rap of her walking stick. "Never!"

"Here, Mama, your *sal volatile*." Beatrice held the bottle to her mother's nose, but was pushed away for her efforts.

Tonia stamped a satin-shod foot for attention, although it had little effect on the Aubusson carpet. "Please stop this nonsensical scene, all of you! Unless you know a great deal more than I, there is no evidence of any elopement. Inspector Futter was here, but the Metropolitan Police are unlikely to concern themselves with an elopement. He came to arrest Colonel Whitham—which seems absurd in itself. But the Commissioner was called to sort out the matter, which I understand has to do with the murder of Faquir Johal."

"Murder?" The dowager duchess was indignant. "I will not have my family involved in anything so sordid." She grandly ignored the previous crimes Lord and Lady Danvers had helped solve as she made a stately exit.

Tonia sent for Isabella to tend to Agatha, then sank onto the sofa herself. Beatrice held out her mother's smelling salts. "Would you care for these, Aunt Antonia?"

"No thank you, my dear. Who could imagine such a scene? What do you make of it?"

"Whatever happened, Sophia did not elope with the Duke of Penthurst, I know that much."

"How can you be so certain?"

"She would never have consented to such a thing. Sophia is in love with my brother. From the first moment."

"And is her affection returned?"

"I rather think so. I am not in Arthur Emory's confidence, but he has been considerably more stupid than usual of late. I know nothing else to attribute it to."

"That is well then, my dear. I am confident matters will sort themselves out. After all, Charles is with them. Shall we return to the ballroom?"

Tonia shook her head at the memory. She had been so confident then. But that was many hours ago. Now, without the lilting music, the shimmering lights and the gay company to buoy her, Tonia's optimism had dissolved.

Her mind shifted to a darker image of the evening. Lord Ellenborough had complimented her on her guest of honour and she told him something of Sophia's history. The earl became immediately grave. "Cawnpore, you say?"

"Yes. Do you know anything of the current state of affairs?"

He sighed. "In such matters 'current' is an approximate term. Two or three months is the best we can hope for, and in this instance the telegraph lines have not yet been restored. I am assured that the army is giving the matter priority, however. We should have word within five or six weeks."

"So you know nothing beyond what is in the papers?"

"I fear not. I would counsel maintaining hope while preparing for the worst."

Now, thinking back, Antonia recalled the strange feeling that had come over her at his words. As if, in accepting the worst, she could release the past and look to the future.

And be strong for Sophia's sake. She could not help hoping that Beatrice had been right about the state of Sophia and Arthur Emory's hearts. In the past months Tonia had seen a new, very becoming maturity in that young man. She had little doubt that he would be a steadfast support for whatever the girl was required to face in the coming months.

The tray arrived with perfectly brewed tea, crisp, lightly buttered toast and a soft-boiled egg. Antonia found that she was ravenous. "That is quite perfect, Isabella. Thank you."

Tonia had no more than finished her second cup of tea when she heard a carriage stop in the street below. She flew to the landing at the top of the stairs in time to see Danvers and Hardy enter. "Charles!" She was in his arms even before she registered the fact that his coat was torn and that he wore no hat. She pulled back. "Your shirt—blood!"

"Not my own, my love." He laughed, holding her at arm's length. "Permit me to say that you look little better than I do."

Her hand flew to her disarrayed hair. "Isabella begged that I let her tend to me, but I could not. Charles, I was so worried—" She looked into his eyes and gave a stifled cry at the dark swelling above his left brow. "Charles, you're injured."

"A little, but I won. Come." With his arm around her shoulders, he led back up the stairs to their sitting room. "Breakfast, Hardy. A hearty one!" he called over his shoulder.

"Now, tell me all, Charles." They sank onto the sofa side by side, then Charles rose again to secure a footstool for Tonia's feet and reseated himself before recounting the adventures of the night. Other than an occasional gasp or exclamation at the terrors and revelations, Antonia restrained herself admirably, struggling to follow the twists and turns of events.

"Colonel Whitham, investigating for the EIC, uncovered the fact that Penthurst had been smuggling opium from the docks to supply his dens."

"No!" Her outcry held all the opprobrium they both felt.

"Yes, it's quite true. That was the main source of his income. He was desperate when the opium supply fell due to the uprising in Bengal where it is grown. Sophia's fortune offered an easy solution."

"So Penthurst planned to force Sophia into marrying him to get his hands on the money she would inherit from the Staveley estate on her marriage. So he really isn't wealthy?"

"Entirely ruined, it seems. Always at a loss to pay his gambling debts, he had thrown his lot in with Azimoolah Khan, first promising to help him obtain the inheritance he was charged with obtaining for Nana Sahib—for a considerable bribe, of course. Then, when it was clear that would come to nothing, he promised rifles to arm the Nana's household for the mutiny."

"Penthurst supplied Azimoolah Khan with rifles?"

"Only the promise. Once Hardy supplied his information from the Devil's Dyke Hotel to the Brighton police they found letters and accounts our Musselman was careless about having left behind."

"Hardy found them?"

"Apparently Anson found them. And paid dearly for it."

"Anson found them? How?" Tonia was struggling to put the threads of the story together.

"Scotland Yard has Chief Constable White of Brighton to thank for that piece of detection. He learned that when Azimoolah departed for India without her, the brokenhearted Annabelle told her brother about the letters her lover had written to her. Anson followed the trail of the letters back to the Devil's Dyke and found documents under a floorboard in the room Khan had used. The lieutenant took them to the barracks with him. Where White found them."

"And they implicated Penthurst?"

"The police think Anson may have accosted Penthurst— or tried to blackmail him. Either way, it spelled Anson's doom."

"And Chandrika's husband? Did Anson kill him?"

Before Danvers could answer Hardy entered with the substantial breakfast his lord had ordered. When it was set on the table Tonia realized her toast and soft-boiled egg had served merely as an appetizer. She readily accepted her husband's invitation to join him and they were soon break-fasting on sirloin and poached eggs in cream.

After their first hunger had been sated Antonia prompted, "Faquir Johal—he was mixed up with Penthurst's smuggling?"

"With helping his brother-in-law uncover the smuggler for the East India Company."

"But who killed him? And who filled Chandrika's head with that nonsense about suttee?"

"I expect the police will find that was the work of Kabir and Parth—those Eurasian men you saw in the park. As was

Anson's murder. They were Penthurst's men. I doubt he dirtied his hands with any of it."

"Yes, but why scare Chandrika?"

"An inept attempt to scare her into telling them what she knew of her husband's investigations."

"But surely she knew nothing?" Tonia took a final sip of tea and pushed her cup aside.

"As you say, but Penthurst was leaving no stone unturned."

Tonia considered. "No. I rather think he simply enjoyed terrifying her. For the sense of power it gave him." Antonia might have gone on, but a wide yawn split her face.

"Come, my love." Danvers picked her up and carried her to her bedroom. "I don't think we need disturb Isabella, do you?"

With an expertise that amazed Antonia, her husband undid the buttons lining the back of her thoroughly disordered ball gown and then loosened her stays. He slid the silken nightdress from her bed and slipped it over her head. Her eyes were already closing when he pulled down the coverlet and she sank into the depths of her featherbed.

"Your daughter would like a lullaby, my love."

He sat on the edge of her bed.

"*Time is the nurse and breeder of all good.*
Hope is a lover's staff; walk hence with that
And manage it against despairing thoughts."

Tonia smiled and placed her hand on her abdomen. Yes, in spite of all the loss, the future was full of hope. She would name their daughter Emilia after her friend.

"*Hope, like the gleaming taper's light,*
Adorns and cheers our way;
And still, as darker grows the night,
Emits a brighter ray."

AFTERWORD

On 17 July, the morning after the massacre, Nana Sahib sent a burial party to the Bibighar to dispose of the tangle of bodies. All, including those not yet dead, were dumped down an irrigation well near the Bibighar.

A few hours later, General Havelock and his troops defeated Nana Sahib who fled into the hills, never to be heard of again.

English officers entered the Bibighar and found the scene "unspeakably horrible... caked with blood..." One officer who was present picked up a mutilated prayer book, opened to the litany. It was sprinkled with blood.

On 27 August news of the events rocked London. "The Morning Herald" reported:

"On the morning of the 17th July the force marched into Cawnpore. The spectacle there presented beggars description. 88 officers, 190 men of her Majesty's 84th Foot, 70 ladies, 120 women and children and the whole European and Christian population, including civilians shopkeepers, engineers, pensioners, and their families, to the number of about 400 persons, had been massacred by Nana Sahib. The courtyard was swimming in blood. A large number of women and children, who were reserved after the capitulation, had been slaughtered the previous morning, the women having been stripped naked, beheaded, and thrown down a well..."

There were three English survivors of the Cawnpore Massacre: Lieutenant Mowbray Thompson, of the 53rd Bengal native Infantry; William Jonah Shepherd, a Eurasian clerk at the Commissariat Office, who had served as a spy for the British; and Miss Amelia (Amy) Horne, the 18-year-old stepdaughter of a captain in the Royal Navy. All three wrote accounts of the events, very aware of "the importance of bearing witness."

Emilia Landry's time in India is based on the historical account of Isabel White who was persuaded by her friend Louisa Chalwin, to accompany her on her return to India because it was such a fine place to find a husband.

Azimoolah Khan may have died of smallpox en route to Calcutta, or escaped to Istanbul in the company of an Englishwoman named Miss Clayton where he was murdered after Miss Clayton died of old age.

Khan's affair with "Miss A" is historical. Her letters were discovered in Azimoolah's apartments.

Lucie Duff Gordon was unable to reconcile the "enthusiastic Englishman" she had championed with the monster portrayed in the British press. She moved to Egypt and died there in 1869.

The account of the Queen's Drawing-Room is taken almost verbatim from the press of the day, the unnamed lady to whom it happened having sent her account to the papers. The reaction in the press was also as portrayed.

I have tried very hard to track actual events in London and in India as they happened—for this the online British Newspaper Archive has been invaluable. Two things fascinated me most as I wrote: How slow communication was in those days compared to today when we know of events on the other side of the world almost before they happen; and the contrast of the elegance of London society and the horror the women in Cawnpore suffered. One newspaper reported the details of the massacre in one column and next to it an account of the queen's departure for Scotland.

On 28 June 1858, after the Indian Rebellion of 1857, the rule of the British East India Company was transferred to the Crown in the person of Queen Victoria who in 1876, was proclaimed Empress of India. Referred to as the British Rah, the rule lasted until 1947.

REFERENCES

Bassett, Ronald, *Blood of an Englishman*, A Novel of the Siege of Cawnpore, 1975, Macmillan, London Ltd.

Breckon, Ian, "The Bloodiest Record in the Book of Time"; Amy Horne and the Indian Uprising of 1857, in Fact and Fiction, (thesis), Bath Spa University.

Grant, R.C., *The Brighton Garrison 1793-1900*: A Layman's Collection of Information and illustrations, ND, A Layman's Publication, Brighton.

Middleton, Judy, *Brighton and Hove in Old Photographs*, 1988, Alan Sutton, Gloucester.

Northacker, Lt. Col. William H., *Cawnpore*: Ganges Double Massacre, 2011, Lexington, KY.

Shepherd, W. J., *A Personal narrative of the Outbreak and Massacre at Cawnpore*, During the Sepoy Revolt of 1857, 2011, General Books, LLC, Memphis.

Stuart, V. A., *Massacre at Cawnpore*, 1973, Pinnacle Books, New York.

Thompson, Mowbray, *The Story of Cawnpore*, by Captain Mowbray Thompson, one of the Only Two survivors from the Cawnpore Garrison, 1859, Follett, Foster & Co., NG.

Ward, Andrew, *Our Bones are Scattered*, The Cawnpore Massacres and the Indian Mutiny of 1857, 1996, Henry Holt and Co., New York.

www.British Newspaper Archive.co.uk

ABOUT THE AUTHOR

Donna Fletcher Crow has always loved the Victorians. *"I love their energy, their confidence, their optimism. Victorians are often criticized as being repressed and are blamed for the injustices in their society; but I see them as people who sincerely worked for good. There were many difficulties in Victorian society, but when they identified a problem they set about with enormous vigor to correct it. I hope I have portrayed those achievements in some of the novels I have set in that period."*

Crow is a lifelong Anglophile, a former English teacher, and the author of 50 books, mostly novels of British history, including the award-winning Arthurian epic *Glastonbury*, The Novel of Christian England. She currently authors three mystery series: Lord Danvers Investigates, The Monastery Murders, and The Elizabeth and Richard Literary Mysteries.

You can see more about her books and pictures from her research trips at www.DonnaFletcherCrow.com

Subscribe to her newsletter here:
http://www.donnafletchercrow.com/subscribe.php

BOOKS BY DONNA FLETCHER CROW

The Elizabeth & Richard Literary Suspense Mysteries:

The Shadow of Reality

Elizabeth and Richard at a Dorothy L Sayers mystery week high in
the Rocky Mountains

A Midsummer Eve's Nightmare

Elizabeth and Richard honeymoon at a Shakespeare Festival in
Ashland, Oregon

A Jane Austen Encounter

A second honeymoon visit to Jane Austen's homes turns deadly

The Torch Ignites

Elizabeth and Richard look back to their first meeting in a New
England autumn

A Most Singular Venture

Murder in Jane Austen's London

The Monastery Murders, Clerical Mysteries

A Very Private Grave

Legendary buried treasure, a brutal murder and lurking danger—

an itinerary of terror across a holy terrain

A Darkly Hidden Truth

Ancient puzzles, modern murder and breathless chase scenes

through a remote, waterlogged landscape

An Unholy Communion

An idyllic pilgrimage through Wales

becomes a deadly struggle between good and evil

A Newly Crimsoned Reliquary

Murder stalks the shadows of Oxford's hallowed shrines

An All-Consuming Fire

A Christmas wedding in a monastery—

if the bride can defeat the murderer prowling the Yorkshire moors

The Lord Danvers Investigates,
Victorian True-Crime Mysteries

A Most Inconvenient Death

The brutal Stanfield Hall murders shatter a quiet Norwich community and pull Danvers from deep personal grief into a dangerous investigation.

Grave Matters

Lord and Lady Danvers's honeymoon in Scotland is interrupted by the ghosts of Burke and Hare-style grave robbers.

To Dust You Shall Return

Catherine Bacon is murdered in the very shadow of Canterbury Cathedral but Charles and Antonia are overwhelmed with their own problems.

A Tincture of Murder

William Dove is on trial in York for poisoning his wife while Lord and Lady Danvers struggle to assist in a refuge home where fallen women continue to die mysteriously.

Where There is Love Historical Romance

Where Love Begins

Where Love Illumines

Where Love Triumphs

Where Love Restores

Where Love Shines

Where Love Calls

The Daughters of Courage Family Saga

Kathryn, Days of Struggle and Triumph

Elizabeth, Days of Loss and Hope

Stephanie, Days of Turmoil and Victory

Arthurian Epic

Glastonbury, The Novel of Christian England